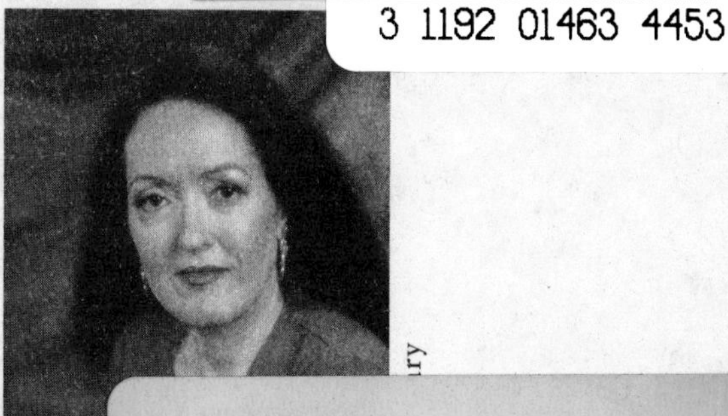

About the Author

ANN HERENDEEN, a native New Yorker and lifelong resident of Brooklyn, received a B.A. in English from Princeton University and an M.L.S. from Pratt Institute. She currently works as a cataloging librarian specializing in natural history. Ann's first novel, *Phyllida and the Brotherhood of Philander*, was published in 2008.

ALSO BY ANN HERENDEEN

Phyllida and the Brotherhood of Philander

Pride / Prejudice

ANN HERENDEEN

HARPER

NEW YORK • LONDON • TORONTO • SYDNEY

HARPER

HarperCollins books may be purchased for educational, business, or sales promotional use. For information, please write: Special Markets Department, HarperCollins Publishers, 10 East 53rd Street, New York, NY 10022.

FIRST EDITION

Designed by Cassandra J. Pappas

Library of Congress Cataloging-in-Publication Data is available upon request.

ISBN 978-0-06-186313-4

10 11 12 13 14 OV/RRD 10 9 8 7 6 5 4 3 2 1

To all the friends I made through my first novel,
Phyllida and the Brotherhood of Philander:
especially Tarra T. Thomas and Karyn R. Pierce,
who accompanied me on so much of this journey,
and Helen and Tom, who inspired me both in
my writing and in my life; and to my father,
Walter Barton (Bart) Herendeen, who would have
enjoyed Phyllida, *not only because I wrote it,*
but because, as I recognized far too late, we shared
the same dark outlook and sick sense of humor.
This one's for you.

Acknowledgments

A book like *Pride / Prejudice*, less the result of research than the spawn of its author's twisted imagination, owes its existence primarily to brain fuel: in this case, coffee. But two people provided essential support that must be acknowledged. My heartfelt thanks go out to Marilyn La Monica for keeping me, if not sane, which might be counterproductive, at least functional; and to my editor, Rakesh Satyal, for giving me the two things a writer can never have enough of: understanding and appreciation of her work.

Pride / Prejudic

One

"IT IS A truth universally acknowledged," Fitz said, "that a single man in possession of a good fortune is in want of a wife."

Charles blinked and sat up. "Lord, Fitz! It's the middle of the night. What do you expect me to make of that? Sounds like another of your epigrams."

"I suppose it is," Fitz said. "But its meaning does not seem particularly obscure."

"You and Caroline going to tie the knot at last? You sly dog."

Fitz grimaced and pulled Charles back down beside him. "My dear," he said, "you have a tendency to levity that, like any disproportion, can be tedious in excess."

"And you," Charles said, "have a way of talking to people as if you were a judge and they the prisoner in the dock."

"Guilty as charged," Fitz said, bestowing a kiss on the pouting lips. "My great uncle might have been pleased at my following his example. Now, what shall my penalty be? I know." He trailed his hand down Charles's slender body until he found what he was searching for, held tight and squeezed.

Charles groaned and arched his back. "God, Fitz, you're a devil. I wish you'd—"

"Don't talk," Fitz said. He moved lower in the bed, opened his mouth, and paid his forfeit with an alacrity bordering dangerously on enthusiasm. He would consider it deplorable if he were not motivated by love. Love of the purest kind.

THEY WOKE TO dawn light. "I'm only leasing the place," Charles said, picking up the argument as if there had been no interruption. "I haven't committed to anything permanent—a few months' tenancy, a year at most."

"The minute you take possession of the house," Fitz said, still groggy from sleep, "nay, the minute you ride into the village, you will be besieged by every fortune-hunting mama and her brood of hideous, squinting, gap-toothed, caterwauling daughters."

"How do you know they will be hideous?" Charles asked. "Or are all women hideous if you think I might find them agreeable?"

"In a way, yes," Fitz said, attempting a lightness of tone he could never feel on this subject. "You are modest in your assessment of your own charms, and too easily flattered by the pitiful arts of any barely respectable female."

"My word," Charles said. "You have a low opinion of my understanding. For someone who calls himself my friend—"

Fitz saw he had wounded where he had hoped merely to inspire wariness. "My dear," he said, kissing the cheek that presented itself as he approached the lips, and stroking the soft brown hair. "I don't question your intellect, merely your judgment, and only on this subject; one that has proven difficult for the wisest philosophers to master, back to antiquity, much less an English gentleman of twenty-two."

"Whereas from the vast experience of twenty-seven, all is revealed," Charles said.

"Twenty-eight, last month," Fitz said. "It is not my age but my temperament that gives me an advantage. I do not immediately assume, because a woman simpers and plies her fan, that she is in love with me, or I with her."

"At last the truth comes out," Charles said. "You don't like women. I've suspected it all along."

"Really?" Fitz said. "In other words, because I show some taste and discrimination, I am supposed not to care for women in general."

Fitz's voice had entered that supercilious register that ordinarily would have led Charles to concede the debate. This time he persevered. "When have you ever looked at a woman but to find fault? As far as marriage is concerned, my fundament is as close to a wife as you'll ever come."

"Don't be coarse, Charles," Fitz said. "If you believe that's all you are to me, your understanding is worse than I thought."

"Deny it all you like," Charles said. "But I begin to pity Caroline."

"And what, may I ask, has your sister to do with this conversation?"

"I am not to be coarse," Charles said, "but you are allowed to be dense. We've talked it over a hundred times. You're to marry Caroline and I'm to marry Georgiana—double brothers-in-law." He shrank back, seeing the truly alarming expression distorting the features of his friend's handsome face.

"Do not," Fitz said, "I repeat, do not bring my sister's name into this bed."

"Why not?" Charles said. "You think she's too good for me? I notice *you* don't scruple to pollute yourself."

Fitz caught himself on the verge of losing his temper and took several deep breaths. Why was it that this subject always upset him, when he knew it was inevitable? "I'm sorry, Charles," he said. "You see, Georgiana is just turned sixteen. With the difference in our ages, and especially since our father died, I am more of a parent to her than a brother."

Charles laid his hand on his friend's muscular chest. "I understand, Fitz. I'm sorry too. I just think you're making too much of this business. You know my father wanted to purchase an estate but died before he could accomplish it. It's the least I can do to follow through on his intentions. You may sneer, from your lofty perch atop the greatest property in Derbyshire—which, you may recall, you inherited—but I, like Lackland, must start from nothing—although I hope I'll do better than King John."

"You could do a lot worse than the Magna Carta," Fitz said.

Charles laughed dutifully. "I'm not rushing into anything. Surely you agree I'm behaving with all the circumspection and prudence you could require."

"My dear boy," Fitz said. "I agree that you think you are. You can't help it that you fell in love with the first house you saw with sufficient rooms, just as you fall in love with every woman who possesses all her teeth and whose hair retains its natural color." He rolled over on Charles, pinning him to the mattress with his larger, heavier form, and kissed him until he gasped for air.

"Brute," Charles said when he was allowed to breathe. "Overbearing, domineering brute." He licked his lips, moving his tongue in a slow circling motion. "Kiss me again, brute."

"If you're going to tease me like that," Fitz said, "I shall be obliged to do more than kiss you."

"Mmm," Charles said, "I was hoping you'd say that. Just try

to take it easy. I want to ride over and look at the place today."

"I will be as gentle with you," Fitz said, "as with a woman."

"Lord help me!" Charles said. "I'm a goner. I won't be able to sit for a week."

And yet, a few hours later, as Charles Bingley rode through the village of Meryton to the manor house of Netherfield Park, he was permeated with a great sense of well-being. Fitz had allowed him to go alone, and to make all the arrangements without interference. "You are no longer the untried youth of our first acquaintance, but are on your way to becoming a man," he said. "I've known it for some time now. Bear with me if on occasion I find the transformation difficult to accept."

"Of course I will," Charles said. "Indeed, I hope—that is—I don't want to give up being your *dear boy* entirely."

The animation that this speech produced in Fitz's austere face and hard body almost led to a repetition of the dawn's activities, until the advancing hour and the possibility of the entrance of servants with shaving water brought things to an abrupt and unsatisfying conclusion.

"Tonight," Charles said, "I will tell you all about it, and you can criticize my decisions and inform me as to how much better you would have managed the business."

"How disagreeable I must be, to be sure," Fitz said. "I wonder you don't take the first chance to marry and seize your freedom."

"I could never be completely free," Charles said. "Just give me credit for some maturity."

"Isn't that what this tiresome conversation has established?" Fitz said, but smiling. "Go on, then. Sign the lease on your manor and invite every female in the neighborhood to a ball. I won't say a word."

"I will hold you to that, Fitz," Charles said. He just might, at that. A ball to celebrate the establishment of his own household. And if he met a pleasant, pretty young lady or two, where was the harm in that? He would have to marry sooner or later, however Fitz jibbed at every mention of the subject. In fact, it might be very nice to have a wife. But he would do nothing rash, nothing to make Fitz jealous or unhappy. The man had the devil's own temper, but he was the truest friend, and there was no doubt he had Charles's interests at heart. And he made love like—like a demon and an angel, both, in one body.

Charles sighed and dismounted in front of the house. It was well kept, in good condition, only recently vacated. He could be happy here. He was sure of it.

THAT FIRST BALL in the Meryton assembly rooms lingered in Fitzwilliam Darcy's late-night torments for weeks. It had all gone as he had foreseen. Every family in the neighborhood had made a point of calling on Charles as soon as he moved in—even before. "I scarcely had my furniture unloaded and my trunks unpacked," he remarked in his cheerful, uncomplaining way, "when the local squires began riding up to 'get acquainted,' as they said."

The ball reflected the fruits of their labor, all the gentry for miles around attending, and worse, all the dreary, middling sort of people, the attorneys and the merchants, anyone who had acquired sufficient capital to retire from business or buy a tiny plot of land and could now call himself a gentleman. That in itself was bad enough, but naturally they all had families, and for some reason their progeny ran to daughters—at least that's how it looked to Fitz.

"My goodness!" Caroline Bingley said, gliding up to take his arm. "It's like a scene from some disreputable opera."

For once Fitz was in agreement, and grateful for her protection. He could only be thankful that he had had the good sense to stay in town until the previous evening and had not had a chance to be introduced to anyone; he could therefore claim to be unable to ask any of this enormous local harem to dance.

Charles was already dangerously entangled, with a plump, glowing girl, all smiles and lush curves, just the sort that would be considered the beauty of this benighted backwater. In London, of course, she'd be dismissed as a country milkmaid, but Charles conversed so spiritedly with her during the dance, and was on the verge of claiming her for an ill-advised second set, that Fitz attempted to intervene.

"Quite a prize, eh?" A vacuous old tradesman who had been elevated to the rank of knight took hold of Fitz's arm as he stepped forward to put a word in Charles's ear.

"I beg your pardon?" Fitz said, lowering his eyelids with disdain at the man's coarse, red face.

"Miss Bennet," Sir William Lucas said. "Our own native rose, you know. It seems your friend hasn't wasted any time. We may see some interesting developments soon, eh, what?"

Fighting the urge to plant the mushroom a facer, Fitz turned away and almost collided with Charles. "Not dancing, Fitz? How can you be so stupid?"

Fitz shrugged. "You are dancing with the only handsome girl in the room, other than your sisters."

"Oh, Miss Bennet is the most beautiful creature I ever beheld!" Charles exclaimed, his voice unnecessarily loud over the thin strains of music from the small orchestra. "But there's her sister forced to sit down, and almost as pretty. Why not ask her?"

Despite his best efforts, Fitz couldn't help sliding his eyes in the direction of the seated girl, curious as to how the *sister* of a country beauty would appear—buck teeth, perhaps, or a giggler, or spotty—and by the worst of bad luck his eyes met hers as, sensing his covert scrutiny, she turned her head toward his side of the room. *Wide, dark brown eyes, fringed with delicate lashes; expressive, humorous eyes, yet earnest; lively but honest. Gentle and innocent as a doe's but with the wit of a philosopher. Playful and seductive as a kitten's but with humanity and Christian grace to temper any impropriety . . .*

Fitz felt himself blushing like a schoolboy, frowned, and looked away. By God! He would not be made a fool of! "I'm afraid she is not handsome enough to tempt me," he said, ashamed of the words as soon as they left his mouth. "You had much better return to your charming partner and leave me to my uncharitable solitude." He watched Charles follow his advice, annoyed at being obeyed so promptly, and became aware of Caroline standing nearby, apparently having witnessed the entire disgraceful incident.

"Miss Bingley," Fitz said, giving a slight bow and attempting a smile. "Will you do me the honor?"

"Why, Mr. Darcy," she said, "I worried, for one breathless moment, that Cupid's arrow had pierced your heart."

"What the de— I mean, whatever are you talking about?" Fitz said.

"But then I recalled," Caroline continued, "that you do not possess a heart to be wounded."

Fitz was grinding his teeth as he led her out to form the quadrille.

THAT NIGHT WAS pure torture, and only the fact that mortals rarely possess the gift of foresight, and Fitz could not, thankfully, anticipate that worse was to follow, allowed him to bear his trials with gentlemanly composure.

"Wasn't it splendid!" Charles said, standing so temptingly

naked in the center of the bedroom, arms outflung in rapture, twirling slowly and tilting his head up to stare for some reason at the ceiling.

"Very nice," Fitz said.

"Nice?" Charles repeated. "Nice? That is the most mewling, pathetic, inadequate word in the English language. The ball shall be anything you say, except nice."

"Very well," Fitz said. "It was not nice in the least. It was horrid. It was hot, crowded, dreary, noisy—and noisome."

"You mean it stank?" Charles was diverted. "Now you're teasing. Explain yourself."

Fitz stretched his long limbs on the bed, artfully displaying the beginning of tumescence over the curve of a muscular thigh. "Come here, you provoking creature, and I'll explain *at length.*"

Charles let his arms fall to his sides, and his mouth drooped. He was not hard—a disturbing and unwelcome development. "You know, Fitz, I've been wondering if we're getting too old for this."

Something pierced Fitz's heart, and it wasn't Cupid's arrow. He willed himself into control. "What do you mean, my dear?" he asked.

"Surely I don't have to recite your lessons back to you," Charles said. "This. Us. All that Achilles-and-Patroclus, Damon-and-Piteous stuff you talk about."

"Pythias," Fitz corrected. "What is it, Charles? Do you doubt my feelings for you?"

"No, never," Charles said. "But Fitz, you always called it a youthful love." He paused, looking down at himself, as if the question had arisen within his body, in his chest, covered with silky hair, or his slim waist with its trail of that same dark hair leading to the dense thatch at his crotch. When he spoke again, his words tumbled out in a nervous rush. "That beautiful girl tonight. Miss Bennet. She made me think that maybe it's time for me to put aside childish things."

Fitz took several breaths and counted to ten, then to twenty and backward to one. "I see," he said, when he had his voice so modulated that his desire to commit brutal murder did not leak through. "A scheming, mercenary female, who from the look of her is on the cusp of becoming an old maid, finds that Providence has dropped a handsome, unattached young man with a considerable fortune into her sphere. Even before her first dance with this savior is finished, she has so poisoned her innocent victim's mind with thoughts of matrimony that he—"

"Stop it!" Charles shouted. "Just stop it! It's not amusing in the least." He strode to the door, yanked it open with such force that he almost struck himself in the face, remembered he was naked and slammed it shut again. "Just let me find my dressing gown and I'll leave you to your poisonous thoughts."

Fitz had already risen to the occasion. He wrapped Charles in a strong embrace, pressing what was left of his by now dwindling erection against his friend's equally flaccid member. "My dear," he whispered. "My dearest, sweet man. Forgive me. I think only of you, of your welfare. You know I never wish to hurt you."

Charles tried to free himself but was no match for Fitz's strength. "Let me go, Darcy," he said. His voice was icy, as Fitz had never heard it.

Fitz released Charles and stepped back, as one does instinctively from attack. "Please, Charles," he said. "Let's not quarrel over this."

"It's too late," Charles said. "We already have. Haven't we?"

"Not if we don't allow a trivial exchange to enlarge into a disagreement," Fitz said. "Whatever I said was meant in kindness to you. And I humbly and deeply apologize for any unintended affront to your beautiful Miss Bennet." This time his voice shook with the lie, but it worked to his advantage.

"Oh, Fitz," Charles said, remorse flooding him at last. "You know I can never stay angry with you." He lay down on the bed.

Hallelujah! Fitz thought, blasphemously and with Low Church vulgarity.

"She is lovely, though, isn't she?"

"What?" Fitz's hand was involuntarily arrested on its path to Charles's lovely thick cock.

"Miss Bennet. Isn't she the most beautiful lady you've ever seen? And do you want to hear what's even better?"

"Please," Fitz said, the last vestige of arousal draining from him like bilge from a beached ship's hold. "I'm all aquiver with curiosity."

"She has the sweetest disposition of any woman I've ever known," Charles replied, oblivious to any sarcasm.

"She would, naturally," Fitz muttered, but softly, so Charles heard nothing of the words.

"Let me tell you everything she said," Charles said, nestling into Fitz's arms, resting his head on Fitz's shoulder as if they had already fucked themselves into exhaustion instead of having stopped everything dead from some sort of willful perversity.

"Yes, do," Fitz said. "Tell me everything." He might as well get it over with, he thought, giving the night up for lost. Dawn was almost here anyway, and they'd have only a precious couple of hours of sleep. Pity what little time they had was wasted on hearing that, amazing as it seemed, this aging country maiden was possessed of every virtue and free of every vice.

In the end, Charles allowed Fitz one quick romp before snuffing out the candle, but it was an unsatisfying, hasty business, and Fitz was so discomposed by the insipid narration preceding it that it turned into a dry bob instead of the real thing. He could tell Charles's heart and soul were far away, across the meadows in the neighboring village of Longbourn, where this damnable Miss Bennet was no doubt lying equally chastely in her sister's arms and enumerating dear Charles's considerable and genuine good qualities . . .

Which was what led to his body's failure, Fitz realized later. The sister's beautiful eyes had intruded on his mental vision just at what should have been the height of pleasure. Fitz imagined her watching him, those innocent but wise orbs staring unblinking while he groaned and sweated over Charles's firm buttocks, and he lost whatever meager strength he had regained.

"Never mind, love," Charles said. "It's late. You're tired, that's all."

"Yes," Fitz agreed, taking the path of least resistance. "But I am sorry."

"Don't be," Charles said, stroking Fitz's damp hair back from his high brow. "It's only what I said before. We're too old for this."

This time the voice in Fitz's brain rang its clarion warning, unmistakable: *Get out now. Take Charles and get away.*

He gave thanks every day since that he hadn't listened.

Two

UNFORTUNATELY FOR FITZ'S resolve, the situation improved, in a dangerous but subtle way that left him completely unguarded. Over the next several weeks, the gentlemen of Netherfield and the ladies of Longbourn came into frequent but public association—dinners, card parties, and the like—in which any sort of private conversation was impossible. Charles's continued praise of Miss Bennet grew tiresome, verging on the insupportable, but as it was all based on so insubstantial a foundation Fitz didn't attempt to argue his friend out of what could only be hardened into obstinacy by opposition; so fragile a structure would crumble easily enough on its own once the chance at greater intimacy was achieved and the lady's shallow character was exposed.

This occasion arose unexpectedly. Fitz, with Charles and his brother-in-law, Mr. Hurst, had gone to dine with the newly arrived officers of the local militia. Fitz had been greatly looking forward to this outing, a chance to spend an informal evening in the company of men, no need to watch his every word—and, if he was very lucky indeed, he might find someone compatible, more than likely in the all-male world of the military, a surrogate for Charles when he was in one of his moods, which were becoming increasingly frequent. Not that there could be a substitute for love. But for mere sport, what harm in that?

The ladies, left to themselves, and indulging their brother in his partiality, invited the eldest Miss Bennet to dinner, and what must the bitch do but travel on horseback, uncovered during autumn rain, and deliberately, as it seemed, catch cold?

It would be inhuman to send her home—even Fitz was forced to admit that—and the next day her sister felt obligated to see how the invalid was doing. And that's when the trouble began.

The woman walked—*walked*—the entire three miles, through the mud and dirt, residue of the rain that had laid her sister low. She tripped daintily into the breakfast parlor, her eyes bright, her delicate complexion rosy and translucent. Fitz was aware not only of her face but of her body, her chest expanding and contracting with deep breaths, so slender and light she could be a boy. But no boy had such trim ankles, or little budding breasts with those sharp peaks of nipples pointing through the thin muslin of her gown; and no boy could look so graceful in the damp folds of drapery; and no boy had ever smelled quite like that . . .

"Did you see her petticoat?" Louisa Hurst exclaimed in glee after Elizabeth Bennet had been directed upstairs to her sister's chamber.

"My dear!" Caroline Bingley replied. "Six inches deep in mud. And her shoes!"

"Sweating like a plow horse," Louisa said.

"Louisa, Caroline." Charles, his courage steeled by first love, dared to admonish his formidable sisters. "Miss Elizabeth's concern for her sister, if nothing else, demands our admiration, not our censure."

Caroline, not at all chastened, turned to Fitz. "I'm sure, Mr. Darcy, *you* noticed her deplorable state."

Fitz had one of those moments, rare for him, of spurious inspiration. "All I noticed," he said, allowing his voice to purr just a little, "is how the exercise heightened the glow in her very fine eyes."

That gave those two cats something to think about. Oh yes.

BUT IT WAS Fitz who was burdened with some rather troublesome thoughts after a day or two of the Bennet sisters' enforced stay. However dull the elder, the younger was unlike anything Fitz had encountered among the supposedly highest level of cultured society in town. Elizabeth Bennet seemed determined to make an impression. Not content with proving her country fortitude by walking, she took every opportunity to show off her unique and often contrary views on any commonplace subject that arose. She spent her time with her sister rather than enjoying the conversation in the downstairs parlor and chose a book over a game of loo, yet disdained the notion that she was any great reader or preferred reading to all other pastimes. She took on Fitz at every turn, matching each of his attempted witticisms with her own adroit turn of phrase.

What astonished Fitz more than anything was that her words were clearly original. He had never heard anything like them in the salons and ballrooms of London; she was not repeating the voguish phrases and the manner of forming them that prevailed in the fashionable soirées, nor was she likely to have spent enough time there to have studied them. And although she was undoubtedly well educated, Fitz had read widely enough to know she was not following any strange conversational plans out of some obsolete primer.

On the second day, when the mother and younger sisters visited, exhibiting their lamentable and pitiable lack of intelligence, grace, and good manners, Fitz was jolted rudely awake from his unwary fascination. Mrs. Bennet was an unmitigated horror, and the thought that she had produced five daughters, three of them as empty-headed and shameless as herself, was enough to make Fitz give up the notion of having any more congress with females for the rest of his life. "There is quite as much of *that* in the country as in town," she said with vulgar frankness, appearing to read Fitz's thoughts, and relishing the amount of immorality to be met with in her small village, before going on to boast of dining with twenty-four families as if it were some great number.

Seeing Elizabeth so quick to divert attention from her mother's worst lapses by serving them up as humorous vignettes of country life, Fitz could only turn away in sympathetic mortification. It was bizarre, revolting, like catching sight of a cripple or a leper, made all the worse by the contrast with her wit and feminine form. When the deformed creature is in other respects a beautiful woman, Fitz discovered, one's disgust is infinitely magnified.

Once the mother and sisters were gone, however, Fitz found himself forgetting the distasteful incidents, surrounded as he was by all the new charms. It was when Elizabeth, innocently as it seemed, touched on his natural concern for Charles that Fitz at last became rattled. He had been startled but amused at her rejection of poetry as encouragement to love, intrigued by her assertion that "a puny love could be entirely starved away by one good sonnet." By then, no doubt encouraged by her mild success, and overconfident of her audience's goodwill, Elizabeth drew poor Charles, already in well over his head, into a pathetic and endearing assertion of his own headstrong disregard for caution. Charles declared, with a fervor that he no doubt fancied was showing himself as one of these fiery, passionate souls celebrated in the latest poetry and popular novels, that were he to resolve to quit Netherfield he would be gone at once, with no second thoughts. Despite Fitz's misgivings that he was making too much of insignificant chat, he couldn't help stepping in.

He heard the scorn in his voice, the affectionate criticism, but was unable to suppress it, as he reminded Charles that, in fact, were "a friend" to request that he change his mind, he would acquiesce.

Charles had been abashed then defiant, and Elizabeth had come to his defense, as if Fitz had been attacking him, when his only intent had been to prevent Charles from looking ridiculous.

It was intolerable, Fitz thought, as he realized that she was laughing at him. A mere chit of a girl, not a beauty in the established mode, with a meager portion and a most tenuous position on the lowest rung of the country gentry. And with the sharpest tongue off a London stage he had ever had the pleasure of being assailed by. And the most striking dark, large, and luminous eyes. And a very fetching, petite figure. Fitz could hardly keep his eyes off her. *That* was a disgrace, more his fault than hers. After all, he was an experienced man of the world, whereas she—

It was not until the third day that Fitz understood she was flirting. How slow he had been! Her unorthodox tactics had almost outmaneuvered him. The revelation had come when Miss Bingley enticed Elizabeth into strolling up and down the room, as if for exercise. Poor Caroline had so little finesse that she readily and happily fell into Fitz's trap, begging to hear his interpretation of why the women did better to walk without him. He had enjoyed confronting them with the truth, that they either wished to tell secrets or show themselves off before the gentlemen.

Elizabeth had striven hard to avoid any such easy capitulation, and it was clear to see that the ignominy of Caroline's surrender had provoked the stronger mind almost to rudeness. "Mr. Darcy has no defect," Elizabeth said in the odd discussion that followed, a deliberation on what minor sins constituted allowable targets for her arrows of wit. "He owns it himself without disguise."

Fitz tried to dwell on this slight, to hold its venomous barb deep in his flesh until it festered and turned black, in hopes of effecting a rough cure from the dangerous attraction. After six years of town life, he had despaired of finding a woman who was both pretty and intelligent, whose mental abilities matched her physical allure. The fact that the younger daughter of an impoverished country gentleman was weaving such a spell proved merely that he had set his ideal too high, and had disqualified any eligible contestants from the start. But, oh, it was hard to resist. Fitz could only hope for the elder sister's swift recovery, and release from the bonds of enchantment—both for himself and for Charles.

THAT FIRST NIGHT of the eldest Miss Bennet's stay, Charles was awash in agony and terror that a serious illness afflicted his inamorata, and the second night was little better. But by the third day, when it seemed that she would, in fact, recover from a head cold, Charles was suddenly up again, in ecstasy with his love, and with no other means to express it, receptive to Fitz's attentions as he had not been in weeks.

"Oh God, Fitz," Charles said, lying in Fitz's arms, sweaty and dirty and so adorable Fitz could have licked him clean for the sheer joy of soiling him all over again, "I've missed this."

"It was not by my choice that you took aversion to our pleasures," Fitz reminded him.

"I know." Charles lifted his head from where it rested on Fitz's chest and stared into his friend's hooded eyes. "I hope you don't take it the wrong way that—that—" He stuttered on the dangerous admission he was about to make. "—that this resumption of my—our—love is because of her."

"Miss Bennet?" Fitz asked. "In other words, you allow me to do with you what you'd rather be doing with her, if the rules of society allowed it?"

"I wouldn't put it so crudely, but yes."

"Naturally, I wish you to desire my love for its own sake," Fitz said after contemplating his answer. "For my sake, and for the sake of our friendship over this past year and more. But I do want you, and will take you in whatever way, and for whatever reason, I am permitted to have you." He paused, watching his protégé for any sign of shame or discomfort. Heartened to see no reaction, good or bad, he decided to try an experiment. Give Charles a taste of his own medicine, see how he liked that. "If it makes it easier for you, I confess that the sister has had a similar effect on me."

"Elizabeth?" Charles asked. "That's excellent!" He lay down again, but on his back, hands behind his head, a prudent distance from Fitz. "Do you mean you imagine it's her you're fucking when you fuck me? Or do you mean that you'd like to have us both, together?"

Fitz laughed. Although he might have preferred a little jealousy on Charles's part, some wounded pride, still, it was going to be all right. "My dear Charles! Such depravity! No, not the two of you at once. At least, not until I've had a chance to try her alone." Little danger of that. One of her most appealing qualities was her rock-solid virtue. Playful she might be, flirtatious even, with a quicker wit than any female Fitz had ever known, but there was not the slightest appearance of immodesty.

No, she was safe. Utterly, delightfully safe. He could enjoy the look of her dark, wide eyes and the surprising, arousing delicacy of her slight form and slender figure—such a contrast to the blowsy, overripe sister—and feel immune from any worry that she might seduce him, tempt him to "ruin" her, and blackmail him into keeping her. And she had more than enough sense to know that, on such very different social levels as they were, there was not the least possibility of marriage between them.

She was the perfect object for Fitz's admiration. So refreshing after Caroline and even Louisa's constant, wearying sycophancy. It was so deliciously satisfying to be able to taunt them with his genuine appreciation of another woman. Shake them out of their complacency. Caroline needn't be so damned sure of him. It had been comforting at first, knowing that when he reached an age—thirty, thirty-five, perhaps—when remaining a bachelor was becoming problematic, he could resign himself to matrimony and she would be there for him, always willing. She'd be an aging spinster by then, but what matter? She would be grateful and happy, and would accept any terms he chose to make. There'd be time to get a brat or two on her, and, eager as she was, she'd do whatever was required—take him in her mouth or go on all fours—to rouse him to hardness.

Now it was becoming stultifying. At least Caroline had her supposed virginity to protect. But Louisa, safely married, could throw herself at Fitz with abandon, and with no fear of any embarrassing consequences. Damn! He hadn't thought of that when Charles had explained that his elder sister, Mrs. Hurst, and her husband would be staying with him in his household. "Household," indeed. It was Fitz she liked living with, Fitz she tormented with her constant adulation, egging Caroline on in her hopes of eventual wedded bliss, and implying, with every word, every look, that in marrying one sister he would gain the favors of both.

Charles rolled over and kissed Fitz on the lips, interrupting his thoughts. "Are you going to lie there like a log all night? Or can a man hope for some help with his trouble?"

"What trouble?" Fitz asked, the corners of his mouth curling up in a smile. He knew the answer to this old joke, but what joy to hear it again.

"Why, this stiff thing," Charles said, waving his erection almost in Fitz's face. "It just keeps growing and growing, and I don't know what to do with it."

"Oh, you poor man," Fitz said, playing the scene out to the end. "Let me see what I can do." He sat up, rolling Charles onto his back again, and knelt between his friend's spread thighs. Charles's engorged cock was leaping and drooling in a state of near release, all without any help from Fitz, just from the presence of Miss Bennet under the same roof. Fitz thought a silent apology to the woman and grasped Charles in a loose fist. "Is this the root of the trouble, do you think?"

"Please, Fitz," Charles said. "I can't hold on much longer."

"So I see," Fitz said. "And yet it seems to me we've had more than enough exertion for two tired old men this night."

"I wish I'd never said anything," Charles said.

"Not at all," Fitz said. "As you so wisely suggested, we ought to consider putting away childish things." He studied the live member, oozing clear liquid from its tip, the head already jutting out from the foreskin, and jerking in its own uncontrollable rhythm. "By the way, is this one of those childish things?"

"Please, Fitz," Charles said again. His voice was suppliant, almost tearful. "Whatever I said before, I humbly beg your pardon. Just, please, *please*, do what you want."

"Are you sure?" Fitz asked. "Do you know what I want?"

"I can guess," Charles muttered, but laughing despite his distress.

Fitz took pity on him. "My dear," he murmured. "I shall

do only what *you* want. And I'm fairly certain you want this." He licked and kissed, then took the head in his mouth. He felt Charles's explosion almost upon him and tried to prolong it, removing his mouth, making Charles moan in agony and lift his hips from the bed. Fitz could not draw things out forever, nor could he hold back his own desire, and he put his hands under Charles's firm buttocks, lifting him up with his muscular arms, opening his mouth and throat in a practiced, smooth motion. When Charles discharged, Fitz swallowed it all, up to the balls.

"Oh," Charles sighed and groaned in ecstasy. "Oh God, Fitz, you're a wonder." He turned onto his stomach without being asked or cajoled, knowing he owed his lover his reward.

Fitz decided to try something else. "No," he said. "Let me see your face."

"Damn it, Fitz. You know I hate that."

"But you promised I could do what I want, after," Fitz reminded him.

"Bugger it, so I did," Charles admitted.

"Not *it*," Fitz said. "You. I shall bugger you face to face, as I prefer, and you will like it."

"You can't make me like it," Charles said. "You can force me to submit, but no one can make someone like something he detests."

"If he truly detests it, no," Fitz said. He was already lifting Charles's legs, placing the ankles over his shoulders, spitting into his hand and readying himself and Charles's bum for his possession. "But if you merely find it embarrassing or improper," he raised his voice to a mincing, effeminate drawl, "then I think I can make you like it very well, despite all your maidenly objections."

"Not such a maiden," Charles said, sucking in his breath as Fitz entered him.

"No," Fitz said. "Precisely my point." He pushed in further, going slowly but inexorably forward, until he had buried his entire shaft in Charles's interior. "How do you like that?" Fitz whispered. He pulled out a few inches and pushed back in, still gently, but increasing the force incrementally.

Charles found himself responding to the familiar amorous technique. "Damn it, Fitz," he complained. "You're a devil."

"And you are a tease," Fitz answered. "But this time you will not escape the consequences of your actions."

He picked up the rhythm, working steadily until Charles was lost in the sensation, pushing up to Fitz's body so that they slammed together, hips to buttocks, with each thrust. Charles's eyes that had been shut like a child's against a dreaded punishment came open, eyelids drooping but irises focused on Fitz's face, and his mouth that had been screwed up tighter than his puckered arse opened in slack, sensual acceptance of the glorious pounding he was receiving. And his cock, that had so recently been drained, rose again, brought to precipitate resurrection by the deep penetration that found and repeatedly struck that mysterious place.

As Fitz came, Charles's mouth stretched into a wide grimace of mingled pain and pleasure, and Fitz leaned down for a tender kiss. Charles discharged again, the effusion trapped between their bellies and heaving chests, gluing them together in a sticky, love-scented mess. Fitz allowed Charles's legs to descend, but remained inside him, his cock slowly deflating.

"Did you like that, you little tease?" he asked.

"You know I did, damn you," Charles said. "You know I can deny you nothing."

"I know," Fitz said. He was purring with pleasure. "I know."

Three

ELIZABETH BENNET WATCHED her sister sleep, recalling the past days' disastrous if amusing conversational exchanges. Jane had enjoyed her first visit downstairs but had become fatigued and had retired early. If it weren't for Jane's potential happiness, Elizabeth would press Mama to take her home as soon as she was able to travel. In a proper closed carriage, that could be as early as tomorrow. But meeting Mr. Bingley was the best thing that had happened to Jane in almost seven years, since before she came out in society. There was so little to choose from in a small village, and then having no portion to speak of—no, if this Mr. Bingley loved Jane, and he showed every appearance of doing so, and of being worthy of the term *love*, then it was Elizabeth's duty to help things along as much as decently possible.

Jane's eyelids fluttered and she emerged slowly to consciousness.

"How are you feeling, dear?" Elizabeth asked. "Any better?"

"A little," Jane said. "Do you think they will mind terribly if I impose on their hospitality a bit longer?"

"I know one person who will be delighted," Elizabeth said.

Jane blushed. "You must not encourage me in false hopes after so short an acquaintance."

"If they were false, my dear, I would not encourage them. I will therefore amend my answer to say that if you leave too soon you will endanger not only your health but the happiness of one other person."

Jane smiled and bowed her head.

"And if an honest assessment allays your worries of my painting the scene rosier than I ought, I can say with certainty that by staying you will sow a great deal of dissension into the rest of the household, and substantially increase my enjoyment of this visit."

"I think," Jane said, speaking slowly in her desire to find a way to express an opinion while avoiding taking sides and offending anyone, "you are unfair to Miss Bingley."

Elizabeth grinned. "I doubt that's possible. But I was not referring principally to Miss Bingley's displeasure, but to a certain gentleman's."

Jane gasped in dismay. "*Mr.* Bingley! But you just led me to believe—"

"Oh, Jane, please. Do be sensible." Elizabeth was constantly reminded how far apart their temperaments were, but grateful for the inseparable devotion that had begun, it seemed, the minute Jane had accepted her first sibling, not as a rival, but as an ally and friend. "I meant that cold, high-and-mighty Mr. Darcy."

"Mr. Darcy! Why should he mind that I am here? Surely I cannot inconvenience him."

"Now there you underestimate your powers," Elizabeth said. "If you are feeling strong enough, I shall attempt to divert you and raise your spirits by relating all the conversation you have missed these past few days. When I am done, I dare you to challenge my interpretation."

"Of what?" Jane asked.

"Only a very interesting love affair in danger of ending due to one party's attempting to retain the waning affections of his beloved, and the other party's determination to assert his independence."

Jane frowned in concentration, then looked up with triumph. The vivacity in her face gladdened Elizabeth's heart. Jane was truly on the mend. "I have caught you in an error, Lizzy! You have spoken of both parties with the masculine pronoun. And here I thought you were going to tell me of Mr. Darcy and Miss Bingley."

"Of Mr. Darcy, yes. But not Miss Bingley."

Jane gasped again and covered her mouth. "Surely Mrs. Hurst cannot be so lost to virtue that she—"

"I'm sure Mrs. Hurst and virtue parted ways years ago," Elizabeth said. "But, no, desirous though she may be of losing her good name and her position in the world, *she* is not Mr. Darcy's object."

"I am at a loss, then," Jane said.

"Why, Mr. Bingley, of course. You will not have had occasion to see it, confined to your bed most of the time. But I have had many opportunities to observe, and I tell you that Mr. Darcy could not be more jealous of a new bride than he is of your nice Mr. Bingley."

Jane laughed but looked unhappy. "Much as I have resented Mr. Darcy's slighting of you, and deplored his lack of both taste and judgment in expressing it, still I think it is beneath you to say such things of him in retaliation. Revenge is never justified, especially when a person must stoop to pettiness to accomplish it."

"It is not revenge. In truth, I do not resent Mr. Darcy's disdain, for after spending three days in his company I see that in that trifling incident at the Meryton assembly I have been treated no worse by him, and in some ways better, than he treats all of womankind."

Jane, conscious of some inside knowledge, was moved to explain. "Mr. Bingley has apologized to me for his friend's behavior."

"To you?" Elizabeth said.

Jane studied her lap, unable to look her sister in the face. "He could not address you directly on this subject, after all. But with his natural kindness he knew how I would feel your hurt as my own, and he does not wish me to think ill of his friend."

"Whatever did he say?" Elizabeth asked.

"Only that he knew Mr. Darcy is overly severe on the subject of ladies, but that he hopes his manners will improve as he spends more time in such congenial company. Oh, Lizzy, don't laugh like that. Those were Mr. Bingley's exact words."

"I can't help it," Elizabeth said. "And I'm afraid Mr. Bingley is doomed to disappointment, as there is no improvement so far. It is all too obvious that Mr. Darcy considers none of us fit to mingle with the educated and intelligent, by which he means his sex alone. In fact, I suspect he would much prefer to inhabit an exclusive company, like a regiment of guards, where no females of any condition are allowed to sully the purity of superior masculine society."

"You are just as severe yourself, you know," Jane murmured. "Mr. Bingley assures me that Mr. Darcy has an excellent character and is a devoted and loyal friend, who has nothing but Mr. Bingley's best interests at heart."

"So does a good husband have his wife's interests at heart," Elizabeth replied. "Come. I will put the case to you. You shall be the judge, whether I have presented a convincing argument."

"Very well." Jane sat up straight in the bed and folded her hands on the bedclothes.

"I would say the first piece of evidence I have to bring is a negative one," Elizabeth began. "That is, it speaks not so much to Mr. Darcy's love for his friend as to his lack of regard for women in general. When the subject of Mr. Darcy's sister arose, Mr. Bingley spoke so glowingly of ladies' accomplishments that Mr. Darcy was moved to challenge his friend's generous assessment, and most vehemently. It was almost more than I could do to keep my countenance."

"But might not Mr. Darcy's words, ungallant as they appeared," Jane offered with her usual diffidence, "simply be his way of praising his sister, contrasting her merits with the deficiencies of other ladies?"

"Indeed," Elizabeth said. "But he went too far, assisted by his acolyte, Miss Bingley. She imagines herself an exception, the ideal of her sex—in addition to Miss Darcy, naturally."

"Miss Bingley *is* very elegant," Jane said.

"Oh yes," Elizabeth said, waving her hand. "She has been to a fashionable ladies' seminary, and she can afford to wear new gowns every season. But you should have heard their requirements for a lady to be considered accomplished. The inventory of scholarly achievements alone was absurd. When they started in on 'a certain something in her manner,' and 'her way of walking and speaking'—well, it was so ridiculous I had to say that no living woman ever met such impossible standards. And, I ask you, if such a creature existed, would she deign to marry an ordinary, flawed, mortal man? Not even Mr. Darcy himself could match her in perfection!"

"I imagine Miss Darcy's education and understanding are superior," Jane said. "She probably favors her brother in both beauty and intellect."

"She may be a paragon," Elizabeth said, "but the inconvenient fact remains that Mr. Bingley does not wish to marry a school headmistress or a marble statue. He has that most annoying trait, common sense, and values instead goodness of heart, sweetness of temper, and, because he is but human himself, physical beauty—that is, you."

Jane flushed again. "Mr. Bingley does sometimes give the impression of being flighty or frivolous, but it is just his natural modesty. He really is quite levelheaded."

"Yes," Elizabeth said. "It was obvious that Mr. Darcy's words sprang from a fear of Mr. Bingley's being in love with *you*."

"I know Miss Bingley and Mrs. Hurst would dearly love to see their brother married to Miss Darcy," Jane said.

"Yet I suspect that the desire arises on their part, as well as on Mr. Darcy's, to create a close tie between the two families, rather than from any concern for their brother's happiness or genuine appreciation of Miss Darcy's merits."

Jane frowned. "I think there is some truth in what you say."

"They forget that, in such an important matter as a man's choice of wife, their wishes will inevitably carry less weight than his," Elizabeth said.

"But Mr. Bingley does speak very highly of his friend's discernment," Jane said. "You yourself told me that Mr. Darcy is said to have an impressive library at his home in Derbyshire, and everybody praises his extraordinary learning. I should think the two of you ought to find a great many subjects for conversation."

Elizabeth grimaced. "I doubt very much whether Mr. Darcy's library contains any novels. And he would deem *anything* written by a female not worth the cost of the rags that make up the paper."

"Oh, Lizzy," Jane said. "All I know is that Mr. Bingley values his friend's advice, and that Miss Bingley shares her brother's opinion."

"And wishes herself in his place," Elizabeth said.

"I will pretend not to understand that," Jane said.

"You cannot misunderstand this next item," Elizabeth said. "You would have laughed out loud watching Mr. Darcy trying to compose a letter to his sister, accosted at every line by Miss Bingley. She deluged him with interruptions, from compliments on his penmanship to requests to be remembered to Miss Darcy. And he rebuffed each intrusion with serene detachment."

"It may simply be courtesy," Jane said.

"A courteous gentleman would not allow Miss Bingley to deceive herself by fancying that her regard is reciprocated," Elizabeth said. "Watching Miss Bingley's attack on all sides, deflected by Mr. Darcy's unconcealed and unchecked derision, I could only wonder. How can Miss Bingley, a resident of this household, be totally unaware of what I have so easily discovered after only three days? Or does the poor woman hope that by constant bombardment she can force a breach in an impenetrable wall? She must see that every cannonball flies wide of the target, and that the defender is hard at work reinforcing the already impressive fortifications."

"You have changed your metaphor," Jane said. "You began with a trial at law and have now turned instead to a siege."

"It seems more fitting," Elizabeth said.

"Besides, it merely demonstrates that Mr. Darcy feels no partiality for Miss Bingley, not that he harbors an inappropriate fondness for her brother."

"True. But now we come to the crux of my argument. You know how I like to attempt to draw a person's character. I had only started when Mr. Bingley, in a fit of exaggerated humility, claimed to be not worth the effort, calling himself shallow and direct, and chose as his example the idea that if he took it into his head to quit Netherfield he would be gone at a moment's notice. Mr. Darcy, just like the clever husband with the simple wife, sneered at such an uncomplicated nature. He insisted that, rather than sticking to his resolve, Mr. Bingley would give in at once if 'a friend' asked him to. Mr. Darcy is so fond of Mr. Bingley, yet he seemed to think the less of him for his willingness to accommodate his own wishes." Elizabeth shook her head at such incomprehensible behavior.

"But what is the great significance of this exchange?" Jane asked. "I don't see it."

"I haven't related the whole yet," Elizabeth said. "I thought your Mr. Bingley deserved some support. He can't stand up to Mr. Darcy's badinage."

"I'm sure he can do very well without your help," Jane said with uncharacteristic sharpness.

"Well, no, I don't think he can," Elizabeth said, not at all displeased at her sister's defense of her suitor. "But in this instance I'm afraid I did more harm than good. 'All you have done is prove Mr. Bingley's amiability,' I said, 'far better than his own modesty will allow. That he would readily change his plans because his friend asked him to, and require no other explanation, is but testimony of affection.' You see, they weren't really arguing over whether Mr. Bingley would leave Hertfordshire or stay at Netherfield, but over something much more momentous."

"What do you mean?"

"Marriage. Mr. Bingley's to you, to be precise."

"Oh, that's absurd. Besides, I would never want my happiness to come at the expense of someone else's," Jane said with a sigh.

"That's nonsense! You can't mean it!"

"Think, Lizzy. What chance of contentment could we have in our marriage if by choosing me Mr. Bingley lost the friendship of Mr. Darcy?"

"What kind of friend is Mr. Darcy if he ends a friendship

because his friend marries?" Elizabeth asked. "Besides, I don't think it's you he objects to so much as the idea of his friend's marrying at all. What could he possibly find objectionable in you?"

"What else did he say, exactly?"

"It wasn't what he said but the expression on his face," Elizabeth said, pausing to recall. "After I spoke my little piece, Mr. Bingley declared that if Mr. Darcy 'were not such a great tall fellow, in comparison with myself, I should not pay him half so much deference.' Mr. Darcy looked angry enough to spit."

"Oh! That's dreadful!"

"Not as bad as all that," Elizabeth said. "Whatever else one may say against him, Mr. Darcy's manners are too elegant to allow him to spit in the presence of ladies."

"I wish you would be serious," Jane remonstrated, as so often.

"I am perfectly serious. But I haven't finished the account. If that were all, no harm done. If Mr. Darcy is angry with me, I don't care *that* for it." Elizabeth snapped her fingers. "But I did care that, by attempting to help Mr. Bingley, I caused a quarrel between him and his redoubtable friend."

"Whatever have you done *now*?"

"Only encouraged Mr. Bingley to stand up for himself, which Mr. Darcy took as insolence. Mr. Bingley was emboldened to speak freely, much in the manner of a schoolboy taunting his tutor in front of company, saying that nothing was so frightening as Mr. Darcy on a Sunday afternoon when he had nothing to do. *Then* I felt sorry, and wished I had not spoken, for Mr. Darcy turned a rather unhealthy shade of white and glowered at his friend until I was convinced that poor Mr. Bingley will pay for it later."

"They will make it up," Jane said. "You mustn't tease yourself over a silly remark. But it is a lesson, all the same. You do have a tendency to say whatever pops into your head."

"Unfair! After I study so hard to find a bon mot, something clever and original, and to make it seem as if I had just thought of it that instant. You of all people should know I resemble our sister Mary in that regard, not Kitty or Lydia, who truly utter whatever words happen to be on their tongue at the moment of opening their mouth."

Jane laughed. "Now you are expecting me to cry foul and to tell you how far superior in wit you are to all our sisters. But I will simply let it stand, Lizzy."

"You have found me out at last," Elizabeth said. "The truth is, I was carried away by the pleasures of a real contest. I've never encountered such an opponent as this Mr. Darcy. Every other man just crumbles at the first show of spirit, as if with all his education and knowledge of the world he can't put two sensible words together when addressing one paltry female."

"Not so paltry. But be careful, Lizzy. You will go too far."

"It's true. Mr. Darcy brings out the worst in me. I want to burst his bubble of pride, put a crack in that solid wall of his contempt, just as badly as Miss Bingley, although for different motives." She couldn't help laughing, even now, at the memory. It had been startling, frightening, but somehow exhilarating, every time she had guessed correctly and provoked a reaction in that tall, fair iceberg.

"All I ask," Jane said, "is that you not come between Mr. Darcy and his friend."

"That I can safely promise," Elizabeth said with a smile. "It's you who is doing that."

"But I don't wish to."

"You will have to make up your mind to it," Elizabeth said, "unless you want to lose your chance at a happy marriage. I know you don't like to put yourself forward, but if ever you were to fight, now is the time. Mr. Darcy loves Mr. Bingley as possessively as any man with a pretty, wayward young wife, and is outraged at his friend's least show of independence. This love for you is probably the first time Mr. Bingley has ever stood up for himself over a woman—or at least a young lady worthy of matrimony."

"Even if I were willing to *fight*, as you call it," Jane said, "I don't see what more I can do and remain within the bounds of propriety."

"Dearest Jane," Elizabeth said. "All you need do is support Mr. Bingley. Nothing improper. He has undertaken all the combat so far. He has made a declaration, as bold as a rebellious colony's defiance of its imperial government, and as likely to result in the usual consequences—military occupation and greater restrictions on trade."

"From a trial to a siege and now a revolution," Jane said.

"That's exactly what it is," Elizabeth said. "Mr. Bingley has proclaimed his autonomy and announced his desire to separate from the former monarch of his affections. Now Mr. Darcy is sending out the recruiting officers and the press gangs, readying for a prolonged and bitter war and quashing of an insurrection. But remember which side prevailed in the last such contest."

"If you are speaking of the French Revolution," Jane said, "I refuse to be responsible for loosing the Terror and the guillotine upon Netherfield."

"I can think of some heads that ought to roll," Elizabeth said. "But I was referring to the Americans."

"WERE THOSE YOUR true sentiments?" Fitz asked Charles that night. "Is that the only reason you allow me my pleasures—that I am a great tall fellow who bullies you into surrender?"

"Of course not," Charles said. "But you must admit that you sometimes talk as if you don't like me very much. And you certainly don't respect me. I feel less like your friend than your whore: pretty and accommodating enough for use in private, but not fit to be seen in polite society."

"Good God!" Fitz said. "All this from a bit of drawing-room nonsense. I meant only that you are not some wild Lochinvar or roaring boy out of Walter Scott or Wordsworth, but a rational, unpretentious young Englishman, a respectable gentleman of property and fortune, if anything too prone to follow the counsel of others."

"And I was merely trying to introduce some sense into that ridiculous discussion, bring it down to earth instead of that up-in-the-air, philosophical tone of all your conversation," Charles said. After a strained pause he added, "You know, Fitz, I've often wished I were more the heroic ideal. You'd have to woo me then, instead of . . ." His mouth closed in a sad little smile.

"So you do feel coerced." Fitz lay down on the bed and stared at the underside of the canopy. "What do you want—a declaration of love? Last night, as I recall, you practically begged me to help you with your *trouble*. In fact, your entire mood was extremely abject."

"Oh, now you're baiting me," Charles said. "I'm sorry, Fitz. At the moment, all I can think about is Miss Bennet. I told you before, I think of her when you—when we—"

"Thank you," Fitz said, "for reminding me."

"*You* said you think of Elizabeth. I wasn't sure I believed you at first, but after these past couple of days I'm convinced. You goad her with your superior manner and exalted language."

"And look how she stands up to me," Fitz said. "I've never met a woman—or a man, come to think of it—who could hold her own in debate with me."

"It's not my idea of lovers' talk," Charles said.

"And your Miss Bennet is not my idea of an interesting woman."

"How fortunate, then," Charles replied, "that you are not courting her."

"Courting," Fitz repeated with what was becoming a habitual sneer whenever he spoke of the woman. "You will have to stop, you know, before she begins to believe you have serious intentions."

"I do," Charles said. "After this ball I promised to hold, I'm going to ask her to marry me."

Fitz's heart leapt in his breast and his breathing became labored. He could feel the color rise into his face, the whoosh of blood in the veins of his neck like a whisper of warning. Apoplexy, they called it. "Don't be silly, Charles," Fitz said when he could speak.

"Silly?" Charles shouted. "I am not silly. You are jealous and cruel and spiteful."

"On the contrary, I am attempting to look at the situation from a perspective of reason and detachment. You're in no condition to ask any woman to marry you—you lack the experience to tell when a lady returns your regard and when she is merely dazzled by your fortune and youthful vigor."

"Yet you're willing to let Georgiana marry me in this deplorable *condition*," Charles said.

Fitz gave a snort of dry laughter. "Don't bank on it, Charles. My consent to an understanding between the two of you would depend entirely on your assurance that all attentions to other women were at an end."

Charles at least had the decency to look abashed. "I'm sorry, Fitz. But honestly, that's only this idea that you and my sisters cooked up between you. I've been happy to go along with it when I was unattached, but where love is concerned I must choose for myself."

"Yet surely I can advise, in this most important decision of a man's life."

"I've heard your advice, Fitz. And browbeat me as you will, subdue me with your superior strength, this time I will make up my own mind and please myself." Charles's tone and manner were all calm resolution, no longer the protesting, eager boy.

As he readied himself for sleep, Fitz reminded himself yet again that he must tread very carefully. From inconvenience to mortal danger was but a distance of a few missteps.

Four

NOW THAT SHE was awake, Jane asked Elizabeth, with great apologies and hesitation, if she would mind very much going to the kitchen to look after some barley water the cook had made and had forgotten to send up. Elizabeth would have to brave the corridors and the stairs in her nightdress, or put her clothes on all over again. Recalling her earlier ruminations, she saw no reason to worry, and slinging her dressing gown over her shoulders, opened the door to the bedchamber and glided noiselessly along in her slippers.

Passing another bedchamber, the door of which had swung free from the jamb a few inches, Elizabeth could not help overhearing. "I am grateful, my dear, that you changed your mind, at least for tonight." There was no mistaking the voice of Mr. Darcy. "It's fortunate we retired early. We can still enjoy a good long revel."

"I never like to make you unhappy, Fitz," Mr. Bingley said. "If only I could just look in on Miss Bennet first. I think coming downstairs was fatiguing for her."

"That's an excellent plan," Mr. Darcy said, "if your aim is

to compromise her and be forced into marriage—entering a young lady's bedchamber late at night, completely unclothed. Or were you intending to put your shirt on first? I wonder Caroline doesn't try that with me. Thank goodness I always remember to lock my door."

"I wish you wouldn't mock my sister so," Mr. Bingley said.

"She positively invites it," Mr. Darcy said. "You know she does. Just as you invite all the tender attentions I pay to you."

"It's not the same."

"No, of course not. I care for you. And when, in addition to your amiable character, I am reminded of all your considerable corporeal charms, that lovely thick rod and those firm round mounds behind, I can do nothing but show my admiration in the clearest way I know how."

The men, both naked, moved slowly into Elizabeth's line of vision. Mr. Darcy was every bit as imposing unadorned as he was in full regalia of coat and pantaloons and cravat. His skin was white and smooth, with muscles well defined by the shadows from the flickering light. He had very little hair, or perhaps, as he was fair, it did not show. Mr. Bingley was slender and dark, sinewy and lithe, with a downy coat of hair on his chest and shaggy legs like a hound's. His appearance was more virile than Elizabeth had expected from his gentle, unassuming nature.

Elizabeth wanted to run away but was paralyzed with something that was not exactly fear. Her thighs felt sticky, as if viscous liquid was leaking out of her, although it was not that time of the month. Her heartbeat thudded so loud she was certain the men would hear it, and her breath became shallow and rapid.

Mr. Darcy embraced his friend from behind, pulling him close with hands wrapped across his chest. He licked Mr. Bingley's neck like a cat, then nipped with his teeth. Mr. Bingley yelped and laughed, turning in the embrace, affording Elizabeth a generous and unconcealed view of both men. That part of Mr. Darcy that Elizabeth had never seen on any man, that young wives made jokes about while shooing the unmarried girls from the room, lived up and more to the descriptions that Elizabeth had been certain were but exaggerations designed to frighten maidens into chastity. So thick, and that *color*! Although perhaps it was a trick of the firelight . . .

It had all happened in a second or two. She gasped, and the men startled at the faint sound. She had the advantage of the dark, where the men were exposed by the lighted room. Ducking her head and clutching her dressing gown tightly around her hunched shoulders, Elizabeth darted down the corridor and turned the corner into safety. By the time Mr. Darcy had moved to the door, there was nothing to be seen.

Elizabeth stood just beyond the corner. Surely he wouldn't come after her. And safer not to make any more noise by running now.

"Damn it!" Mr. Darcy's well-bred voice resounded in the silent passageway. "I told you to see about getting this door fixed. It doesn't close properly."

"Fitz!" Mr. Bingley whispered. "Was somebody there? We'd better not—" The rest was lost in low murmurs behind the thick wood of the door.

Elizabeth headed back toward her sister's bedchamber, too nervous to complete the long journey to the kitchen. "I'm sorry," she told Jane. "I couldn't find it."

"Never mind," Jane said. "I'll do very well with this cold tea and warm water. Perhaps I'll be well enough to go down to breakfast tomorrow."

ELIZABETH SLEPT LITTLE that night, less even than her sister. She had heard of "men who did not like women." But the implications behind the phrase could never have been made so clear to her as in tonight's impromptu tableau. A man who did not like women was also a man who *did* like men—in a way he should not. Why the one should follow from the other Elizabeth had not understood until now, despite all her humorous words on the subject.

There was one incident she had not related to Jane, one piece of evidence she had left out, because it did not help her cause but rather contradicted her argument. It had happened after dinner while Jane and Mr. Bingley sat a little apart from the others, engrossed in their own low-voiced talk. Miss Bingley had invited Elizabeth to join her in walking around the parlor, an obvious ploy to give the gentlemen—or one in particular—a full view of their forms that sitting at a table could not provide.

Ordinarily, Elizabeth would never take part in such a vulgar scheme. But there was no one to be modest before. Mr. Hurst was a nonentity—a fribble, a man of fashion whose concerns encompassed nothing beyond food and cards. Mr. Bingley cared for no one but Jane. Elizabeth felt certain she could disrobe in front of him and fall backward onto a sofa with her legs in the air, and he would merely inquire whether her sister was feeling better. No, it was only this woman-hating Mr. Darcy they would be attempting to beguile, as Miss Bingley well knew.

Elizabeth stood up, suddenly all too conscious of the man's eyes on her, and resolving to be brave, linked arms with Miss Bingley and paraded up and down the room.

Mr. Darcy, lest she should miss any of the connotations of her action, remarked that he knew full well why the ladies walked—a comment totally unnecessary unless to inform Elizabeth that she was the object of his interest.

Miss Bingley, unsurprisingly, blundered happily into the snare, querying Mr. Darcy as to his mysterious meaning, destroying any gains from Elizabeth's deliberate silence. Elizabeth could not recall the rest of the conversation; her head swam with the consciousness of his eyes on her until she felt like a veiled odalisque displayed before a fastidious Oriental sultan searching out replacements for his depleted seraglio.

It was such an effort to regain her composure that she had an overwhelming desire to pierce and draw blood in recompense. Bad enough to refer obliquely in the ensuing discussion to the vices of pride and vanity, but she had not stopped there. When he denied the latter and made a virtue out of the former, "Mr. Darcy has no defect," she said, sinking to the level of insolence. "He owns it himself without disguise." She sensed his recoil and was abashed, but could not take the words back, nor would she if given the chance.

He had behaved almost as badly when Mrs. Hurst played on the pianoforte, suggesting with unbecoming slyness that Elizabeth was so moved by the lively tune that she must wish to dance a reel. What if she had been incautious enough to agree? Considering his lack of courtesy at that first Meryton assembly, it seemed a calculated insult. Or had he already forgotten that insignificant event?

How could he love his friend, to the rejection of all others, and yet watch her so closely? How could he hate women and yet admire her? What did it mean, to "hate women"? Whatever he was, he hated women's minds and natures, not their bodies. At least, not her body.

Just as she felt about him. He was odious, overbearing, arrogant. And beautiful. And amusing, an opponent worthy of her skill. Oh, he was far above her slight talents, and impervious to anything she could say to wound him, but at least she had someone to joust with, someone she could not defeat on the first try.

It would be bad enough if it was just a physical attraction that had sprung up, so quickly conceived and as quickly dispelled with the revelation of weak character or deficient wit. But this was dangerous. He was like a sleek, muscular tiger, something with claws and sharp teeth that must be left alone, while all the time one's hand was reaching out, tempted to stroke the striped coat, only to be bitten off. He knew exactly the effect he had on her—on all women, apparently—and scorned them all. That was some comfort, at any rate, that he had as great a contempt for his friend's snobbish, rude sisters as for her.

After his dismissal of her at the Meryton assembly as "not handsome enough to tempt me," Elizabeth had been very glad to give him no more reason to find her lacking. When Sir William Lucas, hosting his own gathering, had tried to pair them for a dance, she had refused on principle. And apparently done herself some good, because the hateful man had not pressed.

Why, then, did she care that he notice her here at Netherfield? She should stay out of sight, keep quiet, instead of answering his acerbic witticisms with her own, as close to impertinence as she had ever come with anyone. She knew he liked it, knew he had never been spoken to in that way.

Elizabeth was certain now. They must leave this house, but only to gain reinforcements, waging the war for Mr. Bingley's liberation, and Jane's happiness, from their own camp. It could all work out very well. Mr. Bingley was announcing his intentions to set up his own establishment. He and Jane were a perfect match, in age, in temperament—anyone could see that. Even Mr. Darcy would be forced to recognize that the time had come to let his friend decide this matter for himself. It might not have to mean the end of their friendship, after all. Why should he not love a married man as well as a single one? Only he would have to share, that's all.

She must help Jane in her struggle, should they face a whole legion of Mr. Darcys; she shuddered, suddenly in a cold sweat every bit as bad as Jane's, at the image of a battalion of tall, fair, handsome, proud men, advancing in line across like soldiers on the field of battle, but instead of muskets leveled, ready to fire, they had their breeches open, and—

What was the matter with her? When had she ever thought in such lewd images? Never—but only because she had never before seen anything to inspire them. And there had never been anyone worth thinking lewdly about. She had never felt it, this reaction to a man's face or voice, this strange tightness between her thighs, this wetness.

She would not let herself become as pathetic as Miss Bingley.

ONCE BACK AT home, Elizabeth tried a dozen times to tell Jane of what she had heard—and seen—but could not bring herself to do it. Jane was sweet and innocent and trusting. She would be too ready to forgive, to understand, and to hope, where hope was not, perhaps, her ally. No, someone else was better suited to hear Elizabeth's concerns.

"You acted rightly," Charlotte Lucas said with her unflappable serenity, "the only way you could have. Jane is, in some respects, the younger sister to you. *You* can comprehend complexity in a man's character where she, with her untried, unworldly nature, would only be confused."

"Can I?" Elizabeth said. "But suppose it to fall out as I wish. Suppose Mr. Bingley does love Jane, and they marry. How are they to live together with this unspoken transgression between them?"

"Oh!" Charlotte laughed and shook her head. "I forget

our difference of age in our souls' equal companionship. How should any marriage succeed? What man of the world comes to his bride unproven in the field of *amour*? What gentleman of twenty-three has committed no indiscretions? But he does not insult his wife by cataloging them for her."

"But this!" Elizabeth said. "Surely this is worse."

"How so?" Charlotte replied. "How is being loved by a handsome, wealthy friend, a gentleman of the highest standing, any worse than the usual run of such affairs?"

"Because," Elizabeth said, listening to her answer as if to test for the flaw, "to commit a youthful indiscretion or two, with a woman, may be seen as the natural course of a gentleman's maturation. But to do *that* with one of his own sex—"

Charlotte hushed her with a touch of gloved hand on her lips. "Lizzy," she whispered. "Think. How is it different from what we share?"

Elizabeth felt herself blushing. "You swore," she said, "as did I, never to speak of it out loud."

"I am speaking of it now," Charlotte said, her face looking somehow prettier and more dignified as she lost her habitual placid smile, "because you seem to have renounced it. Were all your sighs of pleasure, your protestations of devotion, merely the ploys of a fickle girl?"

"No!" Elizabeth said, more forcefully than intended. She glanced about, afraid that, behind a thick tree trunk, or around the edge of the field, hidden by the stand of corn, there lurked a listener, as she in the corridor that fateful night, but was reassured by the lonely vista, the solitude of the country lane they had chosen for their conversation. "Charlotte, you know my feelings. I would never pretend with you. I just don't see that the innocent love between women is the same as men's—you know I can't say the word."

"Sodomy?" Charlotte said. "No, in law you are correct.

Men are prosecuted for loving one another, while we women are ignored. It is one of the very few times, perhaps the only one, where the law errs in our favor. But in spirit, Lizzy, in spirit. Use your wits and tell me—just how is what your amiable, comfortable Mr. Bingley and your clever, scornful Mr. Darcy do with each other so different from our intimacies, and unforgivable?"

"Unforgivable?" Elizabeth looked up from the ground in surprise. "I don't think that."

"You implied that Jane would not forgive it if she knew."

"Not at all. I'm afraid she will forgive and accept too easily. *I* can forgive, but it is she who is wronged by it."

"How wronged?" Charlotte said. "But it is for him to tell, if he chooses, although I would not recommend it. There is no reason they cannot have a happy marriage. It is common enough, I assure you, and has little effect on a gentleman's eventual choice to marry or remain single."

"If you say so," Elizabeth said. "But you speak with such authority on a subject where it seems you can have no more direct knowledge than I."

Charlotte shrugged. "One of the advantages of having brothers; I am given a window into the minds of young men, whether I wish it or not. Even my father contributes to my education. From everything he says, if all the sodomites in London were not to marry, the city would be a vast unpopulated desert, its business and trade dwindled to little more than the barter of a primitive tribe, the court unattended and the theaters boarded up, as bad as in the time of Noll Cromwell."

"Stop," Elizabeth said, choking on her laughter. "You're shamming me. He can't say such things. I don't believe it." Thinking of pompous, silly Sir William Lucas, with his endless and repetitive stories of his brief, glorious presentation at St. James's, expounding to his wife and children on the natural acceptability of sodomy in London, she felt ready to expire with hilarity.

"I am not shamming," Charlotte said. "Oh, he does not say it quite so openly, but I can put two and two together, and I read the newspapers. When he relays the tittle-tattle from his old associates in town, how this Lord So-and-So and that Mr. Such-and-Such are perpetually in each other's company, and how they and their friends frequent this house or that, and all of them with wives and families, I do not see how Mr. Bingley will suffer any hardship."

"It is Jane's hardship I worry about, not his."

"I still don't see how it matters," Charlotte said. "Once they marry, he and Jane will set up their own household."

"Like Mr. Bingley's married sister, Mrs. Hurst, and her husband?" Elizabeth said.

"Hmm, I hadn't thought of that," Charlotte said. "But most likely Mr. Darcy would go back to his own estate, or to town. He would resent the affront."

"Yes, you're right about that," Elizabeth said. "In fact, it would probably be prudent if Mr. Bingley and Jane went abroad directly after the wedding. Somewhere very far away. Just to be on the safe side."

It was only when Elizabeth returned home, flushed and languid with the afterglow of pleasure, and was roundly scolded by her mother for her "green gown," the inevitable result of lying on damp grass, that she felt genuine fear. "If I had not seen you with that poor, plain Charlotte Lucas, I would suppose you were meeting some man, although who there could be other than that disagreeable, proud Mr. Whatever-His-Fine-Name who snubbed you at the assembly, I can't imagine," Mrs. Bennet rattled on, while Kitty and Lydia sniggered.

"The dangers of a *particular* friendship"—Mary had to utter her tuppence-worth of specious philosophy for the day—

"are well known for men, but of equal if not greater peril for women. Man is the master in matrimony; should a woman demonstrate an independence of masculine rule, she renders herself unfit for the wifely station."

"Oh, do shut up," Lydia said. "You're just being spiteful because you don't have a *particular* friend of your own."

"Thank you, Lydia," Elizabeth said. "I think we've had quite enough of particular friends for one week."

But privately she did not feel so brave. She and Charlotte were not so safe, nor so innocent, as she had thought. And if that sharp-eyed Mr. Darcy were ever to find out about it, she would be reduced to his level.

Perhaps it was time she and Charlotte began to think about renouncing the pleasures of girlhood. Charlotte was twenty-seven. There was little for her to look forward to in life, and Elizabeth did not like to abandon her friend or deprive her of the spinster's only solace. But Elizabeth was not yet one-and-twenty; there was no reason to despair. Surely there were men in the world who liked women, who had fortune enough to marry where they chose, who had wit and humor and were not unpleasant to look at . . . She heard the growing list of requirements. Goodness! The odds against marriage for a woman in her situation were almost insurmountable, unless one were willing to compromise.

What did a little sodomy matter, where everything else was as desirable as one could wish? She would say nothing to Jane, and hope for the best.

Now, if only Elizabeth could find a suitor.

"MR. WICKHAM? I say, is that you, Mr. Wickham?"

George thought for a prolonged minute, continuing to

walk down the dark street until he had placed the voice and determined it would do no harm to claim the acquaintance. Might even lead to some advantage. He turned around and allowed the other man to catch up, registering the red coat. "Mr. Denny! I'll be damned. Sorry for my inattentiveness. I was miles away."

Denny smiled at the beautiful face that confronted him. "Contemplating your many love affairs, I imagine," he said.

George saw no reason to contradict the assumption. "What brings you to town, Denny?"

"Oh, business. Nothing of interest. I say, fancy meeting you like this!"

"Yes," George said. "How's military life treating you?" *Ought to be just up your alley*, he thought.

"Not bad at all," Denny said. "The militia, you know. Never too long in one place. Not like the regulars. Soon as the natives tire of us, or we of them, it's off to the next billet and no danger of being sent somewhere dangerous, like Spain."

"Quite a noble martial sentiment," George said with a gentle laugh. No need to antagonize the man until he saw what he had to offer.

"You know I'm not one of those dashing heroes," Denny said, apparently not offended. "But I'd do my duty if asked and not complain."

"Where are you stationed for the winter?"

"Hertfordshire. Small village, nobody of note." Denny snapped his fingers. "I know—what made me think of you, helped me to recall your name just now—that gentleman whose estate you grew up on, Mr. Darcy—he's there."

"Darcy?" George felt that surefire aphrodisiac, the combination of fear and anger, surge through him at the name. "What's he doing in Hertfordshire? He's a Derbyshire man."

"Staying with a *friend*," Denny said with a wink and a nudge.

A master of subtlety, old Denny. "Anybody I know?" George asked.

"Don't think so. Pretty little fellow named Charles Bingley. But things aren't going so smooth between 'em. Had a few encounters with Darcy myself." Denny preened in the self-effacing manner of a man grateful to have been granted, by chance, the favors of one far above his touch. "Lovely tall man. Very strong. You never mentioned that, Wick," he added in an aggrieved tone.

George raised his eyebrows. "Sorry, but the pleasures of being plowed up the back field by Fitzwilliam Darcy have long faded for me." Had he pushed too far? Hearing that name again so soon had put him off balance. "And since when do you need me to help you to sport?"

Denny chose to take it in a friendly spirit. "Ah, Wick, you were always the master. The rest of us were just the poor 'prentices. You know that."

"Well, it's been delightful, seeing you again, but I must be going," George said.

"Oh, don't leave it like this," Denny said. "Let me stand you a drink at least, regale you with tales of the officers' mess. We have some good times, I can tell you. Lots of pretty girls in Meryton. Not that I care overmuch for that, but admiration is a pleasant thing, wherever it comes from." He studied the slim figure in front of him. "You know, you'd look damned smart in regimentals. If you're seeking a position, you could do a lot worse. And a commission in the militia don't cost anything, you know."

There was the rub. George had endured weeks of torment, the last payment having run out weeks ago and uncertain where to turn next. Mrs. Younge's charity would last only so long. The name was fictitious, of course, the woman being neither encumbered by a husband nor anywhere near what could be called, by any stretch of the imagination, youth. But even an overeager whore of middle years had her limits, and Jenny Younge was close to reaching hers. And then what? Making a decent living as a sharp was an entirely more demanding proposition in town than in the provinces; but life in the country was insupportable after a week. No sport, the palatable women kept close, the farm wives prematurely aged by hard work, about as appealing as the cattle they tended. And just as you were on the verge of getting inside one of the few tolerable girls, her father or brother was apt to turn up with a blunderbuss . . .

"Tell you what, Denny," George said, "I think I'll take that drink you were offering. Might be a good idea at that. Always wanted to be the one giving the orders."

"If that's what you're looking for, you won't find it as a lowly ensign in a militia regiment," Denny said. "But it has its compensations. Everyone loves a man in a red coat."

"So they do," George said. "I know a snug little tavern just a few streets over where a handsome officer and his friend can get a private room, no questions asked, and no danger of interference provided you have the wherewithal."

"A lieutenant's pay isn't much," Denny said, "but I can stand the ready in a good cause. Lead on, Wick. What a lucky thing it was, running into you like this."

Five

"GEORGE WICKHAM!" CHARLES said. "I don't know how he has the gall to show his face within a hundred miles."

"Oh," Fitz said, "he has gall, all right. He's a living, breathing, walking gallstone. I have no doubt he went to great pains to discover that you had leased Netherfield and that I was staying here, and determined to join this particular company of militia merely to spite me."

"That's absurd," Charles said. "He doesn't even know me, nor I him. Besides, you can leave any time, while he will be required to fulfill the terms of his commission."

"I assure you," Fitz said, "if anyone runs from this encounter, it will not be me."

"You never told me," Charles said, "the whole story of you and Wickham."

"And I never will," Fitz said. "And did we not agree never to mention his name?"

"But now that he's here—"

"Now that he's here, he will simply have to go away again,"

Fitz said. "If you insist on holding this damned ball, then there is one assembly he will not attend, one gathering he will not spoil with his loathsome presence."

"Such vehemence," Charles said. "Methinks the gentleman doth protest too much."

"Leave it alone," Fitz said.

"First love," Charles said, not heeding the advice. "A beautiful face, an enormous prick, and then—ah, the falseness of men."

"An enormous prick," Fitz said. "You're right on that score. He's a walking, breathing, goddamned prick."

"I've never heard you talk like this," Charles said. "Why can't you just ignore him?"

"Why can't you just shut it?" Fitz said.

Charles saw the look on his friend's face and regretted his careless, teasing words. "Did he hurt you very badly?" He dared to lay a hand on Fitz's arm, noting the bulging biceps and clenched fist, and felt the vibration of intense and suppressed emotion.

"I can't speak of it to anyone," Fitz said. "If you care for me at all, you will never refer to him again. Do you understand?"

"No," Charles said. "I don't. But I will do as you ask, Fitz. My God, to think of you burdened with all this rage. Is there anything I can do?"

"You know there is," Fitz said, feeling the anger flowing like water from a broken cistern, draining down out of his mind and pooling in his nether regions at the sympathetic words and touch. He kissed Charles with fierce hunger, devouring him with his longing, his wounded pride, his humiliation. And the worst of it all was, Fitz thought, as he rolled Charles over and entered his firm bum-hole, so tight and hot and ringed with dark fur, the worst of it was, when he had recognized George Wickham in the street this afternoon, his body had betrayed him. Knowing who it was, recalling all that had passed between them, yet Fitz had gone hard immediately, like—like a stallion sniffing out a mare or a bull brought to service the heifer. Like an animal. Not a rational, intelligent being, but just one rutting prick scenting another.

He thrust with rough, angry motions until Charles was moved to cry out. "Damn it, Fitz, I want to dance at the ball, not spend a week lying on my stomach."

No, even that was not the worst. Fitz reached the height of pleasure, pressing deeper into Charles's guts, provoking more moans and complaints, made inarticulate with pain and smothered by Charles's face being pushed into the pillow. The worst of it was, even here, with his dear, sweet Charles accommodating his ugly mood, it was George whom Fitz imagined, George's perfect, slim body, his skill at all the attitudes of passion, and his delicate responsiveness. Had all that really been feigned? Had he felt nothing of Fitz's love?

Fitz groaned as the last of his hardness spent itself in poor Charles's receptive arse. He slumped over his friend's back, as Charles manfully tried to control his breathing, not to show how he had been roughly used, not to whimper or cry.

That was the worst. Even now, Fitz wanted him. *Him.* George.

Start with the greatest hurdle, George had always told himself. After he jumped the broad stone wall, the lower, narrower fences would seem like molehills by comparison, and offer as little challenge. Only he had not expected to encounter that bastard Darcy quite so soon. That had been a facer, just in the process of getting acquainted with some of the daintiest bits of muslin he had met in quite some time—pity they none of them seemed to have much in the way of blunt—and seeing that proud, aristocratic sack of shit and his pretty little Ganymede come riding along . . . George could almost blush at the reaction that untoward meeting had caused in him, but he shrugged it off. It was human nature—at least men's nature. The man was good-looking, George was willing to give him that, active, strong as a blacksmith, and possessed of the sort of hauteur that never failed to arouse one's antipathy—and desire.

But things were in the way to turning out just as well as George had hoped. He couldn't quite see it as yet, but there was clearly a wide range of possibilities opening in front of him, like a line of opera dancers all spreading their legs at once. Typically, Darcy had done most of George's work for him, somehow managing to alienate all the goodwill to which he would naturally have been entitled by his immense fortune, handsome features, and noble bearing. All George had to do was fill in the particulars. The same sad story, much of it true. Son of old Mr. Darcy's steward, but godson to the master and reared with the master's son. Treated like a younger brother, educated and provided for, until the death of his benefactor had left George at the mercy of the firstborn, through whose jealousy and resentment he had been cheated of his inheritance and robbed of the living he had been promised.

"I have said something amusing?" George asked as his narration was interrupted by an inappropriate giggle.

"Oh no," Elizabeth assured him. "Please forgive me." Elizabeth was savoring the contrast between the lively conversation of Mr. Wickham and the coldness of that last Sunday at Netherfield. She had spent an entire half hour alone with Mr. Darcy without exchanging a word. Not one single word, while he attended steadfastly to his book. Something scholarly and dull, she was certain. Not a novel or even poetry. Sermons, probably, or philosophical essays. Latin or Greek for all she knew. Greek, undoubtedly, she decided, which had led to her laughter. "I was recalling the last time I was in your supposed patron's company. He could not bring himself even to look at me, much less speak. I am convinced he does not care for women."

Mr. Wickham met her gaze for a quick, meaningful glance, then lowered his eyes along with his voice, softer even than the murmur in which they had been conversing. "Indeed he does not, but it is hardly a subject for a lady."

"No," Elizabeth agreed. "But I have seen for myself, having spent nearly a week at Netherfield, that his romantic attentions are all directed at one who, while perfectly genteel, is not a lady."

"Well put!" Mr. Wickham permitted a gentle, almost melancholy laugh to escape. "Since you have found out that much, I will therefore reward your acumen by adding that, in addition to my wrongs of income withheld and professional advancement thwarted, I have suffered similarly at that gentleman's hands; he has spared me nothing."

Elizabeth gasped and covered her mouth. "Do you mean . . . ?"

"Yes," Mr. Wickham said. "That. Of course, once I was of age I made it quite clear that I would no longer submit to his unnatural demands. That was when he threw me out, with no living as had been promised, no position, and no income."

"And if you had agreed to his terms?"

"I might even now be vicar of my own parish, sufficient for my modest needs, and well situated in a prosperous neighborhood of a southern county."

"Oh!" Elizabeth exclaimed. "This is intolerable! Is there no end to his impositions?" Remembering the nature of the subject, she attempted to moderate her voice. "But surely you can fight. Is it not against the law?"

"My dear Miss Bennet," Mr. Wickham said in a whisper, moving his chair closer to Elizabeth's and taking her hand in both of his. They were sitting apart from the rest of the company, who were engrossed in cards, and the gesture went unnoticed. "You are innocent in the ways of vice. For a man to accuse another of such a crime, he must necessarily admit his own guilt and be prepared to pay the same penalty."

"But if he abused you, forced you, as a youth?"

"The age of consent is thirteen. In my recollection, it was on my very birthday that he began my *initiation*, as he called it."

Elizabeth closed her eyes in sympathy, but found to her consternation that a livelier picture occupied the dark space behind her eyelids: a very young, very pretty Mr. Wickham embraced by a slightly older, robustly handsome Mr. Darcy, much the way Mr. Bingley had been with Mr. Darcy the night she had seen them at Netherfield. This would never do. She opened her eyes and tried to find her place in the conversation. "You said he threatened you, and you refused at first. Is not that in itself a crime, no matter the age of the respective parties?"

"He would not tell it that way, you see," Mr. Wickham said in his unaffected yet knowing manner. "On his side, it would be I who had proposed our sinful activity, or who had acquiesced and was now turning to extortion."

"Still, he would have to account for his misdeeds."

Mr. Wickham shook his head, turning away in partial profile, in the process showing off his fine-boned face and translucent complexion. "It would be his word against mine, and which of us do you imagine would be believed? The son of a steward, or Mr. Fitzwilliam Darcy, master of Pemberley, with ten thousand pounds a year? And even if some of my story was accepted, all it would accomplish is to send us both to the pillory—or the gallows."

"Oh no! You could not, must not, suffer that." Elizabeth removed her hand from Mr. Wickham's, which was squeezing now and attempting to capture her other hand as well. People were looking in their direction. "Impossible! How can he live with himself, with the memory of committing such injustice?"

"How indeed?" Mr. Wickham said with a brave smile. "I rather think our mutual acquaintance revels in his blackness, like Mephistopheles counting up his wicked triumphs." His natural lightheartedness animated his features, rendering what was merely pretty in repose into exceptional beauty.

Elizabeth had to stop and catch her breath at the transformation. "It was generous but reckless of you to share such a secret with me. How do you know that I will not betray you?"

"You?" Mr. Wickham said. "You are all goodness. I would trust you with my life."

"As you have," Elizabeth said. Why was it, the heavier the content, the more flirtatious the conversation? "You may be sure, Mr. Wickham, that your life and your honor are safe with me."

IT WAS DISAPPOINTING somehow, Elizabeth reflected, that the prompt granting of her wish for a suitor should not be more appreciated by her friends. Charlotte's jealousy was understandable, but Jane's unwillingness to participate in righteous indignation at Mr. Wickham's wrongs was the more galling by its reasoned, evenhanded fairness. Jane looked at everything from Mr. Bingley's perspective. If Mr. Darcy was *his* friend, then he could do no wrong. If he had abused and mistreated a man who ought to have had the support and protection owed to a younger brother, it must somehow be due to a fault in the injured party. Mr. Bingley's friend could not be a villain.

"Sometimes I just want to shake some sense into her," Elizabeth complained to Charlotte. "She is my sister and I love her more than anyone—except you—but there are times when her defense of the indefensible makes me want to scream."

"Elizabeth, dear," Charlotte said, stopping for emphasis in their shortcut across the barren field. "I hope you won't scream now, but I must concur with the substance of your sister's objections. Is it not strange that a man, unknown to everyone in the village until a few days ago, should pour out such intimate secrets to a young lady he has only just met?"

Elizabeth waited until she could speak calmly. "Ordinarily I would agree. But you see, Charlotte, I gave him reason to know I would be sympathetic. That I knew about Mr. Darcy and Mr. Bingley."

"That was most imprudent," Charlotte said.

"Why? It was the very thing he was subjected to himself."

"So he claims."

"Why would he allege such a thing if it were not true?"

"Think if it were a woman accusing a man of forcing her," Charlotte said. "If she had truly been mistreated in this way, would she not feel an overwhelming sense of shame and keep the crime to herself? Whereas a woman making a false accusation of that sort proclaims her ruin to the world."

"That's outrageous!" Elizabeth protested. "And unfair. How is anyone to obtain justice in such cases?"

"No one gets justice in such cases," Charlotte said. "All the law allows is further degradation and loss of character to the honest, and a chance of notoriety to the dishonest."

"But if the crime involves two men," Elizabeth said, "there can be no monopoly of ruin or virtue on one side. Both must have a share in the guilt. I can't imagine a man making such an accusation without some truth in it."

"On the contrary," Charlotte said. "With such strict laws against sodomy, there's all the more incentive for desperate men to level baseless charges against the innocent. For the plaintiff, if he has lost everything else, it is a last great gamble, staking all or nothing on one roll of the dice, while his victim, respectable and wealthy, has everything to lose, and will the more readily submit to blackmail."

"Mr. Wickham is neither desperate nor rash," Elizabeth said. "If he is in need of income, and has been prevented from pursuing his true vocation, it is not his own misdeeds that have brought him to this place, but his abuser's."

"I'll grant you this much," Charlotte said. "Mr. Darcy has been doing an excellent job of ruining his own character through his own unaided efforts. Now Mr. Wickham, with your help and that of all the other gossiping women—and men—in the neighborhood, has been provided with the perfect opportunity to accuse him of something far worse than snubbing a lady at a ball or thinking himself above his company at a village assembly. And all behind Mr. Darcy's back, sinking his reputation without giving him the chance to tell his side of things. It's like a Star Chamber of innuendo."

"You certainly take all the pleasure out of rumormongering and backhanded dealing," Elizabeth complained. "But I have virtual proof of the justice of Mr. Wickham's claims. I saw the meeting between them. My sisters and I had walked to Meryton and met Mr. Denny, who was introducing some new officers in the regiment. Well, who should come riding down the street but Mr. Darcy and Mr. Bingley. For one exciting moment it looked as if we would be treated to a first-rate exhibition of the cut indirect, but at the last possible minute Mr. Wickham touched his hat and Mr. Darcy was forced to return the salute. He followed it up by turning an alarming shade of white and cantering off with the look of one who had several dogs and a serf or two to flay alive before dinner."

Charlotte was forced to grudging laughter at the vivid picture, but unconvinced. "How do you know that it is not Mr. Darcy who is wronged, and furious at being trailed by his adversary?"

"Oh, but Mr. Wickham is so handsome and charming, he *must* be another of Mr. Darcy's conquests. There's probably a list long enough to rival Don Giovanni's." Elizabeth blushed rosily at the words, a sight not lost on Charlotte.

"Never tell me you are in love with Mr. Wickham only because he's been subjected to Mr. Darcy's unnatural attentions!"

Elizabeth blushed even brighter at being found out. "Not *only* for that," she said. "Mr. Wickham has been mistreated just enough to merit sympathy, without being so broken as to provoke contempt." She knew better than to feign—not with Charlotte. "But there is something appealing about it, don't you think? I have been going over it in my mind, and although it was most indecent, it made a very pretty picture, Mr. Darcy and Mr. Bingley together. And now, imagining Mr. Wickham, who is more beautiful than Mr. Bingley . . ."

"Scandalous!" Charlotte laughed with genuine pleasure this time and pulled Elizabeth to the edge of the woods. "Come, then. Go over it again with me, and give me kiss for kiss, for I think it makes you amorous."

FITZ KNEW THE ball at Netherfield was not a good idea, but he had to allow dear Charles his simple pleasures. It was only right that the new tenant of a manor should open his house and offer hospitality to the neighborhood, nor would Wickham dare to put in an appearance after that disconcerting meeting on the street. Lord, but Fitz could almost wish he would, just to have the pleasure of throwing him out . . .

Yet as the time drew near for the festive evening, Fitz was surprised how little thought he had wasted on his old nemesis. It was another face he hoped to see, a rather different shape and form he hoped to partner, if only for a country dance or two.

It was her wit he missed. That and her sparkling eyes. Her

intelligence seemed to shine out through her eyes, even if the proof of it necessarily emerged through her small, thin-lipped mouth. Charles was sweet and true, bright enough, pretty and deferential, the perfect combination to arouse Fitz's physical love and the protection due from an older and wiser mentor to a youth. But only this impoverished young lady with a vulgar family and no connections met Fitz's need for an equal. An equal of the mind.

It had been a great relief when the two sisters had quit the house after Miss Bennet's recovery from her cold. Fitz had been careful that last day to repeat nothing of the previous days' indiscretions, the teasing and the prodding, poking at the woman to see what she would do in return, and always rewarded with just that much more than he had expected; enough that he could not resist trying again, but not so much that he must retreat in disorder. Although she had come close to routing him a few times. The remark about the acquiescent friend had been most unfortunate, bolstering poor Charles in all his misguided notions of matrimony and independence. But the worst of it came toward the end of the visit, when she had said, in her arch yet innocent way, that "Mr. Darcy is not to be laughed at." Laughing at him all the while, as such a statement implied.

Only after a week had passed did he begin to miss the pricking of her barbs and the strife of the contest, what the Greeks had called *agon.* The damage she inflicted was not like that of the flesh, which itched and tormented the sufferer, leaving behind a faint scar if one was lucky, and the memory of pain endured and overcome. No, her wounds left one seared to the heart at first, then miraculously healed and wishing for another combat. Even were she to prevail, the result would be not death or bloody defeat, but something sublime, something Fitz had never known, but that all men aspired to . . . the loss of self in the love of another.

Oh, to have a dance with her, and to probe, ever so subtly, attempting to discover her thoughts, perhaps a hint of her true feelings. Just to promenade beside her, to touch the tips of gloved fingers, to press sheathed palm to palm in the turn.

And what had come of that? Nothing but the pain of learning that, like every less discerning intellect, she had fallen under Wickham's spell. That she had no more perception than any other human creature, man or woman. Asking pointed questions about Fitz's *resentment*, and making none-so-subtle allusions to a *certain gentleman*. From anyone else it would have been offensive.

What had he imagined? What had he expected? That she had the ability to recognize Wickham's fabrications for the transparent forgeries they were, while to the rest of the world they remained genuine and opaque? How should a girl of twenty possess the experience and knowledge of the world to distinguish such things, while retaining her innocence and virtue? Yet he had somehow dared to hope . . .

And why should he be disappointed? She was a *woman*, damn it. She was like all women—coy, cloying, secretive, and devious, always going after things in a roundabout manner, like cats. Until his inevitable marriage, Fitz planned to keep his associations with members of that sex to the minimum, allowing himself only the occasional session—an enjoyable method of maintaining his fighting trim—with ladies safely wedded to complaisant husbands. He had never felt himself so drawn to any particular female.

Until now. This girl.

An unfortunate comparison anyway. Fitz had always liked cats.

Six

MISS BINGLEY KNOCKED on Fitz's door a short time after the last guests had left—none other than the appalling Bennet family, the mother already angling to move into Netherfield, along with the rest of her nauseating brood, upon the impending marriage of her eldest daughter.

"Mr. Darcy." Caroline's voice was high and strained, no flirting now. "Mr. Darcy, please come to the door. I'm sorry to disturb you, but it's vitally important."

Fitz, fortunately still wearing his shirt and pantaloons, opened the door a crack. Poor Caroline looked haggard. It had been a long night and her face paint had smeared with the heat. She had not removed so much as her headdress, the once-jaunty feather drooping in disappointment.

"What is it, Miss Bingley? Are you quite well?"

"No, Mr. Darcy, I am not. I am near to collapsing with fatigue, and now Charles is saying the most shocking things and behaving in so eccentric a manner that Louisa and I are afraid."

"Afraid? Had you not better send for the physician?"

"Nothing like that," she said. "He's swearing that he will marry that girl with the dreadful family. Miss Bennet. He says he intends to call on her first thing when he returns from his business in town."

That brought Fitz out into the corridor. "After the appalling exhibition we were treated to tonight he can't be serious."

"I assure you, I would not have disturbed you in your room if I thought it was just a passing mood. He won't listen to me or Louisa, his own sisters, but he listens to you. Please, talk some sense into him."

"I can try," Fitz said. "He has been flaunting a rather touching independence lately."

"We should go up to town with him," Caroline said, running beside him down the corridor, his long strides making her breathless to keep up.

"Yes, yes. Let me just hear it for myself. I wonder he didn't come to me first."

Caroline gasped. "He said he had. He said you knew all about it. Have you been keeping secrets, Mr. Darcy?"

"I don't reveal the substance of our every intimate conversation, Miss Bingley, however you might wish it. Charles is suffering from the common ailment of green youth—lovesickness, an unsuitable romantic passion. I have let him talk and not attempted to dispute; it seemed the more prudent course. He did mention something of this before the ball, but I took it as just another of his hyperbolic enthusiasms. If one good thing could be said to have come from this night's debacle, it's that it should put an end to Charles's absurd matrimonial notions. I'd have staked Pemberley on my certainty that we'd heard the last of it."

"Lucky for you you're not a gambler," Caroline said with more asperity than Fitz had ever heard from her. "But we may *all* reap the rewards of such careless dealing." She eyed Fitz meaningfully.

Fitz restrained his first impulse to snap at the bitch, merely remarking, "We shall see."

". . . declare my intentions, then blave the brist—the blistering wrath of Fitz himself." Charles's loud, slurred speech was audible well before they reached the rooms occupied by Louisa and her husband.

"Ah, there you are, Darcy," Hurst said. "If you would be so kind as to take this Bedlamite away with you, perhaps Mrs. Hurst and I and the rest of this house can enjoy some peace and quiet."

"Gladly," Fitz said. "Come on, Charles. Come and tell me what has you so agitated."

"No, Fitz," Charles said. "I will not come with you. That's what I've been saying. I'm done with that now. Going to marry Miss Bennet. You're welcome to stay on while the banns are being read, but once we're married we shall want to live by ourselves. I'm sure you understand."

"It's merely infatuation," Fitz said to the room at large.

"Am not," Charles said. "Sober as a judge. As sober as your hanging judge of an uncle at the Bloody Assizes."

"Though he was my *great* uncle, Monmouth's Rebellion was, nevertheless, slightly before his time," Fitz couldn't resist murmuring. "Come, let's get you to bed."

"Not with you, Darcy," Charles said. "Won't be getting into my bunghole tonight, old man."

"Language, Charles," Fitz said. "Not in front of your sisters."

"Oh, bugger my sisters," Charles said. He giggled. "They'd let you, you know. We all let you. Except me. Not anymore."

"Charles," Louisa said. "You are being a very naughty boy. If our poor papa were still alive, he'd whip you."

"He'd whip you two sluts all the way to Bridewell and back, is what he'd do," Charles said. "Throwing yourselves at Fitz here, with your husband under the same roof." He turned to

Hurst. "Why don't you put your foot down? Show Louisa you're a man."

"I say," Hurst said. "You have one hell of a nerve barging into my room and telling me how to conduct my marriage. Ought to call you out if you wasn't my brother-in-law, but it's late and we've both had a lot to drink. Forget it all in the morning. Just hope *you* don't take offense, Darcy." It was the longest speech Fitz had ever heard from him.

"Not at all," Fitz said through clenched jaws.

"And as for you, Caroline," Charles continued, Hurst's mumbling not having registered in his preoccupied mind, "I can promise you Fitz won't come up to scratch. Has his eye on my beautiful, sweet Jane's beautiful, not-so-sweet sister, Lizzy. Don't mean sour. What's the course, at the end of meal, ain't sweet, you know, not sugar? Salty?"

"Savory," Hurst suggested, mellowing at the appeal to his epicurean expertise.

"Savory. That's it. Fitz likes the salty-savory Lizzy. Likes to poke her. With words, I mean. Not with his poker. Not yet."

Louisa and Caroline exchanged a significant look. "Now you see what comes of admiring *fine eyes*," Caroline said.

"Not really your style, I'd have thought," Hurst said. Spending most of his days asleep, he was unfortunately wide awake once the clock struck midnight. "Skinny little thing, sharp tongue. None of my affair, I admit, Darcy, but fact is you'd be better off with good old Caroline here. At least she understands about you and Charlie-boy. Can't imagine Miss Eliza Bennet putting up with that, no matter how *savory* she may be. Ha! These provincial gentry are the worst sticklers. No knowledge of the fashionable world. D'ye know I saw her deliberately choose a plain dish over a ragout?"

Fitz felt a headache developing, despite having forced himself to abstain. The desire to drink himself into insensibility had come over him early enough in the evening that he had been able to defend against it, although the horrors that followed had been of such severity and had escalated so steeply it had been a struggle toward the end. "I never seriously admired her," he apologized with poor grace. "It was merely a jest that went too far."

"Was not," Charles said. "He thinks of her. You know, when he rogers me."

The collective and ominous silence that greeted this pronouncement was interrupted again by Hurst, picking up happily on yet another topic on which he felt qualified to express an opinion. "Bad form, Darcy, old fellow. Never think of anyone else when I'm with Louisa. Wouldn't say so if I did, of course. Never think of anything at all."

"True," Louisa said. "Your mind is as void of substance as your cods."

Hurst's stuttering expostulations were overborne by Fitz's roar. "Charles! I expected at least this much consideration, that what was told you in confidence would not be repeated to the world at large. I am tempted to follow your father's example and give you the whipping of your life."

"Too late," Charles said. "The days of my lowering my breeches and bending over for you are . . . over. I'm over bending over. No more indulging for me. Indulging? Not quite right. Endowing?" Hoping the picture would lead to the word, he made a vulgar gesture of fist and bent elbow, smiling in triumph when he achieved success. "I have it! Indorsing!" There was the briefest of pauses until another random thought struck. "I say! Now that your friend George Wickham's in the neighborhood you can go back to indorsing *him*!" He giggled again. The sound made Fitz's teeth hurt.

"I'm warning you, Charles," Fitz said. He passed a hand over his face, in a futile hope that when he opened his eyes his vision would have cleared, that this was all a hallucination brought on by anxiety and the late hour. "One more word from you and—"

"And what?" Charles said. "Only saying Wickham's a damn' fine-looking fellow. Thought you might have been gilding the faded memory a bit, but now I've seen him, all I can say is—see what you mean. And in that red coat, damn' near irresistible, I should think. Better'n that poor little sod Denny you've been making do with. Oh, don't look so surprised. Think I don't notice things. But I see what's in front of my face as well as any man. And I see that your Wickham has charmed all the ladies—even Lizzy Bennet. *Especially* Lizzy Bennet. Now *there's* a picture, eh? The savory Lizzy bending over for the beautiful George Wickham."

Fitz acted by instinct, striking Charles with open palm, unable, despite what would be mortal insult from any other man, to bring himself to hurt the one who had been his *eromenos*, his beloved. Charles's body, loose-limbed and flexible with drink and desire, slumped to the floor.

This time a cacophony of imprecations put a premature end to another shocked silence.

"Just leave me alone," Charles said when the storm had broken over his head and dissipated from lack of energy to sustain it. He sat up shakily from his position on the carpet beside Hurst's stockinged feet. "All of you, just leave me be. I am of age, I am the master of an independent fortune, and as soon as I deal with this stupid business in town I am going to call on the woman I love with all my heart and offer her my hand in marriage. And anyone who doesn't like it can bloody well move out of *my* house."

When Fitz bent down to offer his assistance, Charles pushed him away, his clammy hand slithering against Fitz's like one of those protective sheaths used in brothels. "Don't touch me,"

Charles said. "Can get up without your help. In fact, can get it up a hell of a lot better without you."

"Oh!" Caroline put her hands over her ears. "I don't know what's come over you, Charles."

"Fitz," Charles said, legs sprawled, leaning back on his elbows. "*He* comes all over me, thinking of his Lizzy and her beautiful eyes. Or perhaps of his lost love, George Wickham, of the enormous prick and the even greater insolence. But I'll be the one coming soon enough, in bed with my wife."

In the end Fitz had to hoist Charles to his feet and haul him out into the corridor. Charles didn't fight but he didn't help either. He sagged, limp and unresisting in Fitz's embrace, muttering revolting endearments to his Jane under his breath, radiating spirit-fumes enough to intoxicate the entire household, and collapsed in a stupor on the bed when Fitz dumped him down. His man was standing by and Fitz left him to his distasteful work. Despite Charles's further amusing intimations, Fitz did not enjoy fucking corpses.

THE NEXT MORNING Charles was so sick he left late for town, barely able to sit upright in the chaise. "Can't I put it off a day or two?" he begged Fitz in a piteous voice, his head lolling out the open window.

"You know my feelings on procrastination," Fitz replied.

Charles reached a hand to Fitz's coat sleeve and clung. "I know—that is, I think—I mean—I seem to recall some unpleasant words last night. Please, Fitz, don't hate me for anything I might have said in my cups."

Fitz withdrew his arm. "Drink is no excuse for coarseness, Bingley. An inebriated gentleman ought still to be a gentleman."

"All I can do is apologize, Fitz. Please believe me when I say how very sorry I am. And don't call me Bingley like that, as if we were strangers."

Fitz was damned if he would make this easy. "Friendship without respect is meaningless, and using the outward forms of intimacy when the foundation has rotted away is the kind of sham I abhor. You made your sentiments quite clear, Bingley, and you insulted others besides myself, some of whom were not there to defend themselves. Denying your words now does not undo that damage."

"So were yours quite clear," Charles answered, attempting a brave smile and rubbing his injured if only slightly blemished cheek, "although that damage will be repaired quickly enough. And I've apologized to my sisters, and to Hurst"—he compressed his lips at that indignity—"but as to people who 'weren't there,' I think I know who you mean, and all I can say is how truly sorry I am. I say it to you, because you were the one who was hurt by it." He watched Fitz's face.

Fitz, by great effort, held his face immobile. He had not expected Charles to remember, or to know he was referring to *her.*

Receiving no response, Charles sighed but looked all the more resolute, attempting to sit up straight and square his shoulders. "The one thing I won't do is disown my affections. I shall call on Miss Bennet the minute I return."

As soon as the carriage had gone safely up the drive and around the bend to the lane, Fitz and the ladies went into action. By midday he and Caroline and Louisa had their plan all worked out; by dinnertime they had everything packed, the furniture covered, horses sent ahead to the coaching inns, and were ready to follow Charles to town. Only at the last minute Fitz remembered to write to his sister to give her time to prepare for his arrival and to expect a guest in another day or two. He wrote quickly, unhindered by his usual admirer, Caroline.

My dearest Georgiana,

Please forgive the sudden notice, but I am required to cut short my visit in Hertfordshire and remove to town. I will not burden you with what must remain a private matter, but suffice it to say that my friend Mr. Bingley has suffered an unfortunate entanglement. At the first stage, I shall invite him to stay with us, so as not to overtax the hospitality of his elder sister and her husband, Mr. Hurst.

Mr. Bingley's spirits are very low, nor do I possess the delicacy of touch that is the genius of the gentler sex. I am confident that the easy, friendly atmosphere of a harmonious house, along with the lively company of an unaffected and well-brought-up young lady, will provide the best remedy.

I send all my love and hope that you are, as I am, in the best of health,

Your devoted brother,
Fitzwilliam

THE DRIVE NEXT day was ghastly, crammed in between Hurst and the women and their hot, shifting bodies. As soon as decently possible, at the first stage and change of horses, Fitz took the opportunity to ride alongside.

Once settled in town, Fitz waited a judicious couple of days before calling, after Charles had been persuaded to leave the hotel and stay at Hurst's. Even then Charles was unwilling to receive him, only relenting out of habit and from a pathetic need for company. "I don't see why you all had to follow me," he said. "There's no reason I shouldn't return to Netherfield after this tedium with the agent is resolved. Miss Bennet will be wondering what has become of me."

"I doubt that very much," Fitz said. The words came easily, proof that it was not a lie, merely a slight exaggeration that would become truth in time, helped by absence. "She didn't love you. I could see it in her face. She smiled and looked at everyone the same."

"How would you know?" Charles protested, but already weakening. "She would look the same to you, perhaps, but not to me."

Fitz stroked Charles's cheek. Any lingering hint of a bruise was healed by now, yet the man recoiled as if fearing further blows. "Imagine how mortified you'd be if you declared your intentions, only to have her smile and say in her sweet, serene manner, that she was very sorry but she did not return your affections."

"I don't believe that would have happened," Charles said. "And even if it did, why should I not try? Better to have loved and lost than—"

"Yes, yes, all very well to quote stage plays, but this is life, my dear. You'd have been crushed. Your first real love, so cruelly dispatched."

"Poor old Fitz," Charles said. "I think whatever happened between you and Wickham has given you an aversion. Not all loves are doomed to humiliation and disappointment."

In his all-consuming rage, Fitz did not trust himself to speak. Another few days elapsed before he felt able to extend the invitation that had been his original purpose, and it was a long week before the old mix of affection, concern, and desire began slowly to reassert itself.

IT ALL OCCURRED so quickly, in the span of a few short days, that it took Elizabeth longer than her usual direct penetration to understand that all of them—she, Jane, Charlotte, perhaps even Mr. Bingley—were now bereft of love. Mr. Bingley was gone to town for upward of a fortnight, and judging from the letter Jane had received from Miss Bingley, had apparently every intention of staying there for the rest of the winter. It was pure catastrophe for Jane, but worth putting a brave face on until absolutely certain.

Elizabeth's own sufferings were deceptively mild on the surface, making complaint look like the whining of a spoiled child by comparison. They had begun when she missed Mr. Wickham at the ball at Netherfield, then was surprised into accepting a dance and less than sparkling conversation with Mr. Darcy instead. Next, to her everlasting shame, her entire family, even her dear papa, had seemed to conspire in exposing themselves as the most uncouth, vulgar, ill-mannered family in Hertfordshire—or perhaps in all of the civilized world—and the least desirable as connections for any gentleman contemplating matrimony.

Finally, ensuring that this month would remain, whatever else a long life might bring, the lowest point of her entire existence, she had received the most humiliating proposal imaginable. Mr. Collins was ignorant, conceited, and affected—the sorriest excuse for a clergyman she had ever had the misfortune to meet. The fact that he was her cousin, and in line to inherit after her father's death, changed the encounter from merely humorous to distressing. And just in the event that all this was not bad enough, now Charlotte had accepted this same man's horrendous proposal. She had not wasted so much as half a day, it seemed, in turning away from one whom she had been calling her dearest friend for the better part of ten years, in favor of a pompous, self-satisfied, *stupid* man.

Mr. Collins's proposal would have been nauseating under any circumstances. But now, after Elizabeth's newfound awareness of passion, it was so sickening she had almost vomited up her breakfast three days running since the ordeal of hearing it and refusing him and having to fight her mother on the subject. It was all too vividly clear what a woman would have to endure with him, what would have been the greatest pleasure with Mr. Wickham. His touch, *there* and everywhere. His body inside hers. Oh Lord, she was going to puke again. And to think of Charlotte agreeing to this. The idea was enough to make a fishmonger faint. Charlotte had to know the full truth of what she was entering into, yet she had apparently encouraged the offer.

The worst was there was no one to talk to. It would be cruel to burden Jane with what would seem such trivial grievances when Jane's unhappiness was so much greater. Jane had been on the verge of receiving a proposal from a pleasant young man of good character and great fortune. Elizabeth's only noticeable loss was her friend Charlotte, and Jane would say, rightly, that it was more Elizabeth's fault than anyone's. As to those coarser feelings of bodily passions, Elizabeth could not speak of such things to someone as unworldly as Jane. Yet perhaps she was engaged in the same struggle. Perhaps Mr. Bingley, tame though he seemed to Elizabeth, had aroused the same desires in Jane.

She tried only once before giving it up entirely. "Are you feeling very low?" she asked Jane one night.

"No! Why should I be?"

"No reason, dear. I only wanted to know if you were able to hear my tale of woe."

"Poor Lizzy. What have you suffered?"

"Nothing so terrible. Only the loss of my closest friend."

"You mean Charlotte Lucas? You know my feelings on the subject."

"That it's my own doing."

"Yes, I'm sorry, Lizzy, but how can you expect her to give up her one chance at a home and family—for what? Your friendship? You are the best sister in the world, and my own dearest friend, but I would not give that up for you either, if I had a chance of it."

"You would take Mr. Collins over me?" Elizabeth tried to use a droll tone, but her voice shook.

"Ugh!" Jane made a wry face. "No, I mean if I had a chance at a respectable marriage."

"But that's just what Charlotte did *not* have. Not a respectable marriage. Only Mr. Collins."

Jane looked grave again. "You may laugh, but at her age, with little portion and, forgive me, no great beauty, it is a respectable offer, and the best she could reasonably hope for. It is a pity but a fact of the world, that men often value youth and superficial appearance over character. You wouldn't really expect her to remain unmarried, a burden to her brothers, for the rest of her life, solely to please you? That is not friendship."

"But *Mr. Collins*! I know you think I am animadverting solely on his pretentious manner and laughable self-importance, but the truth is he is not a good person. He is not morally sound, any more than he is witty or charming."

"Now there you have gone too far again," Jane said. "He is a clergyman, and there is absolutely no reason to believe he does not follow the teachings of the church and of his faith."

"I don't agree," Elizabeth said, becoming serious. "I think it is not possible truly to be a good person if one lacks the minimum of understanding."

Jane shook her head. "That is wrong, Lizzy. Would you deny children and illiterate people the possibility of virtue?"

"That's not at all what I mean. Children and the illiterate are merely ignorant—untaught. They can learn. That is why we go to school or have lessons. And even a man who can't read can possess natural aptitude. But think of animals. Look at how a cat toys with a crippled mouse and torments the poor creature for its own amusement instead of slaughtering it cleanly and quickly. Yet no person of sense calls the cat depraved or sinful. Why? Because it does not possess human understanding and does not have the capacity to know right and wrong."

Jane scowled, a rare occurrence. "What about me, Lizzy?" she asked quietly. "And Mr. Bingley? Are we capable of goodness? We are neither of us half as clever as you and Mr. Darcy. Or I daresay your Mr. Wickham."

Elizabeth took her sister's hands. "Look at me, Jane," she said, while her sister kept her head stubbornly turned away. "That is nonsense. You and Mr. Bingley are as far above Mr. Collins as—as—oh, I don't know! All I mean is that there are some people who, whether born deficient or not developing the talents they have, are incapable of choosing the good over the bad. They simply follow the fashion or the outward forms of what to the world signify virtue. And Mr. Collins is a perfect example of that. Whereas Mr. Darcy is an example of the opposite—more than sufficient intellect, but making the choice to do wrong. And while I naturally prefer a good man to a wicked one, I confess to finding informed wickedness more palatable than empty, mechanical conformity, although I leave it to you to decide whether that reflects my own superior understanding or simply my desire to be original."

The two sisters sat in silence while Jane pondered. "You know, Lizzy, I don't like to think you capable of so unchristian a feeling, but I have to say it seems to me you are simply envious."

"Of Charlotte's situation? Never!"

"No, of Mr. Collins, that he won the favors that you had wished to keep for yourself, even though, as a woman, you could not give her what most of us require—marriage, children, a home."

"I would hope not to be so selfish," Elizabeth said. "No, I just think that Charlotte has thrown herself away on someone who doesn't value her. Not as I do."

"Probably not," Jane said. "But she hasn't really thrown herself away. She would be doing that for you, Lizzy, if she chose to forgo her one offer for the sake of your friendship. However great a pleasure it gave you, if you truly love her you will not stand in the way of her happiness."

"Not of her happiness. But this!"

"It is a form of happiness, a more lasting, substantial form than the passing pleasures of dalliance with a friend. If you *are* her friend, you will not add to her woes by condemning her decision, but support her in her brave choice. There are few of us fortunate enough to be loved by men who deserve our regard."

"You are referring to Mr. Wickham?" Elizabeth tried for a careless, laughing manner. "The prettiest, most inconstant man in the world." She had to make a conscious effort every time his name came up not to betray the depth of her feelings.

"Precisely," Jane said. "That is another reason you must not repine. However graceful his manner, however agreeable his conversation, you see by his behavior now that he was not entirely honest with you, despite his *superior understanding*."

"After what Mr. Wickham told me of his ill-treatment by Mr. Darcy, I can't blame him for staying away from the Netherfield ball," Elizabeth replied. The suppressed fury rose so rapidly to the surface of what she had thought to be enforced calm, she was taken by surprise. "Indeed, your Mr. Bingley is no better. He has given up the idea of marriage to you, it seems, in favor of dalliance with *his* friend Mr. Darcy, while Mr. Wickham has merely forfeited the pleasures of one evening's dancing."

"Oh, Lizzy," Jane said. "To speak like that to me—or anyone—is not like you. I will attribute it to your great unhappiness, but I admit to being wounded."

It was as if, Elizabeth thought, the awakening of desire within her had wrought a change in her very nature. To say such things to her own sweet sister! Yet the words would come out; she had no will to keep them in. "All I know is, Mr. Wickham is not the only gentleman abused by Mr. Darcy, and now abusing others in his turn." Why, Elizabeth wondered, should an even cruder statement make up for saying what was already unforgivable?

"Elizabeth, I think you should not talk about things you don't understand. If I was mistaken in Mr. Bingley's regard, I am far better acquainted with the truth of Mr. Darcy and Mr. Bingley's friendship than you are in any position to know. If you have any sisterly love for me, you will not put Mr. Wickham and Mr. Bingley in the same category."

Elizabeth caught herself before saying anything more. She could not afford to lose her one remaining friend.

Seven

CHARLES INSPECTED HIS face in the looking glass. Rather peaked, he thought. Maybe *queasy* was the right word, or *pallid*. He wondered why he was even considering attending this assembly. What could it matter? *She* would not be there. *She* was in Hertfordshire, where he ought to be. Why was he so tired all the time?

"Need help with that cravat?" Fitz said. He sent Charles's man out and took his place, standing behind Charles, pressing so close Charles could feel that ever-present bulge against his crack, through the layers of pantaloons and drawers of two clothed men. Fitz reached around to Charles's neck, breathing on the side of his face, and picked up the ends of the wide piece of starched cloth. "Will you have a waterfall or an Oriental? Or perhaps the clock?"

"I don't care," Charles said. "In fact, I don't really feel like going."

"Think of all the pretty young ladies you can meet," Fitz said. "And all with fortunes to match well with yours." Better Charles should mix with girls of his own sphere in town, he told himself again, instead of falling preposterously "in love" with a penniless nobody from a family that would make Lady Hamilton's seem almost respectable by comparison.

"I thought you didn't approve of being introduced at balls," Charles said.

"Wherever did you get such a misguided notion?" Fitz said. "Lady Finchley's balls are known for having the pick of the *ton*. Now that her eldest son's of age, she invites all the reputable families with marriageable daughters." He laughed, pretending nonchalance. "In fact, she rather defeats her purpose. Every desperate bachelor flocks to her affairs, giving little Peter Finchley some stiff competition."

Charles stared sullenly and indirectly at Fitz, viewing their two reflected faces in the glass. "You go ahead, Fitz," he said. "Maybe I'll meet you there later."

"Nonsense," Fitz said, in the false, jolly air that was becoming routine, like living with an invalid. "Come with me to the opera. There's a very fine soprano I want to hear. We can stop by Lady Finchley's afterward, enjoy a dance or two. How does that sound?"

Charles shrugged and tried to free himself from the confining arms. "I don't know, Fitz. I'd just as soon stay home."

"But you love the opera," Fitz said. He crossed the ends of the neck cloth, then pulled Charles's body sharply back against his own.

"No, I don't," Charles said. "Just like seeing the dancing girls. But I don't even care for that anymore. All I really want is Miss Bennet. I swear to you, if I were to see a whole line of them, kicking up their heels in their short skirts, all I'd think of is how she would look—not that she would ever do anything so indecent, of course."

"Oh, come along," Fitz said. "Picture her in her petticoat, showing her legs. It will cheer you up." He put a wheedle into his voice, as if proposing a treat to a small child. It felt like weeks since Charles had allowed him anything more than a quick pleasuring with his mouth, and then only in the paralysis of near sleep.

"Honestly, Fitz," Charles said. "I don't feel up to much, the state I'm in."

"Is that a challenge?" Fitz said. "I imagine I can make *something* rise with but a little effort." He kissed Charles's cheek and then his mouth. He stripped the untied cravat from Charles's neck in one strong tug and threw it on the chair, tonguing the V of the open shirt, sensing the faint pulse in the hollow under the Adam's apple.

Charles stood still and patient as Fitz fondled him, like a child being undressed by his nursemaid. He barely shifted his stance even as he allowed Fitz to remove his waistcoat and unbutton his breeches.

"Damn it," Fitz said, losing his tightly held composure as he brought forth Charles's lifeless and unresponsive cock. "Don't you feel anything?"

"No, Fitz," Charles said. "It's what I keep telling you, but you don't want to hear it."

Fitz massaged Charles's cock in his fist, still to no effect. He pushed Charles in the direction of the bed, squeezing his balls, until his pert little arse met the edge of the mattress.

"I suppose you want to take your pleasure now," Charles said in a tired voice as Fitz continued to work over his inert member. "Go on. Maybe it will do us both good." He fell backward onto the bed, as flabby and boneless as a jellyfish.

Fitz eyed Charles where he lay, with his unbuttoned breeches and unlaced shirt the picture of the drunken rake. How misleading. And how unappetizing. "If you wished to disgust me, Charles, you've succeeded admirably." He turned to the glass, straightening his cravat and smoothing his hair. "Don't wait up for me," he said over his shoulder on the way out. "I may be very late."

THE OPERA WAS insipid, the soprano not in good voice, and the audience full of claques and cardplayers but few actual music lovers. Fitz didn't wait for the end but slipped out at the second interval and walked briskly to Lady Finchley's. Lord, he needed the exercise! No hunting, no fowling, the only shooting at the indoor gallery at Manton's. No angling in the filthy, stinking Thames. "Riding" on the tame path through Hyde Park, like being a figure in a tableau, with none of the excitement of the chase or the simple satisfactions of travel. A man could turn into a raving lunatic with no outlet for his energies.

He was too early at the ball, from abandoning the opera. The guests were the most eager and desperate of the husband hunters as well as the predatory women who, like Fitz, were looking more for diversion than for a settled position. Caroline Finchley greeted him warmly and with unfeigned delight. "Mr. Darcy! What a surprise. I had not heard you had returned to town." She was too courteous to comment on his glowing face or the slight tang of sweat he exuded, although she cocked a satirical eyebrow at the dirt on his Hessian boots. "Athletic as ever, I see. I hope I shall have the pleasure of at least one set with you, if only for old times' sake."

"The pleasure will be mine," Fitz replied automatically. Actually, it was a genuine joy to see Caro again. She looked, if anything, younger after more than a year of self-imposed exile from society. Her husband's sudden death, collapsing over the hazard table during a high-stakes game at White's, followed, some ten months later, by the birth of her eighth child, had been the gossip of all of London and beyond; nor had it helped matters that the baby had the dark, hirsute look of her last conquest, the youngest

Carrington boy, Richard. But she appeared to have emerged unscathed. Even as Fitz bowed over her hand and awaited his turn at the dance, the room was filling up, visitors being announced with reassuring regularity. No one would seriously consider dropping the fashionable and highly connected Lady Finchley over anything less than witnessed and proven murder—and then only if the victim had been well liked.

"Lord and Lady Swain, Mr. and Mrs. Swain, and Miss Swain," the man at the door enunciated crisply, avoiding any susurrus.

Imagine! Poor old Jimmy married at last. Fitz craned his neck to catch a glimpse of the unfortunate bride, but the three Swains by birth, tall, blond, and bulky, surrounded their catch like fish schooling around a tangle of worms.

Fitz made sure to keep moving through the growing throng. London society was nothing like Meryton, thank goodness; ten thousand pounds a year was not quite so rare—although an income not squandered on gambling, horses, and women was perhaps exceptional—and the lack of a title put him at best in the second tier of desirability. But there was nothing to be gained by standing still and becoming a target.

He saw another familiar form up ahead and took the great chance of approaching without being certain. That glossy black hair was the same, and the slender but curvaceous figure. The clothes were, if anything, even more expensive than those she had been able to afford while under Fitz's protection. He admitted to himself that he felt slightly irked at the knowledge that she was prospering after their connection had come to its natural end. "Miss Waring?" he asked tentatively.

The woman turned at Fitz's voice. "Fitz!" she exclaimed, the public mask of her face collapsing and reforming for one unguarded moment into a wide, sincere smile. She as quickly resumed her cool poise, correcting her original familiarity into

"Mr. Darcy," and adding with something like exasperation, "But it's Mrs. Swain now."

He couldn't quite take it in. "Mrs. Swain? You mean—"

"Yes, Mr. Darcy. Believe it or not, someone from a respectable, wealthy family did, in fact, offer to marry me."

"But Jimmy Swain?" Fitz said, with more emotion in his voice than he intended. "I had thought you sharper than that."

"Oh yes?" she said, her tone a remarkable mimic of Fitz's at his most disdainful. "He proposed *marriage*, you see."

"But how are you? Are you—well?"

"Do you mean have I permitted him to afflict me with the same ailment he suffers from? No, I am indeed sharper than that." She laughed with unforced gaiety and twirled before him, managing not to jostle anyone in the crowd of would-be dancers and seekers of refreshments. "What do you think? Will I make a good peeress?"

"Better than most," Fitz said. "Assuming your husband outlives his father."

Lydia shrugged. "Anything's possible. At least I shall have the perquisites of the future Lady Swain while I'm still young enough to enjoy them."

Fitz was regretting his rash impulse to renew old acquaintance. "You know, Lydia—Mrs. Swain—a peeress, even the daughter-in-law of a peeress, ought not to speak quite so freely in public."

"Thank you, Mr. Darcy," she said, smirking at him. "When I next find myself in public, I will remember all your kind instructions on the subject."

"You do not consider this a public place?"

"Lady Finchley's? Lord, you have been out of town a good while. Nothing I've said here is any worse than what everyone else is saying. In fact, if I were you, I should worry what people are saying about *me*."

"Mr. Darcy." Lady Finchley came gliding through the crowd that parted to make way for her. "I think this is our dance."

Fitz bowed dismissal to Lydia and stepped eagerly forward. "Thank you for the rescue," he said to Caro as the music started up. "That was becoming unpleasant."

"Lydia Swain?" Lady Finchley said. "Since when can Fitzwilliam Darcy not untangle himself from the wiles of a Cyprian?"

"Since she became an anticipated peeress," Fitz answered. "She seems frighteningly self-assured by the transformation."

Lady Finchley smiled. "As she should. It's a good match for her, despite the disadvantages."

"So she was telling me," Fitz said. "It's a pity such a great improvement in her circumstances has to entail such risk."

"Well, Fitz," Lady Finchley said. "You weren't going to marry her, were you?"

"Of course not. How could I? Why would I?"

"Why indeed? No gentleman of property who needs an heir will marry a woman like her. Call her Cyprian or High Impure or what you will, she's still a whore as the world sees it, no matter how exalted her patrons."

"Your meaning?" Fitz asked.

"Only that Jimmy Swain, with his sorry state of health, had but this one chance of a little happiness and he took it. He pays for her clothes and her carriage and her jewels—and her lovers—so that he can hold his head up in the world and pretend, even if everyone knows it's a sham, that he's as capable of keeping a pretty young wife as any man. Lydia allows him every liberty of a husband but one—what he most wants, a child to carry on the name."

Fitz grimaced at the plain speaking. He had forgotten just how frankly and coarsely people spoke in town, especially of those they deemed their inferiors, either by birth or by luck.

He concentrated for a while on the steps of the dance, watching Caro's large breasts that gleamed like ivory globes in the light of a hundred candelabra. She was strapped so tightly into her revealing gown that the vast expanses of soft flesh were given the illusion of firmness, like the rinds of the melons they resembled in size. They barely so much as jiggled, even in the vigorous motion of the reel.

Lady Finchley saw the direction of Fitz's gaze and shook her head. "I ought to be flattered. But I doubt you really want to board this old wreck again."

Fitz smiled, abashed, feeling more than ever like a precocious schoolboy who had scraped together the price of his first visit to a brothel and had no idea what to do next. "I'm sorry, my lady. But—"

"No apologies, Fitz. And please go on calling me Caro. Made me feel quite young again. Know I must seem a worn-out jade to you young stallions, but there's life in me yet. And pardon the jumbled images, but I've a bigger fish on my line."

"Don't speak of yourself that way—Caro," Fitz expostulated with forced politeness. "I have only the fondest memories of a beautiful, generous lady who gave a young, very innocent man the most glorious year of his life."

Lady Finchley laughed at that, snorting in her gruff, aristocratic manner, but looking pleased all the same.

Thankfully the set came to its eventual end and he took the chance to move away. In the interval while the musicians rested there was a growing hubbub of conversation. Over the bowing heads and curtsies Fitz saw a handsome, well-preserved gentleman of fifty sauntering through the crowd like royalty. The man arrived within a few feet of Fitz and gave a slight inclination of the head. "Darcy?" he said. "Lady Finchley mentioned you might put in an appearance. How are you?"

Fitz bowed from the waist, just the right angle required for one of the highest peers of the realm. "Very well, Coverdale, I thank you," he said. "I hope you are well. And how are your sons?"

"Still younger than you, Darcy," the seventh Duke of Coverdale replied, his dry voice turning the most innocuous phrase into a witticism. "I hear your sister is ready to enter society."

"Not quite," Fitz said. "Georgiana is only just sixteen. I'm assisting her in setting up her own establishment."

"Excellent. Does Miss Darcy attend private functions? Alex is giving a small supper and card party next month to mark his coming of age and accession to the title of Marquess of Bellingham. Perhaps he can send her an invitation."

"I'm sure Georgie would be delighted to attend Lord Bellingham's affair," Fitz answered. "As would I."

"Oh, Alex won't do anything to arouse a brother's apprehensions," Coverdale said. "Miss Darcy's companion will of course be made welcome. But I'll warn Alex not to propose marriage on the first visit. Good to see you, Darcy." He moved on, accepting the accolades and the pleas of the crowd as if he had won a great battle or could dispense justice single-handed, Fitz thought with scorn. Yet the man was gracious, polite, patient with everyone who accosted him. He listened to old ladies' encomiums on their debutante granddaughters and to various inebriated men's accounts of their victories over wayward women, unlucky hands of cards, and corked bottles of claret with equal dispassion and forbearance.

He was a true aristocrat, Fitz decided. Noble by birth and breeding. And that business about Georgie was typical. Wealthy she might be by ordinary standards, but Coverdale would be looking higher than a commoner's daughter for his elder son and heir. He must simply have wanted to ease the way for a shy young lady on her first forays outside the schoolroom.

Coverdale approached his hostess and smiled, bowing deeply. "Our dance?" he said, holding out his hand.

"Your Grace," Lady Finchley replied, curtsying with surprising agility and giving the honorific, vaguely improper when coming from a lady of the duke's social sphere, a loving intonation that softened any sting of irony.

Fitz watched as they went through the figures, smiling into each other's eyes throughout the intricate steps and turns. Bigger fish, indeed. Both widowed, fewer than ten years apart in age, they were well matched and, it seemed, genuinely in love.

He need not fear a resumption of that old attachment, whether he wished it or not. A large, buxom blonde, almost old enough to be his mother, was hardly his ideal. Yet Caro's kindness would have been most welcome in his present mood. He scanned the crowd, feeling a strange mix of relief and regret. Perhaps Lydia, he thought. What had she confessed, and Caro corroborated? That she was always careful. If that was true, he might take the chance of seeing if she was interested in rehearsing the past . . .

Fitz saw her skip by, partnered by none other than the same Richard Carrington who had, only a year ago, been known as Caro's latest recruit. Apparently young Carrington had passed his training exercises with flying colors and been promoted out of the ranks to earn his own command. Richard and Lydia, while not as tender as the older couple, were every bit as intimate. Lydia's gown, cut in a flowing style appropriate for a younger lady, did not rein in her flesh so tightly. Her full, shapely breasts rose and fell as she danced, until Fitz was in danger of being mesmerized. He blinked several times and headed for the door. There was nothing to be gained here, nothing except a most exasperating wish to see not quite so much exposed flesh of a rather more slender form, a delicate face with a pair of dark, expressive eyes, and to hear a clear, sweet voice saying that Mr. Darcy was not to be laughed at. Oh, to hear her laugh at him, what joy that would be.

He scowled at his ridiculous thoughts and took his leave.

ALL WAS QUIET when Fitz entered his house and locked the door behind him. He never liked making servants wait up, especially when he might not be home until late, or the next morning . . .

Charles was sound asleep, surprising in one who took no exercise and rarely ventured outside, and who seemed to dream away the days in a dormant state. The slight noise of the door opening and Fitz's careful footsteps did not rouse him so much as one degree above total oblivion; he lay in his usual position, curled on his side, his shirt hiked up conveniently around his waist, and he barely stirred as Fitz undressed and slipped in beside him. Furtive as a twelve-year-old boy, Fitz spat on his hands and began a gentle but purposeful massage of Charles's bum-hole. By the time Charles woke to a sense of what was happening, Fitz was already inside.

"God, Fitz, you do need a bath," Charles said. "Can't you let a man sleep in peace?"

"Hush," Fitz whispered, kissing Charles's neck, unable to waste effort on complicated speech. "I want my own sleep too, you know."

"Then why don't you try *sleeping*," Charles said, "instead of—" He was silenced by Fitz's massive and forceful explosion inside him. He whimpered, lay still, and let Fitz finish.

"I take it the ladies were unreceptive," Charles said a few minutes later.

"What?" Fitz murmured, well on the way to blissful unconsciousness.

"At the ball," Charles said. "Had to come home and abuse me instead."

"Don't be silly," Fitz said. "Just didn't see anyone I wanted half as much as you."

"That's a shame," Charles said. "Because I don't appreciate being treated like your neglected wife, at your disposal any time of day or night, whether or not I'm feeling well, or in the mood—"

"Please, Charles," Fitz said. "Let's discuss this in the morning."

"Very well," Charles said. He sat up and threw off the covers, exposing Fitz's naked, sweat-dampened flesh to the drafty air.

"Damn it!" Fitz exclaimed. "What the hell are you doing?"

"I prefer to sleep alone," Charles said. "If you don't want to talk to me now, please go to your own room."

Fitz groaned and sat up. "You're worse than a greensick girl with the vapors."

"And you wonder why the ladies aren't accommodating," Charles said. "You make Henry VIII seem a model of gentlemanly behavior."

"I begin to have a new appreciation for the chopping block," Fitz said, gathering up his clothes. "I beg your pardon, Miss Anne Boleyn, for disturbing your chaste slumbers." He stumbled wearily to his room and fell into bed, jamming his long legs under the tightly tucked sheet and kicking the corners loose.

CHARLES STAGGERED INTO breakfast when Fitz was done with his meal and perusing the morning paper. Georgiana was not yet down. "You know, Fitz, I don't wish to be ungrateful, but I think perhaps I should consider removing to Hurst's establishment."

"For goodness' sake, Charles." Fitz lowered the paper and observed his friend more closely where he sat huddled like a whipped schoolboy, his shoulders hunched, his eyes fixed steadfastly on his plate. "How I miss my old shooting partner."

"Who do you mean?"

"He was a cheerful, friendly soul, the perfect companion for a walk in the country. No finer way to spend a morning, with convivial masculine conversation, a dog, and a shotgun, bag a few birds . . . Haven't seen him lately." Fitz leaned back in his chair, observing a point a couple of inches above Charles's bowed head.

"If that's what you want, you should have stayed in Hertfordshire. No partridges or pheasants in town."

Fitz laughed. "There's more than one way of hunting, my dear, and many varieties of quarry to flush. Used to have a good friend for that, name of Charles Bingley. Wonder whatever became of him."

"Oh, I see. I'm not cheerful anymore, Fitz. And that sort of 'shooting' doesn't appeal to me now." Charles continued to ignore his breakfast, like a monk at the refectory listening patiently to the long grace and awaiting the signal to eat, the boiled egg congealing in its cup and the rasher of bacon cold and shriveled.

"We made a good pair, though, didn't we, before all this foolishness started?" Fitz said in his purring, seductive voice.

"It's not foolish," Charles said. "Love is not like bagging birds."

"Perhaps not," Fitz said. "But *finding* love is." He stood up and moved to Charles's side, brushing his stubbled cheek with the back of his knuckles. *Too tired even to shave.* At least that made Charles raise his head, although he quickly dropped his eyes to his lap again like a shy country maid. "You must make a bit of an effort, my dear. I could help you, be your pointer, and start the birds for you to take."

Charles held Fitz's hand, keeping it on his cheek. "That's kind of you, Fitz. You've always been a good friend. And yes, we did have some pleasant times." He sighed, let go of Fitz's hand, and stabbed at the egg with his spoon. "If I stay here will I have to lock my door at night?"

"There's no need for that. I won't trespass again."

"Do you promise, Fitz?"

"Damn it, Charles, I have just said so. Don't turn everything into a gothic novel."

"Well, in that case, Fitz, yes, thank you, I would prefer to stay here. At least you don't rant on and on at a fellow about how provincial and dreary everything was at Netherfield. And you don't dragoon me into day-long shopping trips to Bond Street or insist I ingratiate myself with fearsome old ladies I don't know in the hopes they'll be persuaded to confer invitations to Almack's Assembly Rooms."

"You see," Fitz said, smiling, "I do have some good qualities after all."

"I never said you didn't," Charles said. "You're the best of good fellows."

"Not to spoil the sterling character you gave me," Fitz said, "but it so happens I have vouchers for Almack's and I was hoping you would accompany me some evening. It's not really a safe venue for one eligible bachelor alone. No meddling sisters, just you and me, a well-matched team as we used to be. I'll beat the coverts and drive the plump ones to you. What do you say?"

Charles didn't answer directly. "Sometimes I wonder if she couldn't come to town. She has relations here, you know, an aunt and uncle. I don't see why she couldn't visit them, if only for a week or two."

Fitz almost gasped at the articulation of his deepest fears. "Who?" he said, hoping somehow that he had misheard, or that Charles had meant something else—someone else.

"Miss Bennet, of course."

"Why would she do that?" Fitz said when he could speak. "She'd have to stay in the City where her tradesman of an uncle lives, probably above his warehouse. He'd undoubtedly resent the expense of another mouth to feed when there's no chance of her catching a rich husband. It's not as if she'd be close enough to fashionable people to call on them or to attend functions in society."

"God, you're cruel," Charles said. "Don't you have any compassion?"

Fitz shrugged. "The poor are always with us," he murmured. "I can't claim to be a saint, but I do my share of charitable work at home."

"I'm sorry, Fitz. I don't imagine I'll be good company for you at Almack's. There's only one lady I want, and I can't see the point of looking at others." Charles laid his spoon down. "Do you know, Fitz, I'm too tired to eat. I think maybe I'll have a nap, make up for my interrupted night."

Charles climbed the stairs slowly, moving like a man three times his age, head lowered to avoid a misstep and not watching where he was going. He nearly bumped into Georgiana on her way down.

"Mr. Bingley!" Georgiana Darcy said. "Are you quite well?"

"No, Miss Darcy," Charles answered in piteous tones. "I was just telling Fitz that I think I must keep to my bed."

"Good morning, Fitz," Georgiana greeted her brother with a small, formal curtsy and took her place at the table. "Is Mr. Bingley unwell?"

"It's nothing serious," Fitz said. "But I hope you won't mind looking in on him occasionally."

"Of course not, Fitz. He's your friend, and I would like to think he's my friend, too."

"That's right," Fitz said. "You're a good girl, Georgie." He lingered in the doorway as she tucked into her egg and toast. "You will be gratified to hear that the Duke of Coverdale expressly asked you to be one of a select few to celebrate his elder son's coming into his title of Marquess of Bellingham next month."

"Oh, Fitz! I hope you told him I am not yet out." Georgiana's face held the same expression, rigid with terror, that Fitz remembered from her first pony ride, more than a decade ago. Right before she fell off and refused to try again for almost a twelvemonth.

"I did no such thing," Fitz said. "It is not a ball, merely a card party. Mrs. Annesley has assured me many times of your readiness to take the place for which birth and education have fitted you."

"But Bellingham! All the ladies are swooning over his exceptional beauty—or so I have heard. I won't know what to say!"

"Now, Georgie, you know better than to repeat such vulgar sentiments. You will do very well, so long as you repress your childish desire to show off. Young gentlemen don't like a clever female. Just make sure to wear a becoming gown, and let your natural modesty be your guide."

Georgiana set her partially eaten second piece of toast on her plate. "I think I may have caught whatever it is that Mr. Bingley is suffering from," she said. "I seem to have lost my appetite. Perhaps I'll just return to my room."

Fitz decided to go for a walk. What was the matter with

everybody? Charles rejecting balls, of all absurd things—what had been, only a couple of weeks ago, his favorite pastime. Georgie afraid to attend a simple gathering in her natural milieu. At least, the spiritless state Charles was in, Fitz need not fear leaving him alone in the house with Georgie, however much Caroline and Louisa favored anything that would further that cause. He would stroll in St. James's Park, clear his head, then take care of his own business. Perhaps things would improve over time. They usually did.

Eight

IT WAS EASY enough, Elizabeth decided, after suffering a few sleepless and remorse-filled nights, to enjoy the consolations of being in the right. As the days approached for Charlotte's sacrifice, and as Christmas brought her aunt and uncle Gardiner for a visit, she sympathized with Jane in her loss, attempted to treat Charlotte with reasonable consideration, and reveled in Mr. Wickham's continued attention.

Here was living proof that such a man as Elizabeth had only dared dream of existed in the flesh. Mr. Wickham was handsome, intelligent, charming, and open. Where Mr. Darcy looked down his well-shaped nose and sneered, above his company and unconcerned with displaying the sin of pride, Mr. Wickham threw himself into all the lowly pleasures of village society. He did not save himself for whist, but gladly played commerce and lottery tickets with the other young people, laughing at fish won and lost. He danced at assemblies and at family parties where the only music was provided by any girl willing to play the pianoforte for a set or two. He sat with old ladies and children and listened to prattle of weather and high prices and all the housewives' gossip. And always, his eyes followed Elizabeth.

He angled to sit by her at supper and to partner her at cards. When she walked into Meryton, often enough he would have arranged to be free from regimental duties and could escort her and her sisters to shops and the library, then home. Nothing improper, no liberties attempted. The best of it was, he talked. Not for him the silence and implied disparagement of a Mr. Darcy. And now that the Netherfield party was all gone back to town, he made no secret of his mistreatment at that man's hands. Apart from the one most scandalous aspect, which remained Elizabeth's great confidence to hold for him, the rest of his entire story was now common knowledge and the talk of every gossip in the neighborhood.

There was only the one problem in all this felicity: money—or the lack of it. It was what had led to Charlotte's self-immolation, perhaps what had prompted Mr. Bingley's hasty departure. And without it there was no prospect of marriage, the ultimate purpose of such heady pleasures. There could only be disappointment and loss, the same as Charlotte's and Jane's.

But money and marriage couldn't change Elizabeth's feelings. The way her heart leapt when Mr. Wickham entered the room, looked around, and headed straight to her chair. The way his beautiful face lit up at her jokes, and the way he would reach for her hand, forgetting himself in company, then remember just in time, bringing smiles of complicity to their faces, a blush from Elizabeth and the pounding of her heart.

Sometimes she was certain she heard his heart beating with equal force, cutting through the commotion of the laughing cardplayers and the deaf old people conducting their shouted conversations. Then her breath would catch as if her bodice was laced too tightly—which it *never* was, from her being so slender—and she would flush and feel as hot as if she sat near the fire on an unseasonably warm autumn day. Her lower body would clench and secrete moisture, shuddering with a will of its own. She would shift in her chair to relieve the feeling, trying all the while to be unobtrusive, not to let anyone, not even him—*especially* not him—know how greatly she was affected by his presence.

No, she could not talk of these improper urges, the seeds of which had been planted by seeing Mr. Darcy embracing Mr. Bingley, then brought to full flower by learning of Mr. Wickham's own endurance of the same abuse. How did one manage? She could not be the only unmarried young woman who had wrestled with such ungovernable passions, and yet had somehow prevailed over them. Some virtuous spinsters must have known these same desires and had not succumbed. Surely not all of the women who knew such feelings were the fallen ones, the lost ones.

But how?

FITZ DIRECTED THE driver of the hackney to leave him off a couple of streets from his destination. Best not to announce the direction. Not that it was exactly a secret after fifty years. Everyone knew *of* the Brotherhood of Philander, but no one, apart from the members themselves, knew any particulars.

The man at the door bowed Fitz inside, remarking with correct but unmistakable enthusiasm that it was a pleasure to see him again after so long an absence, and informing him as he took Fitz's hat and gloves that most of the members were attending a "sporting event." At Fitz's look of disgust, he assured him it was nothing improper. "Ought to be back soon, sir, if you care to wait."

Even as Fitz settled himself in the large parlor and incautiously pulled the heavy curtains aside to watch the last remains of sunset disperse over Hyde Park, he saw the distinctive group approaching the back entrance. In another minute they came tramping through the garden, laughing and shouting and comporting themselves like rambunctious schoolboys let out for a run.

Sir Frederick Verney, Baronet, beefy and well built, the picture of solid country virtue, led the way, accompanied by the darkly glamorous Andrew Carrington, unusually tall and slim, his allure only accentuated by his swarthy complexion, aquiline nose, and saturnine expression. Lord David Pierce, small and red-haired, who compensated by dressing with the understated elegance of Beau Brummell, and his dear friend, George Witherspoon, a dazzling beauty with a Roman profile and wavy golden hair, followed arm in arm. The Honorable Sylvester Monkton, pretending not to know the others yet reveling in the notoriety, minced along in a typical tailored confection of wasp-waisted coat and pale mauve pantaloons. The physician, Reginald Stevens, looking out of place in his more serviceable garments, and noticeably unhappy, trailed at the end of the procession.

"Who's that?" Verney said, stepping into the parlor, hat in hand.

"Darcy!" Fitz was greeted warmly if distractedly by the others.

"Should have stopped by earlier," Pierce said. "Carrington has treated us to an exhibition of his skill."

Fitz shook his head. Carrington was carrying his brace of dueling pistols, Stevens had his sinister black satchel; it indeed looked as though the men had returned from an affair of honor, although it was a decent hour of the evening, not dawn. What had Fitz hoped for when he joined this odd fraternity five years ago? He was the same age as most of them, a year or two younger, actually, but they held fast to their immaturity, as if by behaving like boys half their age they might somehow stave off the body's inevitable decline. All Fitz wanted today was to sit and have a quiet brandy or two, perhaps a rubber of whist, and pour out his troubles. Maybe, if things worked out especially well, a game of piquet with Verney. Those two-handed contests always seemed to reach a happy conclusion . . . "Not really in the mood for target shooting," he said.

"Don't be such an old dowager," Verney said. "Carrington and I had a capital wager—I said he couldn't shoot the hat off my head at fifty paces at twilight."

Fitz scowled and rolled his eyes. "How did you expect to collect your debt with a gaping hole in your head? Although, for you, might not make that great a difference."

"An academic question, as it turns out," Carrington said in his drawling, supercilious manner.

Verney displayed his high-crowned hat with the neat bullet hole an inch or two from the top, the edges slightly charred. "Finest bit of shooting we ever saw."

"I notice Stevens accompanied you just the same," Fitz said.

"Better safe than sorry," Stevens said. "It was damned lucky we weren't all taken up by the authorities, shooting off pistols in the park, in daylight." His face brightened, his frown smoothing out into his usual bland expression. "But you know, Darcy, just because I have a professional calling doesn't mean I can't take an interest in a wager as well as the next man."

"We were about to settle up," Verney said. He had already untied his cravat and shrugged out of his coat. "But we can wait to hear your news, if you don't mind, Andrew." He looked to Carrington for consent.

Carrington shrugged. "Fine with me, Fred. Every delay is simply interest accruing to my account."

Verney appeared unconcerned. "Works both ways, you know."

"Well, Darcy," Monkton said, when all except Stevens had disposed themselves in the chairs and sofas, drinks in hand. While the physician's services paid for his lodging at the Brotherhood, he also maintained an outside practice for the good of his reputation and the badly needed income. "It's been an age since we had the pleasure of your company."

"You in town for the winter?" Pierce asked.

"Where's your nice friend?" Witherspoon asked. Angelic in appearance, and with a corresponding dullness of wit, he had the gentle manners to match, and had been most comfortable with Charles's undemanding presence. Today Fitz was struck by the vague resemblance to Wickham—like a rough portrait drawn by an unskilled artist who could limn the physiognomy but capture nothing of the spirit.

"Yes indeed, where is he?" Monkton asked in his insinuating way. "Thought you had given us all up, married his sister at last. What was his name? Bingle? Dinghy?"

"Bingley," Fitz said. "Charles Bingley. No, I have not married. And it's Charles who's been talking of matrimony, although fortunately I was able to nip that in the bud."

"Mustn't look so down in the mouth," Monkton said. "Be glad the affair lasted as long as it did. It's not as if he were one of us, after all."

"D'ye know, Monkton," Fitz said, "you've become rather high in the instep all of a sudden. The fact that Charles's father made his fortune in trade is no reason to assume the son is any less a gentleman than I am. He's certainly more a gentleman than you'll ever be."

"Don't play the numbskull with me," Monkton said. "You know perfectly well what I mean. Your Charles was never a genuine sodomite."

"Nor am I," Fitz said. "Yet my money and name are good enough for membership in this exclusive company."

"It's lucky for you I have a strong stomach," Monkton said, "because that is the most nauseating swill I've been subjected to in some time, and I would hate to ruin my new waistcoat by spewing all over it."

"Looks as if you already have," Fitz said, pointing at the intricate pattern embroidered in pale green and jonquil silk.

Monkton's somewhat protuberant eyes stood out even farther at the invitation to battle. "Oh, it's easy for you strapping, tall men to profess the virtues of austerity in dress. We lesser figures must supplement nature's deficiencies with artifice. Let's just say, Darcy, that no man joins the Brotherhood of Philander for the *conversation*."

"I did," Fitz said. "The prospect of enlightened conversation with men like myself, of superior education and from good families, is rare in our degenerate society, unless one is prepared to indulge in gambling or some other unsavory vice."

"Such as eating beefsteaks," Carrington said with a feigned shudder. "Although, have to say, quite fond of a well-marbled cut of beef, myself." He winked at Verney.

"Indeed," Verney said, oblivious to any double meaning.

"What about the Dilettantis?" Pierce said. "Sounds your sort of thing. Roman antiquities and so on."

"Perhaps it used to be," Fitz said. "Yet from what I hear, even by Horry Walpole's day it had become just another gathering of drunkards."

"Whereas sodomy, by contrast, is quite acceptable," Monkton said. "We do agree on that, at any rate."

"Not all love between men is sodomy," Fitz said, "any more than all love between a man and a woman is fornication."

"I only wish magistrates and judges shared your opinion," Carrington said.

"I imagine the liberal ones do," Fitz said. "It's unlikely that men of breeding have anything to fear from outdated laws that were intended more to suppress heresy or insurrection."

"Oh, for the love of Apollo!" Monkton exclaimed. "Tell that to those poor sods from the White Swan!"

Fitz frowned and shook his head. "That is an altogether different matter, regrettable though it was. Those men had no exposure to the ideas of classical learning. Their congregation was formed expressly for the practice of unnatural vice. But for the superior intellect there are other considerations besides one's prick—hard as that may be for you to comprehend."

"Oh, it's *hard* for me, all right," Monkton said.

Fitz felt his temper rising and spoke softly in counteraction. "I warn you, Monkton, I do not put up with deliberate insults, from you or anyone, even here." He caught the amused gaze of the others, apparently eager to witness the duel they had missed earlier; the entire exchange struck him as so ridiculous he was forced almost into good humor. "I'll go so far as to admit that, unfortunately for me, Charles Bingley seems to have lost his taste for *conversation*."

"I don't remember conversation being one of his accomplishments," Pierce said. "Or do you mean something else?"

"You know damned well what he means," Carrington said.

"Then why the devil doesn't he just say it?" Verney said.

"Some of us," Pierce said, "have a natural propriety of speech, regardless of our surroundings."

"And some of us," Carrington said, "have a debt of honor to collect."

Verney and Carrington rose to go upstairs. "Care for a game of piquet, Darcy, when I come down?" Verney said over his shoulder. "This shouldn't take above half an hour."

"I thank you for the low estimate," Carrington said. "A pleasure to see you, Darcy, but what with all this lost time to be made good, Verney and I may actually be engaged a bit longer than that."

"I only meant," Verney said, "that the others had a stake in the wager too, and will be demanding their shares."

"But not on the same terms," Carrington murmured, bowing his good-byes and shutting the door behind him.

"I always had very pleasant conversations with Mr. Bingley," Witherspoon said. "But I never thought he was one of us either."

"He's not," Fitz said. "He's a respectable, innocent young man, somewhat confused at the moment by his lack of experience with females."

"If Witherspoon's artless remark proves anything," Monkton said, "it's that it's absurd to pay the annual equivalent of keeping a king's mistress—assuming anyone in our royal family had better taste in women than a German swineherd—to join the Brotherhood of Philander, only to talk like a maiden aunt telling of her niece's being debauched by a footman. But I am sorry to hear your bad news, Darcy."

"And I'm sorry to hear of your family misfortune," Darcy replied.

"What's that?"

"Why, the constant assaults on their virtue the footmen endure in your sister's household. Suppose she resembles you in that respect."

"Kiss my arse," Monkton said, but smiling. "In fact, I'd be more than willing to return the favor, Darcy. It's been damned tedious here, all the same old faces."

"Since when do you look at faces?" Fitz said.

"Oh, you know what I mean."

"Then why don't you just say it?" Fitz said. "Why pay these exorbitant dues only to talk like a prissy *Miss Thing*?" He screwed his face up and flapped his wrist in Monkton's direction.

"Gentlemen," Pierce said. "This room is a *parlor*, meaning it is intended for genuine conversation, the exchange of words. There are plenty of rooms upstairs to accommodate discussions of a more physical nature." He turned to Witherspoon and cocked his eyebrow. "George, my dear, I am experiencing an urgent and growing need to emulate Carrington and Verney's example. Are you suffering anything similar?"

"Oh, Davey," Witherspoon said, "you know I can never follow all those complicated turns of phrase. But if you mean would I like to go upstairs with you, of course I would."

The two men stood and embraced, sharing a deep kiss. Witherspoon allowed Pierce to unbutton the flap of his pantaloons, then gasped with pleasure as the lean little redhead snaked a hand inside.

Fitz looked away in embarrassment, noting that, however improper, the knowledge that two men were enjoying themselves upstairs and two more were about to follow only made his own situation that much more desperate. He eyed Monkton's slender form in its tight coat. One didn't have to actually *like* a man to engage in sport, after all. "Now that you mention it, Monkton, I might appreciate a more intimate *conversation*."

"Ooh, lovely," Monkton said. "Funny how we go for months with nothing but stale gossip, then have all our excitement in the space of an hour."

Fitz began to have his doubts, however, as they undressed in Monkton's room and the man's sartorial peculiarities came to light. "Damn it, Sylly," he said, "if I wanted something in petticoats I could go to Madame Amélie's."

"Or simply ask Bingley's sister to bend over, as I recall," Monkton said. He showed off the erection blooming beneath his drawers. "I assure you, you won't find this on any woman."

"I should hope not," Fitz said. "Nature has not stinted you

there. But my God, Syl. A corset? It's not as if you have a tendency to corpulence."

"Oh, the fashions these days are impossible," Monkton said. "They're wearing coats so tight, and with such narrow waists. Come on, give me a hand with these laces."

Fitz pulled his penknife from the pocket of his pantaloons and flicked it open.

"No!" Monkton shrieked, stumbling backward. "I'll need to get into the coat again."

"You do make a fellow pay for pleasure," Fitz complained, picking at the knots. "Never expected to find myself working as an abigail."

"Don't worry, love. I'll make it worth your while," Monkton said in the accents of a Covent Garden streetwalker. Once divested of his undergarments, he showed himself off to best advantage, leaning in a carefully posed S-curve against the bedpost. "There. How's that?"

Fitz studied the lithe, supple body before him. "That's what I mean. It leaves such ghastly red marks where you lace it so tight."

"Men," Monkton said, rolling his eyes. "No pleasing you. What can it possibly matter so long as my cock is hard and my arse is open?"

"An excellent point," Fitz said. He moved to stand behind Monkton, who braced himself on the side of the bed. Fitz pulled the stopper from the jar of grease, spread a liberal amount over himself and Monkton, and pushed roughly inside. Monkton inhaled sharply but pressed back against Fitz in encouragement. God, it was a pleasure to have a willing—no, an eager—partner for a change, Fitz thought.

"Oh," Monkton said on a sigh, "you do have an excellent point yourself, Fitz. That Charles Bingley is a fool."

"Leave him out of this, Sylly," Fitz said.

But an hour later Fitz couldn't follow his own advice. It was all he could do not to think of it, the contrast between Monkton's practiced, easy acquiescence and dear Charles's prickly, innocent love. Sylly knew every trick of exciting a man's interest, keeping him aroused, satisfying him—and stirring him to rise yet again. He was like the mythical whore that all men dream of, who does it for pleasure, not for money. Like Wickham without the danger and the malice. But Charles . . . Charles was like a lady. Not in body, and certainly not in performance. But in the way he required courting, never knowing from one day to the next if he would welcome or deny one's attentions. Ordinarily Fitz wouldn't have time for such nonsense, but where love was concerned, it seemed, all one's comfortable assumptions were overset.

Only one other disturbing occurrence clouded Fitz's enjoyment of the first real relief he had known in weeks. Somewhere in the second hour of their tryst he was visited, as after the Meryton assembly, by the memory of a pair of wide, dark eyes, a fascinating, sweet-sharp voice saying, "Mr. Darcy is not to be laughed at," and at the height of his passion he momentarily lost his force.

"It's all right," Monkton said. "I know it's not the same as being with your friend."

The man had intelligence and sensitivity, even if he rarely showed it. "I'm sorry, Syl," Fitz said. "Lie back and let me make it up to you."

"God, Fitz," Monkton said. "It's not as if you have anything to apologize for, after those first two bouts. If I were a woman I'd marry you tomorrow."

"If you were a woman," Fitz said, "we would not be having this conversation."

"Not so sure about that," Monkton said. "I have the feeling

that something curious is going on with you, something more than your Charles contemplating marriage."

"You have a most unhealthy imagination."

"How true," Monkton said, winking. "But you know, Fitz, I'm right more often than I'm wrong. At least I don't lose many wagers."

"Oh, do be quiet," Fitz said. This time he was forced to follow his own advice, as it was impossible to speak with his mouth full.

Nine

CHARLES BLOTTED THE paper again and swore, saw Georgiana in the doorway, and stood up. "I am sorry, Miss Darcy. I didn't know you were there."

"It's all right, Mr. Bingley. Fitz uses words like that all the time when he thinks I'm not listening. Then when I say the most innocuous thing, like *drat* or *deuce*, he scolds me as if I were a child."

"A lady oughtn't to say *drat*," Charles said. "It's vulgar. And *deuce* is highly improper."

"But suppose I hold a *two* at cards?" Georgiana asked innocently. "What am I to say then?" She saw Charles's sad face, realized he was in no condition to endure even her gentle teasing, and took the seat across from him at the small table. "What has you so unhappy, Mr. Bingley?"

Charles felt such a desire to unburden himself to any sympathetic ear that he could not deny even the curiosity of a sixteen-year-old girl. "Do you promise not to tell Fitz?"

"I promise." She pointed to the sheet of paper. "But if that turns out to be a forged commission to the Foot Guards, I'll have to tell him anyway."

Charles laughed. "Not likely. Even a red coat couldn't turn me into a heartbreaker like George Wickham." He noticed her frown and the dark red flush and, assuming this reaction was caused by knowledge of her brother's troubles with the man, quickly changed the subject back to one that could cause embarrassment only to himself. "It's a poem. At least, it's an attempt at an ode, but I can't get the meter right. And I can't think of anything that rhymes with *Jane*."

The diversion worked. Georgiana's face lit up with childish pleasure and she clapped her hands. "Oh, what fun! But there are dozens of words that rhyme with *Jane*. It must be one of the easiest. Let's see. *Plain*, *plane*—there are two words, spelled differently, you know—*pain*, *pane*—two spellings." She sat back and closed her eyes. "Now, let's start from the beginning. *Bane*, *cane*, *chain*, *crane*, *deign*, *drain*, *fain*, *feign*—two spellings—*gain*, *grain*, *lane*, *lain*—two spellings—*main*, *mane*—two spellings—*rain*, *rein*, *reign*—there are three spellings, you recall—*sane*, *seine*—two spellings—*stain*, *wane*, *wain*—two spellings. And if you can take two syllables, *contain*, *disdain*, *explain*, *refrain*, *remain*, *sustain*—"

Charles held up a hand in protest. "I see, Miss Darcy, that I am in an unequal contest. You're so much cleverer than me—like your brother."

"No, you mustn't say that." She shook her head, made uncomfortable by the compliment, then decided to be bold. "But don't *strain* your *brain* or you'll give yourself a *migraine*, if not a *chilblain*."

"Stop!"

"Shall I *constrain* my efforts?"

"Yes! I surrender."

"You are *slain*?"

"Bluestocking!"

Georgiana sat back as if she'd been struck, all her cheerfulness gone in an instant. "I know. I can't seem to help it. Part of the problem is that I still have lessons occasionally, but the truth is I'm never so happy as when I'm reading, or learning something new—or playing the pianoforte." She twisted her hands in her lap, cracking her knuckles.

Charles sat momentarily silenced. How could Fitz imagine he would wish to marry such a child? A precocious child, certainly, but when he compared her coltish awkwardness with Miss Bennet's mature, womanly composure the contrast was devastating. But Miss Darcy was not to blame for her brother's whims. He reached over and lifted her hands to the table, laying his own on top of them to quiet her fidgeting. "Miss Darcy, you'll never play another note if you keep that up. I didn't mean any harm by what I said. I was only joking, because you're so quick and I'm a dolt who can't even think up a simple rhyme."

Georgiana looked at Charles with gratitude. "You're not a dolt. You're so much better at mixing with people. I'll never learn how to be easy in society."

"Of course you will. It just takes practice. Now, let's see if in all that long list of words there's a good rhyme. I don't want an unpleasant meaning. I want something beautiful and kind and sweet-natured. Like the lady in the poem."

"Of course." Georgiana had a revelation. "Mr. Bingley—are you in love?"

Charles felt himself blushing. "Please don't tell Fitz," he said.

"It will be our secret," Georgiana said with girlish solemnity. "What is she like? Sorry, you just said. Beautiful and sweet and kind. Why is Fitz so set against her? Is there something wrong with her?"

"She's perfect. It's just that Fitz doesn't approve of her family. As if that mattered. It's not as if I'm going to marry them."

Georgiana wrinkled her brow. "But that's exactly what Fitz always says. He says, when you marry, you're not only marrying your spouse but his or her entire family and all their connections. It's very important, at least according to him."

"I know. He's been telling me the same thing, over and over. Honestly, I can't see how it has any great significance for me. It's different for you and Fitz, I understand that. Your uncle is an earl, and Fitz has the magnificent Pemberley to keep up, and I suppose you have a good marriage portion."

"Yes," Georgiana admitted, bowing her head.

"Please don't mind that I said it. My sisters have pretty good fortunes, too. All I meant is, my father simply made a lot of money in trade. And some of Miss Ben— Jane's relations are in trade. So she and I are equals on that level."

"But doesn't Fitz think you should move up from that rank? After all, you're not in trade. Your father brought you up as a gentleman and left you a gentleman's fortune. Once you find the right estate you'll be a landed gentleman yourself."

"Well, Jane's father is a gentleman, with a good-size, respectable piece of property. It's not his fault that he has no son and the estate is entailed."

Georgiana recognized the futility of further debate. "May I read the poem?"

Charles, preferring anything to rehashing the same tired arguments with a deceptively young and pretty female Darcy who appeared to have as sharp a mind as her brother, turned the paper face up.

Georgiana read aloud in a soft, clear voice:

When I behold my Jane's sweet face
And all the virtues that her grace,

I think I am in paradise
And never more ~~make~~ need sacrifice
At idols' shrines of brass and ____
When I may worship at my Jane

Georgiana giggled, then looked stricken and covered her mouth. "Oh dear. I'm not good at recitation. Fitz always complains that I give everything a humorous tone."

"What a coincidence," Charles said, delighted to find that they had something in common after all. "He says I have a tendency to levity that is becoming tedious. But he seemed to like it well enough when a certain lady was laughing at *him* in Hertfordshire."

"Really?" Georgiana sounded skeptical. "I would dearly love to see Fitz allowing any lady to laugh at him."

"I've never known him to permit it either. Of course, I've only been his friend for a couple of years. The funny thing is, the lady is Jane's sister. But he doesn't seem to miss her at all now. He said she didn't love me—Jane, I mean—but how would he know? What does he know about love?"

"I think he does know something," Georgiana said, turning her face away and tucking in her chin like a nesting swan. How could Fitz imagine she would ever marry this silly young man? He was sweet, certainly, and very kind, but he was still a boy, even if he was almost seven years her senior. More of a confidant than a suitor. Perhaps there was a way to appear to comply with her brother's wishes without openly defying him. "Fitz is an excellent brother, and I'm sure he's a good friend. You'll see eventually that he means well by you too."

"Yes," Charles said in a dispassionate tone. "Yes, he does."

"I suppose," Georgiana proposed in a hesitant manner, "since you and he are such close friends, he wants us to be friends also."

"Yes, that's it," Charles said, much happier at this turn in the conversation. "And I hope—that is, I would like to be your friend, Miss Darcy." He picked up the crumpled sheet of paper. "I should probably throw this wretched composition on the fire. It's really just—"

"*Profane*," Georgiana said.

"Now hold on a minute. It's not as bad as all that."

"No, the rhyme. Let me see it again. Yes. 'At idols' shrines of brass *profane*.' What do you think? You can contrast your pure love for your perfect lady with the profane idols."

"Oh, I see. That's perfect. I say, you're the best. If I weren't in love with Jane I think I would ask you to marry me after all, the way everybody wants us to."

To Charles's vast discomfort, Miss Darcy responded, not by laughing or cuffing him the way one of his sisters would, but with a stifled sob.

"Now, whatever did I say wrong? Never tell me you're in love with me and I dashed all your girlish hopes."

That raised at least the attempt at a smile. "I think I must tell you my secret," Georgiana said. "If we are to be friends, then you ought to know." She took a deep breath and started in before Charles could forestall her. "Last summer Mr. Wickham proposed to me. No, wait, please don't say anything or I won't be able to tell it all. He said he was very much in love. You see, he was brought up with us, with me and Fitz, and I was used to looking up to him like a brother and felt very comfortable with him—so I was not as cautious as I would have been with a stranger. And he is a personable man, with a pleasing address and—"

"Damned fine-looking," Charles said, before he could stop himself.

"Yes," Georgiana said in a strangled whisper.

"You mustn't be so despondent over a youthful indiscretion," Charles said. "If all the innocent young ladies who'd had their heads turned by a good-looking scoundrel considered themselves ruined, there'd be nobody left for honest gentlemen to marry except the sort of coarse, brazen women who don't care."

Georgiana looked up. "I'm not sure if that makes me feel better or worse. But it is something to bear in mind."

"Please go on," Charles said. "I want to hear the whole—and how you were rescued."

"Mr. Wickham said we ought to elope, because Fitz would disapprove of the match and would try to stop us. And since I'm underage we would need his permission to marry. But I didn't like the idea of sneaking off as if we were doing something shameful, so I wrote to Fitz and he came storming down to Ramsgate and *had words* with Mr. Wickham and that was the end of it."

"And a good thing too," Charles said.

"Yes. Fitz explained that Mr. Wickham was only interested in my fortune. He said that he had offered him the choice of marrying me, with my money to be kept in trust for our children, and we could live on an allowance from Fitz—a very generous one. But Mr. Wickham didn't want that. At least, he never came back."

Charles felt momentarily at a loss. No wonder she was so shy—and no wonder she had been so upset by his witless jest about marrying her. "If it's any comfort, it's the same thing for us men. Fitz is forever warning me off perfectly nice girls, saying they only want me for my money."

"And do they?"

"Well, I suppose most of them. But not Jane."

"How can you tell?"

"I just can," Charles said. "Fitz doesn't want to believe it, but I know. And I think, when you meet a man who loves you for yourself, you'll know. Wickham is simply not a good man, and is out for whatever he can get. But they're not all like him. You'll meet some who are worthy of you. In fact, you'll probably have to fight them off, which means it's a good thing you're so tall." He stood up and put his arm around her bowed shoulders. They were very broad shoulders, he noticed, much like Fitz's.

Georgiana stiffened. "I know we are not in love, but I think you ought not to embrace me like that. Mrs. Annesley is forever reminding me that people tend to misinterpret even the most innocent words and acts."

Charles withdrew his arm, stepped back several feet and reddened like a girl. "I *am* sorry, Miss Darcy. I thought, since we were friends . . ."

Georgiana sighed. Oh, this was impossible! When would she be able to forget the events of last summer and regain her natural poise? It seemed that having a woman's body destroyed any grace she had once possessed. She was always twitchy and nervous now, shying at every friendly gesture like a bird with a broken wing, scuttling into the hedge at the sound of approaching footsteps. "It's all right, Mr. Bingley. I know you were only trying to comfort me. It's just that Mr. Wickham claimed to be my friend too. And I thought he was Fitz's friend, like you."

"Well, I hope I'm a better friend than that," Charles said. God, this was difficult. What the devil was Fitz thinking, bringing him into his house with this sensitive, wounded creature? "And I promise not to take any more liberties."

"Thank you, Mr. Bingley. I assure you, you're the least likely person to take liberties I can imagine."

"Hmm," Charles said. "I'm not sure whether that's a compliment."

"Well, you must admit, you don't seem much like a wild libertine. Would you wish to be?"

"All men do, at least in our imagination," Charles said. "I shall have to be satisfied with being a trustworthy friend. Would you mind helping me with the rest of this poem, so I can chalk up one artistic achievement to my otherwise empty existence?"

Georgiana pursed her lips. "Well, actually, I'm sorry to say I think the fire might be the best place for it. Why don't you let it sit overnight and see how it looks in the morning?"

"That's an excellent idea," Charles said. "What do you say to a friendly game of backgammon instead?"

Georgiana laughed. "I hope you're better at backgammon than poetry."

"I couldn't be worse. We'll play for very high stakes. Tuppence a point."

"Better watch out. I'll have that fortune of yours before the night is out."

"Don't be too sure. It's a game of chance, you know. Luck, not skill, can win the day."

Georgiana let out an exaggerated sigh. "Then you're bound to win."

GEORGE WICKHAM REFLECTED on the good fortune that had followed him all his life. He took pride in the fact that it wasn't merely the common sort of luck that people mistook for "Providence." Most of it was due, as his stern, puritan godfather would have exhorted, to his own efforts. Perhaps not directed precisely in the endeavors that old stiff rump would have recommended, but definitely productive. And always, as one avenue of potential profit was closed off, another opened up for George's exploration . . .

The only woman here with half a brain and looks to match was this Elizabeth Bennet. Funny that sod Darcy hadn't already made a move there, but it was exactly as George had suspected all along—the man was a genuine woman-hater. Didn't just amuse himself with arse like most, but actually preferred it. Once again, George could benefit from this great deficiency in his former foster brother's character. It almost made up for last summer's disaster. *Almost.* If that had succeeded, he'd be set for life with Georgiana's money. No need to do anything but live for pleasure, the way Nature intended, certainly not sign up with some rustic militia. But . . . if he hadn't joined, he'd never have gone to Hertfordshire, never have met *her.*

If George had not spent time in Elizabeth's company and seen that she was truly corporeal, not a phantasm, he would not have believed that such a woman existed. Clever, witty, beautiful, and fascinating, up in the ways of the world, not easily shocked. He had confessed to her the precise nature of his dealings with Darcy. Oh, not in the coarse, unambiguous terms he would use with a man, but unmistakable. Clear enough for anyone, even a carefully brought up female, to get the idea. Any other young lady would have fainted or run crying to her mama at the mere mention of such a subject. But this intrepid Lizzy Bennet not only listened with equanimity, she did not even pretend to confusion or ignorance. In fact, she had contributed her own considerable stock of knowledge on the subject to the conversational pool. George wondered how it was that she was so certain of it.

Well, what matter? It was obvious not only that she knew, but that it gave her an indecent thrill. What a find! George had met women like that before, the debased hags who kept molly houses, and the demireps whose "friends" were sodomites and madge culls, but they were rarely young and pretty, certainly not delectable virgins from country gentry families.

He sighed. A virgin. And chaste. There was the problem, that and her lack of money. He would marry her in an instant if she had the bare minimum of what he required. But she had nothing, not even close. He had made discreet inquires, just to be sure, but there really was no need. Everybody in these little villages was open about such things, however people tried to hide their situation or put on a brave show in town. The Bennet family was spoken of everywhere as a sorry case, five daughters, no son, an entail looming over them, and little left for marriage portions—a thousand apiece. God! The income from that would barely cover an evening at a gentlemen's club once a week. Assuming he could find a patron to pay the dues . . .

As it was, all he could hope for was some weakening of her resolve. If he could not afford to marry her, at least he could enjoy her while he searched for the one who would make him a gentleman of leisure as he deserved. Unless he was very fortunate indeed, and found another extraordinary woman, one with money, George would consider Elizabeth his true wife and the other as merely his bread and butter. Surely, with her superior understanding and her natural wisdom, Elizabeth would acquiesce in the scheme, as the only way for them to have the best of both worlds.

But there was not the least indication of that ever happening. George knew, as he valued his continued survival, he must never allow the magnetic force of his attraction to blind himself to reality, and his instincts for *that* were as sharp as ever. It was infallible, his sense of response, from men and women alike. Never before, in George's experience—and he gave himself credit for having experienced just about every sensation man or woman, or both together, could bring—had he encountered a woman who was both genuinely warm and strictly virtuous. If a woman was truly capable of knowing pleasure, she would seek it out and surrender to it, usually while young enough to enjoy it. It was only the cold ones who held out for marriage.

Yet Elizabeth wanted him very much. She was all aquiver when he entered the room, her animal spirits fluttering like her fan. He could get hard just from imagining her trembling like that beneath him on a bed, or in his lap, in a chair. Or on her knees. Oh God, he had to stop this . . .

Strange the Netherfield party had cleared off so suddenly, leaving the field to him, despite their having all the advantages of terrain and position, not to mention superior numbers. Unlikely that George Wickham, even in his blazingly fine regimentals, could rout so formidable a force. If only he had thought of going into the military sooner; he'd be a general by now, or at least a colonel. He'd have won all his promotions, with Providence on his side like this; wouldn't have had to worry about buying his way up the ranks. It was a genuine stroke of luck, not to have his game exposed at the start.

That consideration jolted him out of his complacency. It *was* a game—it was always a game—and he could not afford to waste any more time in this languorous, love-struck nonsense with Elizabeth Bennet.

"Have you met Miss King?" Colonel Forster said. "Here is Mr. Wickham, a fine fellow, one of my newest officers, eager to make your acquaintance."

"How do you do, Miss King?" George said. He sighed again, hoping the chit would think it from admiration. No elegance, a merely adequate figure, and that frizzy red hair that always goes with skim-milk skin and freckles. But she had one great charm: ten thousand pounds from her uncle. "I do hope you have this dance free."

Ten

AFTER HIS FIRST visit, Fitz was unable to deprive himself for long of the pleasures of male companionship. Not just the physical relief, which was considerable, but the rare opportunity to speak honestly. No need at the Brotherhood of Philander for pretense, for lies and half truths. Despite the loose talk within the walls of the hotel on Park Lane, every man was pledged to the strictest secrecy outside, as if his life depended on it. As it did.

"The thing is, Darcy," Pierce said, "you knew your Charles would marry sooner or later."

"Well, of course," Fitz agreed with counterfeit amiability. "Just thought it would be later. Always intended that he and my sister . . ."

"And you planning to marry Bingley's sister," Pierce mused aloud. "Something rather incestuous about that, don't you think?"

Fitz frowned. "How so? There's no tie of blood between our families. And it's traditional in situations like ours, Charles and mine, going back to ancient times. Aristogeiton was betrothed to Harmodius's sister."

"Who?" Verney asked.

"Oh, the Welsh," Monkton said with a sly smile. "Little better than savages. Irregular in their habits. Don't have marriages and families the way we define them. Didn't even use surnames until recently."

"Stop it, Monkton," Fitz said. "Anyone who's had a proper education has heard of Harmodius and Aristogeiton."

"I haven't," Witherspoon said. Since acquiring Pierce's aggressive protection, Witherspoon had become braver about confessing his ignorance, his lack of education, or even, apparently, his ability to read.

"Famous tyrannicides," Carrington said. "Hardly a felicitous example to follow, Darcy, I should think."

"What's a tyr—" Witherspoon began.

"They killed the ruler of Athens," Pierce explained. "Or rather, his brother."

"That doesn't sound very nice," Witherspoon said.

"They were considered liberators in their time," Fitz said. "Heroes."

"They were lovers," Monkton said. "The beautiful youth, Harmodius, beloved of the noble and manly Aristogeiton. The grateful Athenians erected a statue of the two of them. Naked, of course, as all heroes were portrayed." He paused, a sad look softening his sharp features. "With this tiresome war going on, apparently intended to last our entire lifetime, no one dares travel abroad to enjoy such edifying sights, the way our fathers and grandfathers did."

"The Grand Tour as an excuse to look at indecent sculpture?" Pierce said with a snort.

"It's only your provincial, brutish *Englishness* that leads you to the blasphemy of equating the ideal of masculine beauty with lewdness," Monkton said, rousing himself to the intense hostility he reserved for attacks on what he called his "religion." "And if it's so indecent, what are you doing here, nuzzling in Witherspoon's admittedly beautiful lap? Oughtn't you to be over at the Society for the Reformation of Manners, informing on us all?"

"I only mean," Pierce said, "that there's a vast difference between what was admired in pagan times and what's acceptable now."

"You don't have to be so pleased about it, though," Verney said.

"Oh, Pierce is never happier than when expressing his superior virtue," Carrington said, "even when it's in obvious contradiction to his actions."

"What is that supposed to mean?" Pierce said, standing up.

"What do you think?" Carrington drawled through barely parted lips. "*Hypocrite.*"

"I don't wish to start another war," Fitz said. "All I was trying to say is that when two men love each other, marrying the sister of one's friend is the best way of maintaining the sacred bond."

"Actually," Monkton said, "there is a long tradition, sadly neglected these days, of sworn friendship between men."

"True," Fitz said. "But since, as men of property and position in society, we have a duty to marry, choosing one's friend's sister seems the ideal way to unite the two families."

Monkton, indignation blazing from his eyes, sat up very straight. "I have *never*, in my entire life, been accused of committing such a vulgar, mercantile error as conforming with *duty*."

"Well, in this case, Monkton, you can't claim any extraordinary virtue," Verney interposed. "As younger sons, you and

Pierce are exempt from that duty. The rest of us, however, must eventually accept the obligation of matrimony." The stern voice, ordinarily reserved for his official capacity as justice of the peace at home in Sussex, added to the comical effect of his words, emanating as they did from a muscular and gleaming half-naked man sitting among other casually attired club mates. "But unlike women, we men have the advantage of being able to put off marriage until our middle years," he added, generously commuting a death sentence to life at hard labor.

Carrington, looking for some reason distinctly uncomfortable, turned away from the glowering Pierce, the affronted Monkton, and the splendid form of Verney, and addressed Fitz. "But that, I think, is the core of unpalatable truth at the center of this apple of discord. Doesn't it give you pause when you contemplate lying with the man one night who's been doing the same thing with your sister the night before?"

"Thank you," Pierce said. "I shall take that observation as an apology."

"Take it any way you like," Carrington said. "Preferably red hot and up the arse."

"Do you know, Carrington," Pierce said, "if you didn't have such a notable skill with pistols, you'd have been called to account long ago for all your abuse."

"Yes," Carrington said, "I remind myself of it every morning at Manton's when I put another ball into the bull's-eye. In fact, it's the reason I developed the skill in the first place. So much more enjoyable than having to watch every word. The way you must, Pierce."

"At least, as Verney says, we have time before making any irrevocable decisions." Fitz addressed Carrington's earlier question to turn attention from the quarrels always bubbling below the surface of this ingrown and homogeneous society. "Charles has been of age less than two years. Georgiana's barely sixteen.

Let her at least enjoy her debut in society, and a season or two of freedom."

"But what's your Charles supposed to do in the meantime?" Pierce asked.

Fitz shrugged. "What do any of us do?" The loud guffaws almost made him blush, like a first former admitting in front of upperclassmen that he touched himself. "I don't see what's so funny."

"Oh, use your other head for a change, assuming it still functions," Monkton said. "The one on your neck. *You've* a reputation as a ladies' man. Can get a Lady Finchley or a Lydia Waring with little trouble but the expense—although from what I've heard, now that she's Mrs. Swain, Lydia has given you your marching orders, and Caroline Finchley prefers a ducal crest. But your Charles isn't so practiced, as I recall, nor do I imagine you'll want him risking his health—and yours—by consorting with whores, even the superior merchandise at Madame Amélie's. No, Darcy, if your Charles can't marry the lady of his choice he'll simply mope, or worse"—Monkton lowered his voice to a whisper and looked cautiously around the room, as if spies might be lurking behind the sideboard—"take to writing poetry. You'll have to watch him every minute, lest he leave ballads or even *sonnets* all over your house. And you know what that leads to."

"*Odes*," Verney said, in a similar ominous tone. "All dedicated to a certain unnamed lady."

"The smudged sheet of paper," Pierce said, a sobbing tremolo distorting his clipped speech, "with a couple of tearstains placed just so, beside the words *lost* and *never*."

"And he'll act the part," Carrington said. "Drooping about with limp wrists and long hair, one uncombed lock tumbling negligently over a noble brow to signify a sensitive nature reduced to desolation." He rested his head on his hand and slumped his shoulders in an exaggerated posture of despair.

Monkton clapped a soft, lily-white hand to his own brow. "Oh Lord! Your sister's living in your house, isn't she? You'd better hare on home, Darcy. Just hope you're in time to prevent *poor Charles* from corrupting her with his loathsome practices."

Fitz glared at Monkton. "I'll thank you to leave my sister out of your low japery." He had a hazy memory from a week ago, finding a crumpled sheet of writing paper containing a few lines of feeble, incompetent verse with the name *Jane* smudged and blotted over . . .

"I don't see what's so terrible about writing poetry," Witherspoon said, interrupting at a fortunate moment. "I think it's romantic."

"George, my dear, you know we're just joking," Pierce said.

"Do you think my painting is silly, Davey?"

"Of course not. You're a genuine artist, always have been from the moment you could hold a brush, I imagine."

"Well, yes, Davey. That is, I always wanted to paint."

Witherspoon had quite a reputation among the members of the Brotherhood for his portraits. Fitz had almost agreed to sit for him, until he had gone to Witherspoon's house and seen his works—all the subjects portrayed unclothed, and all standing, some in more ways than one . . . Still, even Fitz had to confess the man had a gift for catching the essence of a person's character in what appeared at first glance to be a mess of disorderly paint and wild brushstrokes.

"But you see," Pierce continued, "sometimes when a young man is thwarted in love he takes up pursuits he showed no previous inclination or talent for."

"Like *conversation*," Monkton said. "That is the root of the problem, isn't it, Darcy? Now that he's seen the *other* side, your Charles has lost his interest in *conversation*?"

"SHE'S HERE," CAROLINE Bingley greeted Fitz in a voice of doom when he returned to his house.

Why was *she* always here? Fitz wondered. Surely Georgie had other friends. "Who is here?" he asked.

"Miss Bennet."

Fitz startled and glanced over his shoulder like Orestes being hunted by the Furies. He despised himself for the lack of control, but he was more afraid now than he had been at the beginning of this dangerous charade, and the shock was truly immense.

"Not *here*," Caroline said. "In town. Fortunately, she's staying with her relations. You know, the ones who live in Gracechurch Street." She let out one of her contemptuous snorts, reminding Fitz unpleasantly of his aunt de Bourgh.

"I fail to see anything fortunate about that," Fitz said.

"Do you?" Caroline said. "Think how much worse it would be if she were living in a more fashionable neighborhood, closer to us. As it is, I barely managed to sit still during her call. I kept worrying that Charles would stop by."

"Why would he?" Fitz asked. "He seems to have developed an altogether healthy fear of the torments that two idle ladies can inflict on a defenseless younger brother. From what he tells me, the minute he walked through your door he'd be hustled off to Bond Street or pressed into escort duty for an Almack's assembly." He paused, taking in the full implications of Caroline's statement. "Wait a minute—you mean Miss Bennet called on you?"

"Yes, Mr. Darcy, that's how it is in society, you may remember. A lady pays morning calls, then her acquaintances return the visits."

"What a damnable business! Pardon my language, Miss Bingley."

"Yes, very tedious," Caroline said, waving her hand amiably at the apology. "But don't worry. I shall stretch it out as long as possible. She'll take the hint soon enough, and that will be the end of it."

"But what will you say to Charles?"

"Nothing, of course. Goodness, how silly do you think me? No, don't answer that. But I am not silly about something as important as this, I promise you, Mr. Darcy."

"And what if—that is—did Miss Bennet ask about Charles? What did you say?"

"She can't, not without sounding like one of her whorish younger sisters. All she can do is inquire after his health, which of course she did, as soon as was decently possible. I replied that he is well, and that's all that can—and will—be said on the subject."

Fitz sighed. "I knew a gift like that would have to be paid for somehow."

"What gift?"

"The business with your late father's estate occurring so providentially, allowing our successful remove to town."

"My dear." Caroline took the chance of putting her hand on his arm. Even beneath the sturdy cloth of his coat and the linen of his shirt Fitz's flesh crawled. "You have worked very hard and been most patient. It will all be resolved soon enough. Just leave it to me. I know how to manage these things. And if you wish to thank me later, I will think of a fitting reward."

She was becoming bolder every day. When would she begin winking and receiving him in dishabille? *Why not just shoot me*, Fitz thought, *like a horse that has stumbled into a rabbit hole and broken its leg*? It would be quicker.

"I WAS WONDERING, Fitz," Charles said the next day over breakfast, "if those vouchers were still good."

Fitz's hand conveying his last bite of egg and toast was involuntarily halted an inch from his mouth. "Vouchers?" he said.

"You know—for Almack's."

"But my dear Charles, you made it quite plain that you have no interest in *game*," Fitz said.

"Well, I've been thinking over what you said, and it seems to me that maybe that is what I need—to get out of the house, enjoy a dance or two with a pretty young lady."

Fitz put the toast down and took a delaying gulp of coffee. "I'll have a look," he said. "I may have lost them or given them away."

Charles stared. "You never misplace things. And surely if you'd given them away you'd remember. What is it, Fitz? Don't you want your old shooting partner anymore? Or have you found a new one? Is that it, eh? Someone at that disreputable club of yours? The Brotherhood of—what was it—Philadelphia? Not such *brotherly* love, though, is it?"

Fitz, thankful that he had never delivered his planned lecture to Georgie about the dangers of keeping fashionable hours, and that the two of them were therefore alone in the breakfast parlor, stood up. "Charles," he said, lowering his voice to its sternest, deepest register. "Remember that my sister is living in this house. It is ill done of you to breathe so much as a word about my private associations in front of her."

"Well, dash it all, Fitz, she's not here now!"

"But she could be," Fitz said. "She could be right outside the door."

"God, Fitz. Anyone would think you—oh! Good morning, Miss Darcy!"

"Good morning, Mr. Bingley," Georgiana said. "Fitz." She kissed her brother on the cheek and sat down. "Did I hear you mention Almack's? That sounds like fun. When are you going?"

Fitz, torn between triumph, exasperation, and imminent heart attack, settled for graceful surrender. It occurred to him that Almack's had one great advantage as a destination. Miss Bennet, while unable to call on Fitz, would be more than likely to venture into this part of town to pay a second visit to Miss Bingley, whereas there was no possible chance her tradesman of an uncle could have obtained vouchers for Almack's. "Tonight, I hope, if I can find the vouchers. I am sorry you won't be able to accompany us."

"Oh no," Georgiana said. "I'm very glad to be still in the schoolroom. Besides, I should only be in the way of you two sportsmen." She looked up from under her lashes at her brother's forbidding countenance, then to his friend's more neutral demeanor. "I hope you bag some very plump partridges tonight, Mr. Bingley. Don't let my brother *constrain* your efforts, or consign all the *plain* ones to your *domain*."

"Georgiana!" Fitz said. "Have you any idea how improper your speech sounds?"

"Oh, it is nothing," Georgiana said. "It is a private joke between Mr. Bingley and me. Merely a rhyming game."

ALMACK'S HAD BEEN a mistake, Fitz discovered early in the evening. Charles, while clearly not in the best of spirits, made an admirable effort to play the eager sportsman. He followed Fitz about like a devoted but untrained puppy, trotting at his heels and trying to discern and obey his master's cryptic commands. But it was always toward Fitz that the game flew. Flush the quarry in whatever direction he tried, the mothers flocked around him to make introductions and he was besieged on all sides by nubile debutantes. And all of them so dull. Slow and stupid and, if not ugly, with no sparkle of originality. It would take a dozen of them together to scrape up the wit of an Elizabeth Bennet. No, even a score of them, ground up and sieved and their essence extracted, could not formulate even one of her quips, simper though they might, and say how dreary Almack's was, but what was one to do, one had to meet suitable acquaintances somehow, and had he heard that Lord Bellingham was to hold a card party for a select company, and wouldn't it be wonderful to secure an invitation . . .

Fitz did everything short of physically pushing them toward Charles, but they recognized superior wealth and position when it was presented to them in so stark a contrast, as easily as they discerned height and aristocratic features. "It's all right, Fitz," Charles said to him once when a large, giggling, *sweaty* female by the unlikely and cloying name of Miss Lucy Lovelace, who had claimed at Charles's inquiry to be sitting down all evening, jumped up and fairly planted herself in Fitz's way when he attempted to find the card room. "I'm just as happy watching the others. You two *great, tall* figures make a very fine pair."

There was nothing to do, Fitz decided, but abandon the field. Sometimes victory was impossible; all that could be achieved was retreat in good order. He apologized to the girl, saying he was fatigued and was on his way home, finding himself strangely disturbed by her incredulous expression. Taking Charles's arm, he moved them in the direction of the entrance, out of earshot of the eager dancers. "I'm sorry I subjected you to this, my dear," he said. "Perhaps a visit to the Brotherhood would be the best remedy. We can have a brandy or two, maybe play a rubber of whist. Then, if you like, we can go upstairs."

"Faugh!" Charles said. His face contracted in what looked like genuine revulsion. "You go, Fitz. I never really cared for that place. Only went for your sake. All those mollies leering at me makes my flesh creep. Perhaps the so-very-obliging Sylvester Monkton will be there. I'm sure he'll be only too happy to give you what you want."

"I don't want Monkton," Fitz said. "I want you. I thought you might feel more comfortable there. More discreet, no servants to spy."

"I'm sorry, Fitz," Charles said, looking over his shoulder at the mention of spies. Nobody was paying any attention, other than a few girls still hoping for a partner. "I don't mean to be a wet blanket. You go ahead and make a night of it. I'm perfectly capable of finding my own way home. And do give my regards to George Witherspoon. That is if any of you exchange any words."

"Bitch!" Fitz whispered in Charles's ear as they said their good-byes. He bowed over Lady Jersey's little hand and bestowed an invited kiss, then headed off at a brisk walk in the direction of Park Lane. The foul weather suited his mood perfectly.

Eleven

"WHAT EXACTLY IS wrong with this Miss Bendover?" Monkton said during an uncomfortable silence.

"Don't call her that," Fitz said. "The situation is not really her fault. If anything, it's due to Charles's immaturity. He fancies himself *disappointed in love.* All so predictable. I've seen it a dozen times. He stands to attention and salutes the first ordinary blond doll he sees, except that in this instance her sister is the most remarkable—" Fitz stopped before he gave too much away. "I've had to use some rather drastic measures to help him see reason."

"Drastic?" Verney said. "Very effective, I should think." He clutched himself in a suggestive way, and in case there were any doubts of his meaning, began making pumping motions with his arm and loosely closed fist.

How puerile. Fitz forced himself not to voice the thought aloud, saying, "Nothing so simple as that. Unfortunately, I've been driven to something close to deception. The woman's been in town for months, but I have kept the fact from Charles, in his best interest. A clean and complete separation is always the easiest."

"For him? Or for you?" Carrington asked, not expecting an answer.

"Well, just what is the matter with Miss Bent?" Monkton said. "Other than the fact that your Charles loves her. We all understand what a tragedy that is—in your eyes."

"Miss Bennet," Fitz said. "Her name is Miss Bennet. And there's nothing really wrong with *her*. It's her family. The most egregious example of the decline of the country gentry you're ever likely to see. The mother is the worst, but the daughters all take after her—that is, all except one."

"My word! How many are there?"

"And what about that one, eh?"

"Elizabeth," Fitz said. Just saying the name gave him an absurd sort of pleasure. "The eldest, Charles's *objet d'amour*, is exactly what you'd expect. Plump, curvaceous, wavy gold hair, like a painting in a brothel, only demure. But the second one, Elizabeth. I never imagined I'd enjoy sparring with a woman."

"You hit her?" Witherspoon asked, his voice high and childish with shock.

"Verbal sparring, Witherspoon. Conversation. Genuine conversation."

"Any society lady can make repartee," Verney said.

"Precisely," Fitz said. "Stale, commonplace phrases, repeated anecdotes and stories, the same caps to the same old jokes. No, this is something quite out of the ordinary. Original, contradictory, acerbic wit just short of impudence. She charged me with a propensity to hate everybody, indirectly laid both vanity and pride to my share of vices, and, as a final paradox, declared that I was not to be laughed at. All the while cackling with internal glee at what she clearly decided was self-importance." He sat back and smiled broadly at the recollection, as pleased with these feats of verbal combat as if he had accomplished them himself.

"A talented artist," Monkton said. "She captured your likeness in one quick sketch."

"My God!" Pierce exclaimed. "Is that what passes for flirtation these days? I'd be sorely tempted to box her ears at least, if nothing more."

Fitz shook his head and frowned. "You wouldn't say such an ungentlemanly thing if you knew her. She does have a predilection for saying things she doesn't mean, but her manner is so innocent and sweet it cushions the blows and just leaves one eager for another round, so to speak."

"How do you know she doesn't mean it?" Verney asked.

After Verney's earlier schoolboy behavior, Fitz decided to ignore him.

"Nothing to look at, I take it," Carrington said.

"No, there you're wrong," Fitz said. "It's her eyes that caught my attention. Very fine, big and bright, and radiant with intelligence. In fact, her entire face is the liveliest, prettiest, most expressive—well. As to the rest of her, at first I thought she had a boyish figure. Then I noticed how light and graceful she is. Very feminine, not like a boy at all; a womanly, soft form, but on a lesser scale. Really, just seeing her walk is enough to make a man catch his breath. And when she dances—"

"*Your* breath, at any rate," Pierce said.

"When shall we wish you joy?" Monkton said with a snigger.

"Yes, yes, I knew I'd be letting myself in for this," Fitz said. "Charles's sisters have already beaten that horse to death. It's nothing, a chimera. I had almost given up finding such a rare combination—a superior mind with youthful, feminine beauty. But no man who values his place in society can afford to ally himself with that appalling family. I do feel sorry for the two eldest, though. They will suffer for it. There's not a respectable gentleman in England up to the rigors of facing down the mother alone—much less the entire brood and all their low connections."

"You're exaggerating, surely," Carrington said. "An excuse not to become entangled."

"If I were exaggerating would I have convinced Charles to move back to town so soon after leasing the manor in Hertfordshire? Over some minor business of his father's estate, something that could have been dealt with in a day or two? No, listen to the account of but one evening, a ball that Charles gave to repay his welcome to the neighborhood . . ." Fitz related the entire sorry litany, the long list of outrages: the vulgar, stupid mother, rattling on during supper about her eldest daughter's imagined prospects, infecting the atmosphere of the entire company with jealousy and resentment at her boasting; the indulgent, ineffectual father, allowing his offspring to run wild, only stepping in when the damage had been done, then compounding it by shaming his one plain daughter, scolding her in company; the spoiled, ignorant younger sisters, practically offering themselves on the dance floor to anything in a red coat; and the middle sister who played the pianoforte abominably and sang worse—and fancied herself a philosopher to boot. "Their nearest relations are a village attorney whose clients are the local shopkeepers, and a merchant who lives in Cheapside. And to round out this commedia dell'arte," Fitz concluded, "there is a clown of a cousin, the stupidest, most obsequious, groveling excrescence I have ever seen, who turns out to be—are you ready—my aunt de Bourgh's vicar, the Reverend Mr. Collins. I know this because he *interrupted* my conversation to inform me of it."

Everyone laughed in the right places, but there was an undertone of discomfort.

"You know, Darcy," Pierce said, "you sound as if you're trying to convince us of something you don't believe yourself."

Verney cleared his throat. "I live in the country much of the time. If I spoke of my tenants and villagers the way you describe these people, I'd be strung up, assuming they were in a charitable mood. Else they'd use tar and feathers like the Americans."

"I can't credit my ears," Fitz said. "Do you honestly think poor Charles would have a chance, mixed up with a mob like that? Good God, he'd be eaten alive."

"He's not like you," Monkton said. "He just wants a wife and his own household. Who's to say this Miss Bedknob wouldn't suit him?"

"Poor Miss Bennet," Witherspoon said. "How hard it must be for her, with no money and a large family. And now when she does find someone, she has to fight a losing contest against a handsome, wealthy man like Darcy."

"Ah, Witherspoon," Fitz said, turning to face the blond beauty. "Are you implying that I am *competing* for Charles? With a village girl?"

Witherspoon swallowed and reached for Pierce's hand. "*You* just now admitted that you—you lied to him. And it just seems unfair. A lady can't win, because she can't do the things that we can do."

Fitz stood up. "You rely too much on your supposed simplicity, Witherspoon. Someday someone will call you on it, and you may not like the way *that* conversation goes."

"Darcy," Pierce said, standing up also. "You may find it easy to intimidate female rustics, but here in town you will learn there are consequences to riding roughshod over defenseless innocents."

Fitz put a hand on his hip and sneered at the small man whose head barely reached his shoulder. "I beg your pardon? You were addressing me, Pierce?"

Carrington laughed. "Not again. Pistols at dawn, gentlemen? Or do you prefer *swords*? I wouldn't mind refereeing that combat."

"Nor I," Monkton said. "In fact, perhaps we ought to settle it now. Shall we draw straws for teams? Or simply match up in *singlestick*?"

"Oh, teams, I think," Verney said.

The others looked ready to follow the disgraceful suggestion, sitting up and removing their coats.

"Better choose by size," Monkton said with a lewd giggle, unbuttoning his flap.

"Haven't used that third-floor room in ages," Carrington said.

"What room?"

"The one with all the beds, like barracks—no doors."

"Oh, for God's sake," Fitz said. "I don't know why I thought to have a sensible conversation here."

"How about a game of piquet instead, Darcy?" Verney said. "I'll give you a ten-point lead if you like." He removed the equivalent article of clothing in the Brotherhood's currency—his cravat—although he had to put it back on first, having already managed to lose several hands earlier in the evening, and began shuffling the cards.

"Thank you, Verney, but until I reach my dotage my skill alone should suffice at cards," Fitz said, heading for the door. "Gentlemen, I am not such a hothead that I am reduced to the level of this imbecilic contest. Good evening—and enjoy your free-for-all."

"Think that is what he needs," Pierce said, moving to take the vacant chair opposite Verney. "A good hot head up his imbecilic arse."

"Just so long as you tell him, not me," Monkton said.

"More the sort of thing you'd say, Monkton," Carrington

said. "Tell you what. I'll wager you don't dare suggest it to Darcy the next time he visits."

Monkton smiled and raised an eyebrow. "What are you staking, Carrington?"

"Oh, the full price, Monkton. The full price. If ever there was a sure thing, this is it."

"You're on," Monkton said, shaking Carrington's hand. "Either way I win. Darcy's favors, or yours."

"I'm flattered," Carrington said. "But I don't think he'll pay up in quite the way you anticipate."

"I think it's dangerous," Witherspoon said. "Look at how close he came to losing his temper tonight. Don't do it, Monkton."

"Nonsense," Pierce said. "Should be an amusing spectacle. I bet Darcy bends Monkton over the sofa and skewers him right here in the drawing room."

"Actually," Monkton said, "we've already done that. His initiation, remember? No, I think this will be a very interesting confrontation indeed."

"Aren't we going to have that contest?" Verney asked.

"No point in it now. Darcy's gone."

"Don't need him."

"It's not worth it without him. No excitement. Just the same old faces."

"Since when do we care about faces?"

"Oh, you know what I mean . . ."

WHEN FITZ ARRIVED home, having taken the long way around, through St. James's Park, Georgiana and Charles were engrossed in a game of backgammon, giggling like two schoolgirls over the rattling of the dice and the clicking of the counters. They looked up at his entrance, as guilty as clandestine lovers.

"Oh, it must be very late," Georgiana said. "Did you dance with lots of beautiful ladies, Fitz? Mr. Bingley said that you were getting all the game—I mean, that you made lots of introductions. I hope you had a pleasant time."

"Charles," Fitz said, using their previously agreed-upon excuse for parting ways, "you claimed to be too tired to bear me company, yet now I find you keeping my sister up long past her bedtime."

"I'm just going now." Georgiana pecked Fitz on the cheek as she went by. "You need a bath, Fitz," she said, wrinkling her nose and running swiftly upstairs before he could reprimand her.

"I'm sorry if I kept Miss Darcy up too late," Charles said. "We were having such fun we lost all track of time."

"How original," Fitz said. He laughed, seeing that perhaps things were on the way to working themselves out without his interference. "It's all right, Charles. It's not so very late. Only a little past midnight." He put an arm around his friend and kissed his cheek. "Perhaps you've reconsidered and would like some company?"

Charles slipped out from under the encircling arm. "Sorry, Fitz. Georgie's right. You really do need a bath."

"JANE," SARAH GARDINER said, "I hope you don't mind another quiet evening with the Pooles."

Jane Bennet looked up from her needlework and immediately assumed the bland smile that was her habitual expression. "No, aunt," she said. "I quite enjoy their company. And their children are a delight."

"I wouldn't go that far," Mrs. Gardiner said. "But at least they are well behaved. And you do seem to have a way with them." Sarah had to fight to keep the pity out of her voice. Jane had held up admirably over the months of her visit. Her composure even as she absorbed the devastating fact of Miss Bingley's rejection had been extraordinary. Sarah wished so often to take her niece in her arms and let her cry her eyes out, but if her brood of young children had taught her anything, it was that all heroism crumbled at the slightest hint of sympathy. Jane's entire existence depended on acting as if her recent loss were only a slight disappointment, when in fact it was, in many ways, the end of the world for her. "I wish we could offer you more exciting excursions occasionally—Almack's or at least a Mayfair ball, but of course we have few acquaintances in that end of town."

"Oh no," Jane said, too quickly. "I'm very happy here." She waited until her aunt had left the room and gone downstairs before putting her work aside and shielding her eyes with one hand. *I will not cry*, she told herself, as she did at least once every day. *I will not. It is pointless, and it spoils the complexion and makes the eyes red.* "As if it mattered anymore," she said aloud, shocking herself into dry-eyed fear.

For no reason she found herself recalling the man—what was his name? Richard? Rupert? She could not remember his Christian name, if she had ever known it. As for his surname, she had decided long ago never to repeat it, even in her thoughts. He had written her poems, courted her as if he were a medieval knight, calling her his Lady Greensleeves, which she had known even then was most improper. But she had been only fifteen, only just become a woman, and it had been flattering, and oh! so exciting. He was too old, almost thirty, and she had been frightened by his passionate pursuit. He had tried to kiss her once, late at night after a card supper, when the other guests had gone home, following her into the corridor and pressing her against the wall. Mama had known, Jane was sure of it, yet had done nothing, said nothing! Jane could still recall the feel of his hands on her, the way his thumb slipped inside her bodice and her nipples had gone hard all at once. And how she had felt the sensation move through her body, inside, to the place between her legs.

She was going to cry again. Charles had felt like that. He had never once touched her other than to hold her hand during a dance, and when she had been recuperating at Netherfield and had been able to come downstairs for dinner, he had naturally taken her hand and bowed and even kissed it, saying how pleased he was that she was better. That had felt just like Mr. Richard-Rupert, only a hundred times nicer, because Charles had done nothing wrong and yet she had felt it, working its way down, shivery and hot at the same time, just from his kissing the back of her hand . . .

And now it was over. She was going to be twenty-three this year, and she had been in love only once and had never had an offer unless you counted Rupert-Richard, which you really couldn't because he hadn't been serious; and anyway, who would want to marry at fifteen before being out or even having danced at a ball? But here she was, her life ended without having ever begun. This was it. Forever. An old maid, stuck living with Mama after Papa died, and bearing her scolding and carping and sighing. And being pushed at every middle-aged, paunchy, balding old widower with ten children.

Stop it, she told herself. *Just stop it*. Women did get married at twenty-three and even older. Look at Charlotte Lucas. Well, that was a mistake, to think of her. Mr. Collins certainly made Richard-Rupert seem like heaven in comparison. At least he had been nice-looking, and with wit enough to write a passable poem or two. He'd be what? Thirty-eight now, probably paunchy and balding. But at least she'd be married and have some children of her own . . .

Oh, this was stupid. She didn't want Richard-Rupert, or

anyone else. Just Charles. She had not known such a feeling existed until she met him. Although she must remember always to think of him only as Mr. Bingley. And she couldn't speak of it with anyone, not even Lizzy, because when a woman loved a man and he didn't return the love it was the most shameful thing she could admit to, other than actually giving in without being married. But it was the same idea, just not all the way. It was halfway to losing one's virtue, because that's how it started. A man who loved you wouldn't ask for that. He would ask you to marry him.

That's what Lizzy didn't quite see: that if Mr. Wickham truly loved her he would propose marriage instead of flirting at assemblies and neglecting his militia duties to hang about in Meryton on the chance of meeting ladies on their errands, all the while making it very clear he couldn't face marriage on less than ten thousand pounds. If you really loved someone money shouldn't stand in your way.

Shouldn't it? Jane thought it over. Well, it wasn't her concern any longer. She wasn't going to be married, because gentlemen did need money to marry, and if they had a good fortune they wanted a woman with a portion equal to theirs. Only Charles hadn't cared, or so she thought. He had told her his secrets, everything. She had been sure he was going to call on her after the ball at Netherfield. And then, instead, he had gone to town and everyone in his household had followed and Caroline had made it clear that now they were back in society where they belonged she had no reason to keep up the acquaintance, because it had only been for her brother's sake and Charles had no interest in Jane anymore. Didn't love her. It had just been amusement, a casual flirtation gone too far. *Not Charles*, she told herself angrily. *Mr. Bingley*.

Perhaps she had been vain. She had been serene, secure in her beauty. Mama had gushed over her eldest daughter's beauty for as long as Jane could remember and she wondered if perhaps she had put too much stock in it. But what else was she to do? A young lady could only trust in her looks, if they were good, and her accomplishments, if any, and hope, and wait. Jane hadn't minded the waiting. She had been certain that he would come along, the one who was meant for her. It had been a long wait, but he had come. And then he had turned out not to be what he seemed. Not *the one* after all.

Never show it, she said to herself, feeling the tears welling up and blinking rapidly. *Never.* What she had told herself every day for eight years and more. Being the eldest was so much responsibility. If she failed, if she ever once let down her guard, they were all doomed to spinsterhood, because the eldest set the pattern. Although surely Lizzy would find someone. Then it wouldn't be so bad. Lizzy would not abandon her. Once Lizzy was married, Jane could live with them and be free of Mama's—

"Oh dear, haven't you started dressing yet?" Aunt Gardiner popped her head in the door without knocking first. "And I was hoping you'd look your best tonight, because Mrs. Poole thought perhaps their eldest, Josiah, will be up from Birmingham. Mr. Poole has often mentioned to Mr. Gardiner and me how lucky he is to have a son like Jos who can take over for him when the time comes. But he'll need a clever wife to manage the household and help run the business. A very promising young man, Josiah Poole. A bit shy with pretty girls, but I'm sure you'll make him feel at ease."

"I will try, aunt. I'm so sorry. I must have been woolgathering. I'll be down directly."

Sarah Gardiner shook her head as she descended the stairs. She would like to march over to Grosvenor Street and shake some sense into that idiot Charles Bingley herself. Of course, if that would do any good she'd have done it by now. It was a pity she had never set eyes on the man to discover what his character was like. Probably decent but weak. And under the thumb—or more—of that Fitzwilliam Darcy. Typical of that world, the men with money and university educations. They always had some friend who would bend over for them, or kiss their arse when commanded. Although what the friend got out of it Sarah never understood. Perhaps it just made them feel loved, as everyone wanted.

Sarah sighed. She would have to go on acting as if Jane had not suffered a great loss. The only way Jane was ever going to get back to her old self was if they all pretended that nothing had happened. After enough time had passed, surely it would feel that way even to her.

She found herself remembering that man, what was his name? Cooper? Hooper? His Christian name had been Richard, she thought. Unless it was Robert? It had been only a couple of years after her marriage to Mr. Gardiner, and she had had other things on her mind. But she remembered the intensity of his look, the way he followed Jane with his eyes wherever she was in the room. He had written poems—disgraceful, but impressive to such a young woman. A girl, really, at fifteen still in the schoolroom, assuming her sister-in-law had ever taught her poor girls anything besides indolence and hypochondria. But that Hooper-Cooper man had claimed to love Jane, and what had come of it? Nothing. And now, seven whole years later, another one not come up to scratch.

Funny to think how it was her sister-in-law, Mrs. Bennet, who had married the gentleman, and look what it had got her. Comparative poverty on two thousand pounds a year, and no prospects for her girls. But Mrs. Bennet's brother, Henry Gardiner, had stayed in trade, and Sarah wouldn't change places with any country gentlewoman for twice that amount! Thank goodness Henry made a decent income and they would bring up their children in the same style, no pretension or false hopes. The boys would go into the business or another respectable trade. The girls would have decent portions, more than enough for any industrious young man of their sphere. They would not have to wait and sigh over irresponsible so-called gentlemen, but would marry men like their father, men who would give them a good home and would not be marrying them solely for their name or their money. Men who expected to work and who needed a wife who was a true helpmeet and companion. Real love, not fairy-tale romance and poetry, or the airs and refinements that made this Mr. Bingley so beguiling that he courted and discarded sweet, innocent young ladies for no better reason than that he *could*. And there wouldn't be any Mr. Darcy hovering in the background to make his friend disdain the best girl in the world, just because some of her family were not of his level . . .

Jane came slowly downstairs, dressed in one of her old gowns that showed off her voluptuous figure, her hair dressed simply, needing no elaborate coiffure to embellish its thick waves of lustrous gold. "There you are," Sarah said. "Looking as beautiful as ever. I do hope that this change of scene has cheered you a little."

"Indeed, aunt," Jane said. "But there is nothing to cheer. I am quite happy. It is good of you to have me to stay all this time." She kept her smile in place all through the short walk to the Pooles' and while Josiah conversed animatedly and at length about the minutiae of expanding a mercer's trade. Strange how Charles could talk of even less momentous topics but it never sounded tedious or dull. The slightest commonplace phrase had an air of grace and charm when Charles . . . *Mr. Bingley*, Jane reminded herself. "How diligent you are, Mr. Poole," she said when there was a split second's break in the flow of words. *And not the least bit shy.*

"You are very kind, Miss Bennet. Do you understand bookkeeping? Now that is a most interesting subject. There are two entries, you see, for each transaction. Then at the end of the month you add everything up and the two sums should match . . ."

Jane smiled and nodded until her neck was so stiff and her jaw so clenched she thought she might never be able to utter another word, not that anyone would notice. Jos and all the Pooles talked enough for the rest of the evening, often all at once, and on several different subjects.

"Did you have a pleasant evening?" Mrs. Gardiner asked. She had to ask twice and then a third time before Jane realized that they were at home and it was just the family again.

"Very nice, aunt, thank you."

"Jos Poole is a most ambitious, hardworking young man. I daresay he'll make something of himself before long."

"Quite an up-and-coming city, Birmingham," Mr. Gardiner said. "If I were thinking of expanding my business, that's where I'd choose. And not too far from the south and London."

"Very true, dear," Mrs. Gardiner said with a wink and a nod in Jane's direction. "But time enough for that. It will be some years before our Henry is ready to branch out."

"Henry?" Mr. Gardiner said. "I thought we were talking about—"

"Yes, dear," Mrs. Gardiner said. "So we were. Do you know, I've always envied mercers' wives. They have first pick of all the new stuffs."

"You don't do so badly as it is," Mr. Gardiner said.

"Never said I did," his wife replied. "I have done very well indeed."

Twelve

THERE WAS NO more gloating now, Elizabeth thought. How her aunt Gardiner must have seen through her blithe denials during her Christmas visit. Mr. Wickham, having apparently discovered, or decided—Elizabeth wasn't sure which was worse—that she had not sufficient charms to overcome her lack of fortune, was in hot pursuit of a Miss King, whose sole claim to his interest was the sudden demise of her uncle and guardian, leading to her acquisition of ten thousand pounds.

Elizabeth reflected on the two men, so very different, who had awakened the same inconvenient desires in her. Both lost to her now. Mr. Darcy she had never had and did not regret. But George Wickham—oh, that was misery indeed, and made almost intolerable from being the kind of loss that a lady can never speak of or admit to having felt.

Charlotte's letters continued to arrive, neatly written, not so much as a tearstain or an inkblot to betray any other emotion than calm satisfaction at her married state. If Elizabeth did dare to infer a slight distress beneath the placid surface in the repeated pleas for a visit, it was no more than she could have expected. She herself would have been long gone, run off to town in disgrace, with Mr. Wickham or alone, sinful or not. *No, you wouldn't*, she told herself. It was unthinkable. Yet marriage to Mr. Collins was just as unthinkable, and Charlotte, so similar to Elizabeth, or so she had once believed, had done it without wasting much thought on the subject. *Probably the only way to swallow him—without thinking.* Like a draught of foul medicine. Close one's eyes, hold one's nose, and perhaps a spoonful of honey after. That worked once or twice. But marriage was forever. Day in, day out, and every night for an eternity of nausea.

As March approached, Elizabeth felt the need to get away. Even a visit to Charlotte was preferable to staying at home, rehearsing her losses, retracing the path to Meryton and back, and always the view toward Netherfield reminding her of her different circumstances such a short time ago. At least the way to Kent and Mrs. Collins led through London, which allowed the two sisters a brief reunion.

Elizabeth was glad to see Jane looking so well, older and wiser in her reassessment of Miss Bingley's character, never once having crossed paths with her erstwhile suitor. Elizabeth found it easier to confide in her sister now that they were in more or less the same abandoned condition, but found she had little inclination. She must try, otherwise the two of them would mope themselves into early spinsterhood, begin wearing caps and neck ruffs, and refuse to stand up with anyone except grandfathers at assemblies. "You have been three months in town, but have gained nothing by it except, I suppose, more soot in your lungs," she said to Jane. "Now it is my turn to visit Kent and sicken myself with the smell of hops."

Jane smiled bravely. "I'm glad to see that you have not given up your friend after all."

"Oh, as to Charlotte," Elizabeth said. "That is finished. But I will enjoy a change of scene, and of course there is so much in Kent that cannot be found in Hertfordshire—such as fat, stupid clergymen and their condescending patronesses."

"If you continue in this sad estrangement with Charlotte," Jane said, "you are putting yourself on the same level as Mr. Wickham, dropping a friendship when you have nothing more to gain from it. Don't behave like that with your friend, but patch things up and wish her well."

"It's too late for that," Elizabeth said. "There is no *well* to wish her, only continued patience in the face of the insufferable, with some added fortitude and selective blindness." Was it her imagination, or did Jane flinch at her careless words? "Don't worry, I promise not to be cold with Charlotte. Whatever is in my power to do, I will. You know I'll try my best to make her laugh, at least."

"Just be kind," Jane insisted. "It can't be easy for her. She understands the full truth of what she has chosen and that she made the decision with open eyes. Don't blame her now that it's too late, but simply let her know you still love her."

"Of course I will," Elizabeth said, surprised at Jane's vehemence. "That is, I will if she'll let me. I daren't love anyone these days, the way things turn out."

"They will improve," Jane said. "I'm sure of it. Perhaps you will meet someone at Rosings."

"Now there's a cheerful thought," Elizabeth said. "Maybe Mr. Collins has a brother."

"Girls!" Mrs. Gardiner called from down the corridor. "What are those dreadful noises? I swear, you two sound worse than my boys. If you don't stop I'll send to the apothecary for an emetic."

ONLY BY THE time spring was approaching did Fitz begin to contemplate leaving Charles on his own with some equanimity. He was not quite back to his old cheerful self, but he no longer sighed every two minutes, nor had Fitz found any more poetic remnants. If Charles did sometimes gaze with unfocused eyes out the window during pauses in conversation or wander aimlessly in the park on Sunday mornings after church, at least he smiled more often and accompanied Fitz regularly to the opera and to concerts, and had regained enough address to partner eligible young ladies at balls. He was careful never to stand up twice with the same girl and showed no preference for anyone. Even a certain Miss Frances Overton, blond and buxom, who from a distance bore a startling resemblance to the eldest Miss Bennet, produced no other effect than to cause him to remark that it was strange how someone can look so much like another person but be so different in character. Fitz had heard the Overton chit had a reputation for sharpness, which no doubt explained her unmarried state at the ripe age of twenty-five.

Charles steadfastly refused to set foot in the Brotherhood of Philander, which was probably just as well. He was more receptive these days, and there were times when he was even eager again, so that Fitz was required to visit so dangerous and unwholesome an environment less frequently. On his last visit, there had been a disturbing and disgraceful incident with Monkton that had led to bruises, bloodshed, and apologies all around. A pity, really. Just when he had begun to think old Sylly a rather decent sort, it was as if the man had deliberately provoked Fitz to behavior that even a common seaman would be ashamed of. And for some reason all the others had been on hand to witness Fitz's less than gentlemanly conduct. Even though Monkton had taken it in good part—in fact, he seemed in an exceptionally good humor about something that would have had Fitz angry enough to risk a duel—on the whole Fitz thought it was time to rusticate, as debt-saddled undergraduates would say. He could at least be sanguine in the thought that Charles was on the mend.

"You know I spend Easter with my aunt, Lady Catherine de Bourgh, in Kent," Fitz told Miss Bingley during one of her frequent morning calls. She always seemed to forget which days Georgiana was at home and ended up in an improper tête-à-tête with Fitz.

"But how will Charles fare without your guidance? It's a pity he can't stay here while you're away, now that he and Georgiana are on such friendly terms."

"Charles is a grown man, Miss Bingley," Fitz said. "Not a child in need of a governor. And surely you would not wish to compromise *Miss Darcy's* reputation, even to advance your brother's interest."

"Oh no! Of course not!" Miss Bingley did not have the grace even to attempt to look abashed. "I suppose," she continued in her insinuating way, "that the pleasure of seeing your cousin again after an entire year outweighs any slight concern you may once have felt for my poor brother."

"Colonel Fitzwilliam?" Fitz said. "It's been almost two years. He does usually visit our aunt at the same time, but he was overseas last year. Yes, he's a very good fellow, but I assure you, Miss Bingley, that your *poor brother* is in no danger of being displaced in my affections."

"Oh!" Miss Bingley was visibly exasperated. "I was speaking of Anne."

"Anne?" Fitz had a hard time bringing an image to mind.

"Miss de Bourgh," Miss Bingley said. "You may recall her, the lady you're betrothed to?"

"Oh." Fitz was taken aback. "Poor little Anne."

Miss Bingley smirked at the epithet, seeming to take comfort from Fitz's lack of enthusiasm. "Is she still sickly, then?"

"As far as I know," Fitz said. "She suffers from a chronic and incurable condition. Very sad, but nothing anyone can do anything about. That is, not within the boundaries of Christian morality."

"*Really?*" Miss Bingley said in a hushed whisper, leaning forward on the edge of her chair and bending at the waist until her face was uncomfortably close to Fitz's crossed knees. "What is it? Was it—that is—did Sir Lewis—Lady Catherine's husband? Do the physicians have any hope?"

"Nothing like that," Fitz said. "I must say, Miss Bingley, you have a wicked disposition." His lips curled in one of his rare smug smiles. He felt almost in charity with Caroline today. Perhaps it was the near prospect of escape to Kent. "No, until her mother expires, which, given her robust state of health, appears to be a distant event, I'm afraid Miss de Bourgh is condemned to a shadow existence as Lady Catherine's only child."

"Goodness, you're cruel," Miss Bingley said in delighted tones. "Quite as catty as a woman." She clapped her hand over her mouth on catching sight of Fitz's expression. "I'm sorry, Mr. Darcy, I only meant—"

"Yes, Miss Bingley," Fitz said, rising from his chair. "I understand completely. Perhaps it's best if you take your leave. I don't wish to be rude, but as my sister is, in fact, not at home today, this imprudent visit of yours could cause some damage to your reputation."

"Oh, pooh," Miss Bingley said. "No one keeps count of my every coming and going—except you, it seems."

"Then," Fitz said, "I am forced to say that I have business to attend to, and will look forward to receiving you another time when Miss Darcy is here also. Good day, Miss Bingley." He rang for the footman and saw his caller and her maid safely out.

Goodness, as Caroline might say. What a sorry state he

must be in, when a visit to Rosings seemed an improvement in his situation.

THE DRIVE DOWN to Rosings Park was a deceptively pleasant introduction to the trials ahead. Fitz shared the carriage with Colonel Fitzwilliam, who had recently arrived in town, on leave from his duties in Spain. He was a childhood friend, a couple of years older, whom Fitz had always looked up to. Now, the passing of time having put them on an equal footing, he proved to be a sympathetic listener as Fitz related the story of his rescue of Charles—naturally concealing most of the particulars. "He still doesn't quite see it," Fitz concluded, "but someday he'll thank me."

"Sounds rather highhanded, Darcy," the colonel said. "I wonder your friend didn't put up more of a fight."

Fitz shook his head. "Charles is very modest," he said. "He has a tendency to, as he would put it, *fall violently in love*, merely because a pretty girl smiles at him or stands up with him at a ball. Now, after almost two years of our friendship, he has begun to recognize the limits of his youth and inexperience, and the prudence of relying on my wiser judgment, especially in so serious a matter as marriage."

"How old did you say he is? Twenty-two?"

"Just turned twenty-three."

"Old enough to make up his own mind," the colonel said. "In my regiment, he'd have his own company. With any initiative, and assuming he'd entered the service at the usual age and had a good five or six years' experience under his belt, he might even have won his major's commission by now."

Fitz felt his color rising. "I think you met him once or twice, did you not? Charles Bingley isn't cut out for the military life. He simply needs a few more years in London society; by then he'll see the advantages of marrying *within the family*, so to speak."

"Oh yes, I remember. Very pleasant young gentleman, but you're right. Not really regimental material. Have him marked out for Georgiana, I take it." The colonel glanced sideways at his cousin. "You know, Darcy, she's a lot like you. She'll want to choose for herself, and nothing you say will alter her opinions. Like the unfortunate business of last summer. You're so used to having your way with your friend, you forget that women—yes, even your sister—have minds of their own."

"I'm unlikely to forget it," Fitz said, scowling at the memory. "Actually, they all seem to be of one mind—that George Wickham is the most charming, delightful creature ever to appear in a red coat—and with the added and irresistible distinction of being the prodigal son."

"I can't believe it," the colonel said, after learning of the man's sudden reappearance and enlistment in the militia. "What could Wickham possibly hope to gain by tailing you? There are more heiresses to choose from in town than in a village."

"I think he's finally found his true calling—spoiling my every chance at happiness."

"Never tell me you've lost your heart at last," the colonel said, laughing in a rather obnoxious, incredulous way.

"It's not entirely out of the question," Fitz said, raising his eyebrows in his most quelling expression.

"Oh, come now, Darcy," the colonel said, unfazed. "Don't use that look on me. I know your views on women and their lack of any worthwhile qualities besides the obvious physical ones. Well, I suppose you have to marry, like every man of independent fortune. What's she like?"

"Nobody," Fitz said. "That is, the one thing I regretted about leaving Netherfield so precipitously was that it looked as if I were running away from Wickham, leaving all his loathsome insinuations unchallenged."

"Ought to have stood up to him," the colonel said. "Called him out or at least told him to clear off."

"How?" Fitz asked. "No gentleman lowers himself to respond to petty gossip."

"You made it sound as if it was a bit more than that."

"That's all Wickham dared do, of course, while I was in the neighborhood, traffic in rumor and innuendo. What he may have said after I left—well, you can imagine." In a softer voice he added, "What I couldn't bear was that *she* believed it."

"She?" the colonel repeated with a smug look. "Is that *she* as in *nobody*?"

"I'll admit," Fitz said, "there was one lady who was something quite remarkable. I was sorry to lose *her* good opinion, if no one else's."

"Could you not take her into your confidence?" the colonel asked.

"How?" Fitz demanded. "Unless one intends to propose marriage, how can a gentleman confide in a young lady? Unfortunately, her family and background are at such an inferior level that marriage is out of the question."

"Yet you speak of her as someone most superior."

"Oh, she is as far above the rest of her family as the sun is above a streetlamp. But few of us have the luxury of marrying a single individual. Take a wife and you take on an entire set of connections."

"Yes, Darcy," the colonel said. "It's called the way of the world. I've had to give a lot of thought to this matter myself, you know. Younger son. Can't marry where I'd like. But I'm a man, with a man's needs. Very trying, sometimes."

"I'm sorry, colonel," Fitz said. "I had not heard of any affairs of the heart for you."

"No, that's just it," the colonel replied. "I know when to enjoy a safe dalliance and when to keep my distance. But it means thwarting one's most natural inclinations. If I meet a lady I truly admire, one who combines beauty, wit, and virtue with open, unaffected manners, then I know—honestly, I just *know* it, the way I know when there are French outriders around the next bend or sharpshooters in the copse—that she'll have no fortune, certainly not sufficient to allow me to make her an offer. But let her be coarse and buxom and bawdy, not in her first youth and known to have slipped once or twice, but nothing proved—*then* of course she'll be an heiress."

"I wonder how long it will take George Wickham to learn that lesson," Fitz said, after they'd shared a cathartic long minute of loud laughter.

"At least another ten years," the colonel said. "He had the beginner's luck of starting with one of the few exceptions—your sister."

"Not such a beginner," Fitz said. "He'd been studying the subject for years. But I'm just thankful I had some luck on my side as well—and your reinforcement—to thwart that. You know, I resented it at first when you were made co-guardian of Georgiana, but I see now what a good choice my father made. Seems he possessed some solid judgment of character after all."

The two men arrived at Rosings in good humor, which, like all anarchic tendencies, Lady Catherine de Bourgh was determined to put down.

THE COMPANY WAS every bit as dull as could be expected: Lady Catherine; Anne, her only child; Mrs. Jenkinson, Miss de Bourgh's companion, a typical impoverished widow, oppressed by her dependent position and middle years into obsequious whispering; and a sparse selection of local gentry, just enough to make up a decent dinner party without having to use the entire length of the table. Under the cover of their aunt's long opening sermon during dinner on the subject of young men's disrespect for their elders, their lack of responsibility in general, and, in particular, their disinclination to marry before the onset of middle age, the colonel regaled Fitz with some of his war adventures.

"I see what you're about," Fitz said. "By telling all these bloodcurdling stories you're teaching me to put my minor tribulations in perspective."

"Not at all," the colonel said. "Just creating a diversion. Frankly, I'd rather try to hold a broken square against a regiment of the Imperial Guard than come between you and Wickham over a woman. Wouldn't know which way to turn, whether to guard my front or my rear or both at once." He tilted his head back to savor a thin spear of early asparagus, letting it slide slowly down his throat.

"Careful," Fitz whispered. "You look as if you've had a great deal of practice at that."

The colonel started to choke, swallowed hard, then laughed in his booming, officers' mess guffaw, causing Lady Catherine to pause in her lecture and frown in their direction. "Pardon me, aunt," he said. "Your turn of expression just now was very apt."

"What, colonel?" Lady Catherine said. "Do you mean to say you found the words *setting up a nursery* amusing?"

"Very," the colonel said. "Considering that I already have an extensive nursery to oversee, with some fifteen hundred inmates that I must somehow coddle through to maturity, all without losing too many to the various childhood ailments common to the infantry, such as bullet wounds, cannonballs, bayonets, cholera, and typhus."

"Hmph. You know very well I don't expect any such thing on your part just now. Younger son, in the military, doing just as you ought. No, it's Darcy I'm addressing. Pay attention, nephew."

"Yes, aunt," Fitz said, smiling at her harsh tone. "I'm listening."

The colonel lowered his voice as Lady Catherine resumed speaking, and leaned closer to Fitz. "Here's a thought. Introduce Wickham to Miss de Bourgh." He nodded ever so slightly in the direction of their cousin, whose head drooped at the end of a slender neck as she picked at her food. "See who wins that fight—although I'm betting on Lady Catherine for a knock-down in the first round."

Fitz's shout of laughter brought the dinner-table conversation to complete silence. He bowed his head to the table at large. "Sorry, the colonel was telling me an interesting campaign story. Please don't let me interrupt."

"Colonel!" Lady Catherine said. "Surely you don't need me to remind you that such matters are not suitable for the dinner table. As for you, Darcy, I find you much altered this year, and not for the better. You would do well to attend to my words, as your situation is a glaring example of the deplorable state of affairs I am attempting to correct."

"Yes, aunt," Fitz said. "Please do continue." He waited until the lecture resumed. "Colonel, you are wasted in the army. A man of your courage might do worse than a certain unmarried lady, the sister of a very good friend of mine. I won't paint the picture prettier than life—she is a man-eater—but an officer who's faced down Bonaparte's best troops for the better part of three years should be able to handle her. And she has fortune enough, I think, to make it worth your while."

The colonel coughed into his napkin. "God, Darcy. If I survive the Peninsula, the last thing I'll be looking for is another campaign. I'll want some peace and quiet, a pleasant, easygoing sort of woman. And why should you play at matchmaking? You heard our aunt. You're the one shirking your duty—not me."

"Just putting you on to a good thing. Miss Bingley might suit you very well. Not to my taste, but—"

"Oh no," the colonel said. "You're not fobbing off one of your worshipping attendants on me. Don't know why the most ghastly clinging females always prefer the disdainful sort of man who'd as soon mount the stallion as the mare, but there it is. She'd be sorely disappointed in me, anyway. Only kind of cock I enjoy is roast fowl."

"Darcy! Colonel Fitzwilliam!" Lady Catherine's roar rose above the two men's delirious laughter and subdued it. "If you can't behave yourselves at a civilized dinner table I suggest you finish your meal at the public house."

"Yes, aunt," Fitz said. "Won't happen again." He picked up his knife and fork, crooked his little finger at the colonel, and stuck out the tip of his tongue.

The colonel remained unmoved. "Good thing I'm not in Spain right now," he said. "If I'd been caught napping like this over there, I'd have been done for."

FITZ REGRETTED HIS inattentiveness and laughter the next morning. Had his badinage with the colonel caused him to miss something his aunt had said at dinner? Probably not. It would be more typical of his aunt to have kept him in the dark for an entire dreary evening. "Did you say Miss Bennet?" he interrupted Mr. Collins's endless speech of welcome, long string of fulsome compliments, and account of visitors at the parsonage. Hateful little toady. If the man had been subjected to the same regimen Fitz had suffered at school, from just one of the masters, he'd have learned to keep his words to the minimum and on the subject at hand or he'd not sit for a week. "Miss Elizabeth Bennet?"

"Yes, Darcy," Lady Catherine answered. "Said she knew you too. Impertinent, sharp little thing, and with so small a portion she's unlikely to marry. She'll learn in time to curb her high spirits and fit herself for her situation in life, as a companion or a governess. I thought we might have her and the Collinses come for coffee some evening after dinner."

"Well, colonel," Fitz said, as Mr. Collins was taking his leave, which at the rate he was going might occur sometime before dawn of the next day, "it's turning out very fine weather. What do you say to a walk? I'm sure Mr. Collins here would be grateful for some company on the way home."

The colonel, ever alert to the need for covert action, was quick on the uptake. "Good idea, Darcy. Could do with some exercise myself."

The visit to the parsonage didn't last long. The colonel had never seen his cousin so quiet. The object of his attention—or seemingly, lack of it—was indeed something quite fine, a small, vivacious dark-haired lady, who was happy to discuss the latest novels, unconcerned at the colonel's obvious lack of familiarity with the authors she admired. Only one exchange stood out. Miss Bennet asked Darcy an innocuous question, something about her sister staying in town over the winter and had he never met her there—the sort of thing anyone asked in company when there were acquaintances in common—and Darcy had drawn back as if struck, recovering only enough to stammer that he had not.

Once safely outside, the colonel linked arms with Fitz and demanded the full story. "Going to have to acquire some discretion, Darcy, around our perspicacious aunt. She doesn't miss much, for all her self-absorption. You pricked up like a wolf scenting a penned lamb when Collins mentioned Miss Bennet."

"Did I?" Fitz replied. "As you saw, colonel, that lamb is more than a match for this wolf."

"Yes, what happened there? It looked as if she drew blood when she mentioned her sister." Fitz held his breath, but naturally the colonel made the connection. "Good God! She's the one you saved your dear Charles from, isn't she? That's rather too much, even given what you've told me of his uncomplaining nature—stealing her for yourself."

"Allow me some credit, colonel," Fitz said. "This is the younger sister. The fact is, if Charles had fallen in love with *her* I could hardly have blamed him, nor would I have rated my chances of spoiling *that* match very high. Fortunately, his taste runs to the conventional, whereas this lady is the most extraordinary I've ever come across."

"I see." The colonel nodded as if he had solved a great puzzle. "That's why you spoke so little. Worshipping from afar. Unfit to address the object of your devotions directly."

"Don't be absurd," Fitz said.

"If I didn't know better, I'd say you were hooked at last," the colonel said.

"Oh, go ahead, laugh at me," Fitz said. "I suppose I deserve it. She certainly thinks so."

Thirteen

"SHALL WE ASK your cousin, colonel," Elizabeth said in response to one of Fitz's particularly inept phrases, "why a man of sense and education, and who has lived in the world, is ill-qualified to recommend himself to strangers?"

"I can answer your question," the colonel replied, "without applying to him. It is because he will not give himself the trouble."

Fitz, mute as a block of wood, apparently unaware that an idiotic smile was plastered across his face, stood by while Colonel Fitzwilliam and Elizabeth Bennet flirted and conversed and laughed at him.

It had been mere curiosity, and the frightening realization that he was trapped for a fortnight at Rosings, that had led to his impromptu visit to the parsonage last week. Just looking for escape from the tedium, although the colonel ought to be companion enough. But today it was all he could do not to fall over in a faint when the visitors arrived at Rosings. The usual discipline of anticipation, of memory and reflection, could not prepare him for this meeting. That first brief call, surrounded by the lesser beings of pustulant vicar, his pitiable wife, her tedious father and unremarkable sister, was like the hazy impression of the deity glimpsed through a veil. Now, after months of mental isolation, living like a hermit in a cave amid the sordid bustle and clamor of London society, the only light having to be laboriously produced by striking a spark from Charles's tepid and damp affections—now he was in the presence of the sacred flame . . .

He had felt the dizziness like a swoon. *She. Her. The eyes. The wit.* He was afraid he might disintegrate at any moment, indecent to stand up, his excitement showing, but not allowed to sit down, the ladies not yet seated. "Miss Bennet," he had replied to the unnecessary introductions, bending over to kiss her hand with its delicately tapered fingers. "What a lovely, unlooked-for surprise."

"Lady Catherine did not tell you we were to visit?" She smiled up at him. "I suppose we do not rank very high in the calendar of events at Rosings. After all, we have had far greater occurrences, even at the parsonage. On several occasions, Miss de Bourgh drove by in her carriage. And one time—I promise you, I am embellishing only a little—the pigs got into the garden! Well! After that, a visit by the family and friend of the vicar's wife can hardly be said to be worthy of attention."

"You are teasing, Miss Bennet," was all Fitz could think to say.

"You are most observant, Mr. Darcy." Her pink, bowed lips stretched in a grin, showing her small, even teeth. "I shall have to be very careful in my speech."

The rest of the visit went by in a blur. Fitz could see nothing but her face and what little of her bosom showed above the modest cut of her gown. Her neck was long and slender, but had nothing of the wilting frailty of his cousin Anne's. Miss Bennet carried her slight form so upright and gracefully it was as if she barely touched the ground when she walked. Fitz doubted that her beautiful arse even met the surface of the chair, more likely hovering just an inch or so above it. He wondered how he knew her arse was beautiful, and as quickly chided himself for such stupidity. What else could it be? How could it be any less lovely than the rest of her? Probably a most exquisite example of the female form, very white, round and firm, but not wide . . .

He forced his mind away from such a dangerous subject. He stared, entranced, as she put a biscuit between her lips, took a neat bite, clamping down smartly with her teeth, and chewed lustily. Did she eat as much here in Kent as she had in Hertfordshire? How did she maintain her slim figure with such a robust appetite? Obviously, hovering or flying or skimming or whatever it was she did must use an enormous amount of energy, far more than mere mortals expended in the most demanding activity. But such a small mouth! Could it possibly encompass him, and would those sharp little teeth get in the way . . .

"You will never become adept if you don't practice," Lady Catherine barked at her.

"I beg your pardon?" Fitz began to rise in defense of Miss Bennet, then realized in time that the instruction, his aunt not having been privy to his thoughts, referred to the pianoforte.

"You are welcome to use the instrument in Mrs. Jenkinson's room. You will be out of the way there, and inconvenience nobody."

Why had no one yet strangled Lady Catherine, or smothered her in her sleep, put poison in her coffee, hammered her head with a fire iron . . .

Later she played on the pianoforte, despite Lady Catherine's criticism. Miss Bennet had a clever trick of starting up the music—lively dance tunes or popular airs requiring vocal accompaniment—whenever his aunt intruded on the conversation. Fitz couldn't recall ever so enjoying a performance on that overworked instrument, except for the times she had played back at Netherfield. Thank goodness he was sitting down now, or all would be lost. Eventually, however, it was safe to approach, and he stood leaning against the back of the pianoforte, watching her face, sometimes moving to her side, turning the pages of the music and drinking in the warmth of her skin, the scent of her hair.

What could he say that would not betray him, that would not disgust her? But she did not appear to be the least disconcerted by anything. She laughed at him and answered his diffident questions with her barbed ripostes, and all was bliss until Lady Catherine put a stop to it. She would not have pleasure and beauty and joy in her house, not if she could help it. And she had never met a happy group that she had failed to rout into disordered retreat and, ultimately, unconditional surrender.

She was superb, Miss Bennet. How could his stupid, dense *bitch* of an aunt not see it? Somehow this one small woman bore up against the onslaught of Lady Catherine's incessant barrage. It was like watching a decimated infantry regiment hold off an attack of French cavalry, as the colonel had described. But this battered little red square was all splendor, muslin and lace, brown curls and pink cheeks and laughing wide eyes.

Oh, he just wanted to stare into those eyes until he fell in and drowned. No, they weren't liquid pools, as some asinine poet had written of his insipid ladylove. Miss Bennet's eyes were brilliant like jewels, although without their hardness. More like an animal's eyes, a cat's. That sounded wrong. It didn't sound like a compliment, or convey how warm and luminous they were. But the round, unblinking stare, the wisdom lightened and tempered by mischief—that was like nothing so much as a cat's. And, Fitz recalled again, he had always been partial to cats.

"IF I HAD any doubts before, that lamentable performance dispelled them," the colonel said as he and Fitz enjoyed their nightly stroll in the park.

"What?"

"There's only one reason an otherwise intelligent man behaves like an imbecile in the presence of a beautiful lady, but I promise you that silent, hopeless admiration won't work with Miss Bennet. You'll have to screw up your courage and talk with her. It's not all that difficult."

"Not for you," Fitz said. "You seemed very much at ease. Whatever did you find to occupy her attention all that time?"

"Reading and music," the colonel said.

"Really, colonel," Fitz said. "That's dishing it a bit too hot. I doubt very much you and Miss Bennet have read so much as one single poem in common. She more or less demolished that approach with me months ago, on that basis."

"Actually, Miss Bennet and I were delighted to discover that Madame D'Arblay's *Cecilia* was one of our favorites."

"Now look here, colonel. You may be able to deceive a trusting young lady with an outright lie, but—"

"Not your perceptive Miss Bennet," the colonel said. "There's no fudging it with her. Just because you only read Latin verse or ancient epics in the original Greek doesn't mean the rest of us are so limited."

"When do you have time to read anything but field reports or listen to any other music than the trumpet and the drum?"

"You know, Darcy, there's nothing like a novel for taking one's mind off the rigors of campaigning. To my mind, a good novel, more than any other work of literature, conveys the most thorough knowledge of human nature, the happiest delineation of its varieties, and the liveliest effusions of wit and humor, all in the best chosen language."

"Such vehemence. But *ladies'* novels?" Fitz said, packing a world of opprobrium into the emphasis.

"If you mean those outmoded tales of gothic horrors, I quite agree with you," the colonel said. "But if you mean a good modern story written by a female, you ought to read one before dismissing the entire category. Besides, you are unlikely to win the hearts of many ladies if you take that tone."

"That's fine," Fitz said. "Because I am supremely uninterested in many ladies."

The colonel gave an arch look and put a finger to the side of his nose. "Ah, Darcy, this is where experience tells. You are used to commercial transactions, I imagine, or those clandestine arrangements with adventurous married ladies, where it is only a matter of coming to terms and striking the best *bargain*, as you call it, on both sides. But a young, unattached lady requires attentive and appreciative courtship. Now, let's assume, just for the sake of argument, that a particular lady and I have no reading in common. I simply ask her what she reads. When she tells me, I ask her why she likes it. Then I say I haven't read any of that author's work and which would she recommend for me to start with. Once we've exhausted that topic, by then I'll have been able to recall some other book I did read, and we're off again."

Fitz laughed. "Ingenious. But rather self-defeating, wouldn't you say?"

"Only if one's ultimate objective is to find a woman whose taste in reading is exactly the same as one's own. For most of us, however, it's simply a way of engaging a lady in conversation. A very obvious stratagem, but works every time."

"Then tell me, colonel," Fitz asked, "who is Miss Bennet's

favorite author? Besides Madame D'Arblay, of course. Dr. Johnson? Laurence Sterne?" He snapped his fingers. "I know! Henry Fielding."

"Ha!" The colonel poked his cousin in the ribs. "You won't catch me that easily, Darcy. Didn't make colonel by falling into ambushes. I'll give you one hint, though—you're cold; very cold."

"Never tell me she truly does read ladies' novels," Fitz said.

"Not going to tell you anything more," the colonel replied. "I've revealed enough as it is."

"All you have shown is that you're treating this as a kind of game, with Miss Bennet as the prize. But she deserves better than to be trifled with."

"That sounds a bit like the pot with the kettle," the colonel said. "Just be grateful that, on a colonel's pay, I can't truly compete. Because if it were based purely on merit, I'd meet the challenge head-on, and a paragon like Miss Bennet requires a worthy opponent. If not an equal—Damme! Which of us could measure up?—at least a man who can put two words together in a sensible fashion. Someone like the Fitzwilliam Darcy I used to know. Wonder whatever became of him?"

Fitz shook his head but said nothing. The insipid smile he had worn during the visit from the parsonage company returned, and he walked for several yards in apparently contented silence. "I have one great advantage over you, colonel," he said as they approached the front door.

"I can count three," the colonel said in an unusually melancholy tone. "To list them in descending order of importance: Pemberley, your vast fortune, and being the only son." After a short pause, he added, "To be scrupulously fair, I would add a fourth, which a lady like Miss Bennet wouldn't admit to considering, but which has an effect all the same: you're a damned fine-looking, tall fellow, and it's no shame to the fair sex to say that even the most demure lady must feel her heart flutter when you walk into a room."

"I would be a fool to deny the truth of what you say, colonel," Fitz said, frowning in modest discomfort at the subject, "and with the common run of females it sums up the entirety of my dealings with them. But I do Miss Bennet the justice of asserting that all of these superficial qualities would count for little with her if I did not possess this one consequential advantage."

"Which is?"

"Whether or not we read the same things, Miss Bennet and I understand each other."

"I don't wish to be unduly skeptical," the colonel said. "But in what way?"

"Temperament," Fitz said.

The colonel, who had been indulging in his only vice—cigars—suffered an alarming paroxysm of coughing. Once he was able to speak, he said, "You frighten me, Darcy, you really do. You are too young to be growing senile, and too old to believe in fancies. I can think of no two people who are less alike in temperament."

Fitz, demonstrating again his bizarre new docility, merely smirked at this taunt. "Remember how she spoke of not practicing on the pianoforte? And then launched immediately into one of her most pleasing performances?"

"That was directed at you, Darcy," the colonel said, "as you would know if you had been attending to the conversation and not lost in some sort of dream. Miss Bennet was making a pointed analogy with your unwillingness to extend yourself in company. She does not attribute her imperfect playing to a lack of natural ability, but merely to laziness, just as you are not incapable of intelligent drawing-room discourse, but are simply unwilling to practice."

"Imperfect? *Laziness?*" Fitz fastened on the offensive words. "Miss Bennet is the most industrious individual I have ever met, and her performances are imperfect only to musical pedants. No, colonel, it is clear you misinterpreted her meaning. We neither of us perform for strangers, as I said to her. Practicing is for the rest of the world, which values technical perfection over expressiveness. Superior beings save their best performances for those who can appreciate the deeper significance, the substance. *That's* our understanding, Miss Bennet's and mine."

The colonel rolled his eyes but said nothing, throwing the butt of his cigar away and preparing to enter the house. A disapproving footman clicked his tongue. "Lady Catherine don't hold with that, sir."

"With what?" the colonel asked.

"Your filthy habit," Fitz said, pointing to the soggy object nestled under a rosebush.

"It's a Spanish custom," the colonel said. "Most of the officers and many of the men have adopted it; even Wellington enjoys *blowing a cloud* on occasion."

"Ah, the ravages of war," Fitz said. "What the Armada failed to accomplish, Bonaparte has brought about two centuries later—turning our good English yeomanry into continentals."

"Yes, sir," the footman said. "But Lady Catherine don't allow anyone to muck up her garden."

"Go on, colonel," Fitz said. "Pick it up and let's go in. While we stay at Rosings we serve under a stricter general than your lenient Wellington."

"Wellington lenient?" The colonel permitted himself one last snort of laughter. "Now there's a match for our aunt. I'd like to see those two in single combat! There'd be a perfect understanding *there*, I can tell you." He pocketed the offending butt and went inside.

"That would be something to see," Fitz said as they tiptoed up the stairs.

"Indeed," the colonel replied. "Similar to yours with Miss Bennet, I imagine. A fight to the death." He had reached his room and he jumped inside as he spoke, slamming the door against Fitz's hammering fist. He was still chuckling as he threw the cigar butt out the window and fell into bed.

ANNE DE BOURGH tossed and turned during what was supposed to be her afternoon nap. She would not take more laudanum. Not until she understood what was happening.

Why did Mama want her to marry Mr. Darcy? What was she to do with such an enormous, ferocious brute? What was she to say to him? He was not respectful, and not in the least deferential. Oh, he deceived people, but she knew what he was—clever, sarcastic, and cruel—although you wouldn't have guessed it from the way he usually behaved in company. She had heard him at dinner that first night, him and the colonel. They had been making fun of her and of Mama. Too bad she couldn't tell Mama, but that would only make things worse.

Now he was in love with that nobody, that friend of Mrs. Collins's, Miss Bennet. Mama didn't see that either. They were very much alike, Mama and Mr. Darcy. It was wonderful how Mama never saw anything she didn't want to see, that didn't fit with her ideas of how things ought to be. What a luxury, never to have to pay attention to intrusive, repulsive facts. But that was because Mama was so strong. She thought she could bend the entire world to her will.

Once Mama knew of Mr. Darcy's fickleness she would insist on forcing the match, so as not to be defeated. Lady Catherine had never been defeated. Well, once she had been, but it had been a very convenient defeat, leaving her better off than before. When Papa had died. She had lost her great battle to make him into what she wanted him to be, but she had been left mistress of his estate, his wealth, and their one child.

Mama had always been sympathetic, even gentle, with her frail daughter. That was her one weakness, mother love. But she would not compromise in this, the whole purpose of her existence, reuniting the family through the marriage of the two wealthy cousins, Mr. Darcy and Anne, the children of the Fitzwilliam ladies, the old earl's sisters. What was Anne to do, how was she to stand up to Mama? Anne was her father's child. Quiet, sickly, the least exertion making her gasp for breath. Not really meek and mild, but she pretended to be, because it was easier.

Anne knew she would just die if she had to marry Mr. Darcy—tall and robust and bursting with animal spirits. Why couldn't she find a small, quiet, unobtrusive man who would worship her and be grateful for her fortune and leave her alone? There were men who didn't even desire women, or so she had heard. Why couldn't she have one of them?

She had thought, long ago, Mr. Darcy was one of them. Something Mama had said about his foster brother, Mr. Wickham. Perhaps *he* was one of those men who preferred his own sex. From things she had inferred, as a young girl listening to adults' truncated conversations, the things left unsaid, unfinished sentences, from gestures and facial expressions, she knew there was something not quite right about Mr. Wickham, but she couldn't tell precisely what. Not that it mattered. Mama would never let her marry an obvious fortune hunter. Why that should be so bad Anne could not understand. Surely there would be a favorable settlement. Mama would see to that; she always drove the hardest of bargains. Anne's husband could enjoy his share of the money and leave her in peace, grateful for his freedom. They might not even have to live together. He could stay in town, spend his days in debauchery and dissipation, while Anne dozed away her life at Rosings, unencumbered by any society more demanding than Mrs. Jenkinson. How perfect it might be . . .

Well, there was no harm in preparing the letter. Anne rose quietly and moved to the writing desk. *Please, don't let Mrs. Jenkinson hear.* What a lucky chance that this Mrs. Collins was so kind and so discreet—and needed money. Obviously she hadn't married Mr. Collins for love, poor woman. She had offered her services casually, circumspectly, at their very first meeting, under cover of Anne's bored, dutiful inquiries. *Do you need anything in the village? It's no trouble.* So much better to get the laudanum anonymously, rather than asking the apothecary directly, even if he was willing. Mama would worry and ask questions and would never rest until she discovered what was wrong. This way, all she had to do was explain to Mama where the allowance money went, but perhaps Mrs. Collins would be able to help with that too.

What would Mama say when Mr. Darcy married this Miss Bennet? It was almost comical. Anne permitted herself a brief smile. What fun it would be to see Mr. Darcy take on Mama—except Mama always won in the end. Men were chivalrous, that was the problem. Or else they were simply terrified and gave in to Mama rather than being eaten alive or burned up in her fiery wrath. But Mr. Darcy was tough. If anyone was equal to Mama, he was. He was her nephew, after all. And not so gallant, from what Anne had seen these past two weeks.

Perhaps Mama would have such a great fit of apoplexy that she'd die. Or maybe her heart would burst from being so unexpectedly contradicted and thwarted. Wouldn't that be wonderful? Anne would be left alone. She could do whatever she pleased. She wouldn't have to marry at all. Was that possible? Why not? She must let Mama keep thinking that everything was going as planned, so that when the news came she was so unprepared that . . .

Anne wondered if it was very wicked, picturing her mother's demise in such vivid detail. It didn't signify. Imagining something never made any difference. Unlike Mama, who believed wishing made it so, Anne had long ago learned the futility of hope. Only dreams had any value—escape, however temporary—and laudanum was the surest way to bring them.

Thank goodness the colonel had no great fortune. He would be worse even than Mr. Darcy. So plain, so loud, the stink of cigars—and that horrid uniform. Why did people claim to find a red coat appealing? It was so hard on the eyes. Black was nice. Comfortable to look at. A small, thin man in a black coat, who consorted with other men like himself, but who cared for Anne alone among her sex. A gentle, quiet young man who might sit languid at her feet and read his verses to her or who might paint or draw her portrait. He would hold her hand and whisper how beautiful she was, how precious to him. *Of course you mustn't play the pianoforte*, he would say. *Only silly females who have no higher accomplishments squander their strength on such an empty pastime. Dancing? No, that is far too fatiguing. May I sit beside you and fan you while you read?*

Anne finished the letter for Mrs. Collins, put the money inside, and folded and sealed it. She was tired now, ready for sleep. Moving back to the bed, she tripped over a shoe.

"Oh my heavens!" Mrs. Jenkinson called from the boudoir. "Are you well, Miss de Bourgh?"

Anne reached for the draught on the bedside and drank it down. "Perfectly, Mrs. Jenkinson," she called in the weakest voice that would carry to the next room. "Please don't trouble yourself." She lay back on her pillows, imagining the slight breeze from his fan . . .

Fourteen

"I THINK HE'S in love with you," Charlotte said. The two friends sat at their sewing in Charlotte's chosen room, tucked safely in the back of the cottage. It was dark and plainly furnished, with no view, but it had the one great advantage: Mr. Collins, returning through the front door from visiting parishioners or working in the garden, would give plenty of warning of his approach.

"Don't be silly," Elizabeth said. She poked the needle through the center of an embroidered daisy, like stabbing her finger in an eye. *Day's eye*, it meant. With but a slight change it would be *Darcy*. She had never felt so angry as during these past couple of weeks, the way he spoiled her solitary walks near the Rosings Park with his sudden appearance in the lane, even in company rarely speaking, but merely stared at her, all smiles and feigned innocence, as if nothing had happened, as if he hadn't ruined Jane's life.

"What's silly about it?" Charlotte pursued her argument. "He's as silent and worshipful as an acolyte in the presence of the goddess."

"That's very poetic, Charlotte, but with Mr. Darcy it's far more likely to mean he's bored, or going over his accounts in his head to save time when he returns to Derbyshire." Elizabeth almost wished he were in love with her, to be able to have the power of ruining *his* life, revenge for Mr. Wickham and Jane, and perhaps Mr. Bingley as well. But there was little chance of that. Never had she known anyone less capable of love. She pierced the ragged daisy again, snapping a thread.

"At least you're not pretending not to know who I'm talking about," Charlotte said.

"I haven't lost my wits or my memory," Elizabeth said. "You've been hinting at this for days now. And besides, who else could you mean? If it were Colonel Fitzwilliam we were talking of, you wouldn't have to insinuate. Anyway, he and I have already had that conversation. He's not free to marry where he pleases."

"An earl's son?"

"Younger son," Elizabeth said. "He made it very clear. He's the nicest man, a true gentleman, although he does claim to have read books he's obviously never heard of, and I think I would have him in a minute, even if he is rather plain, *and* he smokes cigars, but he as much as told me that he would offer for me if he could afford to, but he can't, so he won't."

"Very clear, Lizzy," Charlotte said with a hint of her old warm laughter just below the surface of her subdued, married demeanor.

"Clear enough. You understood it."

"Don't bark at me."

"I'm sorry, Charlotte. I know you're being very brave." Elizabeth put her needlework aside along with her anger, shamed into contrition by Charlotte's example. Here was someone suffering genuine hardship, and yet unselfish enough to concern herself with her friend's happiness. True, Charlotte had chosen her own fate, but her generosity deserved better than Elizabeth's sharp tongue.

"Brave? What nonsense." As always, Charlotte shrugged off Elizabeth's demoralizing sympathy. "You see I have just what I always wanted. A husband and an establishment of my own, and perhaps a child. No, I have no need for courage, except for the visits to Lady Catherine. And they will taper off, I'm sure, as my novelty wears off. Oh, Lizzy, I shall miss you when you go."

The desperation in her friend's voice softened the last remaining shreds of Elizabeth's resentment. "Dear Charlotte. I'm here for another three weeks. I should never have been so cold to you." She sat beside Charlotte on the sofa, put her arms around her friend, and kissed her cheek.

"Ah, Lizzy. How I longed for that, back in Hertfordshire," Charlotte said. "In a way I suppose it was easier for both of us. The clean break, instead of the lingering, festering decline of love into pallid friendship, then into the moldering grave of 'my old acquaintance, married and living in Kent.' "

"I wish I could claim credit for so worthy a motive," Elizabeth said. "The truth is, I was hurt."

"You!" Charlotte's voice was less warm and she shifted out of Elizabeth's embrace. "Don't tell me you regretted turning down Mr. Collins's offer."

"Charlotte, please." Elizabeth reached for her friend's hands. "I think you know what I mean. I was hurt that you could so easily give yourself to someone so—so—I'm sorry, but I must speak plainly—lacking in intellect and inelegant in manner—when only the week before you and I had shared—"

"I see." Charlotte slowly withdrew her hands. It seemed all she did these days was pull herself away from those who would possess her.

"But Jane helped me to understand," Elizabeth said. "I know

a little more now, all the reasons that prevent women from marrying for love, and force us to choose a situation where there is little chance of happiness. I had hoped that, perhaps, with all that was between us, that you would draw the line at—"

"Lizzy," Charlotte said. "What are you saying? That unless I can get a Mr. Bingley or a Colonel Fitzwilliam I remain unmarried, for your sake? That's asking too much for any friendship, even for ours."

"Is it? Is it really?"

"Answer me this, Elizabeth Bennet: would you remain a spinster forever, for my sake?"

Elizabeth was caught, unable to lie flat out. "I never promised not to fall in love with a man, whatever our sentiments for each other. But I would not marry a Mr. Collins."

"Not now, at twenty. What about in five or six years? What then?"

Elizabeth squeezed her eyes tight and shut her mouth into a thin line, shaking her head like a child refusing a draught of vile physic. "I couldn't. Not after knowing a very different sort of man."

Charlotte gasped. "Oh my goodness! Mr. Wickham! You have lost your—"

Elizabeth opened her eyes and stared. "Charlotte! If we were men, I would be entitled to call you out merely for suggesting such a thing."

"If we were men," Charlotte said, daring to smile, "we could do as we liked and laugh about it and boast to each other of our conquests."

"Sometimes I wish—" Elizabeth stopped that line of thought, not sure she approved of where it was leading. "Do you really think me so far gone that I would forget everything and—"

"I don't know, Lizzy. You sounded so . . . *practiced*."

"I'm not, Charlotte. Spending time in Mr. Wickham's company gave me a fairly good idea of the pleasures that marriage could bring, but it's only conjecture, I promise you. He has been a perfect gentleman, not even attempted to steal a kiss. He let me know, of course, that if I were to indicate the least willingness, he would not be averse, but I have been strong." There was almost a sob at the back of her throat. If Mr. Darcy hadn't spoiled his prospects, Mr. Wickham would have a living by now and be free to ask her to marry, instead of having to dangle after heiresses. They wouldn't be rich, but they would live as well as Charlotte and Mr. Collins—and be happy into the bargain.

"Poor Lizzy. Such fortitude." Charlotte's voice was bitter. "I wonder what that's like, to actually wish a man to take liberties."

"Haven't you ever wanted anyone?"

"No, I mean, to have a man I wanted be attracted to *me*. It must be lovely to have to fend off a George Wickham or a Colonel Fitzwilliam. And now Mr. Darcy. No, if I had had three such suitors, even if none of them intended marriage, I doubt I could stomach Mr. Collins either."

"Oh, Charlotte. It's just that I'm a little younger, that's all."

"Lizzy, it's all right. I'm not pretty. I never have been. It can't be helped and you've never been insulting about it."

"Don't say that. It's not true. You are lovely—slender and lithe and . . . Men are so blind. All they want are fat, fair, indolent slugs."

"That explains why you have so many admirers, Lizzy," Charlotte said with a laugh at her thin, dark, and lively friend. "You were never a fool. Don't become one now just because you've had your head turned by a rogue in a red coat."

"It sounds to me," Elizabeth said, "as if you're speaking from jealousy."

"That's unkind," Charlotte said. "Most unkind. I have never wished anything for you but what I wished for myself—a good marriage and settlement. You have at least the chance of making a love match."

Elizabeth felt like the lowest sort of creature. "Charlotte, I wasn't going to admit this, not even to you, but now I must. Mr. Wickham is no longer courting me, assuming he ever was. He is pursuing a Miss King—so I hear. It seems that although she has freckles and no accomplishments, she does have a fortune of ten thousand pounds. Perhaps I should have swallowed my gorge and taken your Mr. Collins after all."

Charlotte exclaimed with proper sympathy, looking only slightly smug. "Ah, Lizzy, you'd never have tolerated him, not for long. It's just as well things have worked out as they have."

"I suppose," Elizabeth said. "So long as you're content."

"I am, Lizzy. Truly I am," Charlotte said in a whisper, although the maid was clattering in the kitchen and they were alone in this part of the house. "It's only that, right now, it's very hard for me, having you here, so close and yet out of reach."

The sadness and longing in her friend's voice effected the return to compassion, as a discussion of unwanted suitors could not. "I'm not out of reach," Elizabeth said. "Not at all. I'm right here. See?" She took Charlotte's hand and brought it to her breast, laying a soft kiss on her friend's lips.

Charlotte, to Elizabeth's horror, pushed her hand violently away and stood up, like a girl of twelve pawed by her drunken uncle. "Don't."

Elizabeth rose also, trying to control her weeping. She managed to remain silent, but her back shook with sobs.

Charlotte touched Elizabeth's shoulder, relieved when her friend turned around again and wept in her arms. "I'm sorry, Lizzy. You don't understand. I have made my choice and there is no having it both ways, not for women. Your Mr. Darcy and Mr. Bingley may be free to go on enjoying each other's company after marriage as well as before, but we cannot. Please don't make me say anything more."

"But why, Charlotte? It's not as if—"

"Because marriage is everything for a woman, but only one part of a man's life. Once we accept a man's offer, we are his entirely. Despise him how we may, suffer his mistreatment, if our consent was freely given we are wrong to go outside the marriage for any reason."

"That's slavery," Elizabeth said.

"That may be," Charlotte said, "but it's the law. He can divorce me for adultery, yet the reverse is not true. And if he chooses to assert his authority over me with the rod or the whip, I must endure it, even to bruises or broken bones."

Elizabeth stood before her friend, speechless with horror. Now she was seeing the unvarnished picture of marriage, the shining Holy Grail of every innocent young woman's quest.

Charlotte let an impish smile return. "Besides—how does one endure maggoty beef and sour milk after feasting on cakes and ale? How can I return to his bed if—"

Elizabeth giggled through her tears. "Oh, I do see that. More like rancid butter and game that's hung too long, though, don't you think?" She paused before asking, "Did you say you thought you might be breeding?"

Charlotte lowered her eyes. "I'm hopeful, but it's too early to tell. He'll have to leave me alone then, but until I'm sure we must keep trying. The only way for us both to get what we want."

Mr. Collins, bustling in a few minutes later, found his wife and her friend in the back room as usual. He stared, uncertain as to what seemed *off* in some way, or out of place—heads bent close over needlework in the fading daylight—and had that been a sob or more of a gasp?—but his attention soon returned to more important matters. "You will be delighted to know," he said in his preaching voice, "that we have again been favored with an invitation to Rosings."

As his heavy tread receded along the corridor, Charlotte murmured, "Won't Mr. Darcy be delighted!"

COLONEL FITZWILLIAM HAD at first merely been indulging in the standard raillery between men on learning that a friend's interest was caught by a particular woman, but as he saw his cousin's behavior over the next week or so, in modest gatherings at the parsonage and in the more formal setting of Rosings, he began to take in the reality. Darcy, always in command of his every action, whose wit shone in company, was so quiet, saying little and with a peculiar, vacant smile on his face, that the colonel had to shoulder the burden of the conversation. Not that it was so very heavy. The lady was every bit the paragon his cousin claimed. She was not beautiful, but her finely drawn features were so animated and her slight form so feminine and graceful, it was difficult even to address the required few polite remarks to the other inhabitants of the room. Her presence overshadowed everything around her—all this, without any deliberate attempt to dominate, and with a modesty and humor that both mocked and flattered her admirers.

"It's a damned shame, Miss Bennet's situation, when you think of it," Fitz exclaimed with force during another of their evening strolls. "A damned shame."

"How so?" the colonel asked.

Fitz recited more or less the same speech he had given at the Brotherhood, describing the entire Bennet family and enumerating their various sins. "It's the mother, really," he said in conclusion. "While ultimately the responsibility for any family's conduct lies with its head—the father—almost all of the evils in this instance stem from her ignorance and vulgarity. What makes it so abominable for Elizabeth is not only her superior intellect and her refinement, but that she's so painfully aware of her mother's failings. My God! When I recall how the woman talked of subjects no lady would dare to mention in polite society, in terms no person of breeding, man or woman, would use. And how valiantly the daughter worked to disguise it all, to dress it up in better form or change the subject. All without committing the opposite and equal offense, of appearing to contradict a parent or treat her with disrespect. It must seem like endless, excruciating torture for her, a swan trapped among carrion crows."

The colonel raised an eyebrow. "Miss Bennet does not appear especially oppressed."

"That's just it," Fitz said. "She endures it all, but is not diminished by it. I was certain she could not have spent her entire life in such deprivation, and must have had the benefit of a town education, but she denies it."

After a long silence, the colonel resumed the conversation in a somber tone. "You will receive a word or two of advice without biting my head off?"

"Why should I? Go ahead, man."

The colonel looked worriedly into his cousin's face. "Be careful, Darcy. I don't think you really see her. You see her in the way you'd like to."

"What the devil do you mean?"

"Forgive me, but I'm going to speak frankly now. I think you're in love, probably for the first time in your life. And you don't have the least idea of how to proceed."

"I assure you I have no improper intentions."

"For God's sake, Darcy, I should think not." The colonel felt outrage building in him at the mere thought of the lovely, innocent Miss Bennet, overwhelmed by his cousin's admittedly fine form and handsome face, his fortune, and his high position in society, accepting an indecent arrangement. He thought of her strong character, knew his imaginings were absurd. He laughed to cover his discomfort. "No, I know you better than that. But my guess is you don't even comprehend how critical it is with you. How much longer are you planning to stay here—another week?"

"Just about."

"Well, my advice is, don't do anything rash," the colonel said. "Whatever your feelings, she's not in love with you."

"Yet you see how she behaves with me." Fitz shook his head. "All propriety, nothing coarse, but you remember I spoke of an understanding between us? It's even stronger now. When we walk together in the park, or I call at the parsonage, sometimes we say very little, but there's no constraint, no sense of awkwardness."

"It may simply be that she doesn't care to exert herself if you won't."

"Ah, but she does exert herself when she has an audience. She never wastes an opportunity to tease me in public," Fitz said, that same smug smile on his face the colonel had seen at Miss Bennet's first visit to Rosings.

"I agree, as far as that goes," the colonel said. Miss Bennet did tease his cousin a great deal, far more than himself, for which he felt a strange mix of gratitude, in awe of her sharp wit, and disappointment, knowing she would never waste her abilities on anyone she considered unworthy, or unable to stand up to her enfilading fire. "But I don't see love there, or any pronounced partiality. I'm sorry, Darcy. If I thought for a minute she returned your regard, I would be giving you very different advice."

"Are you certain it's not envy speaking?"

"It most certainly is envy," the colonel said. "But it doesn't change my observations. Still, if you like, I'll sound her out, discreetly of course, and let you know what she says."

"Military interrogation, colonel?" Fitz said.

"Nothing of the sort," the colonel said. "Merely a directed conversation, as we say."

"Oh, she'll hold up," Fitz said. "I'll wager you a pony she won't break."

FITZ SAW IT at last, the solution to her problems—and his. Should he tell his cousin? He thought not. Not yet. The colonel had already reported the results of his "interrogation," for some reason choosing to dwell on yet another instance of Elizabeth's obsession with her sister's thwarted acquaintance with Charles.

"Nearly found you out, Darcy," he said. "Asked a great many pointed questions about your Mr. Bingley. All I could do to act as if I didn't know the particulars. Do me a favor, will you? The next time you meddle in some poor woman's affairs, have the kindness to keep the sordid details to yourself."

No, just because the man commanded a good regiment and wore a smart red coat and had whored around for the past fifteen years didn't mean he knew anything more about an incomparable like Elizabeth Bennet than Fitz did.

He went over it in his head, just to make sure. All the flirtatious, witty remarks and gibes that proved she recognized in him her equal, her chosen mate. Strange how he could recall every conversation, word for word, from the first moment of their meeting, yet in her presence he was as dumb and stupid as a backward schoolboy. He supposed it was the way of love. But *she* showed no such infirmity. No doubt it was a man's weakness, and perhaps she suffered from a very different ailment peculiar to women.

The comment about poetry killing off all but the strongest of loves. "If it be only a slight, thin sort of inclination," she had said, during that revealing visit of her mother and sisters to Netherfield, "I am convinced that one good sonnet will starve it entirely away." That had been his first intimation that she was more than just a bright, pretty girl, but someone who might conceivably comprehend him, share his tastes and his preferences. How could she know his detestation of all the modern drivel unless she felt it too?

And then there was her pleasure in dancing and music, in walking and in reading, the Greek ideal of the health of the body and the mind, neither one to take precedence at the expense of the other. She had scoffed at Miss Bingley's ill-natured remark that she preferred reading to any other pastime. She understood intuitively, not having enjoyed the benefit of a classical education, the sound principle of nothing to excess. The way she had compared Fitz's reluctance to extend himself in company to her own lack of diligence at practicing on the pianoforte. That was the clincher. She wouldn't say such a thing to him if she didn't intend the underlying implication as well as the literal meaning. She was too perceptive to say things and be unaware of the connotations.

She flirted but she was not a tease. She laughed but she was not cruel. She mocked, but with the smooth, neat cut of a scalpel, leaving a clean wound, rather than the pulpy mess of a surgeon's saw, and nothing she said was untrue, at least as it appeared from her perspective. The way she always harked back to Wickham. Now *that* was an irritation. And hinting about her sister, as if Fitz had done something wrong there, when he had clearly only helped his friend out of a difficult situation. But she would come to see Fitz's side of things, once they were engaged and he could open his heart to her.

He had acted rightly. Charles could never stand up to that

family. But it had at last occurred to Fitz that *he* could. My God, since when did *he* give a tinker's damn about a bunch of pushy, vulgar provincials? He'd like to see the woman who could face *him* down. That bawd of a mother would melt like an April snowfall as soon as he directed the full force of his scorn at her.

Lord, what an exhausting, constant battle Elizabeth must have to wage, maintaining her dignity among that flock of scavengers and drabs. No wonder she was so slender and ate so heartily.

No, Charles was well out of it. But poor Elizabeth . . . Not "poor" as in pitiable. There was no woman one felt less sorry for than she. But she did need rescuing, the more so because she didn't repine and look downhearted, but laughed and jousted her way through life as if she were the only daughter of a wealthy peer, with all prospects before her, instead of . . . He spared a sigh for her hopeless circumstances and a sad shake of the head at her courage.

Well, this was where Fitz could step in. He would lay it all before her, his scruples and his doubts, because she would know he was lying if he proclaimed a love that had simply sprung fully formed, like Athena out of Zeus's forehead, with no birth pangs or struggles. And he would present to her all the advantages he was offering, just in the event she hadn't had it drummed into her from all the mercenary talk in Hertfordshire. It was always a good idea to show himself in the best light. He had made a wretched job of it so far, knocked off course as he had been by seeing her clear in all her starry luster, no longer in partial eclipse from the shrouding presence of her family.

How grateful she would be! He lay in bed longer than usual, allowing himself a shameful long moment of indecent pleasure, imagining the extent of her gratitude and the manner in which she would express it. Fitz would tell her, *No my love, that is not appropriate between husband and wife*, but she would insist in her charming, stubborn way, and he would give in, let her do it, just a little. Not all the way, not to the extent of coming in her mouth . . .

He opened his eyes and swore as he soiled the sheets and his nightshirt. Probably the maid would give a detailed report to his aunt on everything, right down to the very condition of the bed linens.

Damn it all, what did it matter? Wasn't that the point? He was Fitzwilliam Darcy, with ten thousand pounds a year, the master of the richest estate in Derbyshire, and he could do as he pleased. He could certainly please himself about marriage, Lady Catherine or no Lady Catherine.

If she said a word to him he'd tell her just what he thought of her offensive manners and her pathetic, sickly daughter. Trying to fob off an invalid wife on a healthy, vigorous man like him. That would shut her up. And he would bring Elizabeth back to finish out her visit here, at Rosings, as his betrothed. He let loose again, another long white string, thinking of her here, in his room, at night, permissible because they were to be married.

He jumped up and called for his man. He must bathe and dress quickly and eat breakfast on the run. He was going to propose to the lady of his choice.

Fifteen

THE PEN BIT into the paper so hard it tore a large jagged hole and lodged itself in the blotting paper beneath like a knife in a butcher's block. "Damn it!" Fitz said. "God *damn* it!"

Colonel Fitzwilliam, passing in the corridor, crept by the doorway unheard and unseen.

Fitz took another sheet of paper and began again. This time the writing came out heavy and ink-splattered, but legible. He pressed on, finding the words poured out of him effortlessly when telling of Wickham's deceit, however distasteful the subject and unfit for a lady's eyes. Paradoxically, what should have been easy—explaining about Charles and how Fitz had not thought Jane really in love—was far more difficult. He got over that as quickly as possible and concentrated on answering the greater charge, of mistreatment of his foster brother.

Her accusation ran in his head, over and over. *Had you behaved in a more gentlemanlike manner.* All because of "poor Mr. Wickham."

Fitz ground his teeth, remembering. So long ago. Years.

And still he could see it all, seared into his memory. *Christ, Fitz, you're such a* gentleman. *You think you're God's gift, don't you?*

The large barn at Pemberley. George naked to the waist and his breeches around his knees, lying facedown in the straw but twisting the top half of his body around to smile up at Fitz behind him. Fitz had finished now, spent and limp, and lay partly on top of his beloved, an arm around his smooth shoulders, the bony, hairless chest. Fitz wondered if George had grown any hair in the five and more years since.

"Do you love me too?" Fitz asked. He had been crying it into George's neck as he made love to him—a boy's passion that had matured and strengthened into a man's. "I love you, I love you."

George lifted his bowed head and turned to look up at Fitz. "Love you? Are you really that stupid, Darcy? Do you honestly think I'd put up with all this swiving and sweating for *love*? God, you're an imbecile. But generous. I'll give you that."

Fitz hadn't had an inkling. Not one suspicion. Had he? All those years, from boyhood on into early manhood. All the whippings and the scoldings, the sad, stern lectures from his father. "Fitzwilliam, I am disappointed in you yet again. I continue to believe you are not wholly bad, not irredeemable, that reformation is still possible, but sometimes I am close to despair."

It had started out so innocently. A stolen apple or two from a farmer's orchard; a broken window from playing baseball too close to the house; the bird shot out of season when they were testing Fitz's new fowling piece. And always George used the same argument—that he was but the steward's son, forever dependent on the favor of his benefactor. The least sign of bad character, even a boyish prank, could be used as reason to relegate him to his rightful lowly position. He could be beaten or severely chastised, perhaps even sent away, but Fitz, son and heir, could confess to the crimes with no real consequences. "He's your dad," George said, deliberately talking like one of the farmhands, emphasizing the distance in their stations, even though his father had been a gentleman and George had been educated the same as Fitz. "You'll get off easy."

At first George had been correct. Old Mr. Darcy had reprimanded them and read them sermons, but he had seen nothing so very wrong in hungry boys plucking apples from a branch overhanging the orchard wall, or in a high-spirited ballgame. The incident with the fowling piece had been another matter. "Nobody hits a partridge by accident," he'd said. "I thought you were old enough to handle firearms responsibly. Seems I was mistaken." He had whipped Fitz himself for that, and taken the piece away for six months. They'd missed the entire shooting season.

But George always made it up to Fitz. That first time, when they were but twelve and thirteen, Fitz had been so unbelieving and ecstatic at the realization of what he had dreamed about for the entire past year as an impossible, unobtainable hope, he'd have committed murder for the chance—the merest chance—of being granted a repetition of the favor. And each time, George barely had to hint at what he expected from Fitz—and what he was prepared to offer in return. Nothing coarse or crude, only the half smile, the lowered eyes, the expression of remorse and the glimpse of tears if Fitz seemed about to balk.

Then, as they grew older, the crimes became more serious. Stolen money, poaching, and last and worst of all, what had almost got Fitz disowned—the trouble with the cotter's wife. Fitz still felt sick when he thought of it. George had been sneaking off every afternoon to some mysterious rendezvous. Unlike their other adventures, he wouldn't let Fitz share in this or even tell him what it was. "Just a little sport," he said when Fitz asked.

"I like sport too," Fitz said, smiling shyly at the reference to their usually unspoken pleasures. "You know I'm not jealous, Wick, but can't you at least let me come along?"

"Not your sort of thing, Fitz," George said, spitting for emphasis like the laborers he emulated. "Just be my eyes and ears, will you?"

God, he'd been naïve. It hadn't crossed his mind that George would want a woman. *Ladies*, that he could understand, but for boys their age ladies were as out of reach as the High Impures maintained in their own establishments by London's wealthy libertines.

Of course, it was inevitable, in such a close-knit community, that the woman's husband caught them in the act. George escaped, running the shortcut through the woods and into the park, but the man followed soon after, dragging his half-naked and sobbing wife right through the gate of Pemberley and across the gravel drive to the front entrance, and demanding to speak to Mr. Darcy himself.

"No, sir," he said to repeated questions. "Not your boy. It's t'other one, the steward's son." The villagers and the farm laborers all knew Fitz and liked him. To them he had always been honest and fair. It was only his father who had been deceived for so long he thought he had raised the devil's spawn as his own.

And Fitz had had to come into the room, tight and uncomfortable in George's too-small breeches and shirt, and stand in front of his outraged accuser, and swear that the man was mistaken, that it had been a natural confusion—both of them fair, less than two years' difference in age. He nearly choked bringing the words out. He thought he was going to spew, that God would strike him down for the lie. That's what finally made it possible for him to do it, the knowledge that he was now lost to salvation, that he had damned himself and that God would punish him.

Hardest of all was saying such a preposterous thing to the woman. It was one thing to lie to his father—he'd been doing that for so long it had almost ceased to trouble him—and the husband was clearly a brute and a bully and unworthy of the truth. But a wronged woman—that was different. Even a willing whore was entitled to be treated fairly, not insulted with an outrageous falsehood.

Fitz dared to meet her eyes, squinting against the horror of her scornful, reproachful gaze, as her wrathful husband forced her head up, all the time saying, "That's right, Betty, you look Master Fitzwilliam in the face and then you tell me it was him." Fitz took one look, the tangled dark hair over the large eyes, red with weeping, one of them blackened and swollen, the full lips, cut and bleeding at the corner . . . *A vision of hell, what he could expect, the demons, the Furies who would torment him for eternity.* He retched, bent over with the dry heaves, but he heard George's pleas in his head. *Oh God, Fitz, you've got to get me out of this one. They'll kill me. Literally. Please, Fitz. I'll do anything. You know I will. I'll be your slave for a month, anything you want, every night.*

He pulled himself together and said, "Yes, I'm sorry. It was I, Father. It was very wrong of me, I know, but I couldn't help it." It sounded so false, so absurd. How could anyone believe it? So he added, "She's so beautiful I couldn't help myself."

And the woman winked at him. Fitz must have recoiled or flinched, because she gave a soft little gasp when her husband shook her, demanding that she corroborate the lie for all to hear. She wrenched herself out of her husband's grasp and said, "Yes, sir, Mr. Darcy. It was your son, Master Fitzwilliam. He pretended to be George Wickham because it's easier for a steward's son to come and go in the village without nobody noticing."

That time the beating was so severe Fitz passed out from the pain. His father hadn't done it himself, but set the blacksmith on him with the bullwhip. Fitz wasn't able to enjoy George's "slavery" for almost two weeks while he healed. And the settlement to the cuckolded husband had been taken out of Fitz's allowance. He'd had to beg George for spending money for the remainder of the school year.

The only good thing to come of it was the visit from the woman, almost a year later, with her child, both turned out of doors. She found the two of them in the barn as usual, marched over to George and shoved the baby in his face. When he stumbled back in disgust she struck him. Just hauled off with the back of one hand and knocked him down, the brat wailing on her hip. "I'd do worse but I don't want to hang and leave the poor babe without a mother." She kicked at George where he lay and looked Fitz up and down with an approving smile. "Wish it *had* been you, love. You'd a done right by me."

Before she went she reached over and stroked Fitz's cheek. He'd thought she was going to hit him too and he stood there, steady and unmoving, ready to take his punishment like a man. Like King Charles I going to his execution, wearing two shirts so he wouldn't shiver from the cold and appear afraid, paying the fee to the man with the ax and giving him his blessing. God knew he deserved whatever she did to him. But all she did was talk. "Give him a good hot poker up the arse for me, love. But stop being so daft. He's a very pretty fellow to be sure, but you don't want to swing for him, neither. He ain't worth it. You're more of a man than he'll ever be."

They said in the village she went to Manchester and opened her own house with twenty girls and a liveried man at the door, but that was just market women's bawdy stories, Fitz decided. Once or twice, riding down the high street, he thought he'd seen her, a hunched figure in rags with a young child, begging to avoid the workhouse. But it was hard to say. Most women looked much the same, and when they were poor and dirty, indistinguishable one from the other.

Things improved when he went to Cambridge. Away from Pemberley, and in a different college, George had a narrower scope for pinning all his misdeeds on Fitz, requiring as it did the corroboration of tutors and deans. It had been a lovely freedom for Fitz to be judged solely on his own merits. More than one master had encouraged him to take orders and pursue a full degree. Old Biggs, his Greek tutor, had written of Fitz to his father, "An excellent scholar and a first-rate mind." It might not be a bad life, but of course out of the question for someone of his wealth and position. Fitz had prolonged his gentleman's course of study as long as he dared, sorry when the two years were up and he had to come home again. George, a year behind, was struggling, fighting the temptations of town wenches and convivial drinking friends, and losing the battle.

And still it went on. George continued to proclaim his love to Fitz, still begged for help in his scrapes, although he knew not to overreach after the episode with Betty, and after forfeiting his foster father's unqualified confidence by his dismal performance at university. Fitz continued to take the blame, the two of them just skirting the edge of disaster, knowing an inch too far and the game would be over—either Fitz would reveal the truth at last or they'd both be ruined.

All for George's crimes. All for love. Fitz had thought the world well lost, then. And almost it had been, until his father died, still hoping for, if not quite believing in, his only son's eventual redemption.

Then the game had ceased to matter to George. He had demanded his "cut," as he called it, as if his entire life had been devoted to some elaborate swindle that was about to pay off. "You don't think I've been bending over for you out of love. Even you aren't that blind—are you?"

"But Wick, you wanted it too, didn't you?" How many times had George initiated another encounter? Not directly, perhaps, not in words—but signaling with his eyes, or his mouth, the tip of the tongue just beginning to show through parted lips, sometimes just a very slight swivel of the hips, that he wanted Fitz. "I would never have done anything, Wick, if I didn't think you wanted it."

George's only answer was another sneer. "Such a gentleman. Next you'll write me sonnets and give me a ring."

God, he wished he had George at his mercy just one last time. He'd show him what real force was. He'd been gentle and loving, even as a boy when his whole body had seemed to surge out of control for a continuous period of five years. He had only to look at George or think of him, his smile, his fine fair hair and his clean profile, his slender limbs with their surprisingly chiseled, muscular look beneath the clothes that softened him. And that amazing large prick, unexpected on such a slender man, and seemingly always hard, or able to get there at a moment's notice, as soon as they had a chance alone . . . But Fitz usually tried to hold back so as not to hurt him, until that last time, after the taunts and the contempt. Then he had laid into George with the full power of his lust—and only then had George shared in the passion, coming into the straw, gasping and moaning just like Fitz.

"You see," Fitz said. "You do like it."

"Oh, any man's pistol will discharge when he's rammed deep enough," George said, trying to appear unmoved by what had just occurred, struggling to keep his voice level. "Doesn't mean *love* any more than that ugly old tomcat of yours loves the pusses he screws on his night prowls."

"But all these years—" Fitz said.

"Yes, Darcy. What else was I supposed to do when my lord's son wanted to have his way with me? And me just the son of the poor steward. But that's finished now. I'll take my share—God knows I've earned it, and more—and I'll have the living I was promised."

WELL, NONE OF this was anything he could write to a lady. There was enough he could say without offense: the generous inheritance misspent and wasted; the demand for more money to study the law; the repeated failures; and the last renunciation of all help, including the living, in return for three thousand pounds. "I knew he ought not to be a clergyman," Fitz wrote, grimacing at the dung heap of depravity concealed by the phrase.

He sat for a long minute or two, letting the pen marinate in the ink bottle, while he debated with himself whether to tell of the attempted elopement with Georgiana. It was the final, damning piece of evidence, and, oddly enough, he felt confident that Elizabeth was the safest person to entrust with such a secret, something he had not shared even with Charles. "I know not in what manner, under what form of falsehood he has imposed on you," he concluded, before advising her to apply to Colonel Fitzwilliam for confirmation if she doubted Fitz's account. He barely admitted to himself that, in love with Wickham as she obviously was, this would destroy any remaining regard for him she might harbor, far more thoroughly than such mundane matters as income and livings.

God, he wished he had *her* in the straw now. He would show her just what a *gentleman* he was . . .

No. No, he did not. There was nothing similar between Elizabeth Bennet and the man who had betrayed his trust. She was innocent and good, while George was wicked and practiced in deceit. Any resemblance between them was superficial, the happenstance of physical likeness. Both slim and full of life, with their quicksilver changes, witty and pretty, teasing and laughing . . .

George had used it all for treachery, for extortion and blackmail, for cheating and lying and letting others take the blame.

But she was all purity. If she had led him on, it was due to her artlessness, not deliberate seduction. It was Fitz's pride that had brought him to the edge of this precipice, so confident of success that he had pursued the distant horizon instead of watching the path under his feet. He was fortunate to have been pulled up before tumbling over the edge, however painful her reining in. What a narrow escape he had had, almost married into that mob of grasping, vulgar jackdaws, his noble family name and lineage forever tainted.

No, he would simply answer her charges and then he would leave Rosings. Go back to town and forget her. As if that were possible.

He wished just once to have George again. But the need passed, and with it the desire.

Sixteen

"I REALLY AM sorry, Jane," Elizabeth said. "I didn't *want* Mr. Darcy to propose to me." Elizabeth had not been able to keep the recent disturbing events at Rosings entirely to herself. Too upset after receiving Mr. Darcy's odious proposal even to tell Charlotte, she had spent the last weeks of her visit in tense silence, allowing her friend to believe it was sorrow at leaving her alone with Mr. Collins that depressed her spirits. The return journey to London and Jane had passed in a blur of unhappy reflections.

Now back at Longbourn, subdued and anxious, Elizabeth wilted under her eldest sister's perceptive questions. To Jane she disclosed everything, only keeping to herself those parts of Mr. Darcy's letter that betrayed his role in Mr. Bingley's deception. During the days she could maintain her customary composure; but the nights were different. Lying in the sisters' shared bed, whispering in the dark, it was impossible for Elizabeth *not* to talk about it, recounting the worst of the exchange, hoping to clear her head of the most inconvenient feelings—the beginnings of respect, of warmth, dare she say, regret?

"You needn't keep on apologizing," Jane said. "I know it's difficult not having Charlotte to confide in, but Lizzy, please, I can't listen to this anymore."

"But I was mistaken," Elizabeth said. "You see? I thought Wickham was the injured party, but it turns out Mr. Bingley was right after all."

Jane sat up in the bed, pushing back the covers, which left Elizabeth exposed as well. "*You* were the one who wouldn't believe that Mr. Bingley could possibly know what he was talking about. *You* were the one who was so sure that Wickham could do no wrong."

"I know," Elizabeth said. "I just thought you'd enjoy being vindicated in your opinion of Mr. Bingley."

"Vindication implies there was doubt," Jane said. "I don't like to believe Wickham is as bad as you say, but I never for a minute doubted Mr. Bingley's account of things. Now I'd like to get some sleep, if that's all right with you, Lizzy." She lay back down and pulled the covers up, taking most of them for herself.

"Of course, dear. I'm sorry." Elizabeth snuggled close to her sister. It *was* hard without Charlotte. Charlotte had always known the right thing to do. She was the one who had recommended not saying anything to Jane about seeing Mr. Bingley and Mr. Darcy together. But had that been the right decision? If Jane had known about that, she might not have taken Mr. Bingley's defection so much to heart. All this time, and bravely as she was bearing up, Jane was not her old serene self. Elizabeth could see it, if others could not. She was thinner, for one thing. And pale. It was a vicious circle: listless from sitting indoors too much, she had no appetite, which made her tired and unwilling to walk outdoors. If by some chance Mr. Bingley did ever come back, he might not find her so appealing . . .

"I didn't tell you everything," Elizabeth said.

Jane sighed and turned her back. "I'm sleeping, Lizzy."

"About why I refused Mr. Darcy's proposal, I mean."

Jane let out an obviously false snore.

"It wasn't just because of how he expressed himself, or because of Wickham, but the way he treats Mr. Bingley," Elizabeth said. "I thought you should know."

"Know what?" Jane said.

Elizabeth considered very carefully before answering. She couldn't tell Jane the entire truth: that Mr. Darcy had masterminded the deceit of Mr. Bingley, keeping from him the fact of Jane's visit to London. It was so tempting to give Jane the comfort of knowing that Mr. Bingley had not spurned her, but it wouldn't solve anything and it would damage Mr. Bingley's reputation more than Mr. Darcy's, showing him to be a dupe, so diffident and silly that he believed his friend's self-interested opinion rather than trusting in his own heart. If there was a chance of his wooing her again, Jane would despise him. On the other hand, if Elizabeth could hint at the true nature of the men's relationship, it might ease some of her sister's pain. "I was wrong about Wickham," she began. "But not about Mr. Bingley. That is, it's Mr. Bingley whom Mr. Darcy abuses—"

"Well, that was worth being woken up for," Jane said. "Lizzy, I have tried to be sympathetic to your situation, receiving an unwelcome proposal—although most women would probably not find a proposal from Mr. Darcy so very disagreeable as you did—but I thought at least such an occurrence would stop you from repeating this offensive jest about Mr. Darcy and Mr. Bingley."

"You didn't hear his proposal," Elizabeth said. "It was the rudest imaginable. I don't suppose any woman has ever had a worse one. He spoke more of his reasons for *not* wishing to marry me and how he was lowering himself by contracting an alliance with our family—"

"If you think about it," Jane said, "instead of simply repeating it, it's all quite true. A man in Mr. Darcy's position is expected to marry a lady of fortune equal to his. The disparity between our family and his is so great that his relations could hardly be expected to approve of such a match or to welcome you as his wife. It's a testament to the intensity of his passion that he wanted to marry you despite all that."

"That's what he said. It's a shame he didn't want to marry *you*, Jane. You and he would suit admirably, he always reminding you of his extraordinary condescension and you eternally grateful."

"And that's my reward for being your confidante—to be abused along with Mr. Bingley and Mr. Darcy."

"Oh, Jane, I am truly sorry. This whole business has upset me terribly and made me cruel." Elizabeth tried to give her sister a hug and kiss, but was rebuffed by a turned back and a bed cap pulled down over the ears. "The only reason I bring up this old business of Mr. Darcy's treatment of Mr. Bingley is that . . . I keep thinking that . . . if you knew the truth . . . you might not feel—feel so bad about losing him." It seemed to take her forever, between pauses for breath and gulping in fear, to get to the end of that sentence, and all for naught.

"I didn't lose Mr. Bingley," Jane said. "That implies I had him. But as to the nature of his friendship with Mr. Darcy, if it will make you keep quiet and allow me some sleep, I'll say what I swore never to tell anyone, not even you: *I know*. I know it, I know it, *I know it*."

"But how?"

"Mr. Bingley told me. He said I deserved honesty. It was a measure of his esteem for me, so I thought."

"I don't believe it. How can a man confess such an intimate thing to a young lady he has known only a few weeks?"

"Are you forgetting that Wickham confessed a most intimate thing to you?" Jane said. "A *false* thing, I might add—after knowing you only a few *days*."

Elizabeth felt her cheeks warming with shame. "I admit, Wickham has been exposed as a deceitful, even immoral man," she said, her voice cracking in the lowest of whispers. "But Mr. Bingley, however impulsively he has behaved, has never been the sort of man to discuss anything improper with a lady."

Jane gasped and sat up again. "Lizzy, honestly, you can be as crude and ignorant as Lydia sometimes. What is improper about love? Mr. Bingley told me that he loves Mr. Darcy and that Mr. Darcy loves him. He made me swear not to tell a soul, not even you, and I never dreamed of breaking my word, but you have driven me to it. Mr. Bingley told me because, he said, if I knew the truth, I would understand that whatever Mr. Darcy said or did that might seem questionable or harsh was from the purest of motives—love. And you have been sneering and making insinuations for months, and now you see that *Mr. Darcy* has been vindicated."

"Did not that confession of Mr. Bingley's, that he was in love with someone else, make you wonder at his courting you?"

Jane sighed. "He did not say he was 'in love.' He said that he and Mr. Darcy *loved* each other—that it's the highest form of love men can know—but that it's not the same as a man being *in love* with a woman."

"I suppose Mr. Darcy taught him that interesting distinction," Elizabeth said. "No doubt he learned of it in his studies at Cambridge."

"Yes, I think so," Jane said. "It was something in Plato, I think. Or was it Plutarch? Mr. Bingley greatly respected Mr. Darcy's scholarship and his reading. And you needn't smirk."

"How do you know I'm smirking?"

"I can always tell," Jane said.

Elizabeth waited a good five minutes, until Jane was almost asleep. "I saw them," she said.

Jane rolled on her back and groaned. "Saw who?"

"I saw Mr. Darcy kiss Mr. Bingley."

"Lizzy!" Jane wailed. "*Why* are you doing this? Why *shouldn't* they kiss? They *love* each other."

"They were naked," Elizabeth said.

"I don't believe it for one minute."

"It's true," Elizabeth said. "Mr. Darcy put his arms around Mr. Bingley from behind, like this"—Elizabeth embraced Jane—"and licked his neck, like a mother cat with a naughty kitten." She demonstrated, with tongue.

Jane giggled and pushed her sister away. "No, Lizzy," she said. "You're making it up."

"I don't think I could make up such an astonishing thing. And why would I?"

"To make me laugh. Which you have succeeded at, admirably. But I don't accept the premise of your story, because how should you see them naked? It's impossible."

"When you had the cold and we stayed at Netherfield, do you remember the night I went to fetch you barley water from the kitchen? Well, their bedroom door was open, just a crack and—"

"It's like something in an indecent novel," Jane said. "I'm surprised they carry books like that in the Meryton library, and even more disappointed at you reading them. Anyway, I know you're making it up because if you had seen something so interesting, back in the autumn, you could never have kept it to yourself all this time."

"Yes, I think I've been most heroic," Elizabeth said. "I wanted to tell you but I thought it would distress you."

"Then why distress me now?"

"Because of Mr. Darcy's proposal, of course. When I saw them, I thought it meant they were not interested in women. In marriage. But if Mr. Darcy lowered himself to propose to me, perhaps I misjudged the matter. Maybe he'll consider allowing Mr. Bingley to come back to Longbourn and propose to you."

"I'm perfectly sure you misjudged the matter," Jane said with the asperity she would only evince in fatigue. "But now you're telling me fairy tales."

"It's possible."

"One should always be optimistic and cheerful," Jane said, "but it's equally unhealthy to yearn for the impractical or unlikely."

"And now you sound like Mary."

"A sentiment is not necessarily false just because our middle sister expresses it."

"Maybe not, but it certainly falls under the heading of unlikely, if not impractical," Elizabeth said.

"I should think, if you turned Mr. Darcy down, if anything it would make Mr. Bingley less likely to return here," Jane said.

"That is assuming Mr. Darcy will tell Mr. Bingley about it."

"Mr. Darcy will want comfort from his friend in his disappointment, just as you would want it from me—or Charlotte."

"You allow nothing for men's vanity," Elizabeth said.

"If they truly love each other," Jane said with another sigh, "they will have no secrets from each other. Love takes precedence over vanity and pride."

"If it really is love and not just another form of delusion—and lust."

"Mr. Bingley is not deluded," Jane said. "Nor, I should imagine, is Mr. Darcy. And I don't think you should pronounce on a subject you can know nothing about."

"Lust?" Elizabeth said. "Why may I not be proficient in the subject? Since becoming acquainted with Wickham I consider myself very well-informed."

"That is a dangerous boast," Jane said. "Someone who doesn't know you might believe it."

"You're right," Elizabeth said in a voice of contrition. "Even Charlotte thought so. Really, I learned nothing of lust from Wickham that I had not already been introduced to by Mr. Darcy."

"Didn't Mr. Darcy's proposal change your feelings for him at all? You mock him still, as you did after he chose not to dance with you at an assembly, before he had even met you. It's time and more to forget such a trivial slight. Since he asked you to marry him, he has clearly changed his opinion of *you*."

"I am not mocking him," Elizabeth said. "I only meant that seeing him as I did, ex tempore, so to speak, I was most forcefully reminded of the truth of Mr. Bingley's remark, that he's such a great tall fellow, one is inclined to defer to his wishes for no better reason than that."

"Never say you would accept a man merely because of his size."

Elizabeth paused before whispering in a dramatic voice, "Mr. Darcy *is* very big." She took her sister's hands and held them an improbable length apart.

"Oh, Lizzy!" Jane shrieked, snatching her hands away. "I won't say you are as bad as Lydia; you are *worse*." When no response was forthcoming, she was forced to ask, "What about Mr. Bingley?"

"No, I think I've said enough for one night."

"Lizzy, you will tell me if I have to badger you all night."

"Aren't you the least bit shocked that their *pure* love encompasses the physical? Surely the whole idea is tarnished for you now."

"See how you betray yourself!" Jane said. "I don't think you turned down Mr. Darcy for the manner of his proposal or for anything to do with Wickham, but only because you are prejudiced against him for loving Mr. Bingley."

"No, truly that's not the reason. In fact, it's one thing in Mr. Darcy's favor. It is a *kind* of love, even if he does treat Mr. Bingley too much like a master with a naughty pupil, and I'm relieved to know he is capable of such an emotion. When I first saw them, I admit I was quite shocked, but after a little while, once I had time to go over it in my mind, it came to seem a very pretty picture. It's only that I thought it would bother *you*."

"Mr. Bingley never said their love wasn't physical. After all, husband and wife share corporeal love in marriage."

"But that's a man and a woman."

"That was the crux of the argument, as I understood it," Jane said, speaking more slowly than usual as she tried to recall Mr. Bingley's words, "that between a man and a woman, all love has an element of the carnal, and that it can only be purified by holy matrimony. Between men, love can be pure without marriage."

"Such philosophy! And such nonsense."

"It made sense when Mr. Bingley explained it. Really, I didn't pay that much attention. I just took it to mean that men are different from us, which any woman knows by the age of twelve. The most important thing Mr. Bingley said was that it wasn't an impediment to marriage, the way a man's having a mistress would be."

"Lord! Those were interesting discussions you two had! And here I thought it was all poetry and flowers."

"Mr. Bingley is not such an inconsequential man as you assume. Just because Mr. Darcy is so clever does not mean everyone else is a fool."

"I never said—"

"Lizzy," Jane said, "I'm glad you're not tired because I want to hear the entire account now, and with nothing left out."

"NEVER FALL IN love with a woman," Fitz declared, falling onto a sofa at the Brotherhood of Philander. "Never." It was more than he could bear, a month after returning to town, the combined assault of Charles's nervous, uncomprehending smiles at Fitz's displays of temper and Miss Bingley's conspicuous relief that no betrothal to Miss de Bourgh had been announced. Ordinary society had become insupportable; the flirtations and intrigues that had been merely annoyances before Fitz's disastrous infatuation and rejected proposal now affected him like torture. Determined though he was to avoid any stain on his reputation, it was only among this equally vulnerable company that he could unburden his heart, confident that nothing of his misadventures in Kent would leak out into town gossip.

"It's safe to assume you're preaching to the converted here, Darcy," Monkton said. "Besides, Carrington has already treated us to a most interesting course of instruction in that very subject. If you deigned to visit occasionally, you might have spared yourself having to recapitulate the lessons."

"How comforting to find oneself among sympathetic friends," Fitz said. "I was visiting my aunt in Kent. Always go at Easter." He sat up. "What's this about Carrington? Other than you, Monkton, there's no one here less likely to succumb to feminine charms."

"I thank you for the compliment," Monkton said.

"We none of us credited it at first," Pierce said. "But he needs an heir, you know. In line to inherit the earldom when his uncle Newburn dies."

"I saw the rather uninformative notice of the marriage in

the papers," Fitz said. "But I supposed he made the standard arrangement. You talked as if he were in love."

"He is," Witherspoon said. "At least, I believe he is."

"So do I," Verney said, "which is particularly gratifying as I am the one who introduced them."

"Anyone can see it," Pierce said. "Despite the, ah, missteps attendant on any such hasty bargain, it looks as if they are on their way to reaching an understanding that would be the envy of most love matches."

"Yes," Monkton said, "even I am forced to admit that Carrington seems to have achieved the impossible—convinced a beautiful, intelligent lady to ignore all the promptings of her better judgment and accept his somewhat tarnished hand—*and* heart—in matrimony."

That's about right, Fitz thought in disgust. Carrington was, in many ways, the most dissolute of all of them, even Monkton, and the least likely to comply with society's dictates. No one on first acquaintance suspected unnatural or irregular desires in so strikingly virile a figure; there was little incentive for him to curtail his worst excesses. Yet he had succeeded in an endeavor he could not have desired for its own sake, where Fitz, on his first foray into passionate and genuine love, anticipating the certain victory due to his character and position, had suffered ignominious defeat. "Then he's accomplished more than I have," Fitz said. "Who is the girl's family?"

"Oh, nobody you'd know," Verney said. "Mother was my father's mistress after Mama died. But her father was a gentleman. Jack Lewis, second son of the Sussex Lewises. Officer in a respectable infantry regiment. Died in India a while back."

"And you twitted me about marrying sisters to friends," Fitz said.

"Phyllida is not my sister," Verney said, looking pained. "Everyone thinks it, but she's the image of Captain Lewis."

"Still, not exactly a connection to boast of," Fitz said.

"Best Carrington could get, though, given his rather stringent terms," Pierce said. "Really, did very well for himself. Whatever the failings of her relations, Mrs. Carrington is a true lady, in every sense of the word."

"I take it you have been contemplating matrimony, Darcy," Monkton said. "Wait, let me guess." He paused for several long drawn-out seconds, then snapped his fingers. "I have it! The witty, pretty, ethereal Miss Bent, younger sister of the one from whom you rescued your *dear* Charles over the winter."

"*Do* stop calling her that," Fitz said. "Besides, she was most unbending at our last encounter."

"Wouldn't have you?" Pierce said. "Not surprised. Ladies these days are too sharp by half. Know all the disreputable secrets of every man in society. It's our own fault, really. We think we're so vigilant and discreet, hiding in our exclusive madge club here, when the fact is the Brotherhood of Philander has been a byword over half a century for every form of unspeakable vice—"

"Oh, give it a rest," Verney said.

"Yes, really," Monkton said. "If you've discovered a religious vocation, by all means divest yourself of your worldly possessions and ask your brother the duke for a living, but spare us the sermons, here of all places. I admit, Darcy, I'm intrigued as to what led a penniless provincial to turn down a man of your not inconsiderable fortune, not to mention impressive figure. Not to mention *Pemberley*. Good God! The woman must be mad! Have to say, Darcy, you're well out of it. The only thing worse than being married to a woman is being married to a madwoman."

"I'll have you know," Fitz said, "that Miss Bennet is a model of good sense and propriety. Her reasons for turning me down, even if mistaken, were based on the noblest of motives and all to her credit. Damn it to hell—I've behaved like a fool and an ass and a pompous, overbearing boor."

"Couldn't have said it better myself," Monkton murmured.

"Don't push it, Monkton," Fitz said. "I'll make you eat your words yet."

"Wouldn't mind eating something of *yours*, Darcy," Monkton said, moving to stand in front of Fitz, his hips at eye level, rocking back and forth ever so slightly. "Something meatier than words. In fact, I rather think we're overdue for a rematch, wouldn't you say? It might be a more even contest this time, what with Carrington occupied elsewhere."

Fitz almost blushed. It had taken him all this time to remember, and only Monkton's lewd performance had put him in mind of it. He held out his hand. "I'm sorry, Sylly. My conduct during my last visit was unpardonable. It's kind of you to overlook it."

"Hardly. Just want to get my own back."

"Well, that's all over with," Fitz said. "From now on I'm giving that up."

"What do you mean? Are you resigning your membership?"

The words came to Fitz like a blinding, Road-to-Damascus revelation. "Yes. That's the answer." He stood up and moved toward the door. "Thank you for helping me see my way clearly."

"Wait a minute," Monkton said. "It's not that easy. You still owe me satisfaction."

"Oh, you had satisfaction," Fitz said in his purring voice. "Several times, as I recall."

"Don't mean to intrude," Pierce said, sounding even more officious than usual, "but quitting the Brotherhood is not a simple transaction."

"I've paid my dues for the full year," Fitz said. "I won't be requesting any remittance of the unused portion, if that's what you're implying."

"It's not the money," Verney said. "It's, well, you see, we rarely have *announced* resignations."

"What about Carrington?" Fitz asked. "Now that he's married he must have quit."

"*Au contraire*," Monkton said. "That was one of his stipulations—not to change his way of life."

"That's absurd," Fitz said. "He can't expect to have it both ways."

"That's exactly what he expects," Pierce said. "Pity you missed all the past month's excitement—although it's not too late to get in on the wager."

"You a member of White's?" Verney asked, ignoring Fitz's scowl of disapproval. "They're laying ten to one odds against Carrington's getting his wife with child by summer. Maybe twenty to one. A sure thing, and there's still time to place a bet."

"*Against* Carrington?" Fitz was diverted despite his distaste. "Surely the odds are in his favor, especially if it's a love match."

Monkton sniggered. "Oh, the world is so ignorant of these things, they confuse buggery with incapability and a sodomite with a hermaphrodite."

"If I were not already determined to resign, that atrocious equation has convinced me," Fitz said. "But surely Carrington isn't the first Philanderer to marry."

"Of course not," Verney said. "Lord Isham, our illustrious founder, is married, as Carrington reminded us. And there must have been dozens since."

"I can't think of anyone," Witherspoon said.

"Oh, there've been any number over the years," Monkton said. "They don't usually burst in here and make a big to-do, that's all. Just slip quietly into limbo and no one ever hears from 'em again. Sad, really."

"What about that fellow Tilney," Pierce said. "Henry Tilney, younger son of the late general. That was one. Before your time, Darcy, almost ten years ago now. He married some country girl, from Wiltshire, I think, much the way you've been going on about. Took up a family living, had a litter of children. Doesn't come up to town much these days, but seems quite happy, for some unfathomable reason."

"Frankly, I don't know what any of this has to do with me," Fitz said. "I am, unfortunately, unlikely to be married, but I am quitting this delightful association. Gentlemen, I can honestly say that my five years in the Brotherhood have been, if not an unmitigated pleasure, at least rarely dull. Now if you will excuse me, I will say farewell, and I don't see how you can stop me."

"Don't you?" Monkton said, scuttling around Fitz and blocking the door.

Verney stood up from the card table and stood shoulder to shoulder with Monkton. Pierce shrugged out of his coat and waistcoat, rolled up his shirtsleeves, and stood on Monkton's other side. Even Witherspoon, looking both scared and eager, loosened his cravat and took Pierce's arm, standing a little behind his lover but tucking in his chin and setting his usually bowed lips into the nearest thing to a fierce expression he could effect.

"What's all this?" Fitz asked. "Some sort of receiving line?"

"Precisely," Verney said.

"It's a little matter of the initiation," Monkton said, hissing out the last word. "Or rather, un-initiation."

Fitz shook his head. "I have no idea what you're talking about."

"Now look here," Pierce said. "You can't pretend you weren't told. I was one of the attendants, you may recall, at your initiation. Very moving ceremony. You swore never to betray a Brother and the oath was sealed by sacred acts of the body."

"Yes," Fitz said. "That oath was binding. I am a man of honor and I keep my word. To suggest that I have any intention of forswearing myself, of betraying men with whom I've been in the most intimate alliance for the past five years and more—it's enough to—"

"Enough to what?" Monkton said, pushing forward until his nose was level with Fitz's neck. "What is it enough to make you do, Darcy?"

"Nothing," Fitz said. "All I want is to take Charles and go back to Pemberley and try to reclaim some measure of honesty and civility."

"Very admirable," Monkton said. "And just as soon as you've convinced us all of your good intentions you can be on your way." Like the others, he had stripped off his upper garments and unbuttoned his flap, so that Fitz faced an obscene phalanx, bare-chested and with pump handles at the ready.

"George," Pierce said in an undertone, "you are not required to participate. No one will blame you."

"But I want to," Witherspoon said. "I can't bear the thought of Darcy leaving and never having had the pleasure—never knowing . . . I—I never even had a chance to paint his picture. But only if you're sure you don't mind." He looked imploringly into Pierce's disapproving face. "Please, Davey. You know I only care for you. It's just that he's so—so fine-looking. And so big."

It dawned on Fitz what the "un-initiation" ceremony was. And he did now vaguely remember hearing references when he joined the Brotherhood to an obscure "penalty" for resigning.

He contemplated telling them all he had changed his mind and just slipping quietly away into limbo—or Pemberley. But they had closed in on him, drawing off his clothes, while the beautiful George Witherspoon, if not quite up to the standard of his namesake Wickham, nevertheless looking most graceful and appetizing, was doing some interesting things with his mouth. Good old Sylly, slippery and agile as always, had positioned himself in a most receptive attitude at Fitz's feet, and even stalwart Verney and stern little Pierce were getting into the spirit of the occasion . . .

Fitz gave up his protests and, allowing the others to drag him down on the thick carpet, swore some very active oaths to all of them, several times during the course of a long afternoon, that wherever he went after this, and for the rest of his life, he would always be, in his heart, a true Brother.

Seventeen

"GOD, DARCY, WE will miss you," Monkton said, lifting his head with effort from somewhere in the middle of the entangled bodies. "Must you resign?"

"Suppose it's necessary," Pierce said, sitting up shakily over to one side of the mélange. "Nasty rumors following you?"

"Nasty people," Fitz said. He moved his legs—or tried to—but found that some faces and a backside or two were weighing him down. "Did I ever tell you about George Wickham?"

A collective groan rose from the assembled heap.

"The well-hung steward's son, companion of your youth?" Monkton said. "Whose compliance with your indorsings has turned to a preference for blackmail? I think we can all recite the particulars from memory. But that's an advantage of this mausoleum—companionship *and* protection, especially from those sorts of people. Come on, Darcy. Have a drink and reconsider."

"I could use one," Fitz said, grunting as he freed his limbs and felt the strained muscles. "But I won't change my mind." He looked around for his drawers and pantaloons.

"You know, come to think of it, I have encountered that

fellow more than once, lurking around here," Verney said a few minutes later, sitting half dressed with the others, knocking back a restorative brandy or two. "Very beautiful. Face like an angel and a slim, perfectly proportioned body. And *very* active, if you know what I mean."

"Yes, we can imagine," Monkton said. "But please don't let me cut short your charming attempts at description."

"George Wickham?" Fitz said. "Here? He's stationed in Hertfordshire, in the militia."

"Well, yes, he was wearing a red coat," Verney said. "Until I got him out of it." The others guffawed.

"What was Wickham doing here?" Fitz said. "And how was he let in?"

"But I thought—we're allowed to bring in military officers as guests. Aren't we?" Witherspoon asked in a worried tone.

Pierce, his eyes narrowing, said, "Yes, George, that's the one exception to the rule of closed membership. But I don't see how it concerns you."

Fitz scowled. "Leave Witherspoon alone, Pierce, for God's sake. You know damned well he's as faithful to you as Patient Griselda—and as obedient. But you see how such laxity in the rules is an invitation to abuse. Just what were you doing with Wickham, Verney?"

The others laughed even louder than before, adding whistles and some rather rude noises.

"What do you think?" Verney said. "Dipping my wick, with Wick."

"I'm quite in earnest," Fitz said. "The man is dangerous. He's not the innocent he appears."

"Oh, he's not innocent," Verney said. "Very practiced indeed."

"At extortion," Fitz said. "He's had me by the short hairs for years."

"Ooooh," Monkton said. "How exciting."

Fitz drained his glass and stood up. "On that note, fellows, I'll say that, while it's been an *exciting* five years, I'm off to the quiet life of Derbyshire without regret." He found his shirt and his waistcoat, made a careless job of the cravat, and shook hands all around, allowing himself a tender kiss with Monkton. "Sylly, my dear, I hope someday you'll know the same happiness I share with Charles. Until then, I wish you a less perilous road to pleasure."

"Thank you, Darcy," Monkton said, "but I'd sooner follow Carrington's example than bury myself alive in the country like you."

"As for the rest," Fitz said, "I leave you with a warning. George Wickham is treacherous and he could ruin a lot of lives. Not just ours, but innocent people. Ladies."

It was only after he had gone that Verney remembered. "You know, that Wick fellow tried to run off with Darcy's sister. Sounded sort of humorous the way he told it, but not really funny at all, when you think of it. She was only fifteen."

FITZ SENT HIS man out and lay back in the warm water. God, it felt good! Like a baptism, cleansing himself of his sins and starting fresh, pure. He ought to have bathed at the Brotherhood, but this afternoon's ceremony had left him with such a desire to be out of there as quickly as possible that he had simply thrown his clothes on over all the dirt and dashed home. He opened his eyes at the knock at the door and motioned Charles in, taking his friend's hand as he knelt beside the tub and kissing the palm.

"What's brought this on?" Charles asked, his heart fluttering at the wet, tickling sensation.

"I know I've been an insupportable tyrant these past months,"

Fitz said in an unusually low, soft voice. "Will you allow me to attempt to make amends?"

"You've been a very good friend to me," Charles said. "*I'm* the one who should apologize for having been so depressed, but I promise you I'm more cheerful now."

"That is just like you," Fitz said, "all Christian forgiveness. But I understand something of what you've been going through, and I'm appalled at how unfeeling I've been."

"You were only looking after me," Charles said. "I oughtn't to have been so cold."

"You were unhappy," Fitz said. "It's the hardest thing in the world, to open your heart to a lady and have all your most tender, passionate sentiments thrown back in your face."

"Fitz! Did something happen at Rosings? Never say Miss de Bourgh rejected you! I won't believe it."

"Anne? What put that idea in your head?" Fitz flicked water at Charles, making him laugh and draw back. "No, it was very quiet at Rosings, little in the way of company, and I was left to my own devices. It gave me a lot of time to think—too much time—and I remembered a similar affair to yours. A clever, pretty young lady, who made me the target for her arrows of wit. I thought she was flirting but it turned out she simply didn't care for me. I was too young, you see, to tell the difference and I poured out all my feelings of love. And she said I had not behaved in a gentlemanlike manner and—"

"You? Not behave like a gentleman? I don't believe it. She can't have been a lady."

"It was a long time ago, Charles. My manners were too impetuous and youthful. But she was a lovely, genuine lady." Fitz stood up, dripping water over the sheets on the floor and flipping more out of his hair, and grabbed Charles in a close embrace when he handed him the towel.

"Dash it, Fitz!" Charles said, writhing in mock terror. "You're all wet!"

"So will you be," Fitz said, "if you continue to struggle like that." He bent Charles backward over the tub in a kiss but held him securely and let him up again, almost as dry as before.

Charles looked down at his stained waistcoat and smiled. What a pleasure to have Fitz his old self again, laughing and playful, as he had not been since the visit to Rosings—to say truly, as he had not been since the sudden remove to town from Netherfield. A ruined waistcoat was a fair price to pay to have his friend back. "Fitz, why are you telling me this now? I'm sorry you had your heart broken in the past, but I never had the chance even to try with Miss Bennet."

"First, because remembering my torment has strengthened my belief that it was kinder to spare you from repeating my error; and second, to say that while I may not have appeared to sympathize with your sufferings, I do. In Sparta, if a boy failed at a test of military prowess, the older one, his lover, was punished for not teaching him better."

"How cruel! But why should you be punished before I've done anything?"

"As the best method for ensuring that you will benefit from my experience. I was chastised severely for my lapse, and I can help you avoid the same mistake."

There was a noble purpose in all this, Fitz felt, that justified the subterfuge of putting his recent trial in a fictional, distant past. Every time he recalled Elizabeth's accusations of interference between her sister and Charles, Fitz had a feeling of discomfort—almost, he thought sometimes, of *guilt*. But he had done what he believed to be right for Charles, even if the acts themselves bordered on deceit, and Elizabeth's rejection proved the accuracy of his judgment after all. If *he* had believed his love returned, who had years of experience to call on, what misapprehension might poor Charles have been laboring under with the sister?

Beyond that, it was instructive to have undergone the very ordeal he had spared Charles. Like an ascetic monk living in a strict order, Fitz had gained strength of character from the denial of the flesh. But Charles was not so robust. He would more likely starve to death from deprivation than derive moral improvement. Fitz could make a sermon out of his humiliation; but like a lesson from Scripture, it was most useful when the particular was enlarged into more general application as a parable.

"I do appreciate all your concern for me, Fitz," Charles said. "But now I'd as soon forget about it."

"Very wise. It's like having a tooth drawn. The greatest pain is in the anticipation. Once the worst is over, you see it was no such agony as you built up beforehand in your mind."

"Well, I wouldn't say that," Charles said. "It really was very painful. But I am recovered now. Truly."

Later that night, after a companionable if intimate dinner—no guests, and only Georgiana at home, Charles crept along the corridor and scratched at Fitz's door. Instead of the usual dark and silent room, he was welcomed by a naked Fitz holding a candle, his muscular form casting distorted shadows against the walls. "It's like *The Mysteries of Udolpho*," Charles said. "Underground passageways, specters . . ."

"Oh, not you too," Fitz said with a groan. "I had hoped to be spared talk of ladies' novels in my own home."

"Surely Georgiana has read it," Charles said. "Caroline and Louisa exclaimed over it and talked about it so much I feel as if I read it myself. I should think just about every lady in England has read it."

"My sister has more sense than most ladies in England," Fitz said. "But never mind. Come to bed and let's forget about ladies and their foolishness for one night." He led Charles to sit on the side of the bed, helped him off with his nightshirt and knelt between his naked legs. Perhaps because he was tired, sated with the afternoon's excess, Fitz felt no urgency, savoring the view from below before pressing his face against Charles's furry stomach and nuzzling the stiff cock that rose at his nearness, quivering and seeming to reach for his attention. It occurred to Fitz that while he had always enjoyed the sense of mastery attendant on the act, there was a simple satisfaction to be derived from putting the other's pleasure ahead of one's own. "You have been a very brave boy," he said, "and I think you deserve your favorite treat."

"What became of the notion that I'm a man?" Charles said.

"Even a man is entitled to compensation for a difficult task accomplished," Fitz said. "In the military they award prize money for cities taken and ships captured."

"But I have given up something," Charles said, "not taken anything."

"The hardest fight of all," Fitz said. He put his lips over the head of Charles's cock, felt the thrill as his beloved clenched the muscles of his thighs and buttocks and began to shake.

"And the best sort of prize," Charles said, his voice fading out as he was lost in the sensation.

"Indeed," Fitz murmured, taking his mouth away for one glorious prolonged moment of triumph, "a prize that can be shared, as was the battle." He suffered a surge of fear, knowing he had betrayed himself.

But Charles was too caught up in the agreeable sensations to notice. "Oh, Fitz." He sighed with delight as his cock was engulfed. "Oh, Fitz, you are good to me."

After their first passion was spent, as the men lay in a loose embrace, Fitz asked, "How would you like to spend the summer with Georgiana and me at Pemberley—and your sisters, and Hurst of course."

"We'd be honored. Are you sure it won't be any bother?"

"I only wish it were," Fitz said, "so that I could offer you something more substantial in the way of reparation."

"Honestly, Fitz, I can't imagine why you're so agitated. If you're thinking of that silliness back during the winter, that night you came home from the ball, really, I'm the one who should apologize. Like a greensick girl with the vapors, you called it. I promise you that's all over with."

"Charles, my dear, you don't owe me your favors. I have been far too cavalier about your acquiescence, when I ought to have been grateful."

"You needn't act like you're courting me," Charles said. "You've always said it's easier between friends. Lord, I missed you those weeks you were away! It was very lonely at Hurst's, despite all their fashionable acquaintances, and Caroline was forever trying to inveigle your sister and me into some dreary party or other." He let his hand wander innocently down Fitz's side until his fingertips were just brushing his friend's flaccid cock. "What's the matter, Fitz? Don't you want me anymore?"

Fitz grabbed the wandering hand and held it away from their entwined bodies as he kissed Charles's mouth. "It's a good thing you don't require courting, my dear, because it seems I lack the necessary address. I merely need a short rest before the next round. Had a rather strenuous day."

"Thought you said you were having a day of leisure."

"Things came up unexpectedly," Fitz said. He raised one eyebrow. "Why don't you give me a hand? Maybe something else will come up."

"Perhaps I could try being the man this time," Charles said with a nervous laugh. "What do you say, Fitz?"

"Charles," Fitz said in his sternest voice. "That is a serious error and I cannot let it stand. You are not a surrogate for a woman. You are my friend because you are a man, and you are *always* a man to me. We share the purest form of love, one that can exist solely between men—disinterested love whose only object is its own fulfillment, that looks for no advantage of money or condition."

"I'm sorry, Fitz," Charles said. "I know you've said this, or something similar, many times, but sometimes it just feels like sport. Fucking. It's not some sacred ritual, and I don't see why we can't take turns."

"Dear Charles. The physical side of our love ought not to be dismissed or undervalued. It is how we, as mortal beings, with bodies as well as minds, demonstrate our love one to another. But we must never forget the underlying principle. I can only assume that your opinions have been warped by those of the uneducated and the unintelligent, who coarsen and pervert all the highest ideals they are incapable of comprehending."

"I did tell you it was dashed dull at Hurst's," Charles said. That provoked a smile, he was glad to see.

"You certainly understated the dangers of your situation." Fitz lay back and put his hands behind his head. "Now, what I want to know is, can't a man have some help with his trouble?"

"STOP IT, GEORGE!" Lydia Bennet pushed Wickham away and swiped at him with her fan, deliberately missing.

George grinned, stepped back and moved to her other side. "Stop what?" he whispered, pulling her left tit from her gown and fastening his mouth on it. God, she was big for sixteen!

"Oh!" Lydia moaned and trembled against the tree. "Oh, Wick! You'll have me all tumbled and tousled!"

"I'll do my best," George said. "You know you like it."

"Of course I like it," Lydia said. "Who wouldn't like it? But Wick, I don't want the others to know."

"Hmm?" George let go of her and looked into her face. It was frightening how she resembled her sister at the oddest moments. "Know what?"

"Silly! That we love each other."

"I see," George said. "You want to be free to go on flirting with all the other officers."

"It doesn't mean anything, Wick. You know I only want you. But I have to be careful. Harriet Forster was so very kind to invite me to stay with her and the colonel. If it had been up to my father, I wouldn't even be here in Brighton. But I can't let anyone know what we're going to do, not just yet."

"What are we going to do?" George asked. He took a quick, careful glance over his shoulder, saw no one approaching, and, using the toe of his boot, hiked up her skirt far enough to get his hand under. "Something like this?"

Lydia squealed with delight and helped, standing on one foot and bracing her knee on his hip. "Oh! Oh, Wick! I think—I think I'm going to—oh! *Oh! Oh!*"

George nearly lost his balance as she slumped against him, still shuddering, her cunt in full spate. "Steady, girl," he said. He freed his hand, managing to wipe it almost clean against her petticoat.

"There you are!" Mrs. Forster appeared as if materializing from the sea. "Come on, you two lovebirds. The dancing's about to start. You can't have Mr. Wickham all to yourself, Lydia."

Letting Mrs. Forster go ahead, they walked slowly back to the camp, the faint sounds of the music growing louder. "I could have you all to myself if we were married," Lydia whispered.

"Aren't you too young to be thinking of marriage?"

"I'm sixteen. It would be the greatest fun imaginable to be married before any of my sisters."

"But to give up all your freedom before you've even been out."

"I don't need freedom if I'm with you, Wick. Don't you want to?"

"You know what I want," George said, nuzzling her ear and putting his hand down the front of her gown. "Can't get enough of these luscious sugar plums." He ought to be careful, but what was a man supposed to do when a girl just laid herself down in front of him, spread her legs, and begged to be ravished. *What?*

"You could get enough if I was your wife. We could do it all the time, whenever we liked, and not have to worry about being seen."

That was a joke, George thought. Lydia never gave a damn about being seen. In fact, he suspected she would much prefer to have an audience, the larger and more varied the better. *He* was the one who didn't like to be seen, making do with this crude paste bauble because he was thwarted of the diamond. Elizabeth had made it very clear that she had learned the truth from Darcy during her visit to Rosings. At least Darcy's version of the truth. And for some reason Elizabeth had believed it this time. Probably because George wasn't there to contradict Darcy's harsh accusations. Imagine holding a grudge over a bit of boyish arse fucking. That was Darcy all over: petty, stingy, and prudish. But lusty. George had to give him that.

They had reached the regiment's camp now, and George allowed Lydia to be swept off by Pratt for a reel. He stood back in the shadows, away from the light of the torches, avoiding the melting, eager looks of the other girls. Here there were plenty of men to go around; no girl need sit down for lack of a partner.

Brighton was certainly an improvement over Meryton, and a necessary one. The regiment's new posting couldn't have come at a more opportune moment. God! It had been a near-run thing after Miss King's family had whisked her home to Yorkshire—all those merchants clamoring for George's nonexistent money to pay their cheating, racked-up, exorbitant bills. He'd had to wheedle and beg the other officers to do his shopping for him those last tedious weeks. And as for the so-called debts of honor—George preferred not to think of the subterfuges and humiliations he'd had to stoop to. Those creditors were no-nonsense country squires who wouldn't be fobbed off with excuses but enjoyed using their fists and preferred breaking a few bones over more conventional methods of extracting payment. He had hoped to recoup his losses among his fellow officers, but all that had accomplished was to accumulate yet another string of debts. Seems the image of the lax, drink-befuddled officer was just one more myth. Bunch of sharps, every last one of them—and damned few gentlemen willing to forgo payment in the interest of comradeship.

The one problem with Brighton was there was too much competition. The place teemed with officers—regulars as well as militia—guards and riflemen in all the best regiments wearing the smartest uniforms. A junior officer in a red coat was just one of hundreds. And most of the women were their counterparts, adventuresses and fancy whores. No respectable heiress would be allowed within five miles of this den of iniquity, this Hell-Fire Club by the sea.

"Not dancing?" Denny joined George by the fence. "Wouldn't hurt to be seen with someone else occasionally, Wick, if you catch my meaning."

"Hard to miss, old fellow. But I can't see it's any of your business."

"Well, you know, Wick, it's becoming pretty obvious that

you and Miss Bennet are an item, as they say. Even Colonel Forster is beginning to look uncomfortable on the subject."

"What if we are? No one takes these Brighton flirtations seriously."

"They do if it turns into more than a flirtation. Seems to me you've already gone a good ways past that."

"Listen, Denny. Keep a lid on things for another week or ten days. At the end of it, shouldn't be a matter of interest to anyone."

"What do you mean? Don't tell me you're running out on us so soon. You still owe some of the fellows for those purchases back in Meryton."

"Including you, Denny, although you're too polite to dun me directly. Look, here's an earnest of my good intentions." George scrounged an old receipt from his pocket and a stub of pencil and scrawled a promise. "You've been a damned good friend, Denny. It was decent of you to bring me in, but I'd say my welcome in the regiment is just about worn out by now, wouldn't you?"

"Ah, Wick. All it takes is to stand a few rounds, a few of the old debts settled, and you'll be in everyone's good graces again."

"Yes. That's the difficult part, though, isn't it?"

The reel ended and Lydia returned like iron to its lodestone without waiting for the second dance of the set.

Denny bowed. "Miss Bennet, may I request the honor of being your next partner?"

"Oh, hello, Mr. Denny. I might be persuaded, if you were to bring me a glass of refreshment." Lydia's words were perfunctory and she turned away as if dismissing a servant. "Aren't you dancing, Wick? Are you tired?"

"No, love," he said. "Just don't fancy a lesser partner after the best."

"Flatterer," Lydia said, smacking him with her fan, hitting him pretty damned hard. "Flirt! I think you just like to watch, hoping some of the sluts aren't wearing petticoats and you can see through in the torchlight."

"You caught me out, Lyd," he said. He wrested the fan from her grasp as she was bringing it down for another blow and threw it out on the sand, putting his hand over her mouth to silence her protests. "But I'd rather look at you, although I can do without any more thumping." He put his arm around her and pulled her close, pressing her against him and letting her feel the erection. No reason for her to know it was caused by memories of her sister.

"Oh, Wick," she said, sighing and cupping her hand over it. "Let's go away together. Please."

"Temptress," George said. "How will I keep my hands off you?"

"Why should you?" she said, genuinely puzzled. She stroked him through his breeches until he was ready to explode, removing her hand at just the opportune moment. How did the bitch *know* such things? Born to it, George supposed, as a cat to sneaking and a horse to running.

"Oh God, Lyd," George said, groaning and bending over with the pain. "You're going to kill me one of these days."

"Not if we get married," she said in a deceptively sweet voice. "I'll do anything you like then, all night long—and all day too." She opened her lips in a slack, liquid O and circled the tip of her tongue slowly around the perimeter.

George remembered his last conversation with Elizabeth, his desperate hope that all was not lost, that she had not succumbed to Darcy's clever misrepresentations. "In essentials, he is very much what he ever was," she had said. And so cold. Never could he have imagined her capable of such icy detachment. Downright frigid. To *him*, to her soul mate. He thought of Elizabeth in Lydia's place, using her tongue like that, and he lost control, discharging in his breeches like one of those shameless halfwits in Bedlam that people paid to watch and mock.

"Now see what you've made me do," George said, forcing Lydia's hand against the wet stain.

"Shocking!" She laughed and wriggled in George's grip, but didn't actually attempt to remove her hand. "When we're married, we can be as debauched as you like."

"As *you* like," he said, waiting for the hypocritical denials that never came. He gave her credit for that much. If men were dogs, always sniffing at arse and cunt, most women were whores. What made them hot wasn't a man's prick but his purse. But Lydia was an honest slut. She wanted George's cock as much as he wanted to give it to her, and she knew all about his lack of money. She was a drab but she didn't pretend to be pure. Unlike her sister, who teased and hinted and then, like all the rest, sold herself to the highest bidder.

That was it, George thought. Darcy must have made Elizabeth an offer. But if he had, the whole world would have heard of it, that a Miss Bennet had snagged the greatest prize in Derbyshire. And if not, had Darcy really prevailed on her to surrender without marriage? Not from what George thought he knew of Elizabeth. But what, then? What, short of marriage, could have led her to change her opinion? How could Darcy have overcome his stony reserve and divulged his deepest secrets to anyone, much less an innocent young lady?

"Come on, Wick," Lydia said. "Dance with me."

"I can't. Not like this." He motioned to his stained uniform. "Besides, you promised Denny."

"Then we'll just have to stay out of sight." She took his hand and led him away from the dancing and the fires, into the scrub that separated the wall from the strand. They found a secluded spot, sheltered from the wind, and settled down, Lydia leaning in the crook of his arm. She was much of a height with him and probably outweighed him by a stone or even two. He let her have her way, unbuttoning him and taking his prick out and fondling it. He shut his eyes, imagining *her.* It was not so very difficult. They had the same dark hair, the same liveliness. Even the eyes had a similar shape, especially if one didn't look too close. "Do you like that, Wick?" she asked again and again, rubbing and stroking. "Do you like that?"

"Yes, love," he said. Safer than using the wrong name by not thinking. And it was getting very hard to think. When she put her mouth on him it was all he could do not to make the great error. *Elizabeth*, he thought. He imagined her sweet little breasts and her tiny mouth. Could she even fit her mouth around him like this? *Oh, my love. Lizzy.* "Liz—" he murmured before correcting himself just in time. "Lydia."

Eighteen

Pemberley, Derbyshire. August 1812

GEORGIANA DARCY SCRATCHED at the door of her brother's dressing room. "Fitz, what is the matter?" she said. "I thought Miss Elizabeth Bennet was to dine with us."

Fitz paused in the act of changing his pantaloons for leather breeches, and sent his man to fetch his riding boots. "I'm sorry, Georgie. Miss Bennet and her aunt and uncle have had some bad news and must return to town immediately."

Georgiana came into the room despite her brother's state of partial undress. "Oh, I am sorry. Is it a death?"

"No, not so bad as that."

"Is somebody ill?"

"Georgie, please don't press. It's not the sort of thing one can talk about—I promised Miss Bennet, and it would not be proper in any event. But she is perfectly healthy and no one has died." He added under his breath, "Although someone will *wish* he had died when I catch up with him."

"Who?" Georgiana asked.

"Who what?" Fitz said. "Really, Georgie, you oughtn't to be in the room when I'm dressing. You're not a child anymore."

"Please don't scold, Fitz," Georgiana said. "*You* haven't been a child for the last ten years, and there's nothing to see that I haven't seen a hundred times before. And who will wish he had died?"

"Someday those sharp ears of yours will hear something you'll wish you hadn't," Fitz said.

"You sound just like my old governess," Georgiana said. "And I always hear things I wish I hadn't, because people persist in saying things they shouldn't. Especially Miss Bingley. Who will wish he had died?"

"If you must know, George Wickham. There, are you happy now?"

"Oh my goodness! But how does this affect Miss Bennet?"

Fitz sat down on the bed and waved away his man, who was attempting to enter with the boots. "Very well, Georgie. Come sit beside me and I'll tell you. I promised Miss Bennet I would say nothing to anybody, but because of your history I think she won't mind that I make this one exception. You must give me your word that this will go no further." He held out his hand. "I want your solemn oath, Georgiana."

Georgiana took her brother's hand, tears of indignation stinging her eyes. "Oh, Fitz, this isn't necessary. You just agreed I'm not a child."

"So I did. I don't have a lot of time to spare, so I'll have to keep it short. Miss Bennet has received a letter from her eldest sister saying that her youngest sister, Lydia, has run off with Wickham and is living with him in town. Her father has been searching for them without success and now her uncle will want to help. And of course they won't be able to find him, and even if they do they won't have the means to force him to marry her."

"Oh, Fitz, how dreadful! But I thought the Miss Bennets had very small portions. Why would Mr. Wickham run away with one of them? I suppose he truly loves her." The last sentence was expressed on a sigh and a lowered voice, whether of shame or longing Fitz was too preoccupied to discern.

"Love? Wickham? My dear Georgie, the man is incapable of the sentiment."

"I don't understand," Georgiana said.

"It does pass all understanding, doesn't it? Let's just say that men like him are not always governed by the rational desires of the mind but are often at the mercy of their lower body's instincts."

"That's an edifying thought to share with your sister," Charles said, knocking at the door but pushing in without waiting for a reply. "Especially given the condition of *your* lower body at the moment, Fitz. Georgie, do you really think you should be here when your brother is dressing?"

"Oh, stop it, Charles," Georgiana said. "You're just hoping I'll come in on you when *you're* dressing."

Fitz glanced from his sister to his friend and back again. "Since when are you two so familiar?"

"Since we decided always to be friends and never to marry," Georgiana said.

"Is that not somewhat extreme?" Fitz asked. "Might you not regret your chastity as old age approaches, say at twenty-five?"

"Each other," Charles said. "We resolved not to marry each other. I'm sorry, Fitz. I know the scheme is dear to your heart, but—"

"Oh, never mind that now. Listen, Charles, I was just explaining to Georgie. I've become aware of a serious situation and I am forced to dash to town tomorrow. You mustn't tease Georgie to death to find out what it is. It concerns Miss Bennet's family and I don't want it bruited all over Derbyshire and beyond."

"Well, thank you very much for your low opinion of my ability to keep my mouth shut," Charles said.

Fitz smiled. "In the presence of my sister, I'll deny myself the pleasure of the appropriate reply to that. I'll merely say, Charles, that I'm sure you intend to be the soul of discretion, but your sisters have a way of worming the truth out of one that could put the Foreign Office to shame. You know, if they were willing to employ women, Caroline might find her true vocation."

"All right, Fitz. Enough of that joke, if you please," Charles said. "I can't believe you'll tell your sister and not me."

"My dear," Fitz said, "you mustn't take everything so to heart. The matter involves a certain person whom it would be better for Georgie not to hear about by chance. I thought it best to tell her now, myself. But it's no concern of yours."

"I see," Charles said. "It concerns Miss Bennet and therefore it cannot concern me. Might I not wish to express my sympathy to her in her trouble?"

"Miss Lydia Bennet," Fitz said.

"Oh," Charles said, looking oddly deflated.

"She's the youngest sister," Georgiana said.

"Yes, I remember," Charles said. "Big, noisy girl, always chasing after officers."

"Well, she caught one, finally," Fitz said. "And she's creating a wretched scandal for her family."

"Naturally I'm sorry for that," Charles said. "But I don't see how it's any business of yours, either, Fitz, or how you think you can help."

"Let me tell Charles, Fitz," Georgiana said. "I already told him about my—mistake."

"Georgiana," Fitz said in his sternest voice, "after your earlier protestations, that is a very strange confession. You did yourself no good service by breaking your understanding with Mr. Bingley. I hope this will be a lesson."

"Now see here, Fitz," Charles said. "That's quite enough of treating Georgie as if she were ruined, merely because she was deceived into accepting a marriage proposal from a fortune hunter. Could have happened to anybody. And nothing happened anyway."

"How delightful that you are privy to the entire escapade," Fitz said. His face had gone completely white and he was standing very still in a pose that Charles remembered from an incident in the early days of their friendship, when a peculiar person, much the worse for drink, had accosted the two of them in St. James's Park. "Georgiana," Fitz continued in frigid tones, "you may wish to reconsider your situation with regard to Mr. Bingley. Other men will be far less forgiving and might well conceive a disgust—"

"Stop it, Fitz," Charles said with surprising force.

Fitz turned at the sound, opened his mouth wide in something that was not a yawn and took several deep breaths, his chest heaving.

"You see, it's Mr. Wickham that Lydia has gone away with," Georgiana said.

"Wickham! But isn't he—that is—doesn't he—" Charles struggled against the awful tension in the room. His face worked and contorted with the heroic attempt not to laugh, but defeat was inevitable. "Lydia does look a bit like Elizabeth. Maybe he was confused in the dark."

Fitz took two short, controlled steps forward, almost like dancing, and raised his clenched fist. "I could call you out for that." He drew his arm back until the fist was beside his own ear, and took another hopping step slightly to Charles's left.

"No, Fitz!" Georgiana cried, pushing herself between the two men.

"Damn it, Georgie," Fitz said, lowering his arm. "You might have been hurt."

"I didn't want you to hit poor Charles. It's not fair when you're so much bigger."

"Thank you very much, Miss Darcy," Charles said. "As I have now been put in my place by two Darcys at once, I think it best to retire to the company of the other guests. And I sincerely apologize, Fitz. The news took me by surprise, that's all."

"Hell and damnation," Fitz said. He shook out his hand as if he had landed the intended punch and a couple more, and walked briskly around the room, shrugging his shoulders in a rolling motion and swinging his arms. "Georgie, I am truly sorry. It seems if anyone lacks discretion, it is I. Charles, I owe you satisfaction, and you may have it any way you wish, when I return from town."

"Never mind about that, Fitz. I know how you care for Georgie and I don't hold grudges for my own sake. But I think you'd better tell us the whole of this wretched business."

"All right, Charles. Let's get this over with. I'm in a hurry to make the arrangements with my steward, as I expect to be away at least a week, more likely two. George Wickham has indeed run off with Lydia Bennet, eccentric as that seems. They are living somewhere in town, unmarried, and her father is unable to locate them. Now do you see why I need to keep this quiet, and why I am the only person who can help?"

"Of course, Fitz," Charles said. "You know, it's a damned shame you can't tear yourself loose from that clinging vine."

"It seems he will be my responsibility to the grave," Fitz said. "Try as I will to wash my hands of him, if he persists in making messes, I'm the only one capable of cleaning them up."

"Assuming you can."

"Money, Charles. That's all it is with him. Now, if the two of you don't mind, I must finish dressing."

"I'VE NEVER SEEN Fitz so lose command over himself," Charles said. He sat with Georgiana in one of the unused bedchambers, digesting the shocking news before facing the censorious crowd of guests downstairs.

I have, Georgiana thought. When Fitz had "had words" with Mr. Wickham over their intended elopement. She was unable to share the memory with Charles; even after a year it was too painful.

"Although he was in a pretty bad way after his return from Rosings," Charles continued, perfectly capable of sustaining a one-sided conversation.

"Yes," Georgiana agreed. Where last summer's events had brought out the harsh, paternal side of him, asserting his rights over family and property, this time he had seemed like a rogue animal, divorced from all connections. Like an angry cat, balked of its prey, lashing its tail and wishing to pounce on something to tear apart with teeth and claws. For almost a month he had been terrifying. Georgiana had crept about the house, trying to keep from drawing his attention, the least little failing or misstep bringing down his wrath. He had even been out of temper with Mr. Bingley, not greeting him with a kiss at breakfast or going to his room at night. It was sad and disturbing to see a loving friendship diminish over time instead of strengthening, made all the worse for there being no reason for the change that Georgiana could see.

Then, somehow, Fitz had regained his composure, even a kind of contentment. By the time they were ready to remove to Pemberley for the summer he had been his old self, more like the kind, protective older brother she remembered from her childhood. Softer, more forgiving, not so sarcastic and disdainful as he had grown in recent years. "I wondered if he had fallen in love," she ventured to suggest.

"I say, you do have a pretty dismal notion of love," Charles said. "I suppose, after Wickham, that's only to be expected."

"I'd just as soon not hear that name again," Georgiana said. "But now I begin to comprehend your sister. Did you hear her yesterday? She was very droll on the subject of the militia leaving Hertfordshire, and how the Bennet family must feel the loss."

It had all begun to make sense at Pemberley. Fitz had gone on ahead by a day, to prepare for the rest of the party. When Georgiana arrived, the first words Fitz said to her were that Miss Elizabeth Bennet and her aunt and uncle were in the neighborhood, and instructing Georgiana on her duties as hostess when they called. As if she hadn't been acting as Fitz's hostess from the age of twelve. Between Fitz's almost boyish eagerness, and Miss Bingley's incessant censure, Georgiana had been nervous—no, terrified—about meeting Miss Bennet, convinced she would be provincial, sharp-tongued, possessed of neither beauty nor grace, and with a very high opinion of herself. But Miss Bennet turned out to suffer from none of these faults. She was positively charming. Younger than Miss Bingley, polite, clearly intelligent, and basically kind. You could see it in her face.

And the way Fitz looked at her. No wonder poor Miss Bingley lost all sense of discretion. She was the one who showed her ill breeding at every turn, while Miss Bennet had been a model of comportment. When Miss Bingley made her spiteful remark about the militia, Georgiana was so mortified she couldn't say a word, just stared at the floor, not comprehending why Caroline should wish to hurt her so, when she was still desperately hoping for at least one marriage into the family, if not two. But

Miss Bennet, almost as if she knew how painful the subject was to Georgiana, and sympathized without judging, adroitly changed the subject.

Wouldn't it be wonderful if Fitz were to marry her? Georgiana had become almost resigned to the idea that she and Caroline Bingley would be sisters-in-law, especially as Fitz seemed to regard it as inevitable. Georgiana's only escape then would be her own establishment, as Fitz had been promising before the events of last winter had overset everyone's plans. But a man only made a point of introducing a lady to his sister if he intended something serious. And if Fitz married Miss Bennet—oh, how perfect! It would be like having the older sister she had always wanted, someone to confide in, to advise her on all the things a brother couldn't, even as excellent a brother as Fitz . . .

"What a lucky chance," Charles said, as if reading her thoughts, "Miss Elizabeth Bennet traveling in Derbyshire at the same time we came to Pemberley. Eight months since we were at Netherfield, and now to meet again here." God, he thought, it was like something out of the Bible, a miracle or an apparition. He had never seen Fitz so—what was the word? Almost soft. Smiling, agreeable, making gentle, undemanding conversation. Until poor Caroline betrayed herself. Why couldn't she just accept the fact that Fitz preferred Miss Bennet to her? What man wouldn't? And then, what really got Charles thinking—if Fitz received Elizabeth and her relatives so graciously, who were just a town merchant and his wife, then perhaps he had revised his opinion of Charles's marrying into the family. Was it possible? For the first time in months, Charles allowed himself a glimmer of hope.

"Fitz was so eager to introduce us," Georgiana said, "I developed an absurd fear of her. He kept saying how witty and clever she is, and warning me not to hang back in the conversation, until I was terrified she'd bite my head off. But she has excellent manners and she's not frightening at all." She sighed, still stunned at the feeling of intense relief.

"Well, you see," Charles said, "she was very different when we knew her in Hertfordshire. She was the lady I told you about, always laughing at Fitz, and topping his epigrams with her own. But you'd never guess it from her behavior now. To my mind, much improved. More like her eldest sister, Jane."

As her dearest imaginings received confirmation of a sort, Georgiana began to comprehend how Charles could be so genuinely glad to see Elizabeth and yet oblivious to Fitz's attentions to her. "Is she the Jane you're in love with? The one Fitz doesn't want you to marry?"

"Well, yes," Charles said, smiling shyly like a girl. "But perhaps he's of a different mind now."

Georgiana shook her head. "I'm sorry, Charles. After what we've just learned, that will be impossible." She thought of Wickham with something approaching hatred, an emotion that, despite everything, would have been inconceivable in connection with him as recently as a week ago. Now he had ruined more than just one girl's future. He had destroyed so many people's happiness by this one careless act, six at least: hers, Fitz's, Charles's, and no fewer than three Miss Bennets—probably all five of them. Georgiana didn't know whether she wished Fitz to find Wickham and Lydia in town or not. Lydia's disgrace tainted her sisters and rendered them unsuitable for marriage to any respectable man. But a Miss Bennet *married* to Wickham was an even greater impediment to Fitz's marrying another one, because then they would be tied forever, brothers-in-law . . .

"What?" Charles said. "Why?" Seeing Georgiana's crushing embarrassment, he refrained from further questioning and was able to puzzle it out for himself. "Oh, that wouldn't matter to me. Ridiculous, as if Jane were responsible for her younger sister's foolishness. If you knew Jane you'd see what I mean." He recalled the previous day's revelatory conversations. "And look here. When Caroline was so hateful about Elizabeth, refusing to allow her any degree of beauty, and teased Fitz about having once admired her a little, what did Fitz say? Something about, 'that was only when he first knew her, because it was long since he had come to consider her as one of the handsomest women of his acquaintance.' Lord, that was marvelous! I wish I could come up with perfect set-downs like that unrehearsed."

Georgiana smiled but remained grave. "That was before we learned about Lydia," she reminded Charles.

"But he's going off to town to help," Charles said. "You heard him. He knows what Wickham is like, and he won't lay all the blame on poor Lydia."

"No," Georgiana said, "but he could never bring himself to be brother-in-law to Mr. Wickham."

"Of course not!" Charles exclaimed, swiveling in the chair to goggle at Georgiana's wild suggestion. "But it shouldn't matter to him if *I* am. You know, this visit of the Gardiners is the first time I saw him so friendly with people not of his level. He actually invited Mr. Gardiner to fish in the stream."

"That is unfair to Fitz," Georgiana said, accepting the fact that what was to her the most important aspect of the conversation was a dead end. "He is always civil, if not gracious."

"But he sneers at low connections and people in trade," Charles said. "I'm grateful that he befriended me, as I'm really nothing more than a wealthy tradesman's son."

"Now you're just hoping for a compliment on your gentlemanlike character," Georgiana said. "Fitz does not disdain anyone for his position in life, but only those whose manners are lacking. He confessed to me yesterday that he took Mr. and

Mrs. Gardiner for people of fashion at first, and I have to say I felt very easy in conversation with them."

"They certainly have better manners than a lot of people I know," Charles said. "Including members of my own family."

"You can say that," Georgiana said. "I dare not."

"ARE WE NOT to enjoy the great favor of Eliza Bennet's company for dinner?" Miss Bingley said as Georgiana and Charles entered the drawing room. "Mr. Darcy will be sorry to miss her sparkling wit and tanned complexion. Especially after informing us in the strongest terms yesterday how greatly he admires her beauty. Perhaps he's had a bit too much sun himself."

"Miss Bennet and her aunt and uncle have had to cut their tour short and leave for town," Georgiana said.

"*Have* they?" Miss Bingley said. "What a pity! And after timing their arrival in Lambton village so neatly to coincide with Mr. Darcy's at Pemberley. Only think if they had chosen the Lake District or the seaside for their little holiday instead, how differently things would have worked out. And now all for naught."

"Enough, Caroline," Charles said. "Surely you heard Miss Bennet explain. She and her aunt and uncle had originally planned to visit the Lakes, but Mr. Gardiner's business affairs necessitated a shorter trip, and that's how they settled on Derbyshire."

"Oh yes," Miss Bingley said. "That was a charming little speech, and she recited it most correctly. I especially liked the part about daring to visit Pemberley because they had been assured by people in the village that the master was away."

"Nobody knew my brother was coming that day," Georgiana said. "He only decided at the last minute."

"I do hope nothing has gone wrong with the uncle's business

now," Miss Bingley continued as if she hadn't heard. "What is it he does? A mercer? Or is he a clerk, perhaps at law? Oh no, that's the other uncle."

"Stop being such a cat, Caroline," Charles said. "It's really something very serious. Fitz is going to follow them tomorrow. *Oof*," he added as Georgiana elbowed him in the ribs.

"Really?" Caroline said in delighted tones. "Is it some kind of party? No, let me guess. It's an elopement, isn't it? They'll stop at a justice of the peace on the way to town and celebrate with a masquerade ball at Vauxhall Gardens."

"I'm sorry, Miss Bingley." Georgiana decided it was time to step in. "My brother expressly forbade me or Mr. Bingley to discuss the matter. I'm afraid we simply can't say another word about it. My brother will tell you what he can when he returns from consulting with his steward. Now, may I direct your attention to the fruit bowl? We have more of those lovely ripe peaches and nectarines, just picked from the greenhouse this morning, and a few early grapes."

"Very nicely done," Charles whispered. "You'll be a duchess a year after your coming out, I'll wager."

Nineteen

"NOW I UNDERSTAND," Elizabeth said. "Only now, after seeing his estate, and speaking with his housekeeper."

"Understand what?" Jane said.

"That it is virtue that makes a man attractive, just as much as a woman."

"Better to have learned that lesson late than never, I suppose," Jane said.

Back at Longbourn after the painfully truncated summer holiday, Elizabeth could barely bring herself to talk to anyone, even Jane. The memory of those visits to Pemberley, the magnificent reality surpassing anything imagination had supplied, and the revelation of Mr. Darcy's improved behavior, had begun a sequence of thoughts that sprouted up overnight. Like a mushroom after rain, without any planted seeds of hope or preparation of the soil with deliberation, the idea had bloomed, ripe and ready for harvesting, before she had even noticed new growth in a barren field. And then to have it all spoiled by Lydia. It was so absurd as to be funny—if the sudden destruction of carefully rebuilt prospects could be humorous. It was like laboring for years to restore a sacked city, only to have everything undone in an instant of natural disaster, an earthquake or a tidal wave. And all from the heedless act of a sixteen-year-old girl.

"Too late," Elizabeth said. "Mr. Darcy will want nothing more to do with us after Lydia's disgracing us all like this. I should not have revealed Lydia's shame, but I was caught by surprise. I had just received your letters when he arrived at the inn to escort us to Pemberley to dine." That was the most painful recollection. She squirmed with embarrassment even now, remembering how he had come into the dark little parlor at the moment of her taking in the contents of Jane's letter, how they had almost collided, he stooping slightly to pass under the low doorway, and she running after her aunt and uncle who had gone for a walk. How his sympathetic questions at her obvious distress had brought the whole story pouring out of her, coupled with the most unladylike tears, when she ought to have had the sense, if not the decency, to conceal such a scandal, something that reflected so poorly on her entire family it ought never to be mentioned. But no, she had held nothing back, not even Wickham's name—and look what it had gained her. His silence, probably from disgust, and his leaving her with but a look, whether of contempt or curiosity, no doubt appalled to have been on such intimate, even friendly terms with those contaminated by association.

"Selfish little bitch," she spat out, unclear even to her own mind, if she meant her sister or herself.

"Elizabeth!" Jane exclaimed. "I am ashamed of you, more than I am of Lydia. She is merely thoughtless and silly. You are becoming hard. It's not as if Mr. Darcy was going to ask you to marry him again, whatever Lydia did or did not do."

"But he was so different this time. So polite and benevolent.

Did I tell you how he conversed with my aunt and uncle? And escorted us all around the park? How he introduced me to his sister?"

"Yes, Lizzy. You told me at least ten times. I'm sorry, but I don't find it so very surprising that a gentleman showed good manners, and I honestly don't comprehend how you can think of yourself at a time like this. Poor Mama is sick with worry and—"

"And all the burden of her care falls on you," Elizabeth said. "I know I'm selfish. But when I think of how things might have turned out if only Papa had not let Lydia go to Brighton. We should have told people about Wickham."

"How?" Jane said. "Mr. Darcy wouldn't want his sister to be a subject of gossip."

"We could have told the other things, his debts and his gambling, and turning down the living in favor of three thousand pounds to study the law. And then not studying and leaving university. And blaming Mr. Darcy for his own extravagance."

"But that is merely spiteful, and allows no chance for his improvement," Jane said, repeating the arguments they had only half believed in the winter, when little but good was thought of Wickham and it hadn't mattered. "If his reputation is destroyed ahead of his arrival anywhere, he can never redeem himself or start fresh."

"That was our justification then," Elizabeth said. "But look at what our silence has accomplished. A sister ruined, and no hope now of ever getting decent husbands ourselves. I blamed Charlotte for being cold-blooded and stooping to a kind of prostitution. Now I see why she chose as she did."

"Mr. Collins again? Well, he is very happy not to be connected to us now."

"Lord, wasn't that a wonderful letter?" Elizabeth said, momentarily diverted. "Saying it was better for Lydia to have died, and writing all those phrases stolen from fusty old stage plays of a century ago."

"Lizzy, I can't take pleasure in anything to do with this."

"Nor can I, truly. Oh, Jane, you should have seen the park. It was ten miles around, and everything landscaped so well it looked entirely natural. Everyone—the maids, the menservants—spoke nothing but praise of Mr. Darcy. Of course he pays them well, but I doubt I would hear such encomiums from Lady Catherine's people. Mrs. Reynolds, the housekeeper, said she had never had a cross word from Mr. Darcy since he was four years old. Can you imagine?"

"Why should he speak crossly to the housekeeper? If he was brought up a gentleman, he would learn early to mind his temper."

"True," Elizabeth said, smiling at Jane's refusal to grant the reformed Mr. Darcy any extraordinary virtue. "But everything spoke of such responsible management. That's the real proof. A steward or an agent can keep things running after a fashion, but only the master's touch can maintain a great estate like Pemberley in such excellent order. Mr. Darcy's father has been dead at least five years, and it's clear the son's been handling all the business himself. Yet it's more than simply doing his duty. The place shows the effects of, I think you'd have to call it love, or genius. It's not just industry, it's—"

"There's the bell again," Jane said, sounding almost relieved. "Mama must need something, and Hill is overburdened and can't go to her every time."

"—inspiration," Elizabeth finished on a whisper. "I'll go this time."

"No, she's more comfortable with me. You are too sarcastic, like Papa."

Elizabeth, alone in fact as she had been alone in thought since the news of Lydia's folly had forced everyone to put all other consideration aside, was left to her painful ruminations. Visiting Pemberley had been a great mistake. But if she hadn't seen where he lived, what had formed him, what determined who he was, she could never have made sense of everything else that had come before. Even Wickham. Especially Wickham.

People would laugh in their knowing way and say she had fallen in love with an estate, with land, with money and everything it bought. They would both despise her for it and sympathize, a common weakness and in many ways an admirable one. If she could get such a wealthy man, why not? Good for her.

Only now could she see it as it must have been. Growing up heir to all that, such a great fortune, with its consequent responsibilities. For twelve years the only son—the only child. Now along comes a foster brother, the father's favored godson, only a year or two younger, beautiful and charming. And a liar and a cheat. Elizabeth pictured Wickham, unlike most boys in those most awkward of years—scrawny and spotty, grubby, shifty-eyed, and inarticulate—but only a slightly less dazzling version of his current self. Imagine living with that comparison. Surely young Mr. Darcy had been a worthy heir—well grown, sturdy, clever, honest, and brave. Why should the father prefer the *other* to his own fine son? Who wouldn't resent such caprice, just a little? And who wouldn't take advantage?

If she, as a woman, had had to fight not to give way to temptation, how much harder must it have been for a young man, a boy, who had no such female dangers as loss of virtue to hold him back. He would see it as the natural rite of youth. At school, at university, in the army, such affairs must occur frequently, and were given little thought. Oh, it was disgraceful, no doubt. Elizabeth could not condone it. Yet all her sympathies lay with Mr. Darcy, although it had been his fault too, a little. Just a little.

But no, she thought more deeply, *that wasn't it at all*. Visiting Pemberley and its village, hearing Mr. Darcy universally praised—proud certainly, but honest and just; while Wickham, it was suggested, in the closemouthed way of country folk unwilling to speak ill of their own to outsiders, had been wayward and prone to debt—she knew it was not Mr. Darcy who had taken advantage. It was Wickham, of course. He would have sold himself like a woman in order to gain—what? Everything. What whores always got. Money. Preferential treatment, escape from punishment, avoidance of work or study. Whatever he needed.

And Mr. Darcy had taken the bait. He had eaten the apple, as all mankind had done since Adam. Now he had come to expect it, being seduced by the one who submitted for material reward. He had thought of Elizabeth like that, because that's how it usually was between man and woman. Between most people.

Whether such an association was wrong or merely the way of the world, it wasn't hers. That was the root of the original estrangement between them. He had treated her like an inferior, like Wickham. Like a whore, although Mr. Darcy would never think such a word, much less its reality, of her. But that's what it was. Whether it was two young men in a dalliance based on extortion, or a woman agreeing to marriage without affection, it was the same thing. Favors of the flesh sold, in return for wealth and position. She had been right and would always be right in rejecting such a connection, one based on exploitation, not love.

But if love was there too, was it still wrong? Learning of Wickham's bad character had been a shock, one she had resisted. Mr. Darcy's letter had taught her the truth, but it had been a lesson learned by rote, not comprehended. Only Wickham's ruin of Lydia had made Elizabeth know him for what he was—rotten, depraved, and weak—and it had killed any desire she had felt for him. It had once burned so hot she had been afraid of being consumed by it, frizzling up like a thread of gossamer drawn into the hearth. She had thought nothing could quench this flame but the satisfaction of the blaze itself, scorching and blistering her flesh, but now . . .

Discovering Mr. Darcy's virtue had been like a bucket of cold water, sluicing off the soot and reducing that Wickham-fire to sodden ashes. But *seeing* Mr. Darcy as his true self, in this honorable manifestation, was like . . . like a newly laid fire with dry wood in a clean-swept hearth . . . like seeing him that time with Mr. Bingley, naked and aroused. All it needed was kindling. It was the one thing that had been lacking, that had left her unmoved despite his fine person, noble features, and superior mind. Only now that he was worthy did she desire him as a woman with a man. Let silly creatures like Lydia pursue the rakes and libertines. For Elizabeth, goodness was the greatest aphrodisiac of all.

Alone in her room, she touched herself, as she and Charlotte had once enjoyed, and thought themselves so innocent. She imagined Mr. Darcy touching her, Mr. Darcy making love to her, saying it, the word *love* while he fondled her, here on her breast and there, below, and entered her body with that enormous, red—

That was wrong, to think such things of a man who had been spurned. He would never be willing to risk refusal a second time—no man would. A man who had already been humiliated by such a one as George Wickham would be as guarded and suspicious as a knight-at-arms's proud, fiery steed, stolen by tinkers and used as a carthorse, broken, gelded, and whipped. He had been brought up like a lord and had been treated worse than a beggar or a vagabond.

The one person who might understand a little of this was his sister. Sweet, shy Georgiana, who seemed as unapproachable as her brother only because she was tall for her age and had her brother's air of reserve. She had been seduced by Wickham too, although, thank goodness, spared from ruin. But her heart was wounded. Anyone with a heart could sympathize—which left out Miss Bingley.

But what am I to do now? Is there any way to regain his love? He had admired her once, Elizabeth told herself. He recognized her struggle in maintaining her good character against a family that dragged her down, and he was willing to marry her. *Surely, as a man who had lost his heart to the same Wickham, he can find it in himself to sympathize and forgive. Or can he? Does he perhaps think that men are allowed some weakness in this area that women cannot afford? By society's standards he is right. We are always judged harshly for the failings that are indulged, even encouraged in men. But in his soul, in his own private thoughts—does he truly believe this? Can he not see that in our mistakes of the past we are as alike as any husband and wife can be?*

For they had a greater similarity even than that. Anyone can be beguiled and misled by a pretty face, a handsome form, and accommodating ways. But what of the deepest, most passionate, and essential friendship? *There*, she thought, *we are most alike, and not at all like the common run of people, men or women. Mr. Darcy with Charles Bingley, and Elizabeth with Charlotte Lucas. We both loved our friend above all others and sought to retain their love for ourselves against their own desires and their best advantage. It was selfishness, masked as disinterested love. It was the jealousy of passion, but disguised so deeply within our minds as generosity that we failed to recognize it.*

And now she knew that a second chance of happiness, so rare and delicate a moment as few people were ever granted, had been shattered beyond repair. You *had changed*, she thought to Mr. Darcy as if he stood before her, looking down on her with that warm, tender smile on his face, the way he looked in the picture in the gallery at Pemberley. You *had softened your entire demeanor to prove to me that you had listened to my harsh words. I was trying my best to show that I had changed too, had reconsidered my hasty judgment and was willing to be courted. Must a younger sister's folly wreck everything? Is there nothing I can do?*

Oh, Fitzwilliam Darcy, what can I do?

IT WAS AT Cambridge that Fitz began to learn the complex truth of love. At school, the masters withheld the interesting verses, the philosophy and the dialogues. But at university, no man who sought knowledge for its own sake need go away hungry. The Greeks had not one but three words for love: *eros*, *philia*, and *agape*. Desire, friendship, and all-consuming love, that can redeem man by self-sacrifice or destroy him with obsession. They saw the love between a young man, the *erastes*, and a youth, his *eromenos*, as the highest expression of earthly love, the only proper one for their citizens, forbidden for slaves. That told you everything right there.

The Romans were more like us, with the greatest empire the world had known to that time, and the same kind of sophisticated urban society as modern England. For them, the love of man for youth was natural, at worst a minor vice that, unlike with man and female whore, left no bastards to suffer and ruined no woman's life and reputation.

It wasn't all theory; there was flesh and blood to consider and to honor. What a cure for Fitz's wounded soul to learn that the favor he had once committed every sort of crime short of murder to gain from George Wickham could be an act of love between men who enjoyed it for its own sake; for pleasure, not for gain. Men who wanted him, who apparently found him as beautiful and desirable as he had found George.

It had started with old Biggs, his Greek tutor. One day over a ferocious session of translation from the *Iliad*, Biggs had lowered his hand to brush Fitz's inner thigh and remarked, as if it were a part of the lesson, "There is, sadly, but a surviving fragment or two of a play by Aeschylus, *The Myrmidons*, in which Achilles mourns Patroclus by praising his beautiful thighs. I can't imagine his were any finer than yours."

Fitz had startled with revulsion—such an old man, with a belly so huge his waistcoat could not completely button—and Biggs had removed his hand and, coughing and stammering, returned to criticizing Fitz's translation. Poor old sod. Fitz wished now he'd been a little kinder. It wouldn't have killed him to let the man have a feel. He'd been a good tutor, and fair, never penalized Fitz for his refusal. Unlike some. Lots of fellows grumbled about tutors demanding various favors, although most of the complainers were dull scholars who were simply paying for a year or two so as to make useful connections. If they wouldn't learn, the only way for them to get through was by submitting. Yet they resented the price.

But there were others. Intelligent, studious young men like himself, who were interested in academic subjects. Now Fitz discovered Catullus and Horace, Ovid and Virgil and the rest. And especially Plato and the followers of Socrates. Fitz had read some of it at school, but it had been so expurgated that he had never really understood. Even when some of the boys had made jokes, it was just coarse stuff, the same as they said about girls.

This was different. The love of a man for a youth. The affectionate master and the beloved apprentice; the knowledgeable teacher and the devoted pupil. The mentor guiding his young charge through the perils of those years when one's body fights to be let loose and the head swims with unattainable desires. "Yes, it's sexual," Carew said, flicking over the pages until he found the right passage. "Look here—Socrates is always lusting after Alcibiades."

"It's just talk," Ford said. "They didn't do anything."

"Why not? It wasn't like now, with laws and hanging."

"It was against the law for slaves."

"Precisely my point," Carew said. "It's because it was physical *and* the highest form of love. It was only for citizens, their aristocracy. With slaves, it would merely be the same as with women—exploitation and necessity."

"I pity your wife," Ford said, laughing.

Fitz had listened in silence, following the conversation, not daring to breathe. They all wanted the same thing, the love of a beautiful youth, or at least of each other. What he had wanted with George, but that had been so ugly. These men claimed it could be beautiful, *was* beautiful. Pure love.

"What do you think, Darcy?"

"I—I don't know. I haven't thought about it."

"Oh, pull the other one. A big fine fellow like you. Must have had everyone bending over for you, all through school."

"No, I—not at all. That is, I had a friend."

"Oh, I see. How fortunate. For the friend, I mean."

Later, Carew, whose rooms they were in, whispered, "Stay after the others leave."

It had taken some doing, as no one appeared to have any urgent reason to return to his own lodgings anytime before dawn, but finally Fitz was alone with Carew. "At last," Carew said. "I was afraid you wouldn't stay."

Fitz studied Carew's face. He wasn't handsome, but he was nice-looking, with smooth dark hair that he wore in the old-fashioned queue that dandies were already beginning to cut short. "Why did you want me to stay?"

Carew didn't answer, just rested his hand on Fitz's thigh, like old Biggs. But it didn't feel like Biggs. It felt more like George. And when Carew began to unbutton Fitz's breeches, Fitz didn't stop him. He didn't say a word, just tried to keep his breathing even as Carew released Fitz's by now embarrassingly swollen cock and it leapt like a hooked trout in his loose fist.

"I'm sorry," Fitz said.

Carew snatched his hand away. "For what?"

"For being so big, and moving like that," Fitz said. "I can't help it. When you touch me I—"

"Oh, good God. You poor thing. I thought you meant you had the pox."

Fitz scowled, shaking his head, the shame of it making it impossible to speak.

"What did that so-called friend do to you?" Carew said. "Never mind. Shall I tell you what I would like to do?" At Fitz's wary nod, he said, "I should like to kiss it. Has anyone ever done that for you? Yes? Well, I'm glad for your sake, but I bet no one has made as good a job of it as I will."

He was right.

Carew had gone the next term, his debts too high to continue, but there had been others. Fitz had never dreamed that his height and his muscles and most of all his large cock were something that other men might want, might see as attractive, just the way they liked women with shapely tits or a plump, rounded arse.

Always George had made him feel that what they did was disgusting, a perversion. If George sometimes seemed to enjoy it, well, that was how men are, he implied. Vile, debased creatures, at the mercy of their appetites. Laughing all the time as if it was a great joke.

But here were scholars and masters, men of learning and virtue, and they taught of a different time, when love between men was the basis of all that was noblest and virile in a great civilization. When warriors fought side by side with their lovers and when democracy was giving birth to the greatest art the Western world would see in over a thousand years.

It hadn't been one big molly paradise, of course. There were many, both students and tutors, who were vehement in their hatred and condemnation of what they called the sin of sodomy, a term Fitz had heard all his life but had never connected with his boyhood passion. Still, friends sought each other out, introducing likeminded friends, and everybody as circumspect as college men can be, which is to say, not very. But wealth and connections meant something, even here, and Fitz and his friends were left alone. That was one valuable lesson Fitz learned from his father, to behave responsibly with the great fortune they were privileged to enjoy, to husband their riches and not squander it on fleeting pleasures and dangerous indulgence.

In Fitz's first year down from university, his father passed away, leaving Fitz the master of the entire estate, free to pay Wickham his inheritance and send him off. What a glorious liberation that had been! Taking up his residence in the house on Grosvenor Street, entering London society. And finding that a tall, well-built, wealthy young man from a noble family need not work very hard to win the favors of ladies. Not the country girls and cotters' wives of George's youthful indiscretion. Not even the clean but businesslike denizens of a house like Madame Amélie's. Real ladies, like Caroline Finchley, who knew the same people as Fitz, who came from a similar sort of family and spoke the same language.

That had been an astonishing initiation. Caro was careful never to talk of love, treating the whole episode as a charming amusement, but all her gestures, her entire manner, spoke of deep affection. Fitz had not believed that women could truly enjoy the physical act. The famous argument of the Greeks, the gods debating which sex had greater pleasure and deciding in favor of women, had not been convincing to many a young Englishman. Always Fitz had been told it was the man who took his pleasure, the woman who tolerated it, trading her compliance for material reward—money, or a situation, or, in the best of circumstances, when she was of equal rank, marriage. It was the way of nature, of animals. Look at horses, dogs, bulls. The male snorted and sniffed and pawed the ground in his eagerness. The female was tied in place, stood still, endured and produced a foal or a litter or a calf. Yet here was a beautiful, voluptuous woman, wife of one of the country's wealthiest knights, moaning and writhing in unfeigned ecstasy at Fitz's increasingly accomplished touch. "Oh Lord, Fitz," she would say, interspersing her words with cries and gasps of delight. "Your little head is as clever as your big one. Although with you, the two are much of a size. When my heart gives out one of these nights, I will die happy."

After his year of training, Fitz had been subtly eased out of the lady's graces, as a newer, greener youth took his place. It had been so neatly done, Fitz barely realized what had happened until it was over. There had been no farcical meetings on the stairs or mix-ups of time and place to create jealousy or suspicion. Just a few odd moments when Fitz was told the lady was not at home, even though the memory of making the assignation was fresh in his mind from the night before. And seeing another man's hat and gloves on the table in the foyer. Not Sir Peter's, who dressed twenty years behind the fashions . . .

But meeting Lydia Waring, the introduction made by Caro herself, more than assuaged any feeling of rejection. Sharp, quick-witted Lydia, with a curvaceous, well-developed figure and possessed of strong animal spirits, was more than happy to accommodate Fitz's desires. Lydia found a pleasant suite of rooms in Chelsea at a reasonable rent, and she kept it in good order, opening the door, and her person, for him alone. She was rarely tired or out of sorts. Even her monthly courses never ran heavy or long. Lydia welcomed Fitz at all hours of the day or night and she needed no prompting or coaxing to fulfill her end of the bargain. She made him laugh, imitating the fashionable people she came across, and she had a keen ear for accents and mannerisms—and hypocrisy.

It was a pity she hadn't been able to attend school or acquire an education, Fitz often thought, even going so far as to voice his concern once to Lydia. She dismissed that idea with contempt. "So I could be a governess and live worse than a slavey, neither upstairs nor down, at some pinchpenny family's beck and call? I make a much better living as I am, and I enjoy my work." She opened Fitz's pantaloons as she spoke, leading him toward the bedroom, where she soon proved the truth of her words. It suited Fitz far better that she was honest about their relationship instead of playing at a travesty of love, as many women of her sort preferred. Yes, she had a temper, especially if it had been a while since Fitz had given her a new gown or a piece of jewelry. But that was infrequent, and even then she had the prettiest tricks for reminding him, and for thanking him when the error was rectified . . .

If there was sometimes a sense of emptiness, promptings of the heart, memories of those enchanted two years at Cambridge, that led Fitz to wish for more, he ignored it as best he could. But there were times when a stroll in St. James's Park led to the quick easing, if only for a brief half an hour, of the loneliness. One day, in an awkward, perhaps inevitable meeting, he chanced upon Carew, looking far worse than the passing of a mere three years should account for.

They had gone for a drink and dinner at a decent inn, but nothing beyond that. "If I had money and connections, I would have belonged to a club like this," Carew said, handing Fitz a gentleman's calling card, "instead of ending up sick and rotten." Fitz had almost thrown the card away—what did he care for some poxed old earl's dissolute younger son? But he went around one day out of curiosity and met the Honorable Sylvester Monkton. After a rather stilted conversation, the topic had touched on mutual friends, to Carew, and to Fitz's time at Cambridge, and in another week's time he was being initiated into the Brotherhood of Philander.

Twenty

WHERE WAS PROVIDENCE now? George wondered. How had all his plans evaporated into empty air? Running from debts yet again, abandoning his regiment and fellow officers. Here he was, George Wickham, who had had hopes of heiresses, and who had dreamed of Elizabeth Bennet, reduced to hiding out in squalid lodgings in the worst part of town with her whore of a sister.

When Darcy finally found them, it was all George could do not to shake the man's hand and thank him in the most piteous terms. It had been a miserable two weeks and no end in sight. At first it had seemed like all his other larks. A willing, lusty wench, the escape from importuning tradesmen and those ridiculous sums called "debts of honor" that self-styled gentlemen took so seriously. But Lydia Bennet had the sticking power that a girl of her tender years rarely showed. More like Mrs. Younge, with three decades of hard experience. No matter how many tricks George tried on Lydia, things most whores demanded extra payment for, her appetite only increased. He should be glad of her company, he supposed, instead of an empty bed at night, and yet, like most men, he preferred to be the pursuer, not the prey.

He hadn't been gentle with Lydia when he took her maidenhead. He was rough and quick, using her like the cheap goods she was. That would teach her for stealing what belonged by rights to her sister.

She didn't cry, just stared up at him, her lips trembling, and reminding him, as almost made him spew, of Elizabeth's bright, expressive eyes. And then, to his amazement, grabbing him *there*. "Can we try it again, Wick? I think I'll like it better the second time."

And she had.

"Wick, darling," she said, "here's your old friend Mr. Darcy to see you."

There he was, handsomer than George recalled and looking both stern and benign, as if something wonderful had happened to him since they had last encountered each other, on Meryton's high street.

"Why don't you go for a walk, George," Darcy said. "Let me talk to Miss Bennet alone."

"No," Lydia said. "Whatever you have to say to me, Wick can hear it too."

Darcy turned, allowing his eyes to rest briefly on her face. He did not bow, but merely inclined his head from his great height as if to address her on her level. "I beg your pardon, Miss Bennet," he said. "You are too young to know what is in your best interest."

"I may be young," Lydia said, "but I'm a woman now. My Wick has seen to that, and made a good job of it too, so he should hear whatever it is you're proposing."

"For God's sake, Lyd," George said. "Listen to what Mr. Darcy has to say. It might be valuable advice." He gestured like an innkeeper or a thieves' tout, rubbing his fingertips together. That silenced her. "I'll be most appreciative of anything you can do," he whispered in Darcy's ear as he passed by on his way to wait in the other room.

Darcy wasn't alone with her long. He wrenched open the door after about five minutes, letting it bang against the wall with the force. Lydia slipped past him into the bedroom, for once in her life looking abashed, and George sauntered back into the sitting room. "My God," Darcy said. "She has absolutely no sense of the situation she's got herself into."

"No," George said. "I was afraid of that. If she doesn't give a fig for what Fitzwilliam Darcy of Pemberley has to say—"

"Why should she?" Darcy asked. "I suppose you taught her that."

"She's a quick learner when it suits her," George said. "The only person she listens to is me, and then only when I'm saying something she cares to hear, such as how I'm going to warm her arse all night."

"That's enough," Darcy said, his face taking on the familiar expression of distaste. "You could have told me that going in."

"Thought you'd need to hear it for yourself," George said. "Still, I expect you tried."

"I did," Darcy said. "I represented to her all the dangers of—"

"Please, don't repeat it," George said. "Look, Fitz, I truly am grateful, but I didn't expect you to succeed. Just tell me what you think I should do now."

"Grateful," Darcy said with a snort. "I gave up expecting gratitude from you years ago. Right around the time you told me just what you thought of my lovelorn sentiments, and what I could do with myself."

George smiled up at Darcy. *God, he really was a beautiful*

man. "As you should, Fitz. As you should. But honestly, this time it's different. She's like a barnacle. Can't scrape her off no matter how hard I scratch."

"Serves you right," Darcy said. There was none of his old smirk, none of that self-righteous, overbearing hauteur. Almost a kind of sympathy. His next words blew that thought to pieces. "Marry her, George. You'll have to marry her if I can't convince her to return to her family."

"Jesus Christ, Fitz! I can't marry her. You know that. You of all people. You know I've no more money than she has—"

"That was my argument," Darcy said. "But I rather suspect you've met your match at last." He showed his teeth in a repellent, unusually sunny smile.

"Perhaps," George said. "But it'll take at least ten thousand—"

Darcy let loose with a peal of laughter that threatened to bring down the rafters of the rickety old building that had somehow survived the plague, the Great Fire, and the Gordon Riots more than a century later. "God, George," he said. "You're priceless. Here you are in a situation where you should be down on your knees begging for anything I can do—and yes, I mean every improper implication of the expression—and instead you cry for the moon. You are not going to get anything close to ten thousand for marrying Lydia Bennet."

"Fine," George said. "Then I wash my hands of her. Let her go back to her family and explain how she got her swollen belly."

"Wouldn't lay too much on those odds," Darcy said. "It's only been two weeks."

"A very busy two weeks," George said. "Do you want to take that chance?"

"Me?" Darcy said. "You'll be taking the chance when her family comes after you for ruining her."

"That's the funny thing, though, isn't it?" George said. "Her family didn't come after me—at least, they didn't find me. You did. What's it to you, Fitz? Revenge for Georgiana?" He stepped back hurriedly as Darcy raised a fist.

"Do not mention my sister's name, George. I can promise you, you won't do yourself any good that way."

"All right, all right," George said, shielding his face with his hands, just to be on the safe side. "By the way, I met some friends of yours recently. A very pleasant baronet—Verney, I think his name was. That's right—Sir Frederick Verney. And an extremely obliging individual, younger son of an earl—Monk-something-or-other? Although not at all monklike in behavior. Then again, 'Monk' Lewis would no doubt see the resemblance. And now that I think about it, those supposedly celibate brothers in monasteries are notorious for their addiction to the same vice so heartily *indorsed* by that delightful fraternity of yours—what is it called? The Brotherhood of Philander?" He watched from under half-lowered lids, awaiting the explosion.

Nothing. Perhaps a slight twitch at the reference to Monkton, but not the outburst he had braced himself for. He had not thought Darcy would have allowed him to get this far without a forceful interruption, but he soldiered on, attempting to put a crack in that inscrutable façade. "Quite a luxurious establishment you fellows have there. Park Lane. Used to be called Tyburn Lane not all that long ago, wasn't it? Where they had the gallows. More appropriate, eh, Fitz?"

Darcy shrugged. "You know, George, you're becoming rather tedious on the subject. I haven't been anywhere near Park Lane. Only reason I'm in town is to assist Miss Lydia Bennet in her difficulty."

George could see Darcy was telling the truth, more or less. It was clearly the truth as he saw it. But there had to be something . . . He thought back to his time in Meryton, putting things together in his mind. And he got it—so obvious and clear—how he could come out of this ahead after all. Just a question of playing the man the right way—but hadn't he always known that? It took more courage than he had ever needed, and he worked at keeping his voice steady. "I have it—Elizabeth Bennet! That's where this tender concern for the virtue of a natural-born strumpet comes from."

This time there was a violent flinch, almost immediately contained, but unmistakable. George smiled to himself and pursued his quarry with renewed vigor. "Well, well. Fitzwilliam Darcy in love with Lizzy Bennet. Never thought you had such discerning taste in the petticoat line. No wonder you're in such a state—I've suffered that same torment myself. Making you stiff with her wit and her pretty tricks one minute, the next protesting her virtue, until you're doubled over in a constant state of aching balls. Still, if you can catch her, she'll be worth it, yes indeed. A very hot little piece, judging by the sister. Ever noticed the resemblance? Only real difference between them, Lydia doesn't tease, just gives a man what he wants. In fact, when I'm with her, I picture Lizzy to myself, most of the time. Lydia's built on more generous lines, a wallowing barge compared to Lizzy's trim little yacht, but they have the same dark hair, and those eyes. Those wide, innocent eyes that just beg for it." He raised his voice an octave. "*Please, George. Oh, please, give it to me hard because I've such an itch in my cunt I can't bear it*—unh."

George went down with a thud.

FITZ SHOOK OUT his fist and watched as George scrambled to his feet, stumbling over the overturned chair, working his jaw and holding out his arm for protection. It would never do to be caught off guard. George looked vulnerable now, but that was just when he would be most likely to kick a man in the balls or pull a knife. "I'm warning you, Wick," Fitz said, unaware he'd reverted to their boyhood name, "dragging a lady's name into this isn't going to help you."

George grinned. "As I was trying to say, Fitz, Lizzy Bennet's too sharp to fall for a confirmed sodomite like you."

Fitz saw George's ethereal smile with a strange sense of relief. Thank goodness the man's jaw wasn't broken, although Fitz suspected his blow might have loosened a tooth or two. He contemplated opening the door, walking out and downstairs. Better a knife in the back than to listen to any more of this. And he couldn't very well strike George again, not with his mouth all bloody like that. "Your words are beneath my notice or that of any gentleman. But once I make your whereabouts known to Miss Bennet's father and uncle, they will no doubt find a way to shut you up."

"You leaving?" George said. "Give my love to Lizzy. And tell her, I'm sorry we are not to be brother- and sister-in-law, but Mr. Darcy couldn't spare anything to make it possible. No, wait—her sister can deliver that message herself, along with her nameless bastard."

Fitz cursed under his breath. "What do you want from me, Wick? Name a reasonable price and I'll meet it."

"Five thousand," George said. "And I'll bend over for you, like old times."

Fitz laughed again. "Poor old Wick. I've had dreams of that for years. Now, seeing you in all this dirt, with that young whore draped around your neck like a noose, all I can say is, five thousand pounds is one hell of an exorbitant price for admission through the rear entrance."

"Can't get it up, Darcy? Got the pox from those madge culls at the Brotherhood?"

"You'll find out," Fitz said. "Five hundred."

"Two thousand," George said, closing the distance between them.

Fitz tried to back away, but George hooked his leg around Fitz's calf, grabbing his arm and toppling them over onto the sofa. George poked around in the melee, found Fitz's nuts, gave a good squeeze—and Fitz knew Wick was going to come out on top, as he always did.

Fitz groaned at his growing excitement. The rivalry of the verbal contest and the wrestling—it was just like their old days in the barn at Pemberley. They'd have to resolve this sometime, and here was the opportunity. He worked the buttons on his flap, spat into his palm, and rubbed the spittle on his prick. "One thousand," he said as he pushed into George, who had managed, fishlike as always, to twist around and wriggle free of his breeches, offering up his bum like a target. "And settling of your debts."

George gasped and made a strange noise as Fitz entered him. "Fifteen hundred," he said.

The man must be in real pain, Fitz thought. The knowledge only made him harder. This time the little sod would earn his pay. "One thousand," he said, beginning to pump. "That's as high as I'll go. And the debts." His thrusts deepened with every moan and sigh from George.

George fought to retain his concentration, remembering his purpose, the reason for this great sacrifice, as he was pressed into the sofa's seat, his cheek rubbing up and down on the stained fabric with the force of Fitz's actions. "I'm sure Lydia—unh—will want to regale her sisters—unh—with every detail—unh—unh—of how this match was arranged. Unh. Lyd tells me she and—unh—unh—Elizabeth—Christ, Fitz! Take it easy!—are very close."

"And a commission in a good regiment of regulars," Fitz

said. He was pounding George so furiously and in such a rhythm that the sofa walked in a drunken, gimpy-legged shuffle across the bare, uneven floor. "That's my best offer. Take the whore with it or without it."

George gave a strangled cry as he was roused to pleasure despite the pain. There was something feminine, passive about his situation. Pinned beneath Fitz's muscular limbs and trunk, he could only resign himself to the inevitable. It was a rare and precious adventure, the ultimate gamble: starting a course of events then letting it run, beyond his power to stop or swerve. The ball knocked through the window, the fowling piece shot out of season, the woman taken because he was hard and she was willing. "Agreed," he said, when he had discharged, and could talk again. "But a lieutenant's commission, not just an ensign."

"Done," Fitz said. "And I'll have you the rest of the week. And Lydia will swear silence. To me."

"It's a bargain," George said, settling in to enjoy the rest of the ride. As Fitz slumped on top of him at the finish, George was flattened against the worn, hard upholstery. He struggled for air but his chest had no room to expand. Staring sideways across the room, he saw Lydia's dark eyes aglow with lust, peeping through the open bedroom door. Her eyes shot bright fireworks, then became two black holes that grew and grew until they swallowed all the light. *Elizabeth smiled at him, beckoning, naked to the waist and lifting her skirts . . .*

Fitz awoke from his swoon, pulled out of George, and sat up. "Congratulations," he said, holding out his spit-sticky hand. "You're engaged to be married."

George rose onto hands and knees, arching his back to suck in air. The strange vision receded, the black giving way to gray as the world resumed its customary light and colors. Eventually he was able to turn over and sit next to Fitz, taking the offered hand and clasping it in both of his with genuine goodwill. "Worth it," George said. "By God, Fitz. You really do know how to fuck."

"OH, WICK," LYDIA said, her eyes wide and her red lips gaping, when George staggered into the bedroom. "I knew you'd do right by me."

"What do you know about it?" George said, the weariness overtaking him like an attack of ague. He'd certainly earned the money this time. But what was a little work when he had a chance of gaining something from this appalling mess? If there was any justice in the world he should have been finished after getting himself into such a hopeless predicament. No, it was a very fair price, not to mention this unplanned but enjoyable bargaining . . .

"That was a rare treat to watch," Lydia said, "you and Mr. Darcy. Lord! What a big man! Still, as Mrs. Younge says, it's what a man can do with it that matters, and I guess he's had plenty of practice." She had opened her gown, exposing her full breasts, and she shook them in George's face. "Come on, Wick. If you're going to strike sparks like that you have to lay on plenty of wood." She leered and winked at him, like Mrs. Younge with a prospective customer.

"For God's sake, Lyd. Can't you see I'm worn out?"

"Oh, I shouldn't think so, just lying there and taking it up the back alley. Besides, you're strong, Wick. You've always been good for more than once a night."

He knew he'd have to satisfy her or he'd never have any peace. "At least help me get started, Lyd."

"All right," she said, amenable now that things were moving in her direction. "Suppose if you can do that to get us our thousand pounds, I can give you a suck." She went down on her knees, but the stupid bitch used her mouth for talking instead. "Did you mean that, Wick? About pretending I'm Lizzy?"

"Don't be daft. Just said it because I knew it would get a rise from him."

"Well, it did and all! But, Wick . . . you don't really think I'm a barge? You want a real woman, like me, don't you? Lizzy's thin as a girl."

"Now, Lyd," George said. "You know what I like. Didn't you promise that if we married you'd give me what I want all the time?"

"Yes, Wick," Lydia said, happy again. She applied herself with admirable enthusiasm until, just as he had almost regained his full strength, she took her mouth off him to exclaim, "Lord! You think Mr. Darcy's really going to marry Lizzy? You'll have to be quick, then. 'Cause I won't take second place to any of them, especially not Lizzy."

Somewhere George found a remaining reserve of energy. He hoisted her up and laid her on the bed, where her squeals of pleasure added to the din in his skull.

FITZ RAN DOWN the stairs, buttoning as he went. He couldn't spend another minute in that hole.

An unsavory man, reeking of spirits even at this early hour, sidled up to Fitz as he emerged into the street. "A real goer, eh, mate?" he said. "Wot's 'er price?"

Fitz noticed some flecks of a disgusting substance on his pantaloons and scraped at them with a fingernail. "Two shillings," he said. "I was—overgenerous."

"That's the way with you nobs," the man said, looking Fitz up and down in a disapproving way. "Pay too much for wot you could get for 'arf a pint and a promise. A fine gent like you. Even a young, juicy cunt ain't worth two shillings."

"There's two of them," Fitz said. He gave up the scraping. The clothes would simply have to be burned.

"Oh, aye?" the man said. "You don't mean t'owd bitch, the bawd?"

"Not at all," Fitz said. "The other one's only a year or two younger than me."

"Wot they do, then? Let you 'ave 'em both together?"

"Something like that," Fitz said.

The man spat. "Wouldn't mind that. But two shillings. That's more'n I can raise."

Fitz found a half crown in his pocket. "There you go. A gift. Make sure you get your change." The man was so effusive in his thanks Fitz thought he'd never get rid of him. "Tell them Fitz sent you. Got that? Fitz. Ask for Wick."

" 'Oo's that?"

"The whoremonger," Fitz said. "The juiciest cunt of all. Give him the half crown and you can have him any way you like." He left the man staring wrathfully at his back as he walked off. Apart from the slight hollowness in his loins, Fitz felt wonderfully, gloriously vigorous, and alive—free, as if he'd spent the last five years laced into one of Monkton's tight stomachers and only now could take a deep breath and fill his lungs. He was a good thousand pounds poorer, with much business yet to do, but this time *he* had come out on top.

George caught in his own schemes at last, about to be married, not to an heiress or even an eligible young lady, but to a poor ruined jade little better than a whore. Elizabeth no longer deceived. Fitz's heart turned over when he remembered her tears and stifled sobs, the heroic way she had tried to contain her emotions. It had been the sweetest, most unexpected gift that she had felt able to confide in him. He supposed it was simply coincidence, his arriving at the Lambton inn immediately after she received her sister's letter with the bad news, but it was lovely to think he would be the source of her eventual comfort, just as he had borne unwelcome witness to her distress. She would never know, must never know. Wasn't there something in the Bible about that, that true charity was anonymous? The good man did his work in secret while the hypocrite boasted to all of his generosity.

A plangent, tender tune ran in Fitz's head, a light, pure soprano telling of boyish love, *Voi, che sapete che cosa è amor*, with its contrasts of joy and despair, *Ch'ora è diletto, ch'ora è martir.* As Fitz sang to himself, the perfect coupling of sense and music caused a shiver to run the entire length of his body, tingling the hairs on the back of his neck and working its way down to his toes, still somewhat numb from having left his boots on during the episode with George. How extraordinary, that so sordid an encounter should lead to his first knowledge of true love!

Just to be sure, Fitz would buy George a commission in a regiment stationed as far away from London as possible. Even better, now the forces in the Peninsula were making real headway, regulars were likely to be sent overseas. Fitz recalled the promise he had extracted from George, to continue today's shameful exercise for the next week. His whole being revolted at the prospect; he was cured of that sickness. But he supposed he'd have to keep the appointments, if only to ensure by his continued presence in those fetid rooms that George didn't disappear. What man wouldn't prefer to start fresh with nothing than be saddled with a harlot for a wife and the opportunity to die for his country?

Fitz identified the song, Cherubino's lovely aria from Mozart's *Le nozze di Figaro*, that he had tarried in town to hear before removing to Pemberley for the summer. He pushed his hat to the back of his head like a Bond Street beau and strutted westward, chest out, hands in his pockets, whistling his song of hard-won happiness. No chance of running into any acquaintances here. *Donne, vedete s'io l'ho nel cor.* Not since his father died had he known this sense of a crushing weight lifting from his shoulders.

Twenty-One

FITZ AND CHARLES rode slowly home after the dinner at Longbourn. Each man, lost in his own recollections of the past couple of hours, was silent. Even ambling at the comfortable pace demanded by full stomachs and darkness, it was easier without shouted conversation. Charles was contemplating with satisfaction the way Miss Bennet, when the guests were arranging themselves around the table, had looked for him and smiled, as if expecting him to take his habitual place beside her, and without the slightest suggestion of reproach at his long absence and sudden return; and the way Fitz had nodded his permission. After a month of Fitz's new, genial liberality, Charles still dared not take it for granted—not on so momentous an issue.

Fitz's thoughts, as usual, were more complicated. The marriage of Wickham and Lydia, it seemed, was only a stage on his long journey of transformation: a reverse metamorphosis, from the ephemeral beauty of a butterfly, flitting with gaudy wings, dead after a day of epicurean pleasure; or the pride of a peacock, strutting its heavy, shimmering tail, at the mercy of every stalking fox or wolf. That creature could never lower itself to become brother-in-law to Wickham or son-in-law to Mrs. Bennet, nor allow his dearest friend to sink to such a level. But in the weeks since, Fitz was reverting to a less showy, more functional form: the busy, chewing caterpillar, storing up the sustenance for its long winter in the cocoon; or the sober gray dove, emblem of peace and fidelity, that found its equally drab mate and nested in quiet domesticity. If Fitz had lost his chance with Elizabeth, that was no reason to keep Charles from happiness. As shooting season approached, he had suggested a return to Netherfield. They had called on the Bennets their first day back, and been invited to dinner three days later; and Fitz had used the visits to watch and judge . . . .

He had observed Miss Bennet's guarded but, he was now convinced, genuine pleasure at Charles's return, with his own circumspect approbation. He could not have wished for a greater appearance of propriety from his own sister, nor imagined a stronger display of affection on both sides without vulgarity. No, on that score, the mother was still up to her old standards. Fitz repeated to himself Mrs. Bennet's worst transgressions, how she gushed over Charles while doing everything short of holding her nose and pulling her skirts aside in Fitz's presence, making it clear to all that *she*, at least, still held a grudge over his past slights; and how she urged Charles to come to Longbourn and "kill their birds when he had killed all of his own." Unlike last year, it had required little restraint on Fitz's part not to return abuse, cleverly disguised, for offense; the woman would not recognize anything less than blatant insult, and it would cause more distress to the daughter than to the intended target. He had simply shrugged and turned the other cheek, as it were.

Fitz was testing himself, he acknowledged, as much as Miss Bennet or Charles. Mrs. Bennet's words and manners disgusted him, but had no other effect. The idea of allying himself with her, while as repulsive as it had ever been, now appeared to him merely a necessary and bearable ordeal, a trial he must undergo in order to win the prize—Elizabeth. For a reward like that, no sacrifice was too great. In truth, it was better there should be a high price, to counterbalance the pure, shining gold in the other pan of the scales. What did it matter, the existence of this stupid, ignorant woman, once he and Elizabeth were safely at Pemberley? She would be out of sight and out of mind, where she belonged. Like Wickham, away at Newcastle, perhaps overseas. An obstacle to the peacock, perhaps, but no threat to the dove.

No, it was not the mother's behavior that troubled him; it was the daughter's. He had watched Elizabeth but spoken little, looking for a sign that his earlier lack of conduct had been forgiven. But it was impossible to know. She had been quieter than he had ever seen her, displaying none of her former sprightliness or wit, and less forthcoming than at Pemberley—almost as if she too were changing into dovelike modesty. She had allowed no opportunity for him to speak to her alone. They had sat far apart at dinner, and afterward, when the ladies poured coffee and tea, she had kept another girl beside her as a kind of protection, a barrier to his attempted approach. He had taken an unwanted second cup of coffee in the hopes that she might yield to his perseverance, but it had been a wasted effort.

Well, Charles's marriage would clearly proceed apace, and perhaps the enforced proximity, the two friends perpetually in company with the Bennet sisters, would bring about a thaw. Much as Fitz disliked tempting fate, he would go up to town soon and put his affairs in order, so that, in the event of a favorable outcome, he need not take time away from her later in dreary business . . .

As they approached the wide paddock of Netherfield, the

horses, eager to be home, broke into a trot. Fitz had only to touch his spurred heel to the side of his mount and the race was on, but he pulled up slightly at the end to let Charles win by a nose. They were laughing in their old friendly way as they led the sweaty animals into the stable and handed them over to the waiting grooms.

"Happy, my dear?" Fitz said, once they were alone upstairs.

"I don't think I've ever been so happy in my entire life," Charles said. "It was kind of you to allow me to return to Netherfield."

"Nonsense," Fitz said, pleased to have his benevolence acknowledged. "You might as well enjoy your own house, even if it is only leased. And the shooting is as good here as anywhere, although you must be careful not to kill all your birds, at least not in the first week of the season."

"Mrs. Bennet doesn't mean any harm," Charles said. "I'm only grateful she welcomed us so warmly after almost an entire year." He was too engrossed in thoughts of the glorious future to quibble over fatuous remarks, or to notice any difference in warmth between his own reception and that of his friend. "And you truly don't mind about Miss Bennet?"

"Haven't I said so?"

"I just want to be sure. You were so definite before, on the opposing side."

"A man is entitled to change his opinion," Fitz said. "It's not the sole prerogative of the female sex. I observed Miss Bennet's general manner and her comportment with you, tonight and on our previous visit, and I am favorably impressed with the steadiness and intensity of her regard."

"So you were testing us," Charles said.

"Nothing so officious," Fitz said. "Any attachment, if a true one, should strengthen after a year's absence, where a false one will wither. A separation between the parties is not at all a bad way to prove the substance of the connection."

They went to bed early after the long day, wandering in and out of their rooms as they undressed and making desultory conversation in the corridor. It was a bachelor household this season, just the two of them, only a small staff for the house, and without their valets, who had been given a holiday in town. There was no need for formal wear in the country, and a man ought to be able to shave himself for a month or two. Naturally Fitz kept his clothes and his possessions in one of the guestrooms, moving there before dawn so as to rumple the sheets and give the appearance of separate beds—but he was an early riser in any event, and an hour or two of solitude at the beginning of the day was more a boon than a burden.

How comfortable to start out the night in the large bedchamber, no need for the subterfuge of waiting until everyone was in bed, listening for voices or footsteps in the corridor, before sneaking along to Charles's room—or trusting that Charles's courage and caution were sufficient to bring him safely to Fitz. That incident with the faulty lock last autumn had disconcerted them both and forced them to take more care with their arrangements, Fitz arguing for variety to throw off patient spies, Charles preferring a set routine. It was servants, after all, with their rigid notions of propriety and straitened means, who posed the greatest threat, not family and friends.

"I just hope she'll have me after the way I treated her," Charles said as they settled in.

"No woman of sense turns down an offer from a man of your fortune and amiable character," Fitz said as he snuffed the candle.

"Damn it, Fitz! I thought we had got beyond that. I don't want her to be sensible. I want her to love me."

Fitz laughed. "Spoken like a lover. For you, my dear, it is

one and the same. Any sensible person can't help but love you. Like me."

Charles felt Fitz's growing erection thrusting at him and rolled over, sighing with pleasure. "I hope you won't be offended if I think of *her* all the while," he said.

"Not at all," Fitz said. "As you may recall, I have had similar desires. Although how I am expected to know *your* thoughts is a puzzle." He laughed more gently at the absurdity. "Perhaps you meant to cry her name at the height of your passion?"

"Beast!" Charles said, joining in the laughter, until, stilled by Fitz's urgent need, he was breathing in unison with his friend, the deep inhalations and exhalations punctuating the movements of their entwined bodies.

Much later, woken by a sudden, distressing thought, Charles slithered out from under Fitz's heavy arm and rolled onto his back. "I suppose we'll have to give this up after I'm married."

"Mmm," Fitz murmured, roused from the deep slumber that follows great effort. "What happened to the man who was so eager to leave boyhood and its inferior joys behind?"

"I don't know," Charles said. "Things—you—are so different now. I used to think you just wanted someone to bend over for you, and if it hadn't been me it might have been any other obliging fellow. Now, it feels more like—"

"Sounds as if you're on the verge of another proposal," Fitz said, "before you've had the chance to ask Miss Bennet."

"But won't you miss it?" Charles asked. He lowered his voice, whispering so softly Fitz had to strain to hear. "Won't you miss me, just a little?"

"Dear Charles," Fitz said, striving to maintain a lighthearted tone against his own impatience. "Of course I will, at first. But it's not as if we're ending our friendship. Even the Greeks of classical times married in due course. You are not wrong to desire it for yourself." He paused while Charles cogitated. "The one thing I blame myself for is that your generosity to me has kept you from that experience with women that a considerate husband acquires before marriage."

"That was no sacrifice," Charles said. "I never wanted that sort of thing, more like a business contract than affection. In fact, I'm very proud to be coming to Miss Bennet as pure as she in my knowledge of the opposite sex."

"She will not thank you for it," Fitz said, "when you have no idea how to proceed on your wedding night. Virgin young ladies are difficult to please, and need a practiced husband to guide them through their first time."

"I can't believe it's so complicated as all that," Charles said. "But why don't you teach me a few things?"

"If I can," Fitz said. "Really, the most important lesson is self-control. Your natural impulse will be to fall on her and possess her all at once, but—"

"Yours, maybe, but not mine. God, Fitz, allow me some sense."

"You may scoff," Fitz said, "but when you're alone with your beautiful Miss Bennet and you have your first look at an unclothed female form, if you're not careful your cock will make the decisions and the rest of you will merely follow where it leads—or points."

"Thinking with one's prick."

"Precisely. A coarse expression, but true."

"Well, come on, then, and show me what to do."

"Just be patient at first," Fitz said. "Remember, she hasn't been to school or engaged in sport the way we have. This will be the first time that anyone has touched her."

A pleasant half hour went by as Fitz expounded on the finer points of women's anatomy, demonstrating on Charles the various approaches a man could take and the responses they might elicit. The risen moon peeped in at the window through curtains imperfectly drawn, lending the squat, undistinguished furnishings a mysterious, graceful beauty. Caro Finchley's amorous sophistication and Lydia Waring's robust appetite blended in Fitz's memory until, without knowing how or when the change occurred, he was making love to Elizabeth on their wedding night, imagining her small form contrasted with the latent force of her passion, roused to full strength by the skill of an experienced lover.

How different it would be with *her*, Fitz thought, as he kissed and fondled his docile, willing partner. Charles had given Fitz comfort and familiar, easy companionship, but only with Elizabeth might he enjoy the challenge of the mental contest, the spark that could inflame his desire to its hottest. Strange that things should sort themselves out this way, when one would have thought it was the man for love and the woman for the commonplace matters of family and children. But life was a constant surprise, nor were all surprises disagreeable.

As Fitz described that mysterious seat of women's passion and how it varied in size and sensitivity, Charles's eyes shone silver in the faint light, round and unblinking, caught somewhere between fascination and terror, like a child staring at a lion in a cage. "Now you truly are frightening me," Charles said. "My word, according to you, a bridegroom would have to have the intellect of Sir Isaac Newton, the patience of Job, and the conquests of Casanova and Don Juan put together merely to have a one-in-ten chance of ordinary happiness."

"An apt pupil," Fitz said, shaken out of his reverie. "You have learned the lesson perfectly. But don't despair. The mere fact of your willingness to consider her pleasure means you are halfway to achieving it."

Charles said nothing, but his drooping lips and wilting posture reflected lack of confidence—at best, doubt.

"Remember when we met?" Fitz said in an encouraging voice. "You had ventured into St. James's Park one night—"

"And I was so innocent," Charles said, grateful for the different direction the conversation had taken. "I had no idea what went on after dark."

"Or so you always claimed," Fitz said. "It was fortunate I came along when I did."

"But what were you doing there, eh?" Charles asked, giving Fitz the opportunity to complete the familiar anecdote.

"Looking for you," Fitz said, supplying the customary kiss on the lips and caress below. "Yet you became adept in the practices of love readily enough."

Charles sat up. "But that was different," he protested. "At least one of us knew what he was doing."

"Careful, Charles," Fitz said. "That sounds like an accusation."

"Oh, Fitz, I didn't mean it that way. It's just, I can't help thinking how much easier it would be if we could maintain our friendship after—" He stopped, his thoughts overtaken by a monumental epiphany. When he spoke again the words tumbled out in stuttering excitement. "*That's* what you meant about similar desires! Wouldn't it be perfect if you and Elizabeth—that is, remember how you admired her last year? And then when she came to Pemberley over the summer, it seemed as if you two were reaching an understanding. But now, I can't tell—"

"No," Fitz said. "I cannot quite interpret the situation myself."

"That's it, isn't it? Now that you have decided it's acceptable for me to marry Jane, you're planning to marry Elizabeth. I say, that's a wonderful scheme! We'll be brothers-in-law and we can visit as often as we like. The two of you can stay with us at Netherfield half the year, and Jane and I will stay with you the other half—"

"Charles," Fitz interrupted the frenzied outpouring. "Let's not get ahead of ourselves. Things are not so far advanced as I might wish. She was unusually reticent during these visits and—"

"I don't see what you have to worry about," Charles said. "How did you put it? 'No woman of sense turns down an offer from a man of your fortune and amiable character.' And Elizabeth is nothing if not rational. Lord, your aunt de Bourgh will be furious."

"It's a terrifying thought," Fitz agreed with a tight smile. "When I come back from town we'll talk about this some more."

"You're going to town now? Why?"

"I have some business to take care of. And I think you'll find it easier proposing to Miss Bennet without my distracting presence. Won't you?"

"Yes, Fitz, I will. I say, you really are being very decent about this. I hope I shall have excellent news to report when you return."

"I'm sure you will. Look, Charles, before I go there's something I must tell you."

"If it's that you're sorry for your opinion of last autumn, thinking Miss Bennet was not in love with me, I forgive you. I know you had my welfare at heart."

"I'm afraid there's more to it than that," Fitz said. "I must ask a favor, Charles—that you say nothing to her about my belief in her lack of regard for you. For her sister's sake, I would prefer that she not hate me too much."

"And how am I supposed to keep your name out of it?"

"One might as well ask, why would you wish to drag me into it?"

"Think about it, Fitz. I can't very well just turn up again almost a whole year after running off like a shabby, Wickham sort of person, and blurt out some half-arsed proposal. It's not like accepting an invitation to dine. I shall have to explain to Miss Bennet why I went away, and have a credible reason for being in love with her then but disappearing without declaring myself."

"Yes, I suppose so. But Charles, you will need to hear the full account before judging what you may reasonably tell Miss Bennet."

"The full account!" Charles repeated in the giddy accents of a child at a puppet show. "I'm beginning to wonder about you, Fitz. Are you secretly a French agent? Or perhaps you're not really the legitimate master of Pemberley. I know! George Wickham is the rightful heir and you kept him locked in the cellar wearing a mask so no one would see the resemblance to your father, but he escaped and—"

"Enough, Charles," Fitz said. "This is hard for me to say, so I must confess it straight out. When we were in town all those months, and it seemed as if Miss Bennet did not keep up the friendship with your sister, the fact is it was really the other way around."

"Well, damn it all, Fitz! I always knew Caroline took too much upon herself. She's an interfering bitch, to speak plainly. But how is this your confession? Did you suggest it to her? I'm sure she's capable of plotting such a deception all on her own."

"I can't deny it, Charles. But there is something worse that was as much my fault as hers, and which she would not have dared to carry through without my consent and encouragement. Miss Bennet was in town for a time, visiting her aunt and uncle, but Caroline and I decided not to apprise you of that fact."

"You *what*?"

"We thought it imprudent to allow the association to continue, just when you appeared to be on the mend."

"Jane was in town? And you lied to me? For how long?"

"For a few—months." Fitz nearly choked on the word but forced himself to maintain his usual veracity. "And yes, we concealed the truth from you."

Charles leapt out of the bed as if it were crawling with bugs. "You *shit*!" he shouted. "You rotten, filthy *bastard*! You arse-fucking *sodomite*! I don't have words to say what I think of you!" He stood by the side of the bed, chest heaving, hands clenched into fists, his handsome features distorted into glowering ferocity, as if waiting for Fitz to make a move so he could continue the attack on a physical level.

Fitz sat propped on one elbow, watching his friend's eyes. "You appear to be finding a number of appropriate terms," he said.

"Don't, Darcy," Charles said. "Don't you condescend to me. Don't sneer and look down your nose after you have just admitted that you destroyed my happiness as easily as swatting a fly."

"I'm sorry, Charles. It seems I am the one at a loss for words. Only that I am truly sorry and I did it for what I thought was your benefit."

"You can take your 'sorry' and your 'benefit' and your 'concealed the truth' and you can shove them all up your arse."

"Yes, Charles. I understand. It's just as well I left this confession until now. I'll go up to town tomorrow. It will take me a week or more to get through this business. You'll have time to cool off, and if all goes well with Miss Bennet, as I have every reason to believe it should, you'll be in a benevolent mood and ready for forgiveness and reconciliation."

"I'll never forgive you, Darcy. Never."

Fitz sighed and said nothing.

"And I should like you to keep to your own room from now on."

"As you wish."

"And I hope Elizabeth tells you to go to hell."

Fitz put on his dressing gown and shut the door firmly behind him—the same door that had been incompletely closed that night last fall. "She did, Charles," he muttered. "She did." Fitz wondered who had been in the corridor last autumn, if anyone. He had always half hoped, half dreaded, that it had been Elizabeth. Perhaps she had turned down his proposal at Rosings merely from misjudging what she had seen. But no, if that were it, she would have said. That was her great charm—her directness, her lack of pretense, her honesty.

But how could a lady say such a thing? What if the complaint about his rudeness and ungentlemanly behavior was a pretext, the closest she could come to her real objection? Yet God knew his manner had been offensive.

He went over it again, all the discourse he'd had with her, or lack of it, during the recent visits to Longbourn. Still, she had not been cold, merely distant. It might simply be prudence. Fitz sighed. He did not like the thought of a careful, circumspect Elizabeth Bennet. Just because Fitz was turning into a dove didn't mean he wanted a mate of the same lackluster disposition. What had Charles said? He didn't want her to be sensible; he wanted her to love him.

He felt his great need, the interrupted second round of love-making he had not enjoyed with Charles, and he imagined *her* kneeling over him with her slim, light form, naked but for a diaphanous garment like a statue of Aphrodite . . .

Twenty-Two

"SO, DARCY, MRS. Collins tells me you are to be wed."

Fitz looked up from his correspondence, then stood hastily as his aunt de Bourgh burst through the door of his study. "Forgive me, Lady Catherine. I did not hear you come in." *Didn't even know you were in town. Like the Queen of the Night in* The Magic Flute, *spreading gloom and oppression wherever you appear . . .*

"Told the footman not to announce me. None of that formality between aunt and nephew." Lady Catherine waved her hand, heavy with rings. "Oh, sit down, sit down. Don't want some big lump looming over me. Now, what do you mean by going behind my back?"

"I'm sorry, aunt—to what are you referring?"

"None of your hedging, boy. You know very well what I mean. It seems the Bennet family will soon have the good fortune to get rid of not one but two more of their daughters. I have just come from an instructive interview with your light-o'-love, Elizabeth." Lady Catherine's voice shook with sarcasm.

Fitz had no parry to his aunt's unexpected opening lunge. "Elizabeth Bennet?" he said, startled at hearing the name.

Lady Catherine, disappointed at drawing blood so early in the match, and despising any such easy capitulation, was determined on a fight. She stood slightly hunched with her hands on the desk, shouting across the short distance like a fishwife. "The most impertinent, saucy wench I hope never to have to converse with again in my life."

"I am sorry you had an unpleasant conversation," Fitz said. "What did you say to her?"

"Very little, I'm afraid. Hard to get a word in between her insults and impudence and her brazen outright defiance."

"She does tend to speak her mind," Fitz said, struggling to maintain his composure. Curiosity to know the outcome of the encounter outweighed his natural desire to defend Elizabeth.

"It's one thing to allow your friend Bingley to make a fool of himself," Lady Catherine said. "Only a tradesman's son, I understand. But *you* ought to have more sense than to lower yourself to such a piece of country trash."

"Now just a minute, aunt," Fitz said, giving up the attempt at self-control. "I must ask you to refrain from using such terms about a young lady who—"

"Lady! Never in my life have I spoken to anyone who is less a lady than that Miss Cheeky Bitch." She spat the words out with a strange sort of satisfaction, like a badly trained dog retrieving the offal his master has thrown away.

Fitz had to clasp his hands together under the desk so as not to give in to the desire to wipe his face. As the cause of his aunt's indignation began to take shape in his mind, he made a feeble attempt to prevent what felt like hope from showing in his expression.

"And you will wipe that smirk off your face when I'm addressing you."

Fitz wished there was a looking glass in the study. He had never, he was quite sure, smirked in his life. It might be interesting to observe. He folded his lips inward, pressed down with his teeth, then had to undo all his work in order to speak.

"No, Darcy." Lady Catherine held up a hand before he had articulated a syllable. "I will do the talking here. There's one thing you seem to have overlooked. You are betrothed to my daughter. That's right, to Anne. Have you forgotten?"

"I'm sorry, aunt," Fitz said, again settling for the expedience of apology, "but I must tell you that Anne and I will not suit."

"Not suit! Nonsense! You two were betrothed in your cradles. She's your cousin, Darcy, one of us. The person who will not suit is this Bennet creature."

"What exactly did she say?"

"I will not dignify it by repeating it. Suffice it to say she made no attempt to disguise her avaricious gloating at the thought of her impending nuptials. When I warned her of the disapprobation she was inviting, that I and all your family would not acknowledge her, do you know what she had the utter gall to reply?" Lady Catherine paused only long enough to draw another outraged breath. "Said that your wife 'must have such extraordinary sources of happiness necessarily attached to her situation that she could have no cause to repine.' Exactly what the little whore said, word for word."

The full import of the words hit Fitz after a second or two of delay, like downing half a bottle of brandy on an empty stomach. He sat back in his chair and laughed like a lunatic, deep, booming guffaws intermixed with stifled high-pitched giggles. Helpless with joy and the release of so much pent-up tension, nearly half a year's worth, since the humiliation of spring and the sordid arrangements of summer, he needed several long, gasping breaths to regain his voice. "My dear aunt! I know your passion for plain speaking too well to doubt the truthfulness of your account. I can't thank you enough for coming directly to town to share this wonderful news instead of delaying with a letter. Will you stay for tea?"

Lady Catherine stood, arms folded across her chest, observing Fitz's embarrassing display with a jaundiced eye. When she spoke again, she resumed her argument as if there had been no interruption, refusing to acknowledge the deliberate provocation. "Can't you see it's your wealth she's after? If you were to take her as your mistress I should not like it, but better than marrying her. My God, when I think of her at Pemberley, that common, vulgar hussy polluting the grandest of estates with her presence, I want to be sick."

Fitz jumped up and moved to the door. "Let me summon your maid to help you upstairs."

"Do not open that door," Lady Catherine said, sounding reassuringly fit, "unless you want your entire household to hear what I have to say to you. I'm not going to spew all over your Turkey carpet, if that's what you're worried about. Now think, Darcy. The woman you marry will be the mother of your heir. Her blood will mingle with yours in your offspring. Do you want your own blue blood, or do you want this mongrel bitch—"

"Enough." Fitz could no longer indulge his aunt's officiousness. "Better a healthy mongrel than the effete, sickly little doll you've raised." The jibe at his cousin having bought Fitz a moment of stunned, affronted silence, he took the chance to go on the attack, pummeling her with his words like a boxer using both fists to beat his opponent back and down. "Although you feel no qualms at insulting an innocent young lady, I am doubly offended that you would attempt to palm off an invalid wife on a man like me. Since you don't scruple to talk about such things to my face, I'll say without equivocation that I have a robust appetite. In all things. And while I'm sorry for Anne's condition, whatever it is, she could not possibly satisfy a vigorous man. 'In sickness and in health,' they say. That's all fine and good when both parties start out healthy—but to shackle me to someone who would probably faint away from shock on our wedding night, and who, if she did conceive, would be unable to withstand the rigors of childbearing—it's monstrous."

Lady Catherine approached her nephew, her whole body quivering with rage, thrumming like the string of a violin brought to strained vibrato. Her face was such a deep purple it was almost black, her eyes mere slits between narrowed lids, but the pupils showed through like portholes opening onto the depths of hell. Foam bubbled at the corners of her mouth. Fitz saw it again, as with Betty, the cotter's wife—the demon, the Fury who would hound him in the netherworld, the harpy tearing his flesh with her talons . . . He took a step backward but was stopped by the edge of his chair. Lady Catherine poked him in the chest with an outstretched index finger and he collapsed onto the seat.

"How dare you!" she screamed. "How dare you say such things, of your cousin, of your family, to me! I'll tell you this much, Fitzwilliam Darcy. I know things about you and your *appetites*. They may be strong, but they are neither healthy nor natural. I suppose that insolent bitch of yours shares your perversions. She's the perfect partner in vice, eh? Have you been celebrating at your club on Park Lane?"

Fitz felt the blood draining from his face. He tried to speak, to utter the spell that would undo her curse and send her back to the pit of Hades whence she came, but no words emerged.

"Thought I didn't know about that." There was that same expression of satisfaction on Lady Catherine's face, as if the bitter confirmation of even the most unpleasant truth was preferable to the bland taste of ignorance. "To think I would have let my daughter ruin herself by marrying a perverted specimen like you."

The blood hammered in Fitz's neck, restoring the capacity for thought to the blankness in his mind. He would not let this old harridan defeat him, nor would he allow her the advantage of seeing him wounded. "It seems we are in agreement after all," he said, forcing a tight, cold smile onto his face. "You don't want me to marry your daughter and I don't want to marry her. After that, who I choose to marry is none of your concern. I suspect you have nothing more of interest to say to me, aunt, and as I have a great deal of business to get through, I will wish you good day."

Lady Catherine blinked at her nephew's surprising recovery from what was supposed to have been a mortal blow. "I have only this to say, Darcy. You will not get one penny from me after I'm gone. And if that *person* is presiding over it, Pemberley will never see me there."

"Very well, aunt. Why should I want a penny from you? Your entire estate is worth less to me than an honest penny from an honest source. And indeed, we shall get along very well at Pemberley without uninvited visitors. But I do caution you on one point. Whether or not I have the good fortune to marry Elizabeth Bennet, you will refer to her only as Miss Bennet or Mrs. Darcy, as her title may be. Do I make myself clear? There are laws against slander in this country and I will avail myself of them to protect a lady's good name."

Lady Catherine's color had come down slightly and her voice had shrunk to a whisper. "You would threaten me with the law, you filthy sodomite? You are not a fool, Darcy, whatever else is wrong with you. Your situation is most precarious, and I advise you to stay away from the Brotherhood of Philander if you value any remaining shreds of your reputation."

Fitz held the steely smile. He had never countenanced lying, but there were others besides himself to protect, and he had sworn several binding oaths of the body. "I'm afraid I am unacquainted with this brotherhood you refer to. Perhaps Miss de Bourgh might find it a congenial place to get a husband. Shall I make inquiries?"

Lady Catherine slumped visibly at this unanticipated riposte. Fitz felt an odd surge of pity for her haggard cheeks and shaking jowls. "You are treading on dangerous ground, Darcy," she said, without her usual bluster, although she perked up as she turned to leave, glaring at the footman who had opened the door a crack during the shouting. "Out of my way, you little molly."

"Everything all right, sir?" the man asked after Lady Catherine had stormed out the front door.

"Perfectly," Fitz said. "But thank you for asking. In fact, Thomas, is it?"

"Yes, sir. Thomas Watkins, sir."

"I apologize for my aunt's behavior. Take this for your trouble." He handed the man a crown.

"Oh no, sir, I couldn't. Wasn't anything I hadn't heard from me gran."

"I'll bet your gran never called you a molly."

Thomas grinned. "No, sir. That's a new one."

Fitz held out the coin. "Go on, take it. In fact, tell the others to come in when they have a chance and I'll give everyone a gift. You can enjoy an early celebration. I'm going to be married—I hope."

CHARLES, LOST IN a delirium of bliss, was slow to notice that Jane did not seem to share his emotion. It was the moisture rather than the sound of smothered sobs that jolted him to separate their mouths and to snatch his hand away from her breast, although, as he had been in pretty deep, he snagged his cuff on the edge of her bodice and had to spend several awkward moments untangling. "My love! What is the trouble? Did I hurt you?"

"Oh no, Mr. Bingley. No, I am crying from happiness."

"Charles, my love. Now that we are to be married you must call me Charles. But why would happiness make you weep?"

"My dear Charles," Jane whispered. "It is a woman's weakness. I spent so long being in love with you and having to pretend I was not. I had to pretend it even to myself, so that I would not betray my true feelings by any little misstep. And now I am so happy, I can't hold it in any longer. When you touch me like that, it all comes out . . ." She blushed fiery red and would not meet his eyes.

"I am sorry," Charles said. "That was most ungentlemanly of me. I promise not to do that again."

"Ooooh, noooo." The words emerged as another extended moan. "That is not at all what I meant. I like it very much when you touch me. It only made me weep because I had waited so long for this, and now it sometimes seems too perfect, as if I must be dreaming."

"My dear." Charles held Jane in a loose embrace, letting her head rest on his shoulder. "That is exactly how it is with me too. I tried so hard not to think about you for all those months, and all along, if I had only known."

"Known what?" Jane asked.

"That you did love me, as I loved you. We could have been married and doing this for a whole year, almost."

"But why did you go away?" Jane lifted her head and opened her bright blue eyes wide in an expression of innocence that always made Charles's stomach—or perhaps a very different part of him—leap with dangerous excitement. "Why did you not ask me then? If you had asked me—then—I would have given you the same answer I gave you now, and we would not have wasted a whole year."

"I was a coward and a fool," Charles said. "I let Fit—my sisters talk me into thinking you didn't care for me."

"That's why I was crying," Jane said. "I knew you were the right one for me from the start. Even when you only touched my hand, and only in the most chaste, proper way, it still felt to me as if you were—doing something much more. As if you were kissing me or touching me the way you were just now. And I knew that had to mean it was real, and I thought you had to feel it too, or how could I feel it?"

Charles smiled. Even to him this sounded naïve—and yet gloriously true in the way it matched his own sense of their connection. "Oh, I wish I had listened to my heart, or had the courage to stand up for myself!"

"Well, at least you have done it now," Jane said, wiping away her tears. "Let's not dwell on the past but enjoy the present and think of the future. I only hope Elizabeth and Mr. Darcy will know such happiness as we share. But I imagine he must love her very deeply if he was willing to propose a second time after being turned down."

Charles's guts lurched again, but with a rather less charming sensation. "What do you mean, propose a second time?"

"Didn't Mr. Darcy tell you? I thought you two were as close as Lizzy and I are. But perhaps men do not share secrets the same way. When Elizabeth was at Rosings, Mr. Darcy made her an offer, which she declined. Lizzy said . . ." Jane's voice trailed off as she saw her betrothed's unhealthy condition.

Charles leaned against the back of the sofa, his face raised to the ceiling, eyes open but unfocused, limbs dangling as if having lost all their animating force. Jane wondered if gentlemen ever fainted, and what she was supposed to do if one did. Call Mama, of course. But how embarrassing that would be.

Mama would think Jane had been taking advantage of Charles. He was so sweet and so gallant, she was sometimes tempted to . . . hurry things along. But even though they were to be married she could not bear to be thought of as another Lydia, unable to keep her hands off a man. Luckily, she was not forced to make such a call, as the gentleman revived in a minute or two.

"Elizabeth was at Rosings with Fitz?" Charles exclaimed. He sat up, the color coming back into his cheeks with force. "And he made her an offer?"

"Yes," Jane said. "Are you feeling quite well?"

"He never said a word to me," Charles replied by way of answer.

"Lizzy said Mr. Darcy's manner had been—" Jane found it impossible to repeat her sister's harsh description of a man to his friend's face. "Lizzy felt it necessary to decline Mr. Darcy's offer. I think she was most upset because she had not suspected that he had such feelings for her, and I imagine Mr. Darcy was too hurt to wish to confide in anyone, even you."

"No wonder he was in such a foul mood when he got back!" Charles exclaimed.

"If it's any comfort," Jane said, "Mr. Darcy wrote Elizabeth a letter immediately afterward, and she learned she had misjudged him. So although Mr. Darcy could not know it, she had already altered her bad opinion of him."

Charles sat very still, his face set in a grim expression that Jane had not thought it capable of showing. Finally he said, in a harsh, angry voice, "And to think that he had been preaching to me the entire winter of how unsuitable your family is. Yet as soon as he sees Elizabeth again all his arguments fly out the window. And all that time he had been lying to me."

Jane, feeling very bold, reached for Charles's hand and held it loosely between hers. "He probably was humiliated at having his suit turned down."

Charles warmed to the touch, a hazy memory of childhood. A nursemaid, or the long-dead mother? The icy rage melted out of him, replaced by a desire for combat. He wished to defend this gentle, kind lady, who loved him, who put his welfare ahead of her own, from the depredations of the cruel, heartless world. If he had a suit of armor and a battle-steed, he would ride out against an army of Fitzwilliam Darcys and deceitful sisters and beat them back to the dragon's lair where they belonged. "No, I mean he lied about you," he said, looking fiercely into Jane's trusting eyes. "He was the one who never told me you were in town last winter."

Jane heard the devastating words issuing from her lover's mouth that until now had spoken only sweetness, and the contrast hit her with the force of a heart attack. Her face turned greenish-gray, like the first growth of lichen on marble, and as frozen and immobile as any statue. She swayed in her seat, remaining upright only by digging her fingers into the arm of the sofa, then fell back, her eyes rolled up under the fluttering lids and her jaw agape.

What did one do if a lady fainted when you were alone with her? Charles wondered. Call her mother, probably. But Mrs. Bennet would think he had tried to force her. Not that he didn't want to make love to her, and could hardly wait until the wedding day, but he would never press her to the point of losing consciousness. He chafed her hands, vaguely aware of the strange coldness. He wondered what "smelling salts" were, and whether there might be any in the room, so as not to have to summon help and advertise his lack of gentlemanly restraint. Luckily, the lady's complexion improved after a few anxious moments.

"I don't understand," Jane said, her voice as low and tense as Charles's had been at the news of Fitz's rejected proposal. "Why would Mr. Darcy mistreat me so? I was the one who always defended him. When Lizzy said the most scurrilous things of him, I would remind her that he is a gentleman, and your friend. I thought him a most honorable man, because you loved him."

"He is, usually," Charles said, striving to undo what he sensed was irreparable damage. "And as we are all to be sisters- and brothers-in-law, he doesn't want you to despise him. He's ashamed of what he did, and very sorry, and he begged me not to tell you. I shouldn't have broken my promise, but I was caught by surprise. When I think of his colossal hypocrisy—all the way since last spring—I can't give a damn for a promise extracted under false pretenses! Pardon my language."

"That's all right, Charles. It is justified by the circumstances, I believe." Jane felt calm and warmth returning as Charles became more agitated. "And this was because of my family?"

"He said it might have been different if you had returned my feelings." Charles still found it hard not to defend Fitz, just a little. He was in the habit of love, and where affection had been, was not able to let it go so easily. "He claimed he could see that you were not in love with me."

"How was he to judge what I felt for you?" Jane said, with more vehemence than Charles had ever heard from her. "I was not in love with *him*, so why would I show him what I felt? And I thought he loved you. *That* is not love, to spoil your beloved's happiness. I have never been so deceived by anybody. It hurts me to say this about someone you care for, but I don't think I can forgive Mr. Darcy."

"My love. I can't forgive him either. I have already told him so."

"I don't wish to behave in a cruel or unchristian fashion," Jane said, doubting herself at the moment of her lover's agreement. "You know, I wouldn't listen when Lizzy defamed his character and mocked his overbearing manner with you, but it seems she saw the truth more clearly than we did."

They sat in dejected silence, side by side, heads bowed and hands folded in laps, until Jane whispered, "Please, Charles, touch me some more." When he didn't immediately obey, she lifted his hand and placed it on the exposed tops of her breasts, smiling at his uneasiness.

"My goodness," Charles said. "You certainly are not cruel to me. And so much kinder than I had dared hope." His hand worked its way down, in search of that hard little nipple. "But I don't want to make you cry again."

"I am done with crying," Jane said. "And if you're worried about Mama or one of my sisters coming in, I can assure you they will not disturb us. Mama is most understanding about engaged couples and how we like to be alone, and she is very fond of you, Charles."

Things were going so well that Charles didn't like to press his luck, but he couldn't resist. He slowly lowered his free hand the length of Jane's skirts, feeling for the hem, only dimly aware that she was simultaneously gathering them up. He found his way under, encountered stocking and garter, then a rounded, smooth knee. Did he dare move higher?

"Oh, Charles. That's very nice. Don't stop."

He slid up the length of a soft, yielding thigh, the skin like finest satin. Only sighs commented on his progress. His hand ascended until he could go no farther, yet magically the way parted and the road was opened again, leading into humid paradise.

"Oh! Oh, Charles. I do love you, Charles. Oh, I wish we did not have to wait an additional two weeks, just so that we can all be married on the same day."

He had the presence of mind to say her name before speech became impossible for her and unnecessary for him.

Twenty-Three

"MR. DARCY?"

"Fitz, my love. I want you to call me Fitz."

"Yes, Fitz. I cannot quite accustom myself to that name. There is something undignified about it, whereas Mr. Darcy suits you perfectly."

"You would not be comfortable always using the honorific."

"Like my mother, calling my father Mr. Bennet?" Elizabeth felt the involuntary shudder and squeezed her betrothed's arm. "Don't worry. I will make every effort to learn the ways of your exalted society, so that by the time we marry I shall be as odiously familiar as Miss Bingley."

Another tremor brought the trilling laugh Fitz had so longed to hear all those miserable months. "Oh, Fitz, we are perfectly suited, are we not? I know precisely how to ruffle your feathers. But I hope I shall know how to smooth them as well." This last statement was said on a husky note, and Fitz dared not look to see if the unspoken meaning behind the words was as he had guessed.

Elizabeth smiled up at him, drawing his gaze despite his

best intentions. With her bonnet thrown back and secured only loosely around her throat by its ribbons, her teeth shone white against the slight tan of her face, still ruddy from the summer sun, and her eyes sparkled in the dim autumn light.

Fitz wished only to possess her. How ridiculous it was! A mere two weeks remained until their nuptials, yet he was as impatient as a boy. It was undoubtedly a mistake to go on these long walks, but the alternative was to sit in the same house—the same room—as Charles and Jane, and that was clearly insupportable. And so they rambled, every fine day, as far as they could, both energetic walkers who took pleasure in the activity for its own sake, until they were as isolated and adrift as Robinson Crusoe. Oakham Mount was their favorite, the site of their first excursion as an engaged couple, where all the riddles of the past months' misunderstandings had been unraveled. Their conversation flowed like sparkling rivulets around the many companionable silences, so different from what Fitz recognized now as the awkwardness they had endured at Rosings.

They had come to a stile supported at one end by a mossy old oak. As he helped Elizabeth over she fell back against the tree trunk and, still holding his hand, pulled him with her. It was done so neatly he had no chance to prevent his body leaning most improperly along the entire length of hers. She lifted her head, and it was impossible not to kiss her little pink mouth. His cock swelled in a massive and painful erection, but instead of drawing back she nestled her thighs around it, pressing herself even closer.

He forced their mouths to separate, although every part of him protested, and stepped away. "I beg your pardon, Elizabeth."

She reached up and traced the outlines of his lips with the tip of her gloved index finger. His mouth burned at the touch, as if the heat of her peppery skin had worked its way through the kid. "That was a lovely kiss," she said. "There is no reason to apologize."

"You are too innocent," Fitz said. "You do not know what you are risking, what you are tempting."

"I have a fairly good idea," Elizabeth said. "It is I who should beg your pardon for subjecting your gentlemanly honor to such calculated teasing. My own restraint is lacking."

"I must disagree. A gentleman—"

"A gentleman never contradicts a lady," she said. "But you are right in this, as you are in most things. To behave with such abandon so soon before our wedding would be imprudent; if we were not equally delighted by the endeavor, we would have anticipated one of the classic disappointments of life—the unsatisfactory wedding night—and have nothing but repetition to look forward to on the day itself."

Fitz laughed from deep within his chest. She was truly extraordinary, to refer to such indelicate matters with the equanimity of a courtesan and yet retain her innocence. Her courage demanded equal candor. "Your argument is most persuasive, especially as I hope very much not to prove a disappointment. And I have a far better chance of success in a warm, comfortable bed than out here in the cold and the damp."

"You are assuming," Elizabeth said, peeping up at him from under lowered lids, "that you are the one in danger of disappointing, when it is entirely possible that I—"

"Never!" Fitz spoke much louder than necessary.

"The only gallant answer," Elizabeth said. "Indeed, I think here the laws of polite discourse put the gentleman very much at a disadvantage. If you agree with me, you are implying I am cold; if you disagree, you are accusing me of wantonness."

"Your logic is unassailable," Fitz said, "and only goes to prove the unfitness of the subject for conversation, especially between the two people intimately concerned."

Elizabeth dared not pursue it. She had had to take the lead to induce Fitz's proposal, thanking him for arranging Lydia's salvation, despite his natural wish to keep his part in it hidden. That knowledge, gleaned from her sister's careless words and her aunt Gardiner's subsequently coerced explanation, had swept away all her doubts of his regard. Surely a man who undertook so distasteful a task, from which he gained nothing, was a man in love, needing only a little push to overcome the last constraints of shyness and previous rejection. Now it was up to Elizabeth to prove their compatibility, and she must gather the evidence herself. Anything, even a broken engagement, was better than discovering, too late, that they did not suit in this, the most intimate aspect of married life. They walked in silence while she steeled her resolve. "Do I disgust you?" she asked, after a long climb to the top of the scenic viewpoint had revealed only a misty opacity.

"What?" Fitz was so taken aback he could not answer with his usual courtesy. "How can you think that, after what has just passed between us?"

"No, I mean in my character, that I am impatient for our wedding night. Gentlemen rarely expect a lady to be capable of a passion equal to theirs."

Fitz felt his heart pounding. What she was hinting at was more arousing than naked flesh or improper touch. What would be an appropriate answer? And even if he thought of one, his throat would probably close up with excitement and reduce the words to choked gabbling. The image of Caro Finchley, moaning with pleasure at his caresses, came inconveniently yet with benevolence into his unguarded mind, calming him just far enough for coherent reply. "The combination of strong feeling with delicacy of mind and superior intellect is rare in either sex. Few men look for it in a woman, contenting themselves instead with coarse appetite or languid decorum as meets their requirements. But in you, it seems I have found what I thought existed only in imagination." He could not so much as glance in her direction. All his powers of self-command would give way at one glance from those brilliant eyes.

"It feels that way for me, too," she said, finding it easier to speak frankly when he wasn't looking at her face. "But gentlemen often assume that if a woman shows a preference for one man, she is indiscriminate in her affections. And I would be most unhappy if you believed that my earlier, mistaken partiality for Mr. Wickham merely indicated an overfondness for men in general."

"Such a gross misreading of your character is impossible for anyone with an ounce of intelligence," Fitz said, his own tension receding at her discomfiture.

"You give me perhaps greater credit than I deserve." Elizabeth at last dared raise her head, saw Fitz smiling down at her with a very warm expression in his cool gray eyes, and quickly dropped hers to the ground again. "It's one of the many ways you and I are alike, I think, and well suited. Mr. Wickham tempted us both, working on our baser emotions to provoke a desire that we gave the name of love because it was new to us."

Fitz was too shaken by the kiss, the thwarted expression of his love leaving him drained, to wonder how she knew of his disgraceful boyhood attachment. There was no answer he could make, nor did she seem to expect one.

"You loved him, didn't you?" Elizabeth said. This time she watched his face as she spoke, a task made easier by the fact that he would not meet her eyes. "Or confused lust with love. As I did."

"Wickham and I were like brothers, closer," Fitz said. Without any conscious change, he could talk about it, openly and without embarrassment. It was simply there between them—

total and complete understanding. "I thought he must love me as I loved him. I would take the blame for his misdeeds and bear the punishment myself. It was my way of proving my devotion. My poor father went to his death still half believing I was deficient in every moral quality. But Wick—George—Wickham—always showed me his gratitude in a, shall we say, tangible form. And I was weak."

"You were very young," Elizabeth said, her fingertips stroking his forearm where she rested her hand while they walked.

"I was a year or two older than you before I entirely freed myself from that misguided sentiment," Fitz said.

"It's different for men," Elizabeth said. "A man of twenty is but a boy, whereas a woman of the same age is expected to know right from wrong, and have the discernment to tell an honorable man from a fraud. But it took me reading a letter you should not have been forced to write to begin to see the truth. And only when he ran off with my sister did I comprehend what he was. Sometimes I think it is because my vanity was wounded that it was so hard for me to see clearly. I would not admit that if I loved a man, or thought I did, that he could be anything less than admirable."

"You make it sound almost logical," Fitz said. "I only wish I had such reason on my side."

"Men are not made for celibacy. I have often wondered how gentlemen retain their reputation until marriage. And no, I do not expect an answer," she added with a broad smile.

"Thank goodness for that," Fitz said, returning her smile and reveling in the relaxed atmosphere. How had she done it, made all his vice and misbehavior of the past years seem almost trivial? It was, he decided, just as she said: they were well matched—in passion, in understanding, and in temperament. He must write to Colonel Fitzwilliam and crow his triumph, that he had been right all along. Still, it would not do to dwell on this matter. "But I must beg you, Elizabeth, if you care for me, not to continue with this painful subject."

"I am sorry, Fitz," Elizabeth said. "It's only that I need to make sense of things on my own account. The knowledge that you had sought out Wickham, the person you least wanted to meet again, and paid what must have been a huge sum, even for you—it compelled me to accept the truth. The truth about him and the truth about you. And it filled me with gratitude, although I hope I can show it in a less disreputable way than he did." Another mischievous smile nearly undid Fitz's resolve.

"That will not be difficult," he said. "We are to be married. There is nothing disreputable here. And I repeat what I said when we last discussed this unwelcome topic of Wickham and your sister—that the business I conducted with him was bearable because I undertook it solely for your sake and thought only of you during its commission." He barely grimaced at the lie. It concealed, as Elizabeth had just made clear, a deeper truth.

"I wish . . ." she began, remembering her last, odd conversational exchanges with Wickham, the gross suggestions he had hinted at, when he and Lydia had visited after their marriage. It was her fault, she knew, for encouraging his earlier accusations against Fitz, and unlike her original imagining of that connection, the pictures it gave rise to were not pretty. "I hope," she started over, "it makes the memory less painful for you to know that it was when I learned how thoroughly wicked he was, and how—good—you are, that all my feelings for him were extinguished, and blazed up the stronger, for you."

The last words were whispered, so faint he could barely hear. As he leaned down to catch them, it was inevitable that their mouths should meet again, natural that lips should part and tongues touch and taste. She had taken Fitz's hands as she spoke and guided them to her waist. He didn't resist, but continued in the direction she had started, and she lifted herself up into his embrace as soon as he completed the circle. She was so small, and he was so much taller, it was awkward at first—until it wasn't. He lowered her carefully onto the ground as she locked her arms about his neck and raised her knees. He had unbuttoned, God help him, his skill at opening his flap one-handed developed over the years until it had become a mindless reflex, and he parted her thighs with his . . .

Something in her face saved him—a look of longing mingled with fear. Fitz rolled away in the nick of time, convulsing with the discharge he was powerless to contain. He could only pray she did not see, but she was there, leaning over him, her hand caressing his back and flank. "What must you think of me now?" He almost cried in his despair.

"That you are as proficient in the art of love as in conversation, and as unwilling to flaunt your skill until you find the right partner," Elizabeth said. "And that you want me very much. Almost as much as I want you. I doubt I could have drawn back like that if things were reversed. And I wish you need not." She laughed, although with more of a quaver than her usual resonance. "Now what must *you* think of *me*?"

"That you are as quick with an epigram on the brink of disaster as if you were safe in your own drawing room." Fitz answered her with difficulty, his back turned, wishing to shield her—and himself—from the ugly truth of men's unruly flesh. "And that you are kind merely to laugh at me and not condemn."

Elizabeth waited until Fitz had wiped himself on his shirt and stuffed himself back inside his breeches before replying. "You know my way is to laugh whenever morality allows it," she said. She stood up and shook out her gown and cloak, hauled her crushed bonnet up by its strings and attempted to reshape it, the purposeful, jerky movements concealing the trembling of her limbs. "Perhaps I am audacious in making fun of us, but I feel safer that way."

"I should prefer you to feel protected when with me, not to have to constantly guard against my taking liberties," Fitz said. He was able to button and stand up also, brushing the soil from his knees.

"You could take nothing I did not choose to give," Elizabeth said. "I imagine many a marriage has been consummated on this very spot, by couples who had not our—your—strength of will. I used to come here on occasion with my dearest friend, Charlotte Lucas. Mrs. Collins now. My mother would scold me for my 'green gown'—another example of country vulgarity, I suppose, but I am merely quoting."

The abrupt change of subject helped Fitz, as she had intended. He found his hat where it had rolled and knocked it against his palm to dislodge any insects, then replaced it on his head, tapping on the crown to push it firmly into place. "Mrs. Collins," he said. "Do I know her?"

"Surely you remember your aunt's vicar at Rosings?" Elizabeth said, chiding him gaily, her light tone appropriate for the idle chat of a morning call. "Charlotte married him, against all my protestations. But I think she is content with her choice."

They walked again to distract themselves, holding themselves apart. Fitz pursued the inane, harmless line of conversation with gratitude. "Mr. Collins? He is an abomination—an obsequious, arse-kissing fool, utterly lacking in intellect or judgment."

"Precisely. Which is why I turned him down and begged Charlotte to reconsider. Oh, I *am* looking forward to our marriage. You say exactly what one thinks and dare not. I should have so liked to have called Mr. Collins an obsequious fool, although it would probably be better if I did not use that other phrase."

Fitz was shocked out of his newfound calm. "Are you serious?" At Elizabeth's nod, he exclaimed, "But there are laws against such things!"

"Against my saying that Mr. Collins is an arse-kisser?"

"Of course not. There ought to be a law requiring that he be stood in the pillory for an hour every week and proclaimed one with a sign around his neck. No, against bestiality. Men—or women—having improper relations with animals." He was again rewarded with her laughter.

"That is cruel!" Elizabeth exclaimed. "And so very true. I only wish I had thought of it at the time."

"You say the man, and I use the term very loosely, proposed marriage to you?"

Elizabeth gave a stiff little nod. She could barely bring herself to acknowledge the shame of it, even now. "But after I refused him, and convinced him that I was not being overmodest—the work of a very long morning, I promise you—he sneaked off to Lucas Lodge the next day and proposed to Charlotte, and was accepted immediately. I was heartbroken when she told me."

"I should think so. A good friend of yours." Fitz tried to put a face or a form to the vicar's wife, and could not. He had seen only *her*, the flame of his desire embodied. "But she likely has none of your beauty and, although I do not know her, I expect but half of your wit."

"No, Fitz. Don't dismiss her so coldly. She was my closest friend, and I couldn't have loved her if she lacked all good qualities, and she deserved far better than that—abomination. I imagine it's the way you must feel about Mr. Bingley, and that's why you worked so hard to keep him from my sister."

"Now that is underhanded," Fitz said, "comparing your sister Jane to a man little better than a beast."

"I mean only that you perceived her as not good enough for Mr. Bingley. I think my assessment of Mr. Collins was better than yours of Jane, but the moral of my story, if any, is that sometimes our friends know what is best for them, despite our misgivings. And also that our own happiness must not come at the expense of others. Selfish as I am, I cannot be content in my marriage if I do not think everyone rejoices in it as much as I do."

"If you are referring to my aunt de Bourgh," Fitz said, glad of a subject less weighted with dangerous emotions, "I assure you her opinion is immaterial. She has no power over me, and you need not let her disapproval worry you."

"Oh no, Fitz. I quite agree with you there. No, I should qualify my sentiment by saying that my wishes are restricted to those people I am fond of and whose goodwill matters to me. Specifically, my sister Jane, and the man she is to marry, your friend Mr. Bingley."

"So long as you have forgiven me, that is all that matters." Fitz stared into her eyes, suspecting he was, as usual, missing the deeper implications of her words, was again overcome by passionate longing, and turned quickly away.

"But you love Mr. Bingley, I think, and would be sorry to lose his friendship," Elizabeth said, daring to move closer. "I was so very angry with you for so long, but now that I have come to know you, I flatter myself that I understand you. Although what you did was wrong, you did it for a noble reason."

Fitz looked steadfastly out over the shallow hills of Hertfordshire in the far distance, feeling the slight breeze ruffling his hair around his ears. "Not entirely, Elizabeth. Much as I would like your good opinion, honesty is more important. I was selfish. I wanted to keep him to myself, and I had this foolish notion that he and Georgiana would marry. We would be brothers that way, and it was all to be years in the future."

Elizabeth took his hand. "I do see, Fitz. You need not apologize anymore. I did much the same thing, with Charlotte. It's another reason I think we are so well matched."

Fitz was jolted once more by the surge of energy between them, even through their gloves. He pulled his hand from hers with regret, conscious of the necessity. "Please, my love. Don't tempt me again."

"Oh, Fitz, how will we ever wait two more weeks?"

He laughed in loud, wheezing gasps, glancing sideways at her flushed face and rumpled gown, her curls tumbling down her back tangled up with her bonnet strings. "I don't know, Elizabeth. Brisk walks, cold baths."

"Perhaps it will rain tomorrow and we will be forced indoors and into propriety," Elizabeth said as they started down the path that led toward Longbourn.

Twenty-Four

TWO WEEKS LATER, two wedding parties shared a feast at Netherfield. Everyone remarked on the glowing good looks of Mrs. Bingley and the radiant joy of Mr. Darcy. As to their respective partners, it was frequently observed how Mr. Bingley had acquired steadiness along with a wife, while Mrs. Darcy was complimented primarily on her great good fortune. No one, besides those immediately concerned, noticed how little the two couples intermingled or exchanged words. Even the dancing, where tradition dictated that each friend dance with the other's bride, was stiff and formal, and the men returned gratefully to their own wives after one short quadrille. By the end of the evening, as the Bingleys and the Darcys retired to their separate chambers, it was as if an armed truce between two great forces had been negotiated with difficulty, to last the duration of one night, with the hostilities scheduled to resume at dawn.

Elizabeth undressed quickly and sent the maid out. She peeped around the door to the bedchamber, saw it empty, and tiptoed to the enormous bed, climbing the two steps and throwing back the bedclothes. Her impatience, while tempered with a lesser but gnawing degree of trepidation, threatened to overwhelm her; nor would it help matters to keep him waiting. Before she had registered the soft knock at the door, or recalled bidding him enter, there he was, standing at the foot of the bed, its height giving her an advantage she rarely enjoyed. Her breath caught in her throat. "It was good of my sister to allow us to spend our first night here," she said.

"Yes." Fitz, attempting to behave like a civilized man in the presence of his bride, was incapable of uttering anything beyond monosyllables.

"I have never known my sister to hold a grudge," Elizabeth said, "and she would deny it even now if pressed, but the fact is, only your Mr. Bingley's wishes, as her husband, prevailed on her to allow it."

Fitz stood at the edge of the bed and forced his higher organs of brain and vocal cords to function. "He is not *my* Mr. Bingley. And now that we are related, you may call him Charles."

"Charles, then. He has forgiven you, but she has not."

"Forgiven? What grievous sin have I committed now?"

"It is not a new one. I expect you are quite done with errors of any kind, and I must face the trials of marriage to a paragon of virtue. No, Fitz, it is merely that very old, worn-out matter of having separated Jane from Mr.—from Charles last year."

"I had hoped," Fitz said, "that Charles could have kept that information to himself. But surely Mrs. Bingley will overlook it, now that they are married. May we consider this further on the morrow? I confess I may commit a serious error if I am not soon permitted to fulfill the terms of our marriage vows."

Elizabeth smiled at her imposing husband and the significant protrusion at the front of his nightshirt. "So I see," she said. She knelt in the bed and extended her hands in welcome.

"Would it shock you if I said I am in danger of committing the same error, or whatever is the equivalent for a woman?"

Fitz laughed and gathered her in his arms. "You cannot shock me. And I don't think there is an equivalent error for a woman." He kissed her mouth, starting with chaste closed lips but progressing easily to the play of tongues. Elizabeth followed his lead without shyness or hesitation. When his hand moved from caressing her back to her side and then to her breast, she made no protest or attempt to block.

"Oh, Fitz," she said. "I'm so glad we have time for what you once called 'a good long revel.'"

Fitz's heart seemed to come to a complete stop in his chest. "What did you say?"

"A good— Oh, Fitz, that reminds me. I hope this is not the room with the door that doesn't close properly. Would you mind very much just making sure?"

"So it *was* you," he said softly. He released Elizabeth from his embrace as his urgency receded and sat on the edge of the bed, legs dangling, sorting out his conflicting thoughts. How often had he wondered, and hoped, and dared to imagine she would not be disgusted. Yet now he had his wish, he felt an odd emotion, one rarely experienced since boyhood. It was not so strong as shame; closer, perhaps, to modesty. Was this what ladies felt, or were supposed to feel—an absurd embarrassment at having their nakedness or affections revealed?

"I hope you are not too dreadfully disappointed that it was not Miss Bingley," Elizabeth said.

"Of course not," he began, outraged, then saw she was laughing at him still. *Marvelous, sweet perfection of a woman.* He cocked an eyebrow, just to let her know he was not deceived, or cowed at her presumption. "But surely you were surprised."

Elizabeth nestled beside her husband. He seemed troubled in some way that she didn't quite understand. She put her arm around his shoulders in comfort—or tried to. Lord, he was big! "It was not so very bad, you know. If seeing you unclothed had given me an aversion, I would not have accepted your proposal. Even after I visited Pemberley."

"But it was not only me you saw," he said.

"No," she said, permitting a slight quiver of laughter to escape. Not enough to wound, but merely to sting, like the first breath of ammonia to rouse a fainting lady. "Is that what's bothering you? That I saw Mr.—Charles—as well? I confess I was a little taken aback. But while my attention was at first directed toward him, because of the hopes I had for my sister's happiness, ultimately my memories are all of you."

Fitz said nothing, his face settling into that cold stare, an expression of hauteur that Elizabeth recognized now as self-protection.

"Can you doubt it?" she whispered. "For although Charles is a very well-formed man, appropriate for a respectable four or five thousand a year, your far more magnificent appearance confirmed my every idea of the grandeur of a large estate, a house in town, and a clear ten thousand pounds."

That startled him into action. "Elizabeth! Have you any idea—"

"Of how low, indecent, and offensive I sound? Goodness, yes! I was hoping to laugh you out of your gloom but saw nothing less than brute vulgarity would serve."

"You are wonderful!" he said, turning to face her. "And so long as you didn't mention to anyone else what you saw, I suppose I will simply have to live with your teasing. A very fair price to pay."

"Well, I did confide in my friend Charlotte." She sighed at his blank look. "Mrs. Collins. Just to make sense of what I had discovered. She has brothers, you see, so she was able to dispel any minor worries I had."

"I am ruined," Fitz said with a groan. "Collins will have spread the word of my indiscretions all over the south of England at the very least."

"Nonsense," Elizabeth said. "Charlotte would never share so intimate a piece of news with her husband. Theirs is merely a marriage, not a friendship. Besides, had he learned of it, you can be sure you would have seen him at Pemberley within the week, having rehearsed the most accommodating ways to bend over backward, and with his obsequious speeches all committed to memory, hoping to enjoy a similar pleasure to that of Mr. Bing—Charles."

Fitz permitted himself a snort of laughter. "True enough. Yet my aunt de Bourgh had knowledge of my private associations in town."

Elizabeth looked uncomfortable. "There I am afraid Charlotte may well be the source of her intelligence, but not in the way you think. Mrs. Collins must do what she can to improve her husband's prospects, which he is unlikely to accomplish through his own abilities. Charlotte has become friendly with Miss de Bourgh, and it is perhaps from her that your aunt was apprised. But I swear to you I told no one else—except Jane, later on."

Fitz pursed his lips and scowled. "Now I comprehend why Mrs. Bingley is angry with me! But why, Elizabeth? I thought you wanted them to marry."

"Fitz, listen to me. Jane knew it before I said anything. Charles told her last year."

That explained a great deal, Fitz thought. No wonder Charles had been so certain of Miss Bennet's regard. "As I should have told you, I suppose."

"No, Fitz. That is yet another area where my sister is far superior to me. She accepted the love between you two far more readily than I did. I imagine it's because she was truly in love with Charles, whereas you and I were at odds. I do hope you will always tell me everything you ought, but something like this, a particular friendship between two gentlemen—a man would be breaking his confidence to his friend if he spoke of it, even to the woman he is planning to marry. But if you *had* told me, once we were engaged, I should not have thought any less of you. Rather the reverse."

"Then, my love, you would be suspending your excellent judgment in partiality to an undeserving husband."

"Fitz, you misunderstand. At the risk of your taking exception to my plain speaking, I must tell you that I savored the image of the two of you embracing. In fact, I was hoping you would make up that friendship."

"I take it you do not wish to enjoy our honeymoon alone?" Fitz said, grinning.

This is more like it, Elizabeth thought. She clouted Fitz's chest in mock rage. "On the contrary. If you recall, I requested that you secure the door."

Fitz rattled the doorknob to Elizabeth's satisfaction and returned to the bed. His manhood had revived, she was relieved to see, his shirt tenting out and his walk rather stiff-legged.

Their conversation had given her confidence, once it was his pride that needed bolstering. "No, please," she said, stopping his hand as he reached to snuff the candle. "May I not see you? You are so very beautiful."

"My love," Fitz protested at the strange request. "That is more for the man to say, I would think."

"I do not believe either party can claim a monopoly," Elizabeth said. "That I say it of you does not in the least prevent you saying it of me. In fact, I rather hoped you would. But perhaps you require a better foundation for so definite an opinion. I know your dislike of deceit or empty flattery, and I will therefore help you along." With the nonchalant bravery of the forlorn hope storming the ramparts of an impregnable stronghold, she lifted her gown and pulled it over her head in one swift motion.

Never had Fitz's schooling in self-command been more necessary to him than now, at the sight of her exquisite nakedness. Although he had often pictured to himself the delicate beauty of her form, he was unprepared for the reality of curves and flesh. Her breasts were small but perfect globes, the aureoles large circles of palest fawn, the nipples prominent and pointed. She had the slender waist and hips of his most fervid imaginings, but with the slight belly and the bowed shape that so distinguishes the female from the male. Tendrils of dark hair tumbled around her shoulders, in counterpoint to the lush growth between her legs. There was even a tiny trail, like a feminine version of Charles's, leading down from her navel. "*Beautiful* is a poor, inadequate sort of word in the face of such splendor," he said. "My love. Will you allow me to—"

"It is fair to assume my permission is granted, with so clear an invitation," Elizabeth said, her voice trembling only a little. She gasped as he took her at her word, fastening his mouth on her breast, his tongue running frenzied circles around the nipple. "But will you not show yourself to me?"

Fitz disengaged with difficulty. "You wish me to remove my shirt?"

"Please. It is uncomfortable to be revealed to you so clearly while you are hidden from me. A metaphor for our courtship, don't you think?" This time she dared to laugh, although the sound had the brittleness of incipient tears. "And I should like to compare memory with actuality."

Fitz could not afford to waste so much as a second in indecision or vacillation. Kneeling before his goddess, his weight making a deep depression in the feather mattress, he whipped his shirt over his head and flung it with force into a corner.

Elizabeth fell back on her elbows, her mouth agape. "Oh. Oh! I would have thought recollection to enlarge and embellish over time, but I see if anything I underestimated."

Fitz noticed the direction of her fixed and glassy stare. "Surely you are not afraid of me?"

"Of you? No. But of that enormous instrument of torture, most decidedly." She smiled, but the candlelight flickering in her eyes showed glittering terror.

Here, at last, he was on familiar ground. "It has been thought by some to be an instrument of pleasure." He laughed softly, purring at her the same way he would gentle any creature that bristled at the approach of man—stroking and smoothing until the standing hair was flat, the fighting posture relaxed into calm. "Much depends on the proficiency of its owner."

"And we neither of us perform to strangers," she said, shocking him yet again, despite his chivalric denials—and making him desperate to have her.

Yet now, at the very last, he must delay. "My love," he said, holding himself away from her, every muscle aching with the effort. "Your beauty makes it difficult for me to use the restraint a lady requires. Forgive me if I cause you any distress." His need must have shown in his face, because she blinked rapidly several times and nodded her acquiescence.

"Truly, Fitz, you cannot hurt me." She pulled him down to lie beside her, aiming her breast at his mouth for him to suckle again, and guiding his little finger inside her. "Feel how ready I am for you."

Wet, warm. Tight but yielding. Fitz growled, like a dog picking up the scent of home at the end of a long journey.

She arched her back, neatly removing her breast from his lips and directing his attention to the other. "Oh yes, Fitz. Oh, I do love—" She stopped on a gasp of horror and pushed at him with such force that he knew he must have pressed too deep.

He took his mouth from her. “Did I hurt you?”

“No, Fitz. I must say one last thing. Please don’t moan like that. I will make it as brief as I can. I just want to caution you that, although all the authorities on the subject teach that a wife must never express her feelings for her husband in words, I expect that certain sentiments will emerge during the course of the evening and I don’t want you to take them to heart.”

Fitz laughed, despite his pain. “That is, words of love may pass your lips?”

“Yes,” Elizabeth whispered, raising her eyes to his face, then lowering them as her concentration was once more broken by the large appendage below. Taking a deep breath, she resolutely looked away. “Marriage is so unequal a situation, a lady is compromised merely by accepting a man’s proposal. To declare to her husband the depth of her passions is to put herself so greatly in his power as to prevent any possibility of forming an equal partnership. Now, I intend to follow this advice when we are in company—indeed I will endeavor to tease and make sport of you with even greater freedom, because the position of wife allows far more latitude and far less necessity to moderate my language than mere acquaintance—but here, in the seclusion of the marriage bed, I cannot guarantee such discretion, and I don’t want you to presume more from my carelessness than it warrants.”

“It was kind of you to warn me,” Fitz said. “But I am all too well aware you often say things you don’t mean.”

“Now you are laughing at me.”

“Just this once. I promise not to usurp the privilege to which you have long since acquired sole rights. Now, may I hope to entice you to say a few things you don’t mean?”

“Oh yes, Fitz. No more interruptions, I promise. You were going along so very well.”

He kissed her mouth again and fondled her cleft. Her trust

in him was most gratifying, that she lifted her hips to his hand and moved herself against him. When he inserted his middle finger as far as the second knuckle, her muscles, surprisingly strong, clenched and released repeatedly, as if she had done this before. Yet she was as small and snug as any woman he had ever known—more, as he had known only married or professional women. She tightened herself around him with a sigh as he withdrew, as sorry to let him go as he was to leave her. But he must find that place that would bring her to pleasure. There it was, already red and engorged—and so sensitive he need only flick it with the lightest touch of fingertip. Much sooner than he had dared to hope, she was pulsing and throbbing against his palm, spurting with moisture.

"Please, Fitz," she said on a sob, pressing her face against his shoulder. She locked her sharp little teeth onto the sensitive hollow where neck and collarbone joined, worrying at his flesh like a dog with its favorite stick. He put the head of his cock to her opening, holding back as long as he could, until she spread her legs wide and pushed up to meet him, still biting into him, gasping and panting. There was no help for it now; he must enter her or lose everything. With one powerful thrust they were joined, his shaft buried in her, one flesh, one soul. She opened her eyes wide and loosened her jaws from his neck, crying out so loud he was momentarily petrified, convinced he had caused her irreparable damage.

"Oh, Fitz," she said, staring up at him, mouth quivering in what could be a cry of distress or teary laughter. "Oh, Fitz, I love you. I love you. Please, Fitz, don't make me say it again." Her teeth were pink with his blood.

He felt her spasms, and, responding to her own fierce rhythm, began to move inside her with increasing power, driving her forward against the piled bed cushions.

"Ah, I love you. Wicked, sweet man. I love you, Fitz. I love you." Her fingernails dug into the muscles of his back.

"And I love you, Elizabeth," he said, as he spent himself in her. "I will say it as often as you wish, and still it will not be enough." He eased out of her, already regretting the desolation of separate existence, and fell sideways, rolling onto his back. "My love."

Twenty-Five

IN A ROOM just along the corridor, Charles embraced his Jane. He wanted to devour her, slowly and methodically, the way Fitz was probably doing with Elizabeth. Charles could feel the explosion building within; at any moment he was going to let loose. Only the fear of frightening her or giving her a disgust of him allowed him a measure of restraint, and it took all his concentration. He caressed the luxurious waves of her golden hair, released from their bondage to ripple around her face, then dipped his head for a kiss.

"Charles, stop!" Jane said, leaping out of his arms as if scalded.

"My love," he protested. "Surely I may kiss you? We are married."

"Of course," she said. "But the door is open a crack."

"Oh Lord. Fitz did remind me about that. But I had so many more pressing things to see to."

Jane giggled. "Lizzy told me about it too."

"Lizzy? Your sister? Mrs. Darcy? When could she have—"

"Last autumn," Jane said. "She was very witty about it."

"How wonderful!" Charles stood still in a sort of daze, recalling those frustrating weeks with contentment, as for a long-past ordeal, easily endured. "Fitz decided it was my sister Caroline, you see, and he was scathing on that subject. I hope he is pleased that it was Elizabeth all along."

"Charles, my dear. If you don't shut the door and come to bed, I will put my clothes back on and sleep in the dressing room."

"Jane! Oh, you are teasing." Charles roused from his dream and pushed the door shut, watching in dismay as it sagged on its hinges and opened an inch or two into the room. "I suppose we shall have to find another chamber."

"Just put a chair under the door handle. My sister and Mr. Darcy will be leaving in the morning and we can switch rooms then."

"You know you can call him Fitz," Charles said.

"Since he will very shortly be quitting our house, there is no reason for me to address him at all."

"Jane, my love, you will have to forgive him sometime. Let's discuss it in the morning."

"There's no need to discuss it ever, Charles. No, don't blow out the candle. And would you mind very much removing your shirt? I want to see all that dark hair Lizzy told me of."

Excited by the prospect of naked proximity to his beloved, Charles was able to tamp down the slight disappointment that Elizabeth, not Jane, had been the first lady to see him in the flesh. He wriggled out of his shirt like a schoolboy and stood diffidently before his bride.

"You're blushing," Jane said, laughing with delight. "Everywhere."

"I didn't know that ladies enjoyed the sight of men as much as we do the ladies," Charles said, as his eagerness for his wife was revealed in all its unruly passion.

"We don't," Jane said. "At least, I do not. But once we're married, and to someone we love, it does not seem so very wrong."

"No, why should it? It is just that I was embarrassed to think of your sister."

"Yes, dear," Jane said. "If it makes you feel any better, she had nothing but praise for your person. I see, now, that she did not exaggerate."

"May I not enjoy the sight of you, too? You are modest, I know, but—"

"It seems only fair," Jane said. "And I should like to show myself to you, because I love you and I hope it will please you. Although I will have to start by turning my back, until I find the courage." She took a deep breath before beginning, bunching the material of her nightdress with her fingers, until she had worked the skirt up over her hips.

Charles gasped. "Oh, my word! I had no idea!" Her backside was perfection—like a pale peach, its two large halves divided by the crease, the flesh mottled with fatty indentations. Charles had never seen anything so beautiful . . .

She waited for another two breaths, hoisted the gown above her shoulders, and, stretching the opening with her hands, slipped it neatly over her elaborate coiffure. She turned around. "There, Charles."

. . . until he saw the front of her. Full, deep breasts, small, pink puckered nipples, wide hips, and plump thighs that curved in, away from her cleft, then curved out to meet, forming a neat line down to her knees. The slightest movement made everything shake or wobble, just a little. Just enough to make Charles think he was going to . . .

"Are you quite well?" Jane asked, bending over her husband where he lay on his back in what looked like a faint, while that one part of him stood straight up and grew rapidly in size, darkening in color. Jane watched in fascination to see it jerk with diabolical energy, as if trying to escape its attachment to Charles's body and launch itself into the air.

Charles sat up, winced at the pain in his lower body, and took his wife's hand. "No, my love. I am overcome by your beauty. I had seen only your face until now, and while I thought I could imagine the rest of you, I was unprepared for the goddess that was revealed to me."

"You are sweet," Jane said. "But if we don't do something about it, that rather frightening appendage is going to erupt, or explode."

"Very true," Charles said. "Here's what I propose."

"No," Jane said, "no more talking. Why don't you kiss me again. We both like that. Then we'll—Oh! I didn't know you were going to kiss me *there*! And *there*! Oh, Charles!"

FITZ WOKE WITH an odd sense of being watched. It was like a memory from boyhood, drowsing away a rainy afternoon in the barn, and Rowley, the tomcat . . . He opened his eyes.

"There, you're awake," Elizabeth said, kissing his cheek. "I was debating with myself whether to wake you. I didn't want to deprive you of your well-earned and obviously badly needed rest, but—"

"Elizabeth, is something wrong?" Fitz sat up too hurriedly and collapsed against the pillows as the blood rushed from his head.

"No, no, Fitz. It's just that I know we want to get an early start this morning and—"

"Oh God, what time is it?" Again he sat up and again had to flop back down.

"It's all right, Fitz. It's not yet seven."

"What is the trouble, then, my dear?"

"No trouble. That is, I was hoping we would have time for more pleasure before rejoining the world. But I see you are fatigued."

"More pleasure? Surely you are fatigued yourself." Fitz struggled with his conflicting desires and gave in to his baser nature, looking at his wife's face. Ladies were not at their best first thing in the morning and should be left unseen to repair the night's ravages. A young girl after her first night of love would be all the more fragile, feeling wounded, despoiled, and sullied, perhaps disillusioned. Yet Elizabeth's beauty was no more diminished by the harsh light of dawn than her character had been by her family's stark vulgarity. She was rosy and rumpled, her skin glowing, her hair wild and frizzed, the curls tighter and standing out in all directions around her face. Her eyes shone like twin stars in a vista of night sky. Without conscious thought, Fitz recognized, here beside him in the bed, a younger, softer version of Betty, the Fury's visage of the cotter's adulterous wife, and made peace with its womanly, fulfilled maturity.

"Oh, I'm not at all tired. After last night's three enlightening sessions—or was it four?—I see that you poor men must do most of the hard labor in this business."

"Four, my dear. I apologize for making such a sad job of that last attempt."

"Not at all," Elizabeth said. "It's only that I wasn't sure whether it was considered to be—that is, when the man doesn't—when the male organ—I mean . . ." She blushed and swallowed.

"I never thought to see you at a loss for words," Fitz said, lying back and clasping his hands behind his head, a self-satisfied smile lifting the corners of his mouth. "And so early in our marriage."

"Are there words for—that?" Elizabeth asked in a challenging tone.

"Certainly," Fitz said, "although they are not ones a lady would have reason to use, or even to hear."

"Then you have no right to tease me on the subject," Elizabeth said. "And you ought to tell me some of them, so that I may request it."

"I take it you liked it well enough to want it again?"

"I think it will help to improve my vocabulary," Elizabeth said, "associating the action with the word."

"There are a number of terms, all impolite," Fitz said, certain he would regret this freedom, but unable to deny her anything, even a word. "But 'tipping the velvet' is perhaps the least objectionable."

Elizabeth laughed. "Very pretty. I imagine we will need to examine the etymology of that phrase on occasion."

Fitz sat up to meet her lips, kissing her mouth and snuffling at her neck and breast, remembering his first intrigued scent of her, after her walk from Longbourn. "Is this, do you suppose, such an occasion?" he murmured.

She returned the kisses with equal and ardent inhalations. "Honestly, Fitz, no. You are about to observe that I need a bath. As you are in the same condition, it seems to me we might as well revel in our dirt and match our bodies plow to furrow, as we say in the country, and face to face."

His "plow" turned to furrow-cleaving steel at the plain speaking; as throughout the past year, his whole being was stirred by this unique mix of artlessness and alluring sensuality. He wished there was an exclusive gesture or ritual, something beyond the common marriage ceremony, to mark their union as blessed above all others. "You are the most amazing woman I have ever known," he said. "What have I done to deserve such happiness?"

"That is a very trite statement," Elizabeth said. "But we cannot all conceive original epigrams before breakfast. I will let it pass until you have gathered your wits." She put her hand on him. "Does this help?"

"Not with the wits gathering," Fitz said, while speech remained a possibility. "But no, that was not a request that you stop."

She stroked him up and down, fingering the soft skin that moved so tantalizingly against the hard shaft beneath. Her little fist barely encompassed him as he swelled under her ministrations. When the head began to emerge from the foreskin, she exclaimed, "It is like a sheath of velvet! Can a woman tip the velvet too?"

"No!" He dissolved in uneasy laughter, until his resolve for honesty between them compelled him to admit some of the improper truth. '"Velvet' refers to the tongue; what you are proposing is an undertaking best reserved for men."

"And you doubt a mere wife can do as well. We shall see."

Never, he swore, thereby justifying his indolence, should her stainless honor be sullied with the knowledge that, among her sex, this was the principal business of whores.

Elizabeth, encountering no further resistance, licked tentatively at the shaft, like a cat tasting a dish of porridge left unattended on the kitchen table, then pressed her lips in a wide kiss over the head. By the time she attempted to swallow, he was so engorged as to reach the point of danger. At the last possible moment, before he committed the most shameful deed with his bride, she gave up her efforts, made all the more arousing by her lack of expertise. "You are too big," she said, sounding almost sorry, "and my mouth and my throat cannot stretch like the passageway between my legs."

It was easy enough, Fitz discovered, to exercise self-control when his beloved was uncomfortable or unhappy. "Come here," he said, pulling her up beside him so she could rest in the crook of his arm. "We need not re-create all of Aretino's engravings in one day."

She brightened at his mention of the notorious name. "I suppose you have a copy in the library at Pemberley. Perhaps we can try one each week?"

"In time," he said, unruffled, taking his first steps on the glorious lifelong progress of their marriage: learning to distinguish her innocent barbs from deliberate baiting. "It is kept in a special cabinet, with an admonition that it is not to be opened by those married less than a year. Until then, we shall manage very well on our own."

For a minute or two there was silence, punctuated only by the liquid sounds of deep kisses and the shifting of bodies on tangled sheets.

"It is not such hard work as all that for us poor men," Fitz said. "Why should you think it?"

"You groan and make grunting noises."

"You are not exactly silent yourself," Fitz said.

"Would you wish me to be?" Elizabeth asked. "Is it not a testament to your skill? I suppose Charles was too polite to mention it."

"I wish," Fitz said, "you could leave other people out of our bed, if only for a week or two."

"That," Elizabeth said, "is entirely your decision."

"I begin to have my doubts," Fitz said, preparing to engage in more heavy lifting, "that there will be any decision that is entirely mine from now on."

"There's nothing to doubt," Elizabeth answered. "There will be no such unilateral decisions. Oh! Fitz! Oh no, please—don't stop."

"What did you say to me last night, my love?"

"Oh, you are cruel."

"Yes, that. And something else, I think you said."

"Oh, Fitz. Please. Oh. Oh! Wicked." She thrashed and flailed, trying to escape his hand, but he held her in place, straddling her with his thighs. After much experimentation the night before, he began to have a better gauge of her wiry strength. "Magnificent," she moaned out on a long breath.

"And what else?" He played with her nipples, tonguing and scraping with his teeth, until she was shaking with a passion that was as close to the peak of ecstasy as could be obtained from touching only the breasts.

"I see I will have to earn my every pleasure from now on," Elizabeth said. "I love you, Fitz. I love you. Does that satisfy you?"

"For now," Fitz said, success making him careless.

Quick and agile as the cat she so resembled, Elizabeth escaped from Fitz's restraint, sliding around and rolling him onto his back. She flung one sinewy leg over and clambered neatly on top. "There," she said, laughing with triumph. "That is much better. Lord! What an enormous staff you have, grandfather!" She lifted herself higher on her knees, like a jockey preparing to ride hell-bent for the home stretch, and sat herself down, slowly and deliberately engulfing his cock. She sighed and trembled as she slid into position. "Now what have you to say?"

Fitz lay supine, unable to speak, chest heaving in ecstasy. She began her posting, raising and lowering herself in the saddle. If she had a riding crop she would be whipping him inexorably to that glorious finish line. Never had surrender felt so like victory. As she released him from his torment—and hers—he gasped out, "I love you, my dearest Elizabeth. I love you."

"And you accuse *me* of saying things I don't mean," she said on a soft exhale, collapsing forward onto his broad chest. "But it is sweet to hear, all the same."

Over the next hour, as the manor house of Netherfield creaked, shuddered, and growled its way to morning bustle, in four hearts, in two separate bedchambers, the new day was welcomed with fervent gratitude.

Twenty-Six

FITZ RODE OUT early one morning, three weeks into his marriage, circling the park before heading for the uplands beyond. He needed one morning as he was used to, alone in the dawn mist, considering the tenants and their farms: how the Stowe family would manage after the eldest son's death; what was ailing the cattle on the north pastures; whether the war would keep prices high—and whether there would still *be* a war after the next campaign season ended . . .

"So beautiful," Elizabeth said every night. "Oh, you are so sweet, so beautiful." Always she took the initiative, though never was she less than feminine and generous. What would disgust him in any other woman, inviting contempt and killing his desire, in her inspired only reverence for the honorable purity of her love. It was as if, by possessing a man's animal spirits as well as a man's intellect, she raised herself to his level, made it a true marriage of equals.

He had been prepared to act the supplicant, the lust-driven husband begging for the favors of his coy bride. It was the tradition of man and wife, and he had been happy to assume his role, the more especially as it was no pretense but expressed his honest feelings, that it was a privilege merely to touch her. To possess her was so great a gift, he must earn it each time by humbling himself. After all his pride, his thoughtless condescension, he owed her this much, to do for her what he would do for no other woman. He would do it gladly, wanted to . . .

And here, as in everything, she overturned all his expectations. Each night they retired as soon as decently possible. Sometimes the servants had barely cleared the dinner table before they were slipping away upstairs. They would fall on each other still dressed and wake a few hours later in shift and shirt. And he would be hard again, and she was always willing. She never claimed to be tired or out of sorts, never seemed to be accommodating him from a sense of duty—all the states of connubial discontent that married men complained of. Indeed, it was he who demurred when her monthly bleeding arrived. "Surely you will be uncomfortable."

"If you do not object to the mess," Elizabeth said, "I have heard that it eases the cramps." Afterward she claimed the remedy worked very well.

It was because she was so clever, he thought, and so beautiful. She had not learned the shame or false modesty that stupid, plain females adopted to disguise their want of suitors. She reveled in her physical nature at night, but was as eager during the day to explore Fitz's library and to be guided by his tastes in poetry and history. In fact, they had come close to combining the two pleasures several times, reading the same text while occupying the same chair, hands busy creeping into her bosom or working between his legs. She had developed Fitz's knack for unbuttoning breeches . . . They had nearly ruined a volume of Horace's odes, the good translation by Dryden, crushing it between their bodies and creasing the pages. Fortunately the spine had not broken, although two of the pages were stuck together.

The entire household recognized her superiority. They would accept whomever he brought home, of course, would consider it a point of pride to give the master's choice their respect and cheerful, instant obedience. But there was an easy grace to her manner of command, a sweetness tempering her authority, and without the officiousness or pettiness of those new to wealth, that proved, whatever station she had been born into, it was here she belonged by right. Reynolds, the housekeeper, had taken Fitz aside one morning to say how pleased she was with the new mistress. "All of us, sir, we wanted to say that we're thankful you found the right lady for you, not one of those jumped-up hussies that marries for what she can get. Not that you would be taken in by one of those." Then, even more flustered, twisting her apron in her hands like a young girl in her first position in service, she had finished the speech she had been deputized to deliver as the senior member of the staff. "You go on and enjoy your honeymoon, sir, and don't you worry about us. We know when to make ourselves scarce." Fitz could only shake her hand, express his gratitude, and assure her he intended to follow their advice.

These last weeks he had never been so satisfied, yet never more in thrall to his desires. Fulfillment seemed merely to increase the appetite. He had become accustomed to his pleasure, the three and four times each night and the stolen, laughing moments in secluded walks in the park or by the stream, the winter weather making everything rushed, amusingly imperfect, yet all the more exciting. And that time in the barn with old Rowley looking on in feline curiosity to see his master with a puss instead of a tom. The same old fellow who, little more than a kitten, had observed Fitz's frenzied encounters with Wickham. How was Fitz to return to his life in the world, a leader in the community, to entertain visitors and behave like a civilized gentleman? And, oh my God, what would he do when she began breeding?

Fitz longed more than anything for their child. Boy or girl, from such a pairing it would be a worthy heir to Pemberley and the Fitzwilliam name. He would not give way to the dark terror, the knowledge that women died in this ordeal. No, that was imponderable; he would lose his reason by contemplating that abyss. He allowed himself instead the diversion of worrying over a lesser, selfish fear. How would he bear those last months when she was big and ungainly? And after, when she must be left alone to heal? How did good husbands, with the best will in the world . . .

He laughed aloud, startling his mount, Galahad, who tossed his head and broke from the controlled trot into a gallop. He would be faithful because there was no one else he desired. If he could not have her, he would prefer nobody, alone with his thoughts or—Charles, perhaps, would understand. Strange to think how the future had been foreshadowed; how, a year ago, he and Charles had lain in each other's arms, each thinking of a lady—and now they were married to those ladies. And just when that friendship would be most valuable, there was constraint between them. Fitz sighed, regretting his own indifference on the brink of marriage, in the face of Charles's wish to maintain the connection. Elizabeth had anticipated it, of course . . .

Now he understood what she had tried so tactfully to tell him about her friend Charlotte. My God! To think of her, of them . . . Fitz shook his head at himself, smiling. Surely he was being absurd. It was the sort of thing written in obscene doggerel, like Lord Rochester's scandalous verses. What had she said? All he remembered was her quoting her mother, scolding her daughter for her "green gown." Elizabeth was accustomed to hearing coarse country speech and had grown up amid the crude, forthright attitudes of the older generation, even as her own character remained unbesmirched. There was but one interpretation to put on her words. She had hinted as directly as any lady could.

He laughed again, but this time Galahad took no heed, glad of his master's light hands on the reins and enjoying the freedom to run to the top of the next rise. Ultimately, it was chaste. Two young ladies, not a cock between them. There was no harm in it, nothing to condemn, no danger of illegitimacy or loss of maidenhead. It was but the natural consequence of a passionate nature combined with delicacy of mind. She would need an object for her desires, and there was affection and understanding between members of the female sex that men did not possess—should not—unless effeminate themselves. It explained the paradox of the wedding night, Elizabeth's self-assurance combined with her physical purity.

Fitz wished he could remember what Charlotte looked like. He had not the faintest mental picture, so little impression had she made on him, especially as he had seen her only in Elizabeth's company. Who would notice a sparrow when a phoenix had just sprung, aglow with inner fire, from the ashes? He thought of Elizabeth and this Charlotte, no matter her appearance, kissing, fondling, touching . . . The images made him so hard he felt bruised in the saddle, and he cantered back to the house far more slowly than his impatient thoughts drove him. He left Galahad for the stable hands to rub down and ran up the stairs, not pausing to change out of his riding clothes.

ELIZABETH LAY DOZING after Fitz crept silently from the chamber before the sun was over the horizon. An active man needed air and exercise, while she was content with walks, or riding in the little phaeton Fitz had given her, with its pair of ponies. For a short time it was a treat to be alone in the bed for a change. To roll over and over again and hit nothing but the edge of the mattress instead of the usual solid bulk of flesh. To be able to lie in place without falling into the trough made by that heavy body. To stretch one's limbs wide and feel only the coolness of silk and linen, not the heat of tumescent manhood and taut muscles.

Oh, what would she do when she began breeding? Elizabeth let out a soft moan at the thought. Of course she wanted his child, and she hoped it was a son for his sake. But she did not like to examine the business too closely, the distended, swollen body, all slenderness and attraction gone, perhaps forever. Some women never regained their figures, and some lost far more than their looks—their health, even their lives. She would not think of that. What good could it do? Think of Mama, five children and none the worse for it, despite her claims of "nerves." And her aunt Gardiner, four children and doubtless more to come, still pretty and fashionable. Lady Lucas, with that enormous brood. Ugh! Surely she could manage better than becoming a breeding sow with a litter of piglets. Or was it simply the fate of the female sex?

No, she would think of lesser ills, something she could poke fun at. How would she manage at the end of this honeymoon period, how give up this licentious freedom? How was she to become Mrs. Darcy in earnest, instead of the eager bride with the importunate groom, each the prize for the other's improvement in character? It was a transformation the harder to accomplish as the reward fell equally to both, giver and recipient in turn.

She remembered her sorry state, less than a year ago, in thrall to Wickham's graceful beauty with its hints of virile force beneath the red coat and charming manner. How she had wrestled with the desire she could not safely acknowledge, was not even permitted to feel, much less gratify. And now she was married to the epitome of honorable manliness, someone who combined elegance of form and keenness of wit with the solid virtues of prudence, fairness, and benevolence—and everything was allowed! She could touch him, play with him, enjoy his full favors whenever she wished, wherever and however the mood struck. She still did not quite believe it. Men did not like forward ladies; she had heard that all her life. They were the masters, and in this most intimate part of life they must have dominion. Yet Fitz seemed only to welcome her every immodest advance.

She certainly had to laugh at herself for doubting Fitz's skill. Just because he loved his friend Charles, and had been caught in a young man's desire for the seductive, shallow Wickham, why should that mean he did not know how to please a woman? A vigorous man like Fitz would be more likely to seek out congenial partners of both sexes, rather than confine himself to one.

She had been prepared on their wedding night to help him if he seemed clumsy or ignorant, but he had proved from the beginning that his pride was as justified in this private arena as in the more public spheres of wealth and education. Each time they made love it was as if he found a new way to please her and a different configuration for their bodies to come together. He delighted in surprising her, all the more that she was quick to learn and matched him in stamina. Every night he played the game anew, and try how she might to gain the advantage, he always won, carrying her pell-mell to the edge of ecstasy and holding her there above the perilous drop until she said the words she had vowed never to repeat: "I love you." She must have said them more in these last three weeks than any other words in the English language, and he seemed unlikely to tire of hearing it for the next fifty years. Truth be told, what she could hardly bear to admit even to herself, she would say it with or without his enjoyable coercion. But best not to let him know that.

And all those daylight trysts, in the library and outdoors. The park was so full of hidden groves and shaded nooks it was as if it had been designed for impetuous, breathless lovers who could not walk ten paces without tumbling into an embrace. The cold and the snow denied them leisure and comfort, but it was a revelation how much could be accomplished while wearing cloak and greatcoat, and standing against a tree . . . She ought to feel shame, but with him the owner of it all, it seemed perfectly natural. Certainly the staff treated her with all the deference due to Mrs. Darcy. If anything, they appeared pleased that their reserved young master had found a wife who could free him from his straitlaced, gentlemanly propriety on occasion. Servants withdrew wordlessly from whatever room the master and mistress occupied, and when she and Fitz ventured outside, people always seemed to have duties in another part of the estate, far away in the opposite direction. Nobody ever so much as hinted that there was anything the least bit odd about their returning from "walks" with her gown and his coat all rumpled, roughened from tree bark, or stained with moss, her bonnets shredded and hair tousled. And after that time in the barn there had been bits of straw in everything.

Only there had she felt ill at ease, seeing Fitz stroking that mangy old tomcat, holding it in his arms like a lover and murmuring silly endearments in a voice almost indistinguishable from the loud purring. The creature was so jealous it had bared its yellowed teeth and hissed at her when she approached. "He remembers Wick—Wickham, you see," Fitz had said by way of apology. As if that explained everything. Old Rowley, he called it, the legendary despoiler of maidenheads, feline or human. It had watched them as they coupled, its one good eye drooping half closed, kneading the straw with its front paws and twitching its tail.

She wondered if carrying a child made one's desire decrease, if, once there was no practical value in the coupling, the body no longer sought it out. But she doubted very much that nature arranged anything for people's petty convenience. Look what happened with teeth and wrinkles and gray hair, people who looked old and worn out by the age of forty. Why would so great a thing as desire be made easier for people when *teeth* caused such suffering for no apparent reason other than to try one's faith in a benevolent creator?

There were ways to prevent conception, she had heard, but she suspected they were ineffective or risky, else everyone would use them and no one would have eight or ten children. Those poor women one saw holding a swaddled infant over a swollen belly, while a child barely old enough to work minded a toddler and an even smaller one crawled on the floor. Who would choose that? But Elizabeth dared not think of it. How hurt Fitz would be if he found out! Power was good, just enough to maintain equality, but not so much that she crushed his spirit or lost his admiration. It was a measure of his love that he had chosen her to be the mother of his children. And she wanted it too, to give him that supreme gift that only a woman can give to a man.

She wished she knew how Jane and Charles were faring. Jane's letters had been unusually short, the happiness spilling out through her vague words like blots from too much ink, but sparse on details. It was not the sort of thing one could write in a letter, even to one's sister. If only Jane could forgive Fitz, perhaps they could all be friends again. Surely, after a month of marriage—

Charles, of course! She saw it again, the two naked men, their flesh reddened in the glow of firelight, Fitz's rod pointing straight out toward his friend, and the way he licked Charles's neck. He licked her neck that way too, sometimes. She shuddered, overtaken by another bout of desire, like a fever but not so sweat-drenched, like a toothache without the pain, only that sense of coming uncentered, like a maypole unwinding . . . That was the answer. She would write to Jane again, invite them to Pemberley, see what Jane answered. When she heard the booted footsteps taking the stairs two at a time, she knew he had felt her longing.

ELIZABETH WAS AWAKE when Fitz entered the bedchamber.

"I am glad you are back," she said. "Where have you been all this time?"

"Riding the farms," Fitz answered. "But the sweetest images appeared to me, of you and your friend Charlotte, and the loveliest sensation came over me, and I had the strongest urge to return."

She peeped up at him from under her cap, the tendrils of hair that always escaped forming a flirtatious fringe. He could have sworn she read his thoughts. "How strange! I was just thinking of you and Charles."

"Indeed?" Fitz sat on the side of the bed and slid his fingers over a curl, tucking it under the edge of the cap. "Why should it be, I wonder, that the thought of you with your friend, or of me with mine, creates such heat?"

"Does it?" Elizabeth smiled. "It certainly took you long enough to figure it out."

"And you gave me as clear an indication of your meaning as a lady could. Can you forgive my slowness?"

"You are never slow," Elizabeth said. "Merely purposeful. You reach your destination at your own steady pace." She sat up, allowing the bedclothes to fall away from her rosy nakedness. "And you know, Fitz, there are times when deliberation can be far preferable to a disorderly rush." Her small breasts with the pointy nipples were so close to his face he couldn't help drawing one into his mouth, rasping it with his tongue until she purred with pleasure.

Fitz took his mouth from her and sat on the side of the bed, fumbling with the buttons of his riding breeches. "Nevertheless," he said, "I think I cut it very close this time."

"Perhaps. But you made it safe home." Elizabeth kicked the covers to the end of the bed and exposed her entire body, the narrow waist and hips, the shapely legs spread wide to show the opening to that nether paradise where he had been granted entrance, despite his sins. Fitz extended his booted legs in a helpless gesture, his whole body shaking.

"Come here," she said, tugging on his arm. "Don't waste time with all that now. Come and make love to me."

"I'm sorry, my love," he said. "I'm not able to—"

"Oh, for love's sake, Fitz, just be careful with the spurs is all I ask."

Which is how a new feather ticking had to be sewn, and a set of the best linen sheets, made expressly for the master's nuptials, were turned into dust cloths after only three weeks.

Twenty-Seven

ELIZABETH SAW HER husband reading a book at breakfast instead of his usual newspaper. "Tired of those 'vapid sheets the rattling hawker vends through gaping streets'?"

Fitz stood briefly to acknowledge his wife's entrance before returning to his seat. "I am delighted to hear the words of my old friend George Crabbe again, and issuing from such sweet lips. The truth is, I am so enjoying your gift to me that I cannot put it aside, even with the temptation of a new day's worth of maggots dropped on this trifler's brain."

"You are reading *Cecilia*?" Elizabeth asked.

Fitz held the book up to show the title. "I am once again humbled, my love. It was easy for me to despise what I called 'ladies' novels,' never having read any. But now I am forced to concede the merits of the form. A perfect combination of sharp satire and gentle comedy, yet also an appreciation of the finer human qualities, so as not to fall into the trap of despising all mankind. And written by a woman—a lady."

"And a very moving, absorbing story," Elizabeth said. "It's

not simply an argument or a debate, like a sermon or an essay, but an account of events that could be real. That's what I admire most in Madame D'Arblay's writing."

"I suppose it's why novels are held in low esteem," Fitz said. "Unsophisticated readers no doubt believe they are reading a history, an unembellished account of a young lady's life, and only the discerning appreciate the art that goes into it."

Elizabeth nodded, admiring once again her husband's ability to keep pace with her thoughts. "And why poetry is the more respected. It's not possible to mistake heroic couplets for everyday speech. The reader can never forget that the poet is working hard at his craft of meter and rhyme."

"Now I see the truth," Fitz said, "that a good novel, more than any other work of literature, conveys the most thorough knowledge of human nature, the happiest delineation of its varieties, and the liveliest effusions of wit and humor, all in the best chosen language."

Elizabeth arched her brows. "You cannot in good conscience claim to be the originator of those words."

"You have found me out," Fitz said. "It was my cousin, Colonel Fitzwilliam."

"He is a thief," Elizabeth said. "But of words only. Still they were mine and I labored to produce them."

"I ought to have guessed he couldn't have constructed s
a perfect turn of phrase on his own," Fitz said. "Why did
know it for yours?"

"You and I had never discussed books and music in t
dard way of men and women becoming acquainted.
convinced of our contrary opinions, and had yet t
how much better we agree with our clothes off."

Fitz laughed and shook his head. *Deliberate*
time.

"But I confess I like both forms of litera

said, returning to the safer ground of reading. She had learned that her husband held up better if given an occasional respite. "Crabbe has long been my favorite for verse, and Madame D'Arblay for novels."

"May I infer from that," Fitz said, "that my gift to you was redundant?"

"Do you mean, had I read Crabbe before? Yes, of course. Papa had all of Crabbe's works in his library. But it makes me value your gift all the more. It is every romantic poet's rule that husband and wife must share the same taste in reading or the marriage is doomed to failure."

"You are not merely claiming it now because I have been converted to Madame D'Arblay?" Fitz asked.

"Fitz!" Elizabeth rose from her chair and settled herself in the less comfortable but more stimulating seat of her husband's lap. "We have been married for a whole month."

"Have we?" he said, putting his arm around her and kissing her mouth and her neck. "It feels like a week at most."

"That is the only permissible answer," Elizabeth said, returning the kisses and nibbling on her husband's ear. "But I mention the elapsed time because you ought to know by now I don't dissemble. I thought it was why you married me."

"Yet I have found you to be far gentler in private than the fierce, uncompromising Boadicea you pretend to be in company," Fitz said. "I thought it possible you might occasionally say what you hoped would please me. After all, you *do* so many things to please me." This last statement was punctuated by a hand descending into the front of Elizabeth's gown.

"Oh no," Elizabeth said, her words coming somewhat breathlessly as she lifted her skirts and turned to straddle Fitz's hips. "You misunderstand my motives. I do such things purely to please myself." She flipped open the buttons on Fitz's breeches. "As this." Kneeling on the edges of the chair's seat, she raised herself until her spread thighs just met the tip of her husband's already engorged member.

Fitz groaned as he was released from his drawers and as suddenly captured by her hot opening. "Oh God, Lizzy. Someone might come in."

Elizabeth put her hands on Fitz's shoulders, pushing herself up and sliding down. "Don't worry, Fitz. If anyone does, he will have the sense to go away and come back later."

Later

"There really is no excuse for only now ascertaining our mutual admiration for George Crabbe," Elizabeth said, between mouthfuls of long deferred and greatly needed buttered toast and boiled egg. "When our grandchildren inquire, we will have to hide the awful truth from them."

"That we were too far along in love to bother with the usual manner of determining whether we were compatible?" Fitz said.

"Precisely," Elizabeth answered. "It is such a shocking lapse that our courtship did not originate in a shared poetic preference, and that we only found it out weeks after we were wed, that I will have to save it for a deathbed confession, like a sixth months' child."

"At least we need not fear that." Fitz looked up from his somewhat dry roast beef. "Lizzy. Do you feel that you are—? Have you any of the signs?"

Elizabeth shook her head. "Don't be silly, Fitz. It has been less than a fortnight since I had my—well, you know, that is not a fit subject for the breakfast table."

Fitz laughed. "I am astonished you have found one."

"Oh, I shall be able to think of a dozen, once we are no longer alone." Elizabeth inserted a knife into a pot of raspberry preserves, smeared a large glob onto a strip of toast, and, extending her tongue to draw in the tip with its covering of glistening red, swallowed the rest of the bread in a gulp.

Fitz felt as if he was peeping through a spy hole in the wall of a lady's bedchamber. "We cannot continue like this," he said in a low voice, very much afraid he would be unable to avoid a repetition of this morning's disgraceful lapse.

Elizabeth looked up from her plate. "No," she said, equally glum. "I am sorry, Fitz, for my misdirected enthusiasm."

"Never reproach yourself, my love," Fitz said, putting his hand over hers where it rested on the edge of the table. "As soon blame the idol for her worshipper's excesses."

"But I inspire them," she said. "And I cannot claim ignorance of the effect my actions have on my devoted follower." She stared pointedly at his hand, which, not satisfied with merely grasping, had turned its prize over and was now gently, if persistently, stroking the palm. "I think it's time we allowed a visitor or two to encroach on our cloistered solitude."

Fitz snatched his hand away. "I suppose we must have company," he said. "Nothing else will prevent me from committing idolatry at every canonical hour."

"Surely your sister ought to be allowed to return home from her town exile," Elizabeth said.

Fitz laughed, grateful that the mention of Georgie had subdued his disobedient flesh as reproving words could not. "Dragged back by force, more likely. What sixteen-year-old girl would wish to leave her own establishment in London and live under her married brother's roof?"

"I think Georgiana will prefer it," Elizabeth said. "She has the wit to value guidance over independence; and I will like having a sister again, as I am accustomed. Even though it means curbing my conversation at the breakfast table—and my behavior." She used her spoon to scrape the remainder of preserves from the pot, clamping her lips around the bowl of the spoon and working at it with her tongue. "Of course, we could always take breakfast in bed and come down late."

Hard again, damn it. "You must not sway me from the path of improvement," Fitz said. "I would all too readily let everything fall into disrepair if it meant an extra hour or two of indulgence."

Elizabeth wiped her sticky hands and face. "You forget," she said, "that I married you precisely because you are the master of a well-run and productive estate worth many thousands of pounds. I would never allow things to deteriorate that far, or there would have been no purpose to my polluting the shades of Pemberley in the first place."

"Wretched old sow," Fitz muttered, deflated once more. "I wish, just once, my aunt had kept her offensive opinions to herself."

"Not at all," Elizabeth said. "By speaking frankly, she gave me the perfect excuse not to invite her to add to the pollution. No, Fitz, let us begin with some more deserving visitors, perhaps a couple of them."

"Oh, Lizzy," Fitz said. "Not your parents, please. Not yet."

"I don't think I could stand it either. No, I was thinking of someone who at one time seemed to have a genuine claim on your affection. Someone with the initials C.B." *Counterbalance love with love*, she thought.

"Caroline—that is, Miss Bingley? Lord, that's worse. I do feel sorry for her, but honestly, I was hoping to distance myself from that connection."

"Definitely *not* Miss Bingley," Elizabeth said. "While I most heartily approve your sentiments—a man can never feel a partiality for a woman he pities—I am not yet ready to disturb our perfect equilibrium. Knowing her, the mere fact of your marriage would not necessarily destroy all her hopes."

Fitz laughed. "*You* may say what would appear insufferable vanity in me. But whom have you invited?"

"No one, yet," Elizabeth said, "but I was thinking of my sister Jane. You do remember her? She's married to a former friend of yours, a Mr. Charles Bingley. And if there are no objections on either side, I believe it might help us ease into the wider world if we had Jane and her husband for a short stay—perhaps a month or two."

God, she was astonishing! "It's as if you know my thoughts, as if we are of one mind," Fitz said. "How do you do it?"

"It is not difficult with so attentive and generous a husband," Elizabeth said. "I must say, for a man who does not like women, you have made an excellent beginning at marriage."

"Whatever gave you the idea I do not like women?"

"Oh, Fitz, you know very well that a man who has a *particular friend* can't possibly like women as well."

Fitz frowned. "You go too far with that jest sometimes. I know you take pleasure in this line of teasing, but—"

"But I am perilously close to the border that separates vulgarity from obscenity."

"It is a very narrow line," Fitz said, "and one you frequently enjoy surveying. But you are incapable of saying anything that I find truly objectionable."

"Well, to be fair, you don't have to like *women* in the plural. *One* is really all that is required. In fact, in our society, it is usually recommended that a man love only one woman at a time. The one he is married to."

"I can safely promise there will be no other," Fitz said. "Come, tell me how things stand between you and your sister."

"It's difficult to know. Never have we sent such empty letters, polite words with little of substance. I have written to inform her of my married bliss, and she has shared similar tidings with me, but of deeper sentiments, nothing. In my next letter I hoped to extend an invitation, so that we might talk of those things we cannot write."

"Then she has forgiven me?"

"That I cannot say. You will have to ask her yourself."

JANE WOKE EARLY and sat by the window to read the letter a third time, just to be certain.

> Mr. Darcy has expressed his wish several times now, that his old friendship should not be forgotten in the pleasures of marriage. He is heartily sorry for the wrong he committed and hopes that one more gracious than himself can be persuaded to forgiveness.

All this trouble over something so simple. Charles loved her and she loved him. They were alike in every way except that one that made it most suitable for them to marry: she was a woman and he a man. When she was a girl she had worried sometimes, how it would be to be married. In charge of the household all by herself; managing the money and the staff, making sure they stayed within their budget, and giving orders without being either arbitrary or indecisive; planning the menus and arranging parties and dinners. But with Charles it was all so easy. Any time she had a question she could ask. He didn't make fun of her for not knowing or expect her not to bother him with women's work. Most of the time it turned out she knew the right way all along, better than he did. It was voicing her question out loud that helped her clarify her thoughts. That and having an amiable, kind husband who valued her for her solicitude and caution.

She thought back to their wedding night, how innocent they

had both been, and yet how natural and joyful the consummation. It had not mattered one whit that she had so small a portion or that Mama was sometimes vulgar. Or that Charles's sisters wished him to marry Miss Darcy. No, on that night, and every night since, for an entire month—and even, on several delicious occasions, during the daylight hours as well—all that mattered was that they were husband and wife, man and woman—even, to say it truly, lovers.

It was not wrong, she decided, to admit that she loved his body as well as his character. Before marriage one dared not think such thoughts. Now, it was sanctioned by society and, more important, by the church and by God. Charles's dark, silky hair; his slender yet well-defined limbs; his stomach with those faint ridges of muscle ("from riding, I suppose," he said diffidently when she asked); his little pink nipples peeking through the thick foliage on his chest. Who would have guessed that men's nipples were as exquisitely sensitive as a woman's? Jane could bring her husband to the very edge of release, just by licking him there . . . Even that unmentionable part of him, the male member, was beautiful, sweet, and gentle, just like him, but easily roused to masculine force if required. She giggled to herself. Yes, it was so often required these days!

Her only lack, it seemed, was Elizabeth. How she wished for her sister's friendship and wisdom, to compare their respective states of wedded happiness and see if perhaps Charles had started a child in her. *Lizzy would know.* To be able to talk as they were used to, to say anything—anything at all. Oh, if only there were not this cloud hanging over them of deceit and cruelty.

CHARLES LAY FEIGNING sleep, watching through slitted eyelids as his wife read her letter. How lovely she was, and how kind. How generous to him. And how well matched they were, despite Fitz's worries.

He had known it from the first meeting, at that assembly in Meryton. She was the one for him. Yes, she was more beautiful than any other girl, but that wouldn't have convinced him if she hadn't been *the one* in every other way, too. She was gentle and thoughtful, unhurried and methodical, never out of sorts or in low spirits. She even came to Charles for advice or to ask his opinion. Him! He could laugh if he didn't feel so proud—although, really, when you considered, it was a hell of a lot of responsibility. But there again, Jane proved her superiority, for while she made a show of deferring to Charles's judgment, the truth of it was they always thought alike. Not for Jane the cutting sarcasm of her sister Elizabeth, or the quick, darting movements that matched her sharp wit—what Fitz liked so much.

Charles could smile at his old self, fretting over the wedding night, and now to see how easy it was. It wasn't hard to please a woman; a man didn't need superior intellect or the experience of a libertine—else how would there ever be happy marriages among ordinary folk? All one had to do was pay attention. It was like school, if a thousand times more interesting. You just had to study and apply yourself. He laughed silently in his thoughts, imagining how much better school would have been if they had had lessons like these. Listen to how she breathed: calmly as at rest or rapidly, as if she'd been startled, like a horse at a gate. Touch her and see whether her muscles tensed or stayed slack. Feel her heartbeat hammer and hear her little moans turn to gasps. When her inner walls began to contract and release, oh, then it was bliss. You could push inside her and she welcomed it, begged for it as if she were the one receiving the favor. And the best of it was, a leisurely pace was rewarded. The bedroom was not a steeplechase or an auction.

It was the parable of the tortoise and the hare made real. Slow and steady . . .

He thought of his first sight of her, the revelation of the abundance of rounded shapes, the fleshiness of thighs and breasts, stomach and buttocks, all with the palest, delicate skin and blond curls everywhere, not just on her head but under her arms and between her legs. Even her upper thighs had invisible hairs, as fine as spider silk, except they tasted delicious and weren't sticky. He was one fly who didn't struggle in the web, but was delighted to be captured . . .

That had been an inspired notion, kissing her below the first time, instead of going straight for penetration. It was such a great pleasure for Charles when Fitz used his mouth; why should it not be the same for a woman? Tonguing her deeply and thoroughly, burrowing his way inside her like a mole in a garden, like an earthworm in dense soil, he had churned her, turned her up wet and yielding. If his skill was not yet sufficient to bring her to satisfaction, still, by the time his own need was so great he could not hold back any longer, she was ready for him. He had thrown himself into her flesh like a horse let out to pasture in spring, wallowing in mud.

No poet, indeed, he thought, recalling his one poor attempt. All his comparisons sounded horrid; but he meant only reverence for her motherly warmth, the sense of viscous, yielding liquid, thick and enveloping, that defined her. She surrounded him like the waves of the ocean embracing a floating log, lapping at his sides, spilling over his back, bathing him in love. Every night he began with *the kiss*, and each time he improved in ability. By now he knew her secret pathways, every little fold and covered lane. As she came gushing into his open mouth, he was so hard he could barely move up in time to meet her, rod to cleft and face to face.

Sometimes they tried it with her on top. He could reach up

to her large, soft breasts, quivering and shaking like jellies, the small pink nipples standing out like ripe cherries. He would try to encompass all the flesh, one in each hand, and never quite succeed. But what fun it was to try—for both of them. Everything he did seemed to delight her. It was a miracle. The way Fitz had scoffed and sneered, you'd think . . .

That was the only thing missing from his complete happiness. His friend. He wished he could tell Fitz how fortunate he was, let him know that all his work of separating him from Jane had been senseless, like King Canute commanding the tide to turn. To boast of his growing proficiency, his power to make this gorgeous, languid woman moan with happiness or whimper with need. And, truth be told, it would be comforting to be bullied—just a little—in their old genial manner. It was wearing, always being the man. Not so much for the body, but the mind. Charles would welcome the chance to lie back, so to speak, and let Fitz make the decisions for a while.

He wondered how Fitz was getting along with his clever little bride. Who was the man in that marriage? It was, in many obvious ways, hard to imagine, yet it had a sense of rightness to it, the appropriateness of the unexpected. Somehow, he felt, Fitz was happy. Oh, he'd give a great deal to see that, Fitz content in his marriage, the counterpart to the one he had so despised for his friend. Charles forgot he was supposed to be asleep and laughed out loud.

"I thought you might be awake by now," Jane said, moving from the window to sit on the side of the bed. "I have had another letter from my sister Elizabeth."

Charles blinked and sat up. "Mrs. Darcy?"

"She invites us to Pemberley."

"And what will you answer?" Charles asked.

"That depends on you," Jane said. She leaned over to kiss her husband's sweet, sulky mouth. "I know you would like to see your friend again, and I desire your happiness above all things, but I would prefer not to have to stay in Mr. Darcy's house. Yet I can't bear to be separated from you ever again—" The rest was muffled and hard to distinguish because her mouth was covered. For a long time there were only muffled squeals and yelps. "Oh, Charles," Jane said at last. "You are the best husband. I would rather go to Pemberley than to have to do without you for even a day."

"We don't have to go at all," Charles said, turning his head away so she wouldn't see how much the lie cost him.

"But you want to, don't you?" Jane said, her voice coaxing, as with a child.

"I miss him," he whispered.

Twenty-Eight

THE REUNION OF the two sisters was loud, and entailed much embracing, kissing, and the clasping of hands. The meeting of the two men was quieter. As Jane and Elizabeth wept, laughed, shouted, and whispered all at once, Fitz smiled and held out his hands. Charles, after a quick glance at his wife and receiving a small nod of approval, simply walked into the welcoming circle and kissed Fitz on the mouth. He allowed himself to be enfolded in the strong arms and to luxuriate in the heat radiating from the muscular chest.

"Oh, Fitz," Charles said. "I am pleased to see you."

Fitz lowered his eyes to the significant bulge pressing against him. "So I see," he said, returning the kiss with force. "It's good to have my old shooting partner again."

"Seems to me we're both loaded and primed," Charles said as he snuggled closer.

Fitz acknowledged the fact with a bark of laughter, and held his friend at arm's length. Charles seemed to stand straighter, carrying his slender form with new confidence, yet still with his old grace. "You have grown into marriage, Charles," Fitz said. "From a youth to a man. I admit to liking it very well." He wrapped Charles in his arms again, and kissed the top of his head where it rested against his shoulder.

Once Mrs. Darcy and Mrs. Bingley's first effusions were spent, they drew aside to admire the expressive attitude of their husbands.

"That would make an excellent picture for the gallery," Elizabeth said.

"They do look happy," Jane said.

Fitz gently disengaged from Charles's clinging hands, stepped toward the two ladies, and bowed. "Mrs. Bingley," he said. "It is generous of you to accept our invitation, considering the great wrong I did you a year ago. While I can begin with but words of apology, I hope, during the weeks of your stay, to prove by my conduct how deeply I regret the injustice and impropriety of my misdeeds and the distress they caused."

"Oh!" Jane was unable to give a polite or coherent reply. Only now did she understand the great charm of her sister's formidable husband. It explained everything—Charles's love and Elizabeth's, who had married her dearest sister's enemy. Jane blushed and stammered, looking for guidance to Elizabeth, who merely smiled agreement with her husband's sentiment. She found the strength from her month of marriage, the knowledge of Charles's devotion allowing her to stand up even to him, her nemesis. "Mr. Darcy, I—that is—I know you love Charles and that . . . what you did—that is—of course I forgive you."

Fitz took his sister-in-law's hand and kissed it. "You are too kind. I would prefer that you suspend your judgment of me until you determine whether I am worthy of forgiveness. And if you decide that I am, please call me brother, or best of all, Fitz."

"There, Jane," Charles said, his voice sounding overloud in

the hushed atmosphere. "Didn't I tell you Fitz was the best of good fellows? Go on, kiss him back and let's all be friends."

Jane rose on tiptoe to her brother-in-law, who slouched to meet her halfway, and deposited the lightest of fluttering kisses on his cheek. "You must call me Jane," she said in her soft voice.

"Only when you are ready," Fitz said. "For now, it will give me the greatest pleasure to address you as Mrs. Bingley, so that I will be reminded of the truth, articulated so well in the words of the wedding ceremony: 'what God hath joined let no man put asunder.'"

The ladies walked slowly upstairs, arm in arm. Jane, still in awe of Fitz's performance, let Elizabeth chatter away uninterrupted. "It was silly of me to worry, but I was a little afraid, when I suggested this visit, that your Charles might put on a show of resistance on your behalf. Yet I of all people should know how my Fitz's splendor carries everything before him."

"Actually," Jane found her voice again in defense of her husband, "Charles was quite determined to stand firm this time, for my sake. All the way in the coach, he swore he would not just melt into Mr. Darcy's arms. And surely you saw, Lizzy, for nothing escapes your notice, how he looked to me before greeting his friend."

"I did," Elizabeth said, recalling the way he had looked in the same way to his friend, only a couple of months ago, for permission to sit with Jane at dinner. "You can be proud of him. He has done more than most can manage in the face of such magnificence, certainly more than I am capable of. Indeed, it is one of the reasons I longed for your visit—some badly needed reinforcements against overwhelming odds."

"Goodness, Lizzy!" Jane exclaimed. "You make it sound like a war!"

"It is," Elizabeth said. "Fitz and I are, both of us, in a state of constant conflict: good sense and responsibility, allied but outnumbered, opposing the hordes of animal nature."

Jane looked startled and unhappy. "I had not thought things to be in such a way between you two, since you assured us all of your genuine love for him. But you know it is your duty as a wife to comply with your husband's wishes. You mustn't reproach him if he is importunate, but accept his demands in a submissive spirit." Her voice had sunk to a whisper, so tremulous Elizabeth could barely make out the words.

Elizabeth's ringing laugh almost brought the men out of their embrace. "Oh, Jane!" She lowered her voice with effort. "It is not Fitz's demands that trouble me, but my own."

Jane went bright crimson from her hairline down to her chest. She could not look at her sister. "If that is a fault, then I too am guilty."

Elizabeth slipped an arm around her sister's waist. "That was ill done of me. I had not meant to alarm you with my silliness. And anything *you* do cannot be so very wrong." She made a rounded motion over her middle with her free arm. "I was wondering if you had any notion of—"

"You mean, might I be with child?" Jane's face glowed at the welcome change of subject, and in such a way as left little doubt. "I am not sure, but I rather think I am." She blushed again—hard to see against the previous color, still fading. "And you, Lizzy?"

Elizabeth shook her head. "Thank goodness, not yet."

"Oh, that is not like you! Surely if you love Mr. Darcy you want to give him a child?"

"Of course. It's just that—I admit I prefer to devote yet more time and effort to the process before having to face the consequences."

The two ladies succumbed to mirth again, pausing on the landing to see how the men were doing.

"There's still a week or two left in the season," Fitz was saying, "and the game should be plentiful, as I've been out of doors very little this past month." He looked sideways at Charles to see how he took this.

"Me too," Charles said, apparently unaware of any hidden meaning. "We can go first thing tomorrow, assuming the weather holds. I can't wait to tell you—" He broke off, knowing the ladies were listening.

"Lord!" Elizabeth exclaimed. "It will be a treat to have the house to ourselves. I shall be glad of the opportunity to tell you certain things, too."

"You mustn't make me laugh so," Jane said between giggles. "I'll be as silly as our younger sisters all through dinner, just thinking of it."

THE SHOOTING PARTY was in the old-fashioned style: no beaters or loaders, just the two men, their guns and their dogs, stalking the ground-nesting partridges through the brush. Fitz and Charles set off in the direction of the scrubland above the far end of the park, away from the farms and the tenants' dwellings. There was game here, but widely dispersed. The men walked in an odd arrhythmic manner: a few steps, stop, stand still, then more steps, another halt. It looked hesitant and ungainly, but it flushed the birds more efficiently than regular, continuous pacing, which led them to believe themselves unseen and safe. The dogs, at first cavorting wildly in delight at their freedom, soon settled into their work, scenting and pointing. Before long, the booming sound of the birds' rocket-like launch into startled flight brought the men's guns up. Fitz took the first shot, Charles the second, in their accustomed system. In just a couple of hours they bagged nearly a dozen apiece.

"A good day's work," Fitz said. "Ought to leave some for the rest of the week, and more to breed for next year."

"Pity to go in so soon, though," Charles said.

As if by prior discussion, but with no more words spoken, the men walked out of the scrub, toward the wooded area at the edge of the park. Under the trees there was smoother ground, free of brambles. At the first dry patch of grass they hung the bags of game from a branch to keep them safe from the dogs, spread their greatcoats like a blanket, and lay down side by side. The dogs settled in with a contented sigh, glad of the rest and grateful not to be scolded off. Although the woods sheltered them from the worst of the wind, it was chilly without their coats. The men snuggled for warmth, which led by logical steps to kissing and then to fondling. It was Charles who acted first, surprising Fitz with his eagerness and newfound skill.

Afterward, lying at peace in each other's arms, watching the gray clouds scudding overhead through the naked braches, Charles broke the silence. "Do you know, Fitz, I thought married life was going to be pleasant, but I never guessed it could be this good."

"It is as I said," Fitz said, making a joke of it. "You have grown into marriage—two inches at least, maybe three."

"Can't say the same for you, thank goodness," Charles answered in the same vein. "Any more would be indecent. You could choke a fish hawk as it is."

"And yet," Fitz said, "you have developed a remarkable facility."

"It was marriage taught me that too," Charles said.

"Mmm?" Fitz could tell Charles was in the throes of philosophy, and would talk with or without encouragement.

"Do you remember how you teased me about my inexperience with women? Well, it was all so easy and natural, despite both of us being completely innocent. It occurred to me that I had become a man, not by wishing, or by any particular act of the body, but simply by loving."

"That is almost profound," Fitz said. He was not yet ready to admit having undergone much the same transformation himself. "But I never thought to cede my place as master there."

Charles lifted himself on one elbow to see his friend's face. "Must it always be master and pupil between us, man and boy? Can we not love as equals, both of us men?"

Fitz laughed to cover his discomfort. "The ancients would not have it so. Still, I imagine, then as now, the actuality did not always reflect the ideal."

"Perhaps we can create a new ideal," Charles said.

"Perhaps," Fitz said.

But Charles understood more than he showed. For when Fitz rolled over on him and asked would he mind very much if they made love as they were used to, Charles lifted his hips and raised his knees. "I shall always want that," he said.

Twenty-Nine

Not Quite a Year Later

ELIZABETH AND JANE sat in the nursery at Pemberley. The large room, with its enviable southern exposure, had a crowded feel today, containing as it did two cradles set side by side, the occupants' mothers, and the nursemaids, temporarily banished to the corner where they conversed softly. "It was kind of you to travel in your condition," Elizabeth said. "I ought not to have asked, but I don't think I could have borne it another day without you."

Jane shook her head. "I was glad to come. And I am perfectly well. It has been almost three months, after all."

Elizabeth nodded in the direction of little Charlie Bingley. "Wouldn't Charles allow you to leave him at Netherfield? You must have had a miserable journey—a crying infant, a nursemaid, yards of dirty swaddling clothes. I wonder you didn't hire a third coach."

"Charles?" Jane sounded scandalized. "I wouldn't dream of going so far as Longbourn without my precious child, much less all the way to Derbyshire. Surely you wouldn't want to be separated from Anne."

"Oh, you're as bad as Fitz," Elizabeth said. "Do you know, I had never considered even the possibility of there being disadvantages to marrying into such a great estate until now. Instead of a nursemaid in the village, as you and I and our sisters had, there are so many rooms we must have a nursery right here in the house."

"We do the same at Netherfield," Jane said. "It's so much easier, not having to worry how Charlie's faring." She sneaked a glance over her shoulder at the nursemaids. "Not that our dear Molly gives us any cause for concern."

"Nor our Bridget," Elizabeth said, "although I can't see how it makes any difference, other than to rouse us at all hours, fretting over every little belch and fart. Babies will thrive or not, depending on their constitution. At least the old way, the sounds and smells were kept at a decent remove, and only when the infant was weaned and grown into a child, capable of learning proper conduct, was it allowed to return to the family."

"You won't remember," Jane said, "but when you came home, you were so cross at missing your 'Nana' you cried for an entire fortnight. I believe that's when poor Mama began complaining of nerves."

"And when you and I became such good friends," Elizabeth said. "You must have looked after me then, in place of my nanny. But I never thought to see some merit in Mama's notions. It's a wonder I don't develop nerves myself."

Jane put a comforting hand on her sister's shoulder. "You are tired, Lizzy, that is all. I imagine this is the first time in your life you've ever known such a feeling, or felt ill. How long has it been? A little over a week? You ought not even to be out of bed. I promise you, in a month you'll be yourself again, and then you'll see how lovely it is, having your little girl to hold and fondle whenever you wish." She leaned over Charlie and placed several wet kisses on his face.

"I would never dare do that with Anne," Elizabeth said, somewhat wistfully. "The few times she falls asleep without first creating the most impressive commotion, it's more than our peace is worth to disturb her."

"Girls are supposed to be easier," Jane said.

"Perhaps ordinary girls," Elizabeth said. "But this one is clearly a Darcy, and is determined to make her least discomfort known in the clearest possible terms." The object of her words, obviously intent on making a mockery of her mother, was at the moment lying peacefully on her back, cooing softly to herself.

Fitz entered the nursery on tiptoe and moved to stand over the cradle. "How is my darling girl?" he inquired. "How clever you are to ignore these censorious ladies and remain blissfully above the fray."

"Gggaaa," Anne said, wriggling in delight and smacking her lips. "Ggguuughghgh gugh."

Fitz reached down to stroke his daughter's cheek. "That's right," he murmured. "Glug glug glug. Lizzy, my dear, has Bridget seen to her?"

"Of course, Fitz," Elizabeth said, rolling her eyes. "Do you honestly think she'd be so docile if she were hungry?"

"Oh, Anne loves her papa," Fitz crooned. "She never cries for Papa, does she? Hmmm?"

"It's true," Elizabeth said. "Whenever Fitz talks to her in that ridiculous voice, she's a perfect lamb."

"There you are, Fitz!" Charles said from the doorway. "Thought we were going shooting. I intend to get at least a dozen." He held his hands in the air, mimicking the act of aiming a fowling piece and tracking birds in flight. "Bam! Blam!"

"Shhh, quiet!" Elizabeth said. "You'll disturb—"

Anne Darcy let out a startled wail. Her face went from pink to crimson to beet red, and she gasped several times to catch her breath, before repeating her original assertion several times, in louder, more emphatic tones.

"Honestly, Charles," Jane said. "What is the matter with you?"

"Me?" Charles said. "What's the matter with Fitz's little wench? Our Charlie never cries like that." He leaned over his son, who opened his eyes and let out a long statement of support for his cousin's sentiments, in a similar register.

"Oh!" Elizabeth covered her ears. "Was there ever a more grating sound! It drives all rational thoughts out of a person's head."

The nursemaids rose from their chairs and rushed forward.

Fitz raised a commanding hand. "Let me show you how it's done." He scooped up his swaddled offspring, held her close to his chest and, balancing on the balls of his feet, danced lightly across the room, swaying her in his arms like a hammock. "Did Charles frighten you? What a silly fellow he is, to be sure." The howling subsided to a cry, then a mew. "Whatever shall we do with you?" Fitz continued his murmuring. "Shall we betroth you in your cradle to your uninspiring cousin here? Or would you prefer to choose for yourself?" Amazingly, the child, groggy from her exertions, drifted off to sleep.

Little Charles, fussed over by nursemaid, mother, and father together, soon relapsed into his usual passive calm.

"There, you see?" Fitz whispered to the room. "All it takes is consideration."

"You will spoil her, Fitz," Elizabeth said. "Far worse than you ever were."

"Lizzy, my love," Fitz said, "here is one subject on which

it is fair to say we are equally knowledgeable, which is to say, equally ignorant, this being our first endeavor. And never have I heard it persuasively argued that loving one's child spoils it."

"On the contrary," Elizabeth said, "it is well known that picking up a crying baby only encourages its bad behavior."

"Oh, Lizzy," Jane said, "you must be right, but I can't find it in myself to be so heartless. And Mr. Darcy did look so very sweet rocking Anne like that. I can't see how it could be wrong."

"Thank you, Mrs. Bingley," Fitz said. "Charles, I felicitate you on your intelligent wife and harmonious family."

"Well, Fitz, I always knew that Jane would be the best wife a man could wish for."

"As you have reminded me many times over this past year," Fitz said. He returned his daughter to her cradle and the care of her nursemaid, and leaned down to his wife. "If our daughter had not the look and wit of her mother, I could not care for her half so well as I do," he said in a low voice.

"And you will be wanting a son next," Elizabeth said, shrugging her shoulders at her husband's attempted caress and turning her face away. "It is enough to bend a woman's thoughts to continence, as a parson's most fiery sermons cannot accomplish."

Fitz's face, frozen and aloof, showed the pain he could not speak. "You know I would never force my attentions on you. And until you are healed, I wouldn't dream of—"

Elizabeth blinked and laughed. She reached for Fitz's hand, holding it to her lips, just touching his fingers with the tip of her tongue. "I intended no such cruel reproach. I meant only that a lesson or two in etymology might be most welcome. Perhaps the derivation of 'tipping the velvet' could be examined *in depth*."

If it were possible for an elegant, reserved man of thirty

years to blush, then the room would have witnessed an astonishing event. As it was, Fitz coughed, covering his face with his hand. "Charles," he said, "weren't you saying something at breakfast about new coveys?"

"Indeed," Charles answered with enthusiasm. "One of your tenants—Stowe?—claimed to have seen a nesting pair up beyond the top of the park, and another somewhere on the far side of the stream." The men sauntered out, arm in arm.

"Fitz!" Elizabeth said. "You may wish to take a blanket today. The ground is quite wet after all the rain we've had."

"You see, Charles," Fitz said, "that noisy charade of yours was unnecessary." He raised his voice to call over his shoulder, "Thank you, my dear. Have you any advice on the best position we should take to secure the most game?"

"None that I can share in company," Elizabeth replied.

"A blanket?" Jane asked. "Why would they take a blanket to go shooting?"

"Shooting!" Elizabeth said. "If they bring home so much as one little woodcock I shall be very surprised."

Jane, after mulling over this answer, said, "Well, as long as they enjoy themselves."

"There's little doubt of that," Elizabeth said. "You see what married life is like these days."

"You know you're happy," Jane said. "You just like to tease poor Fitz. What was that about velvet?"

"A most interesting fabric," Elizabeth said, licking her lips, "and one Fitz is inordinately fond of. A pity we didn't live a hundred years ago when it was the fashion for men."

UNLIKE THE PREVIOUS year, Fitz had been at home most of the season, and hosted several shooting parties. Well into her ninth month and despite, or perhaps because of her growing discomfort, Elizabeth had insisted on having company. Nobody thought anything amiss at a breeding wife in the country, she said, however shameful it appeared in town, and there would be plenty of time for solitude later. The quarry was nothing but rabbits, songbirds, hedgehogs, and once, annoyingly, a gray squirrel that scurried up the nearest tree and watched the frantic baying below, its teeth chattering and its tail quirking into a question mark. "Hurst brought the damned thing in a cage as a curiosity," Fitz said. "Probably let it loose rather than go to the bother of taking it away with him." He raised his gun. "Ought to shoot it, lest it breed. I've heard they drive out the native red ones." He had the gun cocked and aimed, when the memory of Wickham and the fowling piece made him lower the barrel and ease the hammer down.

"Fetching little beast," Charles said.

"Rat with a bushy tail," Fitz said. "Won't waste birdshot on vermin."

"Maybe we should try the other side of the park," Charles said.

"Hardly worth it," Fitz said. "The last parties exhausted most of the coverts there. You know, that was an excellent suggestion, bringing some protection from the damp." He unslung the bag from over his shoulder, shook out the heavy horse blanket, and spread it down.

"WE SHOULD GO in soon." Fitz reluctantly broke the drowsy silence of sated appetite.

"It is rather cold," Charles said. "But how will we explain about not getting any birds?"

"Explain?" Fitz raised an eyebrow. "My dear, one does not explain one's poor aim or the scarcity of coveys. One merely apologizes to the cook for failing to provide any game and offers to procure a substitute from the butcher. An offer that is always dismissed with contempt for that sorry individual's wares."

Charles grinned in appreciation. "I suppose we daren't actually share a bed indoors."

Fitz tightened his arm around his friend's shoulders, pulling him closer to conserve heat. "It would be ill-advised," he said. "There's always the barn."

"Ugh." Charles wrinkled his nose. "I can do without that mangy old cat watching us."

"Old Rowley?" Fitz said. "Poor old fellow. Elizabeth doesn't like him either."

"A lady of sense, despite marrying you," Charles said, taking the chance at a jibe he could not have imagined a year ago.

"You are treading on dangerous ground, Charles," Fitz said. "The truth is, I am so fortunate in my marriage, and so undeserving, it almost makes one question the wisdom of Providence, or divine justice."

"That's absurd," Charles said. "There's never been such a perfectly suited couple, except for Jane and me, of course. I shouldn't have assumed you lie to Elizabeth."

Fitz stood up suddenly, pulling the blanket with him, causing Charles to yelp and roll over in the grass, much like the dogs he had also displaced. "No, Charles, you shouldn't."

Charles lay sprawled, smiling into Fitz's eyes that were laughing back at him, not hurt or angry as he had feared. In fact, Charles couldn't remember seeing a softer expression on his friend's face, that had so frequently looked cross, scornful, or downright murderous. He rose and buttoned his breeches, then brushed the leaves out of his hair. "I suppose our wives are grateful to have us out of the house so they can enjoy a good long gossip about us."

Fitz gathered Charles into an awkward one-armed embrace around the blanket, the fowling pieces, and the dogs. "You flatter yourself," he said, leaning in to plant a kiss on Charles's upturned face.

"In that case," Charles said when he had caught his breath, "perhaps we can stay out a little longer."

"No," Fitz said, "we'd best get home while it's still daylight, or our wives will have nothing left to say tomorrow. But it's a pity your visits have to end so soon."

"Well, Fitz, on that subject I have some news you may find interesting. I was planning to announce it at dinner, but I'll say now that Jane and I may be able to visit far more frequently."

GEORGIANA DARCY PLAYED the pianoforte after dinner while the others talked. She had been diligent about her morning's practice; now she needed to think. If she played interesting, difficult pieces, the sort that challenged her ability and improved her technique, she would have to devote all her attention to the fingering; if she tried popular airs, Fitz would demand that Elizabeth have her turn to play and sing; and if she chose dance tunes, the couples would form and she would be chained to the instrument all evening. So she allowed herself the treat of something easy, the well-known Beethoven sonata that she could play from memory. There were so many things in life that didn't make sense unless one reflected on them for days, weeks or even months, sometimes. And there was no better means of contemplation than moving one's fingers over the keyboard, playing by rote and freeing the mind.

"YOU'LL NEVER GUESS who bought the Gowertons' place," Charles said.

"I don't even know what the 'Gowertons' place' refers to," Fitz said, "much less who bought it, or why I should care."

"That's easily answered," Charles said. "Bentwood Grange, in Hertfordshire, not far from Netherfield. Matthew Thornby. And you should care because he claims to know you."

"Never heard of him," Fitz said.

"Well, he doesn't exactly know you. He knows *of* you."

"Lizzy, my dear," Fitz said, "ask Reynolds if she has any of that physic she gives the maids for greensickness. I'm afraid Charles is suffering from the vapors."

"Mr. Thornby is good friends with a Mr. and Mrs. Carrington," Jane interjected, "and Mr. Carrington claims to know you, Fitz."

That beautiful young man, Georgiana thought, letting the music shut out the talk. He kept intruding on her thoughts at all sorts of inconvenient times. Gervaise Alexander Warburton. Alex, he had everybody call him, although he was a marquess, heir to the Duke of Coverdale, and had about ten given names and several titles. She had been so nervous last year when she had received the invitation to his coming of age party. But everything had been pleasant—well, almost everything. There were about eight couples, young men and women of Alex's circle. Georgiana's partner was Peter Finchley, and she knew right away she didn't like him.

There was nothing really wrong, nothing she could put her finger on. He wasn't rude or coarse, but he had an insinuating way about him, making much of how friendly Fitz had been with his mother. His mother! Lady Finchley was old—at least forty—and she had a dubious reputation. Even a sheltered girl like Georgie had heard things. Still, the rumors hadn't stopped Lady Finchley from becoming practically engaged to Alex's father. Now that at least made some sense. Coverdale and Lady Finchley were close in age, and both widowed.

Georgiana had just stared unblinking at Mr. Finchley, not answering his remarks, until he stammered and almost blushed. For the first time in her life she was made aware of how men might suffer from their lack of beauty, as well as women. It must be difficult for a man to be short and slight, *reedy*, some might call it, with dull, sandy hair, when in the same room with someone like Alex, over six feet tall with auburn hair and a face like a statue of Apollo . . .

"HOW DO YOU know Mr. and Mrs. Carrington?" Elizabeth had just asked Charles.

After a long pause, Fitz said, "No, Charles. You landed yourself in this mess, and you must extricate yourself."

"I imagine they are acquaintances from when you were in town," Elizabeth said.

"It's a club they were all members of," Jane said. "It sounded very agreeable. The Brotherhood of Philander."

Fitz coughed rather loudly.

"Fitz, my love," Elizabeth said. "Are you all right? Perhaps you need some of Reynolds's physic?"

MR. FINCHLEY WAS like Wickham in some ways. Georgiana had learned her lesson and she could never have feelings for a man like that again. Men of that sort were obvious—she could see it easily now, when a year ago it had been frightening and mysterious. They chased every young lady with a fortune and pretended to be in love with anyone who was even passably handsome. It was just a game to them, and most young ladies understood that. It was why one waited until eighteen to come out in society, to be old enough to know.

But Alex. His manners were as perfect as his appearance. He

had been to university, like Fitz, except it was Oxford, not Cambridge, and unlike most of the gentlemen scholars, he appeared to have actually studied. How had it happened? He'd been laughing about something, all the responsibility he had as the elder son, the heir. But never vain or boasting. Something about school. That was it. He hadn't been to school, not been allowed. He'd had tutors instead. "You can never fudge a lesson or hope not to be called on when it's just one pupil alone with a master," he'd said, a rueful smile on his face. "I don't know how many times I had it beaten into me. *Arma virumque cano . . .*"

Georgiana couldn't help herself. "*Troiae qui primus ab oris Italiam fato profugus Laviniaque venit litora*," she'd completed the first line of the *Aeneid*. She didn't mean to show off. The words just slipped out, and she fought the urge to clap both hands over her mouth like a child who had shouted a filthy word, and run from the room.

Alex looked around, smiling in that slightly conspiratorial way that people do when they are the only ones in the group who know your secret. "A scholar," he said.

"Never saw such a pretty one," Mr. Finchley said. "Tell me, do you know Catullus and Ovid as well as Virgil?" Typical of Mr. Finchley, to mention the most notorious names, the reason ladies weren't supposed to study Latin in the first place.

"THERE'S NOTHING SO terrible about the Brotherhood," Charles said. "It's just that Thornby and the Carringtons have parties, and they invite everybody from town. A very fast set. Most of them are all right, but I always find Sylvester Monkton a little sly for my taste. Hearn's younger son," he explained for Elizabeth's benefit. "The old earl was a loose fish, and his sons do their best to emulate him."

"Sylly's not a bad sort," Fitz said. "He has at least the virtue of honesty—and that requires courage."

"I liked Lady David Pierce," Jane ventured to add. "I was frightened of her at first, because she's a bit rough, almost mannish in demeanor, but underneath she's really very sweet. When she learned that Charles was a close friend of Fitz's, she treated me with almost motherly affection."

"Pierce married?" Fitz repeated in a faint voice. "To whom?"

"Witherspoon's sister, Agatha Gatling," Charles said.

GEORGIE PLAYED A wrong note, took her hands off the keys, and sat with her fists clenched in her lap. But that was worse, because then the others would know she was listening. She flexed her fingers several times and started the piece from the beginning.

"MISS GATLING?" FITZ said. He indulged in a spate of loud, unpleasant laughter. "That's wonderful. Truly wonderful. I almost wish I were back in town, to twit him for it."

"Odd, isn't it?" Charles said. "Bet she has five years on him, and a face like a pug dog."

"Charles, dear," Jane said. "Lady David can't help her appearance."

"No," Fitz said, as if Jane had reproached him. "It's not that. There was nobody fiercer against the—how did Pierce phrase it?—the *incestuous* nature of marrying the sister of one's friend, and now he's committed the exact same folly."

"Suppose he found it more convenient," Charles said, "always over at her house to visit George."

"I think it's a love match," Jane said. "They have a son, a few months old, and Lord David seems to dote on the child."

"Well, all I can say is, thank goodness it's a boy," Charles said, unrepentant, "because I got a look at it one time and it takes after its mother. If it had been a girl they'd be better off exposing it the way they did in ancient times."

GEORGIANA HADN'T MEANT to lie to Fitz. It was just that, living alone in London, only Mrs. Annesley for companionship, and after the humiliation of Wickham, and with two whole years to wait until her coming out, she needed something besides needlework and the books in the circulating library to occupy her mind. She could not work on improving her drawing and painting—she had reached the limits of her slight talents there—and her knowledge of modern languages was at the stage where it was conversation she needed, not more written exercises. And somehow she'd got the idea of studying Latin.

Everything had been easy at first. She'd bought a beginner's grammar and worked at that, making sure always to have a fashionable novel at hand, for the benefit of Mrs. Annesley and unexpected visitors. The novels were a pleasure, anyway, when her mind was tired. Latin turned out to be much like mathematics, and enjoyable as that was, you had to stop sometimes and allow yourself a respite, use the brain in a different way.

Georgiana had been so excited when she reached the stage of being ready to read texts. She had considered carefully where to start, poetry or prose, and had chosen the *Aeneid*. Everyone learned that, and an expansive, straightforward narrative might be easier than the compact, convoluted forms of poetry. And it was respectable, with none of the unsavory associations of some of the poets and their verses. Her disappointment when she found how almost impossible it was to go from vocabulary lists, verb conjugations, and noun declensions to translating whole sentences and paragraphs still stuck in her throat. She knew she must have a Latin master if she was going to make any progress, and she would need Fitz's permission to put an advertisement in the newspaper to hire one.

It had been but a small lie. When Georgiana spoke about writing to Fitz, Mrs. Annesley thought she meant an Italian master. That's when the idea occurred to her, of asking Fitz if she could engage an "Italian" tutor for conversation. She had composed the advertisement herself, to make certain it was correct, but that's when things went horribly wrong. Once the applicants learned they'd be teaching a young lady—Georgiana still couldn't bear to think of it. Some had been shocked, others incredulous. Worst were the ones who, having heard the Darcy name and getting a look at their prospective pupil, had been all too eager. One man had actually licked his lips, just like a barn cat with cream all over its face.

Georgiana's other masters hadn't behaved like that. Dancing masters and drawing masters knew their pupils would be girls. Act like a fox invited into a pen of clipped-wing geese and not only wouldn't they be hired, their characters would be ruined and no one else would hire them either. But Latin masters expected a boy, or a youth. The only one who wasn't scandalized was so clearly disappointed, like an ardent groom discovering his veiled bride has been scarred by smallpox, that he had declined the position on the spot.

If Miss Gatling, as she was then, hadn't applied the next week, Georgie would have been in despair.

"TELL ME," FITZ said, his voice in that oily, suggestive tone Georgiana hated, the one he used when he tried to trick her into admitting some childish misbehavior he couldn't quite prove, "is everyone in the Brotherhood married now?"

"Certainly not," Charles said. "Monkton's still single, as you can surmise. And Verney. Although if the ladies ever got a look at him he wouldn't be free for long."

"Why?" Elizabeth asked. "Is he a hermit? Or a recluse?"

"What? No, he's a baronet," Charles said. "Sir Frederick Verney, of Sussex."

"He takes his shirt off in company," Jane whispered. "At the card table. I didn't know where to look the first time he did it. When he remembered there were ladies present he was very apologetic. He said it was a custom of the club, which is all gentlemen of course, so it's perfectly all right there."

"I see," Elizabeth said. "Oh, I almost wish we had stayed in Hertfordshire, so we could visit."

Fitz stood up. "I am extremely grateful not to live within easy distance of Hertfordshire."

"Don't worry, Fitz," Elizabeth said. She stood up also and moved to his side to take his arm. "I can't imagine even a shirtless baronet can compare with you."

"No, indeed," Charles said. "Verney's a fine-looking fellow, but—" He thought better of this line of conversation, although the ladies showed only benign interest, and lapsed into red-faced silence.

"THOUGHT IT WAS you," Miss Gatling had begun the interview in a most unconventional way. "Recognized the address."

Georgiana had apologized, at which the older woman had softened considerably. "Sorry? For what? For being clever? For being Miss Darcy? Only meant I didn't suppose your brother needed a Latin tutor after two years at Cambridge."

Georgiana had engaged her immediately. There was no one

else, and Miss Gatling seemed to understand without having to be told that Fitz didn't know. "Wouldn't tutor a boy," she said. "Don't need the money. Only applied because you're a girl. Men think they're the only ones capable of higher learning. Don't suppose you've read any of Mrs. Wollstonecraft's work."

When Georgiana protested about not wanting to be a bluestocking or a radical, Miss Gatling just laughed. "A little *amo, amas, amat* never made a girl unfit for marriage. All the better for it, really, if men had the wits to see it. Damned fools. Pardon my language. I'm a little rough sometimes, take after my father, but I don't mean any harm. Now, show me where you are in the grammar."

The lessons quickly became the highlight of Georgiana's day. Miss Gatling was the cleverest woman she had ever met. Cleverest person, even more than Fitz in some ways. Georgiana insisted on paying the standard fee and Miss Gatling accepted without being pressed. "Keeps everything honest," she said. When Georgiana told her about the "Italian" misunderstanding, Miss Gatling laughed and offered to teach that too. She knew all the modern languages—French and Spanish, Portuguese ("because of the war, you know"), German—even Russian and Greek. When they had worked through the requisite amount of Latin prose, they would discuss the meaning in Italian, then in French, before finally going over any remaining questions in English.

"Best pupil I ever had," Miss Gatling said one day. "Not that I've had many besides my brother, George. Sweetest, best-natured young man you can hope to meet, but not a scholar. Wish I could put the two of you through an examination, side by side, and then ask those stuffy old sods who run the colleges which sex should be educated." She didn't apologize for her language that time.

"THEN THERE WERE the other marriages," Charles said.

"Whose?" Fitz asked.

"Carrington and Thornby's," Charles said. "And Pierce and Witherspoon's."

"Charles," Jane said, in the kind of warning voice she almost never used.

"Oh, we're all friends here," Charles said. "It was Carrington's idea, I think. Hired some peculiar dissenting preacher to perform the ceremony."

"Charles," Fitz said, in the same tone of voice as Jane.

"Well, we didn't go," Charles said. "Wish we could have. That would have been something to see. But didn't seem quite the thing, especially as Jane and I had only just been married ourselves."

"If you don't tell me," Elizabeth said, "I will ask Fitz."

Fitz nodded his head in Georgiana's direction. "Not in front of my sister."

Charles moved over to sit by Elizabeth, speaking in a low voice.

Georgiana kept on playing, making sure to pound the keys harder than usual so as not to seem to be listening. She only caught the word *molly* before the rest of the words were drowned out by Elizabeth's laughter.

GEORGIANA HAD RECOVERED easily enough from her slip of the tongue at Alex's party. "Oh no," she'd said, her blush at Mr. Finchley's wicked taunt making her denial all the more believable. "I'm no scholar. My brother reads a lot and was at university. I must have heard him reciting it so many times that I memorized it myself."

"Yes, that would be it," Alex agreed blandly, that same conspiratorial smile on his face. Then he turned back to his partner, Miss Swain.

Charlotte Swain, daughter of a peer, taller than most of the men, blond and buxom. Really huge. And not very bright. Georgiana told herself that was wrong, almost a sin, to think of someone in that way who hadn't done her any harm. Miss Swain wasn't stupid. Just not educated. And not a reader. Not even novels, as she confessed gaily, almost shamelessly, to the party when the subject of the latest books came up. But Alex showed her more than mere politeness. Every time he looked at her his face warmed, as if she were his partner in life, not just the one assigned to him for the party.

Oh, Georgiana thought, what was wrong with her? Hadn't Fitz said, more times than she could recall, that men don't like clever women?

But that was silly. Because look at Elizabeth. Other than Miss Gatling, Elizabeth was the cleverest woman Georgiana had ever met. She was clever in a different way, and she disguised a great deal of it. Knowledgeable without being studious, she kept up with novels and modern poetry, although of course she didn't have any Latin. She was quick where Georgiana was slow, able to come up with a quip or a witty reply without a moment's hesitation, while Georgiana would be stammering, tongue-tied, her thoughts tangled in her head and making her look to the rest of the world like a complete idiot. For all her learning, Georgiana would never be judged clever if she and Elizabeth were in the same company, yet Elizabeth, because of her playful, easy manner, would never be mistaken for a scholar or accused of being a bluestocking.

And Fitz had married her, in despite of so many impediments: her poverty, her vulgar family, and, worst of all, the shame of becoming Wickham's brother-in-law. In fact, Fitz was so in love with her that Georgiana had sometimes watched, openmouthed in awe, as she said the most scandalous, teasing things to him, and instead of losing his temper, or worse, going all white and silent, he would smile and take her hand or even kiss her right there in the drawing room in front of Georgiana. Even in front of his friends Charles and Jane. Sometimes he laughed or went red in the face, as if he were the woman, to be embarrassed.

So there was no reason Alex, Marquess of Bellingham—"the beautiful Bellingham," everybody called him—mightn't like a clever woman also, except he didn't. He looked at Georgiana as if she were a curiosity, or perhaps a friend, and because he was kind he pretended to flirt, but he was practiced enough to make it very clear he was only playing. He saw how young and innocent she was and was too much of a gentleman to cause hurt. And all the time he was smiling at that enormous Miss Swain and it was obvious that she hadn't been picked for him; he had chosen her. They would probably announce their engagement any day now. Which just showed how hopeless it was going into society because all there was to choose from were married Apollos and free—What was Mr. Finchley? Sort of a Silenus, except not with that horrible pot belly, or old and wrinkled. A satyr, that was it. Goat's feet and horns would suit him perfectly. You couldn't fall in love with Mr. Finchley, but that's who was out there for girls like Georgiana.

"IT GOT ME thinking," Charles said. "Between inconvenient acquaintances on one side, and Jane's family on the other, things were becoming somewhat—crowded—and we thought it might be time to look for something a bit more out of the way."

"Or out of Hertfordshire," Fitz said.

"Yes. And you'll be glad to know that we've found a delightful little manor, just over the border in Staffordshire, and we're going to move in as soon as the weather's better and the roads are clear for travel."

BACK WHEN GEORGIANA was fifteen it hadn't been so bad. She had thought herself in love with Wickham because he was good-looking and charming—and because she had known him all her life. She'd had no idea of "love" except flirting and talking with an attractive, friendly young man. Now, though, things were very different. Now she understood what it meant when you saw a man whose face resembled the engraving of a statue of Apollo she had seen in Fitz's book on antique sculpture. Now she appreciated the joke when Elizabeth and Jane laughed about Sir Frederick Verney taking his shirt off. Imagine the beautiful Bellingham without his shirt!

Thank goodness she had another year before her formal debut. If she had to go to balls and dance with Bellingham she would disgrace herself. And there would be all those Finchley-satyrs pestering her and she would have to choose one of them eventually. How did ladies do it? How did Elizabeth and Fitz meet and fall in love? And Charles and Jane? Well, that could be no solution for her, because it was fine for men with good fortunes to marry penniless ladies, but never the other way around.

That was one benefit of having Elizabeth for a sister. For all her playfulness, she was intuitive, quick to recognize when someone needed kindness and understanding. She had confessed to Georgiana early on her own mistaken partiality for Wickham. "I was lucky," she said, in that smiling, flirtatious manner that was so natural for her she used it even with other ladies. "I had no fortune to tempt him to honesty and matrimony. If I hadn't learned in time the sort of man he is, I might well have ended up in a worse condition than Lydia, as Fitz could hardly have been expected to force him to marry *me*." A loud burst of laughter followed this shocking statement, with its acknowledgment both of Fitz's early love for her and his awareness of her affection for a rival. But what a comfort! From that moment Georgiana was free of her guilt and self-reproaches, and began to accept her lot as a wealthy, handsome young lady who might hope for a husband she could both respect and desire.

Gradually she gave up her childish notions of remaining unmarried. That was not allowed, not when one had thirty thousand pounds. Besides, wouldn't it be better to see a man without his shirt—without anything on at all—than to go through life never knowing . . .

She reached the end of the sonata, let the last note fade away, placed her fingers in position for the opening chord, and started in.

"Oh, not that gloomy thing again," Charles said. "Can't we hear something else for a change?"

Thirty

LADY CATHERINE STOOD over the bed, turning the rings on her fingers and watching her daughter moan in her sleep. "Can't we do something?" she said for the tenth time.

Mrs. Collins put a hand on her patroness's shoulder and guided her toward a chair. "The laudanum will help," she said in a whisper. "Just give it a few minutes."

Lady Catherine allowed herself to sit. Thank goodness for the vicar's wife. How had things gone so long without her? And to think she was the friend of that horrid little chit who'd stolen Darcy—she caught herself on the verge of another apoplexy, took a deep breath, and forced herself to wrench her thoughts away.

Maybe Mrs. Collins was right after all. Darcy wouldn't have been kind to Anne. Even if Lady Catherine had forced the match, what good would it do if he was cruel to her child? Men were so thoughtless. Ignorant, pigheaded, stubborn fools. Even dear Sir Lewis. At least he'd had the good sense and good manners to defer to his wife. But Anne had inherited his poor constitution instead of the Fitzwilliam strength, the noble blue blood that had taken them across the Channel with William the Conqueror to establish their line here in England. And down through all the centuries they'd kept their power and their wealth by their strength. Darcy had it, and his two cousins, the young earl and his brother, Colonel Fitzwilliam. Why did Anne have to suffer?

And why, come to think of it, had she, Lady Catherine, borne only the one child, no son? Because poor dear Lewis had been weak. Couldn't father more than one. Even that much had more or less worn him out. Yet she'd loved him, chosen him herself. She admitted now, years too late, that it had been a mistake, picking a weak man. But it had been a good marriage. Two strong—and strong-willed—people in a marriage was a recipe for sorrow, even divorce. And she'd done well. Rosings was not Pemberley, but it was a fine property, and Kent was a far more desirable location than some bleak northern extremity like Derbyshire.

And Anne. She was her darling girl, conceived in the early days of the marriage, while Lewis could still do his duty as a husband. How proud he had been! As if the one child fulfilled the marriage vows. After that, no matter how Catherine chafed him and scolded him, he kept to his own room most of the time, and when he did venture to share her bed he'd been good for little more than a cuddle. "Tipping the velvet," he called it. Pleasant enough, but not likely to bring a son into the world.

Ah, well, perhaps this marriage was the answer. Thank Mrs. Collins for that too. This George Witherspoon, he wasn't actually weak. You could see it if you looked past the Greek-god exterior and the diffident, gentle manner. If you looked at his hands, those broad-tipped fingers stained with pigment, you could see the power in him. Claimed to be an artist, a painter.

To be fair, he didn't go about announcing it, like some of the vile boasting peacocks in town. But he answered honestly when asked. He didn't display his work, after all, had the decency to keep it in the attic, like a true gentleman. No harm there.

And his sister, Lady David Pierce. She was a woman after Lady Catherine's own heart. Didn't fear to put forth her opinion. Always sensible. Not a pretty, simpering little miss, like that Mrs. Darcy who looked as if butter wouldn't melt. Lord! Lady Catherine could strangle her and him both. But enough. Think of something else. Agatha, Lady David Pierce. She was a worthy connection. No title in her family, but a solid fortune of her own, not a mere sponge on her brother, and married to a duke's younger son. True, an Anglo-Irish nonentity, but a duke is a duke, and it was a connection to be prized. How the ghastly vicar, Collins, would crow. At least Collins recognized the value of titles and ancient families, and gave them the deference they were due, while so many of his generation, even her own nephew, disdained them.

Anne's moaning quieted and she rolled onto her side.

"There," Mrs. Collins said. "What did I tell you? She'll sleep until morning and she won't be troubled by bad dreams."

"Thank you, Mrs. Collins. You will stay with her? I will inform Mr. Collins that your duty is here tonight."

"It's my pleasure," Charlotte said. "More than duty. But if you will, your ladyship, let Mrs. Jenkinson know as well." Lady Catherine laid a soft kiss on her daughter's cheek and turned to leave, acknowledging Charlotte's request and curtsy with a nod. Charlotte quickly locked the door after her. No sense in taking chances. Mrs. Jenkinson was grateful to enjoy her own sleep uninterrupted, but the mother was a hoverer. Charlotte removed her gown and shoes, and slipped under the covers to gather Anne in her arms.

Miss de Bourgh snuggled close and sighed. "Is she gone?"

"All clear and the door bolted. You do that very well. I almost had my heart in my mouth with fear."

Anne giggled. "Years of practice. Now tell me again about this George Witherspoon. Is he really as beautiful as you say? And you're sure he won't want to—"

"Absolutely. He's a member of that same club I was telling you about. Golden hair like waves, springing from a high, noble brow, like a hero in a poem by Walter Scott; blue eyes like summer sky, *and* he's an artist . . ." Charlotte kept the words flowing, embellishing Lady David's prosaic language to create a more enticing picture.

Lord, it was good to hold a woman in her arms again. There was no passion here, no enjoyment of that sort. Anne, for all her tricks and deceptions, was truly unwell. Whenever she walked too far or stayed up too late, her heart would beat so fast she grew faint; sometimes there was a blue tinge around her mouth and her fingernails. The doctor always clicked his tongue when he saw that; Charlotte hadn't even had to prompt him to say that marriage was out of the question.

No, it was like a holiday merely to spend a chaste night with a slender, nicely formed girl, instead of a large, heavy man who never smelled quite clean. She felt a pang for little Willie, left with that slattern of a nursemaid. Well, a night or two once in a while shouldn't hurt. Charlotte wouldn't be allowed to shirk her wifely duties longer than that, even had it been possible for Anne to arrange it.

"And he's in love with his brother-in-law," Charlotte concluded her enumeration of Witherspoon's admirable qualities as prospective husband. "I'm sure he's never kissed a woman in his life, apart from his sister, and he won't start now."

"Oh, Charlotte. You are clever."

Charlotte gave Anne the real medicine, stroking her fine hair until her breathing leveled off and she fell into the deep, laudanum-induced sleep. Her head nestled, surprisingly weighty, on Charlotte's shoulder, cutting off the circulation in her arm. Charlotte didn't move an inch.

"BUT I DON'T wish to be married," George Witherspoon said. Another debate on the merits of matrimony was under way, this one in the richly furnished town house in Berkeley Square belonging to Witherspoon's half sister.

"Nonsense," Lady David Pierce, the former Agatha Gatling said. "Look how happy David and I are."

"But that's because you love each other," Witherspoon said. "Besides, I'm already married to Davey."

"Now George," Lady David said. "We've gone all over that. That marriage is private. As far as the rest of the world is concerned, you're free to take a wife."

"But I don't even like women. I'm sorry, Aggie. Of course I like you. You know what I mean!"

"Perfectly, my dear," Lady David said. "Which is why this marriage is just the thing for you. She doesn't like men, you don't like women, she's an invalid and she's wealthy. A large fortune and a very pretty piece of property in Kent with extensive grounds and a park."

"How do you know she doesn't like men?" Witherspoon asked.

"Dear Charlotte—Mrs. Collins—has written me all about it," Lady David said. "Ever since she married that appalling vicar of hers, she's made it her business to help poor Anne out of her difficult situation. The girl ain't up to much—something wrong with her heart—but that's why you and she should suit, George. Charlotte has become very friendly with Miss de Bourgh, and she assures me that Anne's ideal husband is a kind, gentle soul, preferably an artist or a poet, someone who won't touch her, even on the wedding night, and will live apart from her, in town. It's you to the life, George."

"I don't know," Witherspoon said, on the point of wavering. "What do you think, Davey?" He turned to his friend, who had remained admirably quiet all this time.

"I admit," Lord David Pierce said, "I was skeptical at first. If it wasn't our dear Agatha proposing it I wouldn't have considered it. But everything I've heard about this Miss de Bourgh merely confirms Agatha's portrait. And it never hurts to own property or add to one's wealth, no matter how comfortably off one is to begin with."

"Very true, David," Lady David said with a fond, approving nod in her husband's direction. "You always understand the practical aspects."

"Flatterer." Pierce laughed and kissed his wife's rosy cheek. "You only say that because I'm taking your side in this discussion." Pierce frowned, and drew himself up to his full height, barely an inch or two taller than his wife, and several inches shorter than his statuesque friend. "You know, George, my love, Agatha has always managed your affairs so that you don't have to worry your head over all that accounting gibberish, but the fact is you are the master of a considerable fortune and a very eligible *parti* in the marriage market. If word ever got out just how well-off you are, you'd have unmarried females throwing themselves at your feet every time you stepped out of doors."

Witherspoon's fair countenance paled even further and he stared in alarm from his sister to his lover and back again. "Really, Davey? Are you sure? Because I try to go out every day, to see the light and the colors, you know, and if I couldn't—if—that is, if young ladies were to accost me all the time, I'd have to give it up, and then how would I paint?"

"David." Lady David spoke sternly to her husband. "There's

no need to frighten George to death." She turned to her brother, speaking in the gentle tone used with a child convinced there's a headless ghost hiding under the bed. "George, what David is trying to say is that marriage is so important to most ladies that they always discover who the wealthy, unmarried men are sooner or later. But with an invalid wife safely tucked away in Kent, and the marriage made public, you'd be protected from any trouble of that sort."

"I see." Witherspoon looked thoughtful, a sight rarely seen. "But what happens when she dies?"

"Oh!" A simultaneous groan arose from Lord and Lady David.

"There, Agatha," Pierce said. "You always underestimate George's powers of deduction. He's as quick as you or I, really. He just comes at things from a different direction."

"Yes, the one we're least expecting," Lady David muttered. "Don't worry about that now, George. She's still a young woman, and if she stays at home and doesn't overexert herself, there's no reason she can't live a good many years."

"But how can you be sure?" Witherspoon asked.

"We can't," Pierce said. "All these things are ultimately a gamble."

"Well, I hate gambling," Witherspoon said. "It's just odds and percentages, but people never pay attention to that. They always bet on the queen of diamonds or think nine is their lucky number or something, and then they're disappointed. And they lose a great deal of money and shoot each other and—"

"My goodness," Lady David said. "All this time I thought—"

"You thought I had no sense," Witherspoon said. "But I do have some. I just can't afford to waste it on numbers and reading and writing and cards and dice and horses and all that stuff that men usually waste it on. All I want to do is paint. And if I have as much money as you say, then I think I ought to be able to spend it the way I please and live as I choose, so long as I'm not hurting anybody."

"But this is a way to *help* someone," Pierce said. "Poor Miss de Bourgh isn't well, and she's an heiress, which means she'll have to marry someone so as to keep the property in the family. Do you know her mother wanted her to marry Darcy? Think of what a misery that would have been. On both sides."

"Fitzwilliam Darcy?" Witherspoon said. "Who used to be in the Brotherhood and married that witty Miss Bennet you were all teasing him about? Oh, that would be too bad." He looked earnestly at his sister. "He's very big and strong, you know, Aggie. It's the kind of thing you can't imagine without seeing it for yourself. I saw him—I mean, we all saw him when he left the Brotherhood because we had to have his un-initiation ceremony and Davey said it was all right for me to participate and I'm awfully glad I did, because Darcy was most remarkably vigorous and I had a—"

"George," Pierce said. "That's hardly the way to talk in the presence of a lady."

"Oh, Aggie doesn't mind. Aggie knows me. And anyway, Miss de Bourgh is safe now that Darcy has married someone else."

"Don't you see?" Lady David said. "There will be others. And none of them, I dare to wager—if you don't disapprove, George—will be as perfect a match for her as you are. Ten to one she'll be forced to marry a brute who'll insist on 'perpetuating his line' or some such nonsense, and she'll die giving birth to a misshapen brat—"

Witherspoon's eyes widened and he cringed, turning for comfort to Pierce, who enfolded him in his arms.

"Honestly, Agatha," Pierce said. "And you scolded me for scaring him." He stroked Witherspoon's hair and kissed his cheek. "All we're trying to say, George, is that both you and

Miss de Bourgh have an incentive to marry. You don't have to commit yourself right away. In fact you'd be foolish to appear too eager. But with Mrs. Collins's help, an introduction can be made. We can travel down to Kent, perhaps Lady Catherine will invite us to stay and you can see how things stand."

"What if I don't like her? I won't be forced into marriage."

"Nobody will force you into anything. You have my promise on that," Pierce said. He tightened his arms around Witherspoon and kissed him again, first on the forehead, then the mouth, until Lady David blushed and smiled and looked away. "When we married, I promised to love you and cherish you, and that is what I intend to do. If you decide this marriage won't suit, you have only to say so and that will be the end of it. Isn't that right, Agatha?"

"Absolutely," Lady David said.

"Well, then," Witherspoon said. "When you put it like that, Davey, it all seems very reasonable. Now, can we please go to bed? Or is it Aggie's turn tonight?"

Pierce cocked an eyebrow at his wife. "What do you say, my dear? Will you yield to your brother after he's agreed to such a sacrifice?"

"Hmph!" Lady David said. "But you'll owe me double next time."

"Owe you?" Pierce said in a soft voice. "I'll insist on it."

Summer

The four friends strolled in the park at Pemberley. Birdsong, perfumed flowers, bright colors, and mild temperature—everything delighted the senses. But more than any tangible pleasure, how blissful it was to be alone! Elizabeth savored the freedom. Practically her entire acquaintance had descended on Pemberley over the course of the winter: her parents; the Gardiners; Mr. and Mrs. Hurst, bringing the inevitable Caroline Bingley; even Lydia Wickham, tormenting Fitz with indelicate references to the former friendship between the two men.

Elizabeth had anticipated that being Mrs. Darcy would resemble running a fashionable hotel; what she had not foreseen was that her responsibilities might at times be more accurately compared to those of an opera impresario. Caroline, whose attachment to Fitz showed no signs of abating, even with the evidence of little Anne in the nursery, could be managed like a self-important actress, with crude flattery of her stylish gowns and her stock of town gossip. For Charles's sake, Elizabeth denied her instincts and employed considerable tact; but diplomacy didn't work with Lydia. Elizabeth had found her youngest sister alone one morning after breakfast and, taking an educated guess, asked if she recalled the relative position of their two husbands, the last time they were together. That had shut her mouth. Protection of Fitz outweighed any minor burden of guilt at digging up the buried past; Elizabeth could still smile at the rare memory of Lydia made red-faced and discomfited by someone else's words.

Only the start of the London season had emptied the house. The Hursts and Caroline had decamped after Easter, followed shortly by the Gardiners, whose business profited from the increase in trade. The reluctant Mrs. Bennet, who must chaperone her younger daughters, had gone the next week. Mr. Bennet, blandly ignoring all hints, had lingered yet another week in triumphant "second bachelorhood," as he called it. Finally, Lydia recalled, belatedly and with ill-concealed alarm, that were her "dear Wick" to be left to enjoy the season on his own, even in as remote and dreary a place as Newcastle, the fact that he was married and the father of a infant daughter might occasionally slip his mind.

After a session of mixed couples, Elizabeth with Charles

and Jane with Fitz, they changed partners for ease of pace and conversation, the two sisters hanging back and allowing their husbands to walk ahead. Jane, her second child beginning to show, would soon wish to return indoors, but Elizabeth had something important to discuss first. "I was wondering," she began, "if you had given any thought to what we talked of earlier." She inclined her head in the direction of the slight bulge at Jane's waist.

"Nursing this one myself?" Jane blushed, as any mention of the body's functions seemed to produce in her, but considered her sister's question seriously. "I am divided in my mind, Lizzy," she said. "I admit, the temptation is great, to mother my child in all ways. But I dislike the idea of keeping Charles away." The last words produced the fiery red flush that attended all acknowledgment, even now, of her passionate feelings for her husband.

Elizabeth forbore to laugh this time. "But Charles would never neglect you merely because you used your body for its intended purpose."

Jane shook her head and kept her eyes fastened resolutely on the path. "Whether he would or no, it is not right, surely, for a man to be with his wife while she is . . . ?" She left the sentence unfinished in ladylike ambiguity.

"Oh, nonsense!" Elizabeth answered. "I doubt very much that our nursemaids—or any others, for that matter, who earn their living through their milk—spend their entire lives estranged from their husbands. And have you considered the reason I proposed this?" She stared earnestly into her sister's face.

"Do you mean, because it—?" Even speaking in a whisper, Jane could not express so dangerous a thought.

"Lengthens the interval between conceptions," Elizabeth said. "Yes. Look at us and all our family. Mama, our aunt

Gardiner, you, me. If we go on as we are, we shall be little more than broodmares. But take our Bridget, now. Her husband is quite a stout fellow, and very fond of his wife. Yet she has but two children from ten years of marriage. You see?"

"Oh, Lizzy!" Jane wailed. "That is wicked!"

"How so?" Elizabeth was, if anything, equally shocked at her sister's distress. "It is nature's way. It was Bridget who explained it to me, when I asked how she had managed. In fact, she was quite amazed that Mama had not told us herself, as it seems to be common knowledge among countrywomen. But there it is—our mother had not the sense even of an ignorant Irish peasant."

"Not so ignorant, apparently," Jane said. "And that is hardly the way to talk about a devoted family servant who has been like a mother to your child."

Elizabeth let out a long sigh. "You know I meant nothing by it. I have the greatest respect for Bridget's wisdom, as I thought I had made clear. And she has been a far better mother to Anne than I could ever be."

Jane laid a contrite hand on her sister's arm. "Don't say that, Lizzy. I'm sure you love her very much. I ought not to reproach you for your manner of speaking. I am familiar enough with it after all these years."

"Indeed," Elizabeth said, accepting the implied apology. But she could not resist further teasing. "And yes, I do love Bridget very much. She is a good, kind woman, although her brogue is so impenetrable at times, I worry that when Anne begins to talk she will be mistaken for a tinker's brat and banished to the kitchen."

"Oh!" Jane rolled her eyes, opened her mouth several times, thought better of each retort, and remained silent. The two sisters walked without speaking until the party had reached the edge of the park.

"I always enjoy conversing with Charles," Elizabeth at last

embarked on a safer topic, "especially on questions of estate management. He has far more presence when he is with but one companion than in a group."

"And I am learning not to be afraid of Mr. Darcy," Jane said, responding gratefully to the gesture of peacemaking. "And before you correct me again, I will say that he and I have agreed to go back to calling each other Mr. Darcy and Mrs. Bingley because we are more comfortable that way. It is my choice as well as his."

"Just so long as you are not angry with him," Elizabeth said, "you may call him whatever you like."

"Angry? Lizzy, you must not imagine I would hold on to such a sinful emotion all this time. No, Mr. Darcy and I get along very well. He is so well-read and so clever, yet he treats me with the greatest courtesy and respect, and asks my opinions, as if they matter."

"I am glad," Elizabeth said, "because they do matter, very much. In fact, I was thinking that it's time we allowed our poor husbands into the house."

"What foolishness is this?" Jane said. "It is Mr. Darcy's house."

"No," Elizabeth said. "I meant a room set aside, just for him and Charles. Lord knows we have plenty to spare."

Jane smiled and lowered her eyes. She would have to accept the fact, she told herself, as so many times in the past, that life with her sister would always entail indelicate, unsettling, and contentious conversations. But Elizabeth loved her, almost as much as Charles did—and she returned the love in equal amount—and so she must accustom herself by degrees, separating the completely unspeakable, like nursing and its effect on conception, from the merely embarrassing, like this. "I am afraid I understand your meaning, Lizzy," she said. "But I do not consider it a fit topic for discussion."

Elizabeth slowed the pace further, until the men were well out of earshot. "But I do not understand yours, Jane. After what you have just said, surely you do not dislike the friendship between our husbands? Or do you simply not like to talk about it? Because I had quite made up my mind to this proposal, but didn't want to carry it out without asking you first. Which means you will have to discuss it just a little."

"No," Jane said, "I mean it is for them to decide, not for us. They are the men, and it is Mr. Darcy's house to use as he wishes."

Elizabeth put her free hand, the one not supporting Jane's arm, to her forehead in a gesture of exasperation. "I can't comprehend how you claim to have a happy marriage with such a topsy-turvy view of things."

Jane laughed. "I will never learn when you are joking and when you are serious. But if it will end this uncomfortable subject, I will say that I am delighted with the friendship between our husbands. I would never oppose any of Charles's wishes, so long as it was not morally objectionable or led him into bad habits or company. But beyond that, he and Mr. Darcy were friends long before they married us. A truly happy marriage ought not destroy a longstanding friendship."

Elizabeth was briefly silenced, humbled by the depth of her sister's love and the selfless yet confident way she acknowledged their husbands' attachment. Jane's faith was true, unshaken by doubts. It made Elizabeth's practical viewpoint seem shallow by comparison. She had prided herself on her "philosophical" marriage: correcting her original prejudice with civility and impartiality; moved by gratitude, advancing to affection; finally, through reflection, achieving what she hoped was understanding. But when she said the word to Fitz, did she truly mean love, as Jane so sincerely felt for Charles? Or was it mere passion? *Philia, eros, agape.* Fitz had taught her the classical names for the three emotions that English muddled into the one word, *love*. Perhaps, she decided, what had begun as *philia* and progressed quickly to *eros* would develop over time into the *agape* her sister had known from the beginning. "Then you do not object to my assigning them a room?"

"Of course not," Jane said. "I don't see why it must be announced, that's all, as if you're bestowing some great reward, like Queen Elizabeth with her favorites."

"That's a splendid thought!" Elizabeth seized upon the analogy, and its change in mood, with relief. "I must make more use of my namesake. Which do you suppose Fitz is? He certainly had Leicester's pride when we met, but now there is more of the industry and adventure of Raleigh. I would not like to see him so misguided as Essex."

The men stood waiting for their wives to catch up. "What is this?" Fitz asked, having listened for what followed his wife's telling laugh. "I hope I am not to be conveyed to the Tower."

"Not at all," Elizabeth said. "Although I have decided to give you and Charles your own special lodging, for when the weather is inclement. That small room at the end of the corridor on the second floor. Will that suit, do you think?"

"Admirably," Fitz said. "Do you hear, Charles? We are to put up in style this winter."

"That's very kind," Charles said. He gave a small, graceful bow to Elizabeth, then seeing his own wife ill at ease, adroitly changed the subject. "So, Fitz, did you attend your cousin's wedding?"

"Anne de Bourgh's to George Witherspoon?" Fitz stepped in to back up his friend. "No. Tempted as we were, we were not invited."

"Lady Catherine can't possibly mean to keep up her objections to your marriage forever," Jane said.

"No," Elizabeth said. "I think she felt happier with a private ceremony. As few witnesses as possible."

"What is there to be ashamed of?" Jane asked. "It sounds like an excellent match. Charles says Mr. Witherspoon has an immense fortune." She blushed, embarrassed at the mercenary implication. "I meant only that Lady Catherine need have no fear that her daughter was making an imprudent connection or had been taken in by a fortune hunter. I have met Mr. Witherspoon and I can say that he is of good character, and very pleasant in manner. If Miss de Bourgh—I suppose I must call her Mrs. Witherspoon now—is as great an invalid as you say, he will treat her considerately."

"Well, you know," Charles said. "Lady Catherine had hoped to get Fitz as her son-in-law. Witherspoon can't measure up to that."

"No one can measure up to that," Elizabeth said. She signaled for Fitz to take her arm. The couples, formed up now husband with wife, proceeded in the direction of the house, Fitz's head bent low to hear his wife's urgent, whispered message.

"Truly?" he said, placing a tender kiss on Elizabeth's forehead. "So soon?"

"I'm sorry, Fitz." Elizabeth answered in the regretful tone appropriate for informing the company of an afternoon's outing spoiled by rain. "The way we work at it, it's unavoidable."

"Sorry? Why should you be sorry?"

"What if it's another girl?"

Fitz laughed. "Then there's no help for it. Since we have honored my mother with our first, we'll have to name the second one Catherine."

Charles and Jane, following close behind the other couple, were not allowed to escape hearing the news, and conveyed their heartiest congratulations. "Perhaps it will be a boy this time," Jane suggested. An intense discussion of names, in which Fitzwilliam, George, and Charles figured prominently, was cut short by an interested party.

"All I know," Charles said, "is that it's much better for friends to marry sisters than to marry one's friend to one's sister."

"Excellent!" Fitz exclaimed, clapping Charles on the back as if he were the one who had just heard good news from his wife. "Marriage has been the making of you, Charles. Not merely a man, but a wit. I believe you have coined an epigram."

The Story Behind
Pride / Prejudice

OF JANE AUSTEN'S six published novels, *Pride and Prejudice* is the most popular and the most frequently adapted. It's also the most "romantic," with a Cinderella-like love story; a witty, spirited heroine, Elizabeth Bennet, who, unlike her two-hundred-year-old peers, is still envied and admired by twenty-first-century women; and a hero, Fitzwilliam Darcy, considered by many readers the sexiest of Austen's leading men. What could possess a writer to try her hand at yet another version of this beloved story? Madness, hubris, cynical exploitation aside, my reason is simple: I felt there is a hidden story behind the one Austen shared with us, one she gives readers just enough clues to discover if we will.

The central story of *Pride and Prejudice* follows Elizabeth and Darcy's growth in self-knowledge, as the misunderstandings arising from her prejudice and his pride evolve into genuine love. But intertwined with this story is a parallel one, concerning the friendship between Darcy and his "gentleman-like" friend, Charles Bingley. It too begins with an unequal relationship, here between a slightly older, far more sophisticated man, and an inexperienced "youth," still reliant on his mentor's guidance. Just as Darcy and Elizabeth can know true love only once he has been "humbled," that is, when he realizes how his inflated sense of self-worth has prevented him from seeing her as his equal, so Darcy's continued friendship with Bingley requires acceptance of him as a man, an adult, capable of making his own decisions—especially the all-important choice of wife.

As I read and reread the novel, it seemed to me that this friendship can be interpreted as romantic, or at least sexual, and that in Darcy and Bingley Austen was showing readers what today we might call "bisexual" men. These are not "gay" men; their love exists not as an exclusive, self-contained pairing, but in the context of the society in which they lived, where marriage to a lady of good family was the objective of every gentleman of property, just as marriage to a "gentleman in possession of a good fortune" was necessary for every young lady. This is *the hidden story* I have brought out in *Pride / Prejudice.*

The only thing drearier than reading a political novel is writing one. My motivation for writing *Pride / Prejudice* was the fun of telling a good story, not advancing an argument. But a "bisexual *Pride and Prejudice*" can't expect to escape this sort of analysis entirely. While I may have "queered" Austen's novel, I don't feel I've "changed" it by turning her characters into something different from what they are in the original. As the title indicates, the idea derives from "slash" fiction, in which existing stories are retold with same-sex relationships between some or all of the main characters. (The term refers to the / symbol, which indicates which characters are to enjoy the same-sex treatment.) Like the first slash, based on the original *Star Trek* television show, and featuring stories about Captain Kirk and Mr. Spock (K/S), the concept works best when the source material contains a genuine homoerotic subtext.

To those who feel that making the hidden sexuality explicit "spoils" Austen's work, I would say that because we value sexuality differently than did people in 1800, it's no more wrong to include it in modern retellings of her stories than it is to examine some of her other subtexts, such as the slave trade and the wealth derived from it in *Mansfield Park*. There's no overt sex in Austen's novels, not because her characters lack genitals or hormones, but more because of the different way in which this aspect of life was viewed at the time; as just another bodily function, its depiction was unnecessary. But we have come to recognize that the physical act of love has emotional and psychological components, and showing it allows for a three-dimensional portrayal of character. It's because we don't see sex as inherently sinful or disgusting that we can include it in adaptations of older works without regarding the new material as erotica or obscene.

Yet surely Austen didn't "intend" to write a "bisexual" love story. I must be misinterpreting innocent remarks and behavior in the light of my own contemporary, sex-saturated cultural background. I believe Austen created her deeply sympathetic and carefully detailed human portraits from observation, enhanced by the writer's gift of imagination. As it's highly unlikely that never once in her life did she meet a gay or bisexual man, it's far more probable that she based her characterization of Darcy and Bingley at least partly on some gay or bisexual men of her acquaintance. Whether she "knew" what she was seeing is a meaningless, modern question, like looking at a black-and-white photograph and asking why everybody's wearing gray.

Pride / Prejudice is a way of bringing to light the alternative universe that was invisible in Austen's time. What to us seems explosively subversive, in Austen's time simply didn't matter. Whether Mr. Darcy and Mr. Bingley spent the night in each other's arms or alone in their separate rooms, their friendship would appear exactly the same in public, where Austen and the rest of the world would see them. But just because people couldn't or wouldn't see it doesn't mean the sexual element wasn't there, just as the fact that until recently we were unable to verify the existence of black holes and dark matter in the universe doesn't mean they don't exist. I call *Pride / Prejudice* a yin-yang, reverse-image *Pride and Prejudice* that fills in the blanks by illuminating what was previously obscured.

All authors who write versions of Austen novels are faced with the hellish problem that the Divine Miss A. produced some of the most elegant prose ever to appear in English literature. If we want to tell the same story from a slightly different angle, or by supplying the yang for her yin, we have two unpalatable options: to paraphrase, or to dump vast chunks of her text into our narrative. Neither alternative is attractive to a writer. Copying is, well, copying—not creative at all. Paraphrasing is about as low as a writer can go, taking material that is perfect and turning it into at best mediocre fare. We can steal, or we can spin gold into straw. Both practices merit Truman Capote's dismissal of Jack Kerouac's *On the Road*: "That's not writing, that's typing."

Rather than "type" an entire novel, I have imagined the scenes that Austen didn't show us, what I call "writing in the gaps." Of course, for the story to make sense, some of Austen's crucial scenes must be included, and whenever possible I have a character do the dirty work of paraphrase, as when Elizabeth recounts to her sister Jane the conversations she has missed while recuperating from her cold. Throughout the book, I tried to mesh my own voice comfortably with the original by continuing Austen's jaunty, epigrammatic manner, although without attempting futile imitation. Were Austen to be granted a chance to come back to life, my hope is that her fury at this mangling of her "darling child" would be directed at the content, not the style.

The biggest "gap" in the original story takes place after the disastrous Netherfield ball, when Bingley and his household remove to London for the winter. Austen keeps her attention focused on Elizabeth and the Hertfordshire society, while telling us nothing of what the men are up to during those four or five months in town. This was the section of the story that allowed the greatest scope for my imagination, and where I indulged myself by introducing characters from my first novel, *Phyllida and the Brotherhood of Philander*, along with its eponymous gentlemen's club.

Some readers may protest that since "sodomy" was a capital crime, Darcy, whose only vice is a very reasonable "pride," would be unlikely to commit so immoral an act or to associate with men who do. The natural development of Darcy's sexuality, beginning with the adolescent, exploitative relationship with George Wickham, and progressing in early adulthood to the pleasurable instruction of mistresses, seems implicit even in Austen's chaste original. We tend to forget, in our modern age of hookups and safe sex, the difficulties facing the sexually active gentleman of two hundred years ago. There was no "dating," no casual sex between men and women of the middle and upper classes. Female prostitution, to a much greater extent than now, filled a very real need. Same-sex activity, by contrast, while illegal and dangerous, was readily available and inexpensive—or free. A "heteroflexible" man could find willing partners in the streets and the parks, and in the clubs called molly houses (like a gay bar or bathhouse). Although a "bisexual" man could take the prudent course of action and satisfy his urges with women, a fastidious man like Darcy might sometimes prefer men of his own class—educated, discreet, perhaps even clean—to the coarser female merchandise of brothels.

There is also the way in which people accommodate their desires on the one hand, and the rules of society, including harsh and repressive sexual laws, on the other: by a psychological disconnect. Darcy is "clever" and has been to university, where he has been exposed to the ideas of ancient Greece and Rome, with their very different understanding of love between men. If two gentlemen truly love each other, and express that love physically, then, by definition, this must be an honorable act, not a crime. The law is for the purpose of regulating the conduct of the uneducated lower orders who lack higher moral principles and are simply pursuing "unnatural" sex. That the law would apply equally to all is something Darcy admits only subconsciously.

Darcy is the intelligent woman's elusive ideal: the man who wants a partner on his level, and who values a woman's mind as much as her appearance. In the segregated world of 1800, when men and women pursued separate leisure activities and received very different educations, Darcy expects to find his equal in a man. When he meets Elizabeth, because of the disparity in their social status, it takes him time to recognize in her the embodiment of that other half he has been seeking. Austen has brilliantly conveyed the more cerebral aspects of this perfect match in scenes that read like conversational sexual intercourse, and I have necessarily extended this form of lovemaking into the couple's engagement and married life. But I also enjoyed the chance to portray Elizabeth as Darcy's equal in appetite and energy as well as in intellect.

Elizabeth, as Austen has created her, is, I believe, a passionate woman. The sections where Elizabeth struggles with her attraction to the charming, handsome villain, George Wickham, strike me as Austen's guarded way of showing us the heights of a young lady's sexual excitement over an unworthy and dangerous object. It is for this reason that I included a physical side to Elizabeth's friendship with Charlotte Lucas. Because of the ignorance surrounding female sexuality, both women would consider their love "innocent." With no male organ involved, there could be no "sex," nothing improper. But they would regard all intimacy as private and would be as disinclined to speak openly of their deeper feelings, even to each other, as would two men engaged in far more forbidden same-sex acts.

While it's possible to claim a connection with modern ideas of bisexuality for the men, women's choices were determined more by the economics of marriage and spinsterhood than by sexual orientation. For a woman to live unmarried she needed financial independence; the majority of women living on the lower rungs of the gentry, like Elizabeth and Charlotte, did not have this option. Single, they were dependent for the rest of their lives on their parents and brothers. Elizabeth, with no brothers, faces certain poverty on her father's death. Charlotte can expect only grudging charity and resentment from her brothers in a large family with many obligations. Living together, apart from their families and any financial support, meant certain and extreme poverty even if it had been socially acceptable. Earning a living in the few available jobs, such as governess or schoolteacher, was little better than servitude. Marriage was the only possible choice if it was offered, and choosing it says nothing about a woman's sexuality, merely her "stomach." Thus Charlotte accepts the loathsome Mr. Collins and Elizabeth, while horrified, eventually recognizes Charlotte's necessity, even if she can't quite endorse it.

Charlotte's speech in chapter 14, in which she claims that men can have it "both ways" in marriage while women cannot, does not reflect my own beliefs. It's my opinion that Austen intended Charlotte's marriage as a cautionary tale against the cruelty of a society that makes it impossible for women to live unmarried. Austen is not arguing in favor of sexual freedom, only the choice to marry for genuine love or not at all. I doubt she would agree that men should have it both ways either, but

I see in Darcy and Bingley a couple who will have it so, and I tried in this story to make it work. Where Elizabeth has a husband who will, indeed, be "everything" to her, I couldn't help wanting to give Charlotte a measure of happiness beyond what her creator allowed—thus the chaste but affectionate relationship with Anne de Bourgh.

The one plot change I have made is to have Jane learn of Darcy's direct involvement in separating her and Bingley. It seemed unlikely that this big, ugly secret could be kept forever, especially once she and Charles are engaged and can talk freely. Knowledge on both sides is essential for the success of the "bisexual" love stories. Jane and Elizabeth must understand the true nature of their eventual husbands' friendship if their marriages are to be based on honest, informed choice. Similarly, Darcy's recognition of the enormity of the wrong he did to Jane, and of the need to seek her forgiveness, establish the primacy of both men's marriages in their lives. Loving their wives does not prevent them from loving each other; but the integrity of their marriages demands that they respect each other's choice of wife and acknowledge her as a partner.

Darcy and Bingley complement each other, and their sexual relationship "completes" them, in a way that marriage to women so much like themselves can't. Darcy may enjoy marriage with an equal, but there's an essential part of him that can't help being a master and a mentor. Elizabeth, while she appreciates Darcy's library and the broadening of her intellectual horizons it provides, will never submit to a master, no matter what the morality of the time demands of a wife. Bingley, however, will always be, at heart, Darcy's "dear boy." Bingley loves Jane for the qualities of gentle, easygoing kindness they have in common, but he also needs that direction and decisiveness that only Darcy can supply—and Darcy enjoys having someone to look after.

It's important to note that most bisexual people who live in societies where monogamy is the norm live in monogamous relationships. That they are capable of loving a person of either sex does not mean they have a lover of each sex simultaneously or live in a ménage. My depiction of the married lives of the Darcys and the Bingleys is not meant to be representative of all "bisexual" men, but only a faithful elaboration of Austen's happy ending for her characters. As Alan Bennett says on the DVD of his play *The History Boys*, viewers or readers who criticize his work because the story or its characters aren't "typical" are missing the point. For Bennett, the raison d'être of fiction is to show us what's *not* typical, something different and interesting. The arrangement at the end of *Pride / Prejudice* is not meant to be "typical" of anything, but only what I imagine works best for these particular characters.

Finally, I must apologize for passing off the famous description of a novel from *Northanger Abbey* as Elizabeth's, and for making Henry Tilney a (former) member of the Brotherhood of Philander. In imagining a love match between two clever people, I felt certain that Elizabeth would, in her loosening of Darcy's straitlaced character, expose him to the pleasures of "ladies' novels," and the speech from the other book was too perfect to pass up. It is Austen herself, as the narrator, who defines the novel in *Northanger Abbey*, not a particular character, and I see Elizabeth as sharing many of her creator's opinions, which is why I also gave her George Crabbe for a favorite poet, as he was Austen's. As for Tilney, he seems the sort of witty, sexy man who might enjoy the "conversations" at the Brotherhood. Having come this far along in vice as to be messing with Jane Austen, a little miscegenation between novels didn't seem so bad.

Bibliography

Although, as I claimed in the acknowledgments, this book was not the result of "research," I did refer to some works that should be cited.

Jane Austen, *Pride and Prejudice.* 1813. For the definitive text of Austen's masterpiece, I used the Penguin Classics edition, edited with an introduction and notes by Vivien Jones, with the original Penguin Classics introduction by Tony Tanner, c. 2003. The notes were the source for the advice from John Gregory's 1774 conduct manual, *A Father's Legacy to His Daughters*, with which Elizabeth fortifies herself on her wedding night.

The Annotated Pride and Prejudice, edited and annotated by David M. Shapard. New York: Anchor Books, 2004. This book was invaluable for its explanations of all the minutiae and nagging questions that beset even the most devoted Janeite. Without it, I would still be puzzling over how Darcy could afford to pay ten thousand pounds, an entire year's income, to Wickham and Lydia (he probably paid closer to one thousand) and wondering what birds Darcy and Bingley were shooting at Netherfield and Pemberley (partridges, mostly).

I also found two biographies very helpful for insights into both Austen and her characters:

Jane Aiken Hodge, *Only a Novel: The Double Life of Jane Austen.* New York: Coward, McCann & Geoghegan, 1972.

Claire Tomalin, *Jane Austen: A Life*. New York: Alfred A. Knopf, 1998.

The quotation that Elizabeth and Darcy share at breakfast is from George Crabbe's poem "The Newspaper." Excerpts from the poem appeared in a *New York Times* article on Sunday, June 17, 2007, that claimed it was published in 1812, but all other sources I can find agree it was published in 1785, allowing plenty of time for Darcy, Mr. Bennet, and Elizabeth to have become familiar with it.

On the Web

To learn more about me and my writing, please visit my Web site: www.annherendeen.com

Readers interested in queer history will want to check out Rictor Norton's site: www.rictornorton.co.uk

Readers curious about my views on bisexuality, the "genetics" of sexual orientation, gay men who love women, and other sensitive topics, will find them cogently expressed in some eye-opening essays on Peter Tatchell's Web site: www.petertatchell.net

ENTER THE WORLD OF JANE AUSTEN

DARCY'S STORY
***Pride and Prejudice* Told From a Whole New Perspective**
by Janet Aylmer

ISBN 978-0-06-114870-5 (paperback)

CASSANDRA & JANE
A Jane Austen Novel
by Jill Pitkeathley

ISBN 978-0-06-144639-9 (paperback)

DEAREST COUSIN JANE
A Jane Austen Novel
by Jill Pitkeathley

ISBN 978-0-06-187598-4 (paperback)

Coming in 2010

THE LOST MEMOIRS OF JANE AUSTEN
A Novel
by Syrie James

ISBN 978-0-06-134142-7 (paperback)

TWO HISTORIES OF ENGLAND
by Jane Austen and Charles Dickens

ISBN 978-0-06-135195-2 (hardcover)

PRIDE & PREJUDICE
by Jane Austen

ISBN 978-0-06-196436-7 (paperback)

Visit www.AuthorTracker.com
for exclusive information on your favorite HarperCollins authors.

Available wherever books are sold, or call 1-800-331-3761 to order.